Known for sensuall
emotional Western
New York Times bestse

JOAN JOHNSTON

has long been a reader favorite.
Here are some of the reasons why:

"(Joan Johnston) does short contemporary westerns to perfection."
—*Publishers Weekly*

"...a top-notch craftsman..."
—*Romantic Times Magazine*

"...Ms. Johnston writes of intense emotions and tender passions that seem so real that readers will feel each one of them...(she) writes the very essences of the West..."
—*Rave Reviews*

"A guaranteed good read..."
—*New York Times* bestselling author Heather Graham

"Ms. Johnston always provides high quality entertainment for our reading pleasure."
—*Romantic Times Magazine*

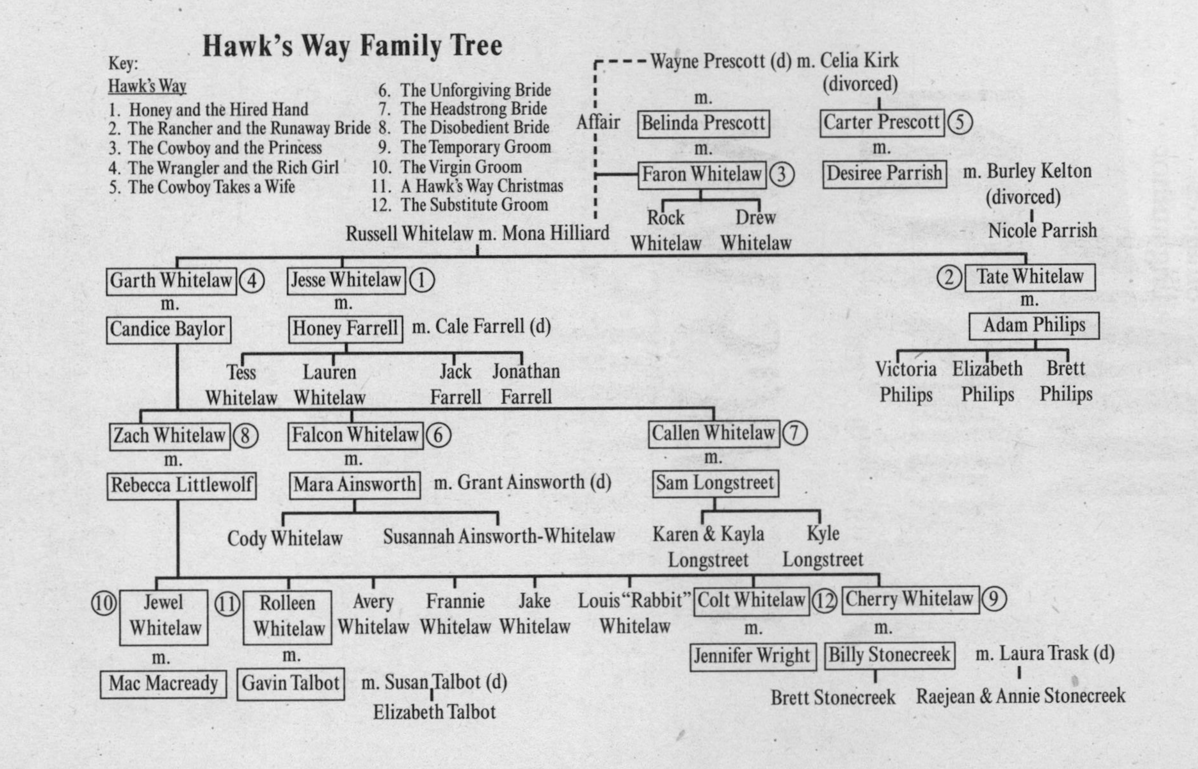

Hawk's Way Family Tree
Key:
Hawk's Way
1. Honey and the Hired Hand
2. The Rancher and the Runaway Bride
3. The Cowboy and the Princess
4. The Wrangler and the Rich Girl
5. The Cowboy Takes a Wife
6. The Unforgiving Bride
7. The Headstrong Bride
8. The Disobedient Bride
9. The Temporary Groom
10. The Virgin Groom
11. A Hawk's Way Christmas
12. The Substitute Groom
Wayne Prescott (d) m. Celia Kirk (divorced)
Affair
Belinda Prescott
m.
Carter Prescott 5
m.
Faron Whitelaw 3
Desiree Parrish
m. Burley Kelton (divorced)
Nicole Parrish
Rock Whitelaw
Drew Whitelaw
Russell Whitelaw m. Mona Hilliard
Garth Whitelaw 4
m.
Candice Baylor
Jesse Whitelaw 1
m.
Honey Farrell
m. Cale Farrell (d)
2 Tate Whitelaw
m.
Adam Philips
Tess Whitelaw
Lauren Whitelaw
Jack Farrell
Jonathan Farrell
Victoria Philips
Elizabeth Philips
Brett Philips
Zach Whitelaw 8
m.
Rebecca Littlewolf
Falcon Whitelaw 6
m.
Mara Ainsworth
m. Grant Ainsworth (d)
Callen Whitelaw 7
m.
Sam Longstreet
Cody Whitelaw
Susannah Ainsworth-Whitelaw
Karen & Kayla Longstreet
Kyle Longstreet
10 Jewel Whitelaw
m.
Mac Macready
11 Rolleen Whitelaw
m.
Gavin Talbot
m. Susan Talbot (d)
Elizabeth Talbot
Avery Whitelaw
Frannie Whitelaw
Jake Whitelaw
Louis "Rabbit" Whitelaw
Colt Whitelaw 12
m.
Jennifer Wright
Cherry Whitelaw 9
m.
Billy Stonecreek
m. Laura Trask (d)
Brett Stonecreek
Raejean & Annie Stonecreek

JOAN JOHNSTON

HAWK'S WAY ROGUES

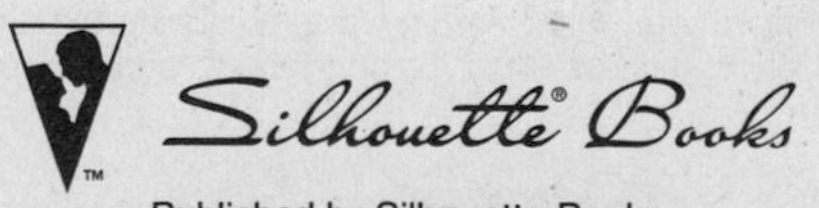

Published by Silhouette Books
America's Publisher of Contemporary Romance

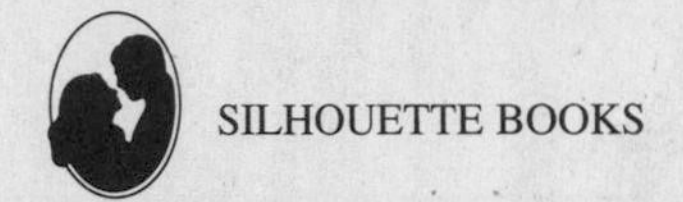

HAWK'S WAY ROGUES

ISBN 0-373-48445-3

This edition published by arrangement with Harlequin Books S.A.

Visit Silhouette at www.eHarlequin.com

Printed in U.S.A.

CONTENTS

Dear Reader,

Honey and the Hired Hand is the first of my books ever to feature one of the Whitelaw Brats from Hawk's Way, a ranch in northwest Texas.

At the time I wrote it, I didn't know Jesse Whitelaw was going to have two brothers (Garth and Faron), and a sister (Tate). Or that Faron would have a half brother, Carter Prescott, who'd turn up in *The Cowboy Takes a Wife.* Or that Garth would have eight (!) adopted children, and that one of them would be a troublemaker named Cherry Whitelaw, who'd get her own story in *The Temporary Groom.*

Like you, I love family stories, and it seemed the most natural thing in the world to keep spinning yarns about the Whitelaws. I never suspected the family would get so large, or that the HAWK'S WAY books would eventually encompass three generations of Whitelaws.

I hope you'll enjoy meeting the Whitelaws as much as I've enjoyed writing about them.

Happy trails,

Joan Johnston

HONEY AND THE HIRED HAND

For my friends, Sally, Sherry and Heather—
the Square Table at JJ's

One

The hairs prickled on the back of Honey Farrell's neck. She was being watched. Again. Surreptitiously she scanned the room looking for someone—anyone—she could blame for the disturbing sensation that had plagued her all evening. But everyone in the room was a friend or acquaintance. There was no one present who could account for the eerie feeling that troubled her.

Her glance caught on the couple across the room from her. How she envied them! Dallas Masterson was standing behind his wife, his hands tenderly circling Angel's once-again-tiny waist. Their three-month-old son was asleep upstairs. Honey felt her throat close with emotion as Dallas leaned down to whisper into his wife's ear. Angel laughed softly and a pink flush rose on her cheeks.

Honey saw before her a couple very much in love. In fact, she had come to the Mastersons' home this evening to help them celebrate their first wedding anniversary. Honey found it a bittersweet event. For, one year and one month ago, Honey's husband, Cale, had been killed saving Dallas Masterson's life.

Honey felt her smile crumbling. A watery sheen blurred her vision of the Texas Rangers and their wives chattering happily around her. Mumbling something incoherent, she shoved her wineglass into the hands of a startled friend.

"Honey, are you all right?"

"I just need some air." Honey bit down on her lower lip to still its quiver as she hastened from the living room.

The overhead light in the kitchen was blinding, and Honey felt exposed. Shying from the worried look of another Ranger's wife, who was putting a tray of canapés into the oven, Honey shoved her way out the back screen door.

"Honey?" the woman called after her. "Is something wrong?"

Honey forced herself to pause on the back porch. She turned back with a brittle smile and said, "I just need some air. I'll be fine."

The woman grinned. "I suppose it's all the speculation about you and Adam Philips. Has he proposed yet? We're expecting an announcement any day."

Honey gritted her teeth to hold the smile in place, hoping it didn't look as much like a grimace as it felt. "I—could we talk about this later? I really do need some air."

She waited until the other woman nodded before pulling the wooden door closed behind her, abruptly shutting out the noise and the painful, though well-intentioned, nosiness of her friends and neighbors.

The early summer evening was blessedly cool with a slight breeze that made the live oaks rustle overhead. Honey sank onto the back porch steps. She leaned forward and lifted the hair off her nape, shivering when the breeze caught a curl and teased it across her skin as gently as a man's hand.

She quickly dropped her hair and clutched her hands together between her knees. She felt bereft. And angry. *How could you have left me alone like this, Cale? I'm trying to forget what it was like to be held in your arms. I'm trying to forget the feel of your mouth on mine.* But seeing Angel in Dallas's arms tonight had been a vivid reminder of what she had lost. And it hurt. It was hard to accept Cale's untimely death and go on with her life. But she was trying.

At least she had learned from her mistake. She would never again love a man who sought out danger the way Cale had. She would never again put herself in the position of knowing that her husband welcomed the risks of a job that might mean his death. Next time she would choose a man who would be there when she needed him. Inevitably Cale had been gone on some assignment for the Texas Rangers whenever a crisis arose. Honey had become adept over the years at handling things on her own.

If her friends and neighbors got their wish, she wouldn't be on her own much longer. Only this time she had chosen more wisely. The man who had brought her to the party tonight, Adam Philips, was a country doctor. Adam would never die from an outlaw's bullet, the way Cale had. And Adam was reliable. Punctual almost to a fault. She would be able to count on him through thick and thin.

That was a definite plus in weighing the decision she had to make. For the good-natured gossip at the party about her and the young doctor was founded in fact. Adam Philips had proposed to her, and Honey was seriously considering his offer. Adam was a handsome, dependable man in a safe occupation. He liked her sons, and they liked—perhaps *tolerated* was a better word to describe how they felt about him. There was only one problem.

Honey didn't love Adam.

Maybe she would never love another man the way she had loved Cale. Maybe she was hoping for too much. Maybe it would be better to marry a man she didn't love. That way her heart could never be broken again if—

The kitchen door rattled behind her. Afraid that someone would find her sitting alone in the dark and start asking more awkward questions, Honey rose and headed toward the corner of the house where the spill of light from the kitchen windows didn't reach. She almost ran into the man before she realized he was there.

He was leaning against Dallas's Victorian house, his booted foot braced against the painted wooden wall, his Stetson tipped forward over his brow so his face was in deep shadow. His thumbs were stuck into the front of his low-slung, beltless jeans. He was wearing a faded western shirt with white piping and pearl snaps that reflected the faint light of a misted moon.

Honey felt breathless. She wasn't exactly frightened, but she was anxious because she didn't recognize the man. He might have been a party guest, but he wasn't dressed for a party. He looked more like a down-on-his-luck cowboy, a drifter. It was better not to take a chance. Honey slowly backed away.

With no wasted movement, the cowboy reached out a hand and

caught her wrist. He didn't hold her tightly, but he held her, all the same.

Honey stood transfixed by the feel of his callused fingers on her flesh. ''I'll scream if you don't let go,'' she said in a miraculously calm voice.

The cowboy grinned, his teeth a white slash in the darkness. ''No you won't.''

There was a coiled tension in the way he held his body that she recognized. Cale had been like that. Ready to react instantly to any threat. Suddenly her curiosity was greater than her fear. She stopped straining against his hold. Instantly his grasp loosened, but he didn't let go.

''I've been standing out on the front porch watching you through the window, waiting for a chance to talk to you,'' the drifter said.

So, she wasn't crazy. Someone *had* been watching her all evening. His eyes weren't visible beneath the brim of his hat, but she felt the hairs rise on her nape. He was watching her right now. She ignored the gooseflesh that rose on her arms as he caressed her wrist with his thumb.

''I'm listening,'' she said. Regrettably the calm was gone from her voice.

''I know you're having some trouble handling things all by yourself at the ranch and—''

''How could you possibly know what's going on at the Flying Diamond?''

''Dallas told me how things are with you.''

She exhaled with a loud sigh. ''I see.'' He was no stranger then, although just who he was remained a mystery.

''It wouldn't have been hard to tell you've got problems just by looking at you.''

''Oh? Are you some kind of mind reader?''

''No. But I can read people.''

She remained silent, so he continued, ''That frown never left your brow all evening.''

Honey consciously relaxed the furrows of worry on her brow.

''Judging from the purple shadows I saw under your eyes, you aren't sleeping too well. You aren't eating much, either. That dress doesn't fit worth beans.''

Honey tugged at the black knit dress she was wearing. Undeniably she had lost weight since Cale's death.

''Not that I don't like what I see,'' the cowboy drawled.

Honey felt a faint irritation—laced with pleasure—when his grin reappeared.

''You're long legged as a newborn filly and curved in all the right places. That curly hair of yours looks fine as corn silk, and your eyes, why I'd swear they're blue as a Texas sky, ma'am.''

Honey was mortified by her body's traitorous reaction as his eyes made a lazy perusal of her face and form. She felt the heat, the anticipation—and the fear. She recognized her attraction to the man even as she fought against it. This tall, dark-eyed drifter would never be reliable. And he had *danger* written all over him.

''Who are you?'' Her voice was raspy and didn't sound at all like her own.

''Jesse Whitelaw, ma'am.'' The drifter reached up with his free hand and tugged the brim of his Stetson.

The name meant nothing to her; his courtesy did nothing to ease her concern. She stared, waiting for him to say why he had sought her out, why he knew so much about her when she knew nothing about him.

He stared back. She felt the tension grow between them, the invisible electrical pulse of desire that streaked from his flesh to hers. Unconsciously she stepped back. His hold on her wrist tightened, keeping her captive.

His voice was low and grated like a rusty gate. ''Dallas told me about your husband's death. I came here tonight hoping to meet you.''

''Why?''

''I need a job.''

The tension eased in Honey's shoulders. She released a gust of air she hadn't realized she'd been holding. Despite what he'd said, the way he'd looked at her, he hadn't sought her out to pursue a physical relationship. She couldn't help the stab of disappointment, when what she ought to feel was relief. At least now she knew how to deal with him.

"I can't afford to hire anyone right now," she said. "Especially not some down-on-his-luck drifter."

The smile was back. "If I wasn't down on my luck, I wouldn't need the job."

She couldn't hire him, but she was curious enough about him to ask, "Where did you work last?"

His shoulders rolled in a negligent shrug. "I've been...around."

"Doing what?" she persisted.

"A little cowboying, some rodeo bull riding, and...some drifting."

Bull riding. She should have known. Even Cale had never ridden bulls because he had thought it was too dangerous. *Drifting.* He was a man who couldn't be tied to any one place or, she suspected, any one woman. The last thing she needed at the Flying Diamond was a drifting cowboy who rode bulls for fun. Not that she could afford to hire him, anyway.

Just today she had discovered over fifty head of cattle missing—apparently rustled—from the Flying Diamond. That loss would cut deep into the profits she had hoped to make this year. "I can't hire anyone right now," she said. "I—"

The back door opened, revealing the silhouette of a large man in the stream of light. "Honey? Are you out here?"

She recognized Dallas, who was joined at the door by Angel.

"Are you coming in?" Dallas asked Honey.

"Yes. Yes, I am." She took advantage of Dallas's interruption to slip from the drifter's grasp. But he followed her. She could feel him right behind her as she stepped onto the porch.

Honey turned to the stranger to excuse herself and gasped. The harsh light from the kitchen doorway revealed the man's features. She was suddenly aware of his bronzed skin, of the high, broad cheekbones, the blade of nose and thin lips that proclaimed his heritage.

"You're Indian!" she exclaimed.

"The best part of me, yes, ma'am."

Honey didn't know what to say. She found him more appealing than she cared to admit, yet the savage look in his eyes frightened her. To her dismay, the drifter put the worst possible face on her silence.

His lips twisted bitterly, his grating voice became cynical as he said,

''I suppose I should have mentioned that my great-grandfather married a Comanche bride. If it makes a difference—''

Honey flushed. ''Not at all. I was just a little surprised when I saw...I mean, I didn't realize...''

''I'm used to it,'' he said. From the harsh sound of his voice it was clear he didn't like it.

Honey wished she had handled the situation better. She didn't think any less of him because he was part Indian, even though she knew there were some who would. She turned back to Angel and saw that the young woman had retreated into the safety of Dallas's arms.

''I came outside for some air,'' Honey explained to Dallas. ''And I met someone who says he's a friend of yours.''

Dallas propelled Angel ahead of him onto the back porch and pulled the kitchen door closed behind him. ''Hello, Jesse. I wasn't expecting you tonight.''

Jesse shrugged again. ''I got free sooner than I thought I would. Anyway, I could have saved myself the trip. Mrs. Farrell says she can't afford to hire anyone right now.''

Dallas pursed his lips in disapproval. ''I don't think you can afford not to hire someone, Honey.''

''I'm not saying I don't need the help,'' Honey argued. ''I just don't have the money right now to—''

''Who said anything about money?'' Jesse asked. ''I'd work for bed and board.''

Honey frowned. ''I really don't—''

''If you're worried about hiring a stranger, I'll vouch for Jesse,'' Dallas said. ''We went to Texas Tech together.''

''How long ago was that?'' Honey asked.

''Fifteen years,'' Dallas admitted. ''But I'd trust Jesse with my life.''

Only it wouldn't be Dallas's life that would be at stake. It was Honey's, and those of her sons, Jack and Jonathan. ''I'll think about it,'' she said.

''I'm afraid I need something a little more definite than that,'' Jesse said. He tipped his hat back and said, ''A drifting man needs a reason to light and set, or else he just keeps on drifting.''

Honey didn't believe from looking at him that Jesse Whitelaw would ever settle anywhere for very long. But another pair of hands to share the load, even for a little while, would be more than welcome. There was some ranch work too heavy for her to handle, even with her older son's help. Honey brushed aside the notion that she would be alone with a stranger all day while the boys were at school. It was only a matter of weeks before her sons would be home for summer vacation.

She took a deep breath and let it out. "All right. When can you start?"

"I've got some things to do first."

Honey felt a sense of relief that she wouldn't have to face him again in the near future. It evaporated when he said, "How about bright and early tomorrow morning?"

Honey sought a reason to keep him away a little longer, to give herself some time to reconsider what she was doing, but nothing came to mind. Anyway, she needed the help now. There was vaccinating to be done, and she needed to make a tally of which cattle were missing so she could make a more complete report to the police.

Also she needed to add some light to improve security around the barn where she kept General, the champion Hereford bull that was the most important asset of the Flying Diamond.

"Tomorrow morning will be fine," she said.

The words were barely out of her mouth when the kitchen door was thrust open and another silhouette appeared. "I've been looking everywhere for you. What are you doing out here?"

Adam Philips joined what was quickly becoming a crowd on the back porch. He strode to Honey's side and slipped a possessive arm around her waist. "I'm Adam Philips," he said by way of introduction to the stranger he found there. "I don't think we've met."

"Jesse Whitelaw," the stranger said.

Honey watched as the two men shook hands. There was nothing cordial about the greeting. She didn't understand the reason for the animosity between them; it existed nonetheless.

"Are you ready to come back inside?" Adam asked.

He had tightened his hold on her waist until it was uncomfortable. Honey tried to step out of his grasp, but he pulled her back against his hip.

"I think the lady wants you to let her go," Jesse said.

''I'll be the judge of what the lady wants,'' Adam retorted.

The drifter's eyes were hard and cold, and Honey felt sure that at any moment he would enforce his words with action. ''Please let go,'' she said to Adam.

At first Adam's grip tightened, but when he glanced over at her, she gave him a speaking look that said she meant business. Reluctantly he let her go.

''It's about time we headed home, don't you think?'' Adam said to Honey.

Honey was irked by Adam's choice of words, which insinuated that they lived together. However, she didn't think now was the moment to take him to task. The drifter was still poised for battle, and Honey didn't want to be the cause of any more of a scene than had already occurred.

''It is getting late,'' she said, ''and I've got a long day tomorrow. It was nice meeting you, Jesse. I'll see you in the morning.''

Honey anticipated Adam's questions and hurried him back inside. It took them a while to get through the kitchen, which now held several women collecting leftover potluck dishes to be carried home.

''Aha! I expect you two were out seeing a little of the moonlight,'' one teased.

''We'll be hearing wedding bells soon,'' another chorused.

Honey didn't bother denying their assumptions. They might very well prove true. But it was hard to smile and make humorous rejoinders right now, because she was still angry with Adam for his caveman behavior on the back porch.

When they reached the living room, a Randy Travis ballad was playing. ''Dance with me?'' Adam asked. His lips curved in the charming smile that had endeared him to her when they first met. Right now it wasn't doing a thing to put her in a romantic mood. However, it would be harder to explain her confused feelings to Adam than it would be to dance with him. ''Sure,'' she said, relenting with a hesitant smile.

At almost the same moment Adam took her into his arms, she spied the drifter entering the living room. He stayed in the shadows, but Honey knew he was there. She could feel him watching her. She stiffened when Adam's palm slid down to the lowest curve in her spine.

It wasn't something he hadn't done before. In the past, she had permitted it. But now, with the drifter watching, Adam's possessive touch felt uncomfortable.

Honey stepped back and said, "I'm really tired, Adam. Do you think we could go now?"

Adam searched her face, looking for signs of fatigue she knew he would find. "You do look tired," he agreed. "All right. Do you need to get anything from the kitchen?"

"I'll pick up my cake plate another time," she said. She felt the drifter's eyes on her as Adam ushered her out the front door to his low-slung sports car. He opened the door for her and she slid inside. Protected by the darkness within the car she was able to look back toward the house without being observed. She felt her nape prickle when she caught sight of the drifter standing at the front window.

Honey knew he couldn't see her, yet she felt as though his eyes pinned her to the seat. They were dark and gleamed with some emotion she couldn't identify. She abruptly turned away when Adam opened the opposite door and the dome light came on.

Adam put a country music tape on low, setting a romantic mood which, before Honey had met the drifter, she would have appreciated. Right now the mellow tones only agitated her, reminding her that Adam had proposed and was waiting for her answer. He expected her to give him a decision tonight. To be honest, she had led him to believe her answer would be yes. They hadn't slept together; she hadn't been ready to face that kind of intimacy with another man. But she had kissed him, and it had been more than pleasant.

"Honey?"

"What?" Her voice was sharp, and she cleared her throat and repeated in a softer tone, "What?"

"Are you sure you want to hire that drifter?"

"I don't see that I have much choice. There's work to be done that I can't do myself."

"You could marry me."

The silence after Adam spoke was an answer in itself. Honey knew she shouldn't give him hope. She ought to tell him right now that she couldn't marry him, that it wasn't right to marry a man she didn't love. But the thought of that drifter, with his dark, haunting eyes, made her hold her tongue. She was too attracted to Jesse Whitelaw for her own good. If she were free, she might be tempted to get involved with him. And that would be disastrous.

But was it fair to leave Adam hanging?

Honey sighed. It seemed she had sighed more in the past evening than she had in the past year. "I can't—"

"You don't have to give me your answer now," Adam said. "I know you still miss Cale. I can wait a little longer. Now that you have that hired hand, it ought to make things easier on you."

They had arrived at the two-story wood frame ranch house built by Cale's grandfather. Adam stopped his car outside the glow of the front porch light. He came around and opened the door and pulled her out of the car and into his arms.

Honey was caught off guard. Even so, as Adam's lips sought her mouth she quickly turned aside so he kissed her cheek instead.

Adam lifted his head and looked down at her, searching her features in the shadows. Something had changed between them tonight. He thought of the stranger he had found with Honey on the Mastersons' back porch and felt a knot form in his stomach. He had always known that his relationship with Honey was precarious. He had hoped that once they were married she would come to love him as much as he loved her. He hadn't counted on another man coming into the picture.

Honey kept her face averted for a moment longer but knew that was the coward's way out. She had to face Adam and tell him what she was feeling.

"Adam, I—"

He put his fingertips on her lips. "Don't say anything. Just kiss me good night, and I'll go."

Honey looked up into his eyes and saw a tenderness that made her ache. Why didn't she love this man? She allowed his lips to touch hers and it was as pleasant as she remembered. But when he tried to deepen the kiss, she backed away.

"Honey?"

"I'm sorry, Adam. It's been a long day."

He looked confused and even a little hurt. But she had tried twice to refuse his proposal and he hadn't let her do it. Maybe her response to his kiss had told him what she hadn't said in words. Then he smiled, and she could have cried because his words were thoughtful, his voice tender. ''Good night, Honey. Get some rest. I'll call you next week.''

He would, too. *Good old reliable Adam.* She was a fool not to leap at the chance to marry such a man.

Honey stood in the shadows until he was gone. When she turned toward the house she saw the living room curtain drop. That would be her older son, Jack. He kept an eagle eye on her, which hadn't helped Adam's courtship. She called out to him as she unlocked the door and stepped inside.

''Come on down, Jack. I know you're still awake.''

The lanky thirteen-year-old ambled back down the stairs he had just raced up. ''He didn't stay long,'' Jack said. ''You tell him no?''

''I haven't given him an answer.''

''But you're going to say no, right?''

She heard the anxiety in Jack's voice. He wasn't ready to let anyone in their closed circle and most certainly not a man to take his father's place. She didn't dare tell him how she really felt before she told Adam, because her son was likely to blurt it out at an inopportune moment. She simply said, ''I haven't made a decision.''

Honey put an arm around her son's shoulder and realized he was nearly as tall as she was. *Oh, Cale. I wish you could see how your sons have grown!* ''Come on,'' she said. ''Let's go make some hot chocolate.''

''I'd rather have coffee,'' Jack said.

She arched a brow at him. ''Coffee will keep me awake, and I need all the rest I can get.''

Jack eyed her and announced somberly, ''School will be out in about three weeks, Mom. I don't think I can do any more around here until then.''

''You don't have to,'' she said. ''I've hired a man to help out.''

''I thought we couldn't afford hired help.''

''He'll be working for room and board.''

''Oh. What's he like?''

Honey wasn't about to answer that question. She couldn't have explained how she felt about the drifter right now. ''He'll be here in the morning and you can ask him all the questions you want.''

From the look her son gave her, she suspected Jack would grill the drifter like a hamburger. She smiled. That, she couldn't wait to see.

Jesse Whitelaw had another big surprise coming if he harbored any notions of pursuing Honey on her home ground. Her teenage son was a better chaperon than a Spanish duenna.

Two

Honey yawned and stretched, forcing the covers off and exposing bare skin to the predawn chill. She scooted back underneath the blanket and pulled it up over her shoulders. She was more tired than she ought to be first thing in the morning, but she hadn't slept well. For the first time in over a year, however, it wasn't memories of Cale that had kept her awake.

The drifter!

Honey bolted upright in her bed. He was supposed to show up bright and early this morning. She glanced out the lace curtains in her upstairs bedroom and realized it was later than she'd thought. Her sons would already be up and getting ready for school. She tossed the covers away, shivering again as the cold air hit flesh exposed by her baby doll pajamas. She grabbed Cale's white terry cloth robe and scuffed her feet into tattered slippers before hurriedly heading downstairs.

Halfway down, she heard Jonathan's excited voice. At eight he still sounded a bit squeaky. Jack's adolescent response was lower-pitched, but his voice occasionally broke when he least expected it. She was already in the kitchen by the time she realized they weren't talking to each other.

The drifter was sitting at the kitchen table, a cup of coffee before him. Honey clutched the robe to her throat, her mouth agape.

''Catch a lot of flies that way,'' the drifter said with a lazy grin.

Her jaws snapped closed.

''Good morning,'' he said, touching a finger to the brim of his Stetson.

''Is it?'' she retorted.

His skin looked golden in the sunlight. There were fine lines around his eyes and deep brackets around his mouth that had been washed out by the artificial light the previous evening. He was older than she'd thought, maybe middle thirties. But his dark eyes were as piercing as she remembered, and he pinned her with his stare. Honey felt naked.

She gripped the front of the masculine robe tighter, conscious of how she was dressed—or rather, not dressed. She thrust a hand into her shoulder-length hair, which tumbled in riotous natural curls around her face. She wondered how her mascara had survived the night. Usually it ended up clumped on the ends of her eyelashes or smudged underneath them. She reached up to wipe at her eyes, then stuck her hand in the pocket of the robe. It wasn't her fault he'd found her looking like something the cat dragged in.

Honey didn't want to admit that the real reason she resented this unsettling man's presence in her kitchen so early in the morning was that she hadn't wanted him to see her looking so...so mussed.

''What are you doing here?'' she demanded.

He raised a brow as though the answer was obvious. And it was.

''I let him in,'' Jack said, his hazel eyes anxious. ''You said the hired hand was coming this morning. I thought it would be okay.''

Honey took several steps into the room and laid a hand on her older son's shoulder. ''You did fine. I'm just a little surprised at how early Mr. Whitelaw got here.''

''He said we can call him Jesse,'' Jonathan volunteered.

Honey bristled. The man had certainly made himself at home.

''Jesse helped me make my sandwich,'' Jonathan added, holding up a brown paper bag.

Honey's left hand curled into a fist in the pocket of the robe. ''That was nice.'' Her voice belied the words.

''Jesse thinks I'm old enough to make my own lunch,'' Jonathan continued, his chest pumped out with pride.

Honey had known for some time that Jonathan could make his own sandwich, but she had kept doing it for him because the routine morning chore kept her from missing Cale so much. She was annoyed by the drifter's interference but couldn't say so without taking away from Jonathan's accomplishment.

"Jesse rides bulls and rodeo broncs," Jack said. "He worked last at a ranch in northwest Texas called Hawk's Way. He's gonna teach me some steer roping tricks. He's never been married but he's had a lot of girlfriends. Oh, and he graduated from Texas Tech with a degree in animal husbandry and ranch management."

It was hard for Honey not to laugh aloud at the chagrined look on Jesse's face as Jack recited all the information he'd garnered. The drifter had been, if not grilled, certainly a little singed around the edges.

The shoe was on the other foot as Jack continued, "I told him how you haven't been coping too well since Dad—well, this past year. Not that you don't try," he backtracked when he spied the horrified look on his mother's face, "but after all, Mom, the work is pretty hard for you."

Honey was abashed by her son's forthrightness. "I've managed fine," she said. She didn't want Jesse Whitelaw thinking she needed him more than she did. After all, a drifter like him wasn't going to be around long. Soon enough she'd be managing on her own again.

She stiffened her back and lifted her chin. Staring Jesse Whitelaw right in the eye she announced, "And I expect I'll still be managing fine long after you've drifted on."

"The fact remains, you need me now, Mrs. Farrell," the drifter said in that rusty gate voice. "So long as I'm here, you'll be getting a fair day's work from me."

The silence that followed was uncomfortable for everyone except the younger boy.

In the breach Jonathan piped up, "Jesse thinks I should have a real horse to ride, not just a pony."

"I'm sure Jesse does," Honey said in as calm a voice as she could manage. "But I'm your mother, and until I decide differently, you'll stick with what you have."

"Aww, Mom."

This was an old argument, and Honey cut it off at the pass. "The school bus will be here in a few minutes," she said. "You boys had better get out to the main road."

Honey gave Jonathan a hug and a quick kiss before he headed out the kitchen door. ''Have a nice day, sweetheart.''

Jack was old enough to pick up the tension that arced between his mother and the drifter. His narrowed glance leapt from her to Jesse and back again. ''Uh, maybe I ought to stay home today. Kind of show Jesse around.''

Honey forced herself to smile reassuringly. ''Nonsense. You have reviews for finals starting this week. You can't afford to miss them. Jesse and I will manage fine. Won't we?''

She turned to Jesse, asking him with her eyes to add his reassurance to hers.

Jesse rose and shoved his chair under the table. ''Appreciate the offer,'' he said to Jack. ''But like your mom said, we'll be just fine.''

''Then I better run, or I'll miss the bus.'' Jack hesitated another instant before he sprinted for the door. Honey would have liked to hug Jack, too, but at thirteen, he resisted her efforts to cosset him.

A moment later they were alone. Jesse was watching her again, and Honey's body was reacting to the appreciation in his dark eyes. She rearranged the robe and pulled the belt tighter, grateful for the thick terry cloth covering. She felt the roses bloom on her cheeks and hurried over to the stove to pour herself a cup of coffee.

Too late she realized she should have excused herself to go upstairs to dress. If she left now without getting her coffee, he would know she was running scared. There was absolutely no reason for her to feel threatened. Dallas wouldn't have recommended Jesse Whitelaw if she had anything to fear from him. But she couldn't help the anxiety she felt.

''Would you like another cup of coffee?'' she asked, holding up the pot.

''Don't mind if I do, Mrs. Farrell,'' Jesse said.

''Please, you might as well call me Honey.''

''All right…Honey.''

Her name sounded far more intimate in that rusty gate voice of his than she was comfortable with. She stared, mesmerized for a moment by the warmth in his dark eyes, then realized what she was doing and repeated her offer.

''More coffee?''

He brought his cup over, and she realized she had made another tactical error. She could actually feel the heat from his body as he stepped close enough for her to pour his coffee. She turned her back on him to pour a cup for herself.

"Those are fine boys you have." Jesse moved a kitchen chair and straddled it, facing her.

She leaned back against the counter rather than join him at the table. "In the future, I'd appreciate it if you don't come inside before I get downstairs," she said.

"I wouldn't have come in except Jack said you were expecting me."

"I was—that is—I didn't expect you quite so early."

That was apparent. Honey's bed-tossed hair and sleepy-eyed look made Jesse want to pick her up and carry her back upstairs. He wasn't sure what—if anything—she was wearing under the man's robe. From the way she kept tightening the belt and clutching at the neck of the thing, he was guessing it wasn't much. His imagination had her stripped bare, and he liked what he saw.

It was too bad about her husband. From what he'd heard, Cale Farrell had died a hero. He supposed a woman left alone to raise two kids wouldn't be thinking much about that. At least he was here to help her with the ranch work. Not that he would be around forever—or even for very long. But while he was here, he intended to do what he could to make her life easier.

He knew it would be easier for her if he didn't let her know he was attracted to her. But he wasn't used to hiding his feelings for a woman. The way he had been raised, part of respecting a woman was being honest with her. Jesse planned to be quite frank about his fascination with Honey Farrell.

He liked the way she'd prickled up last night, not at all intimidated by him. He liked the way she had stood her ground, willing to meet him eye to eye. He bristled when he thought of her with any other man—especially that Philips character. Jesse wasn't sure how serious their relationship was, but he knew Honey couldn't be in love with Philips. Otherwise she wouldn't have reacted so strongly to *his* touch.

At any rate, Jesse didn't intend to let the other man's interest in Honey keep him from pursuing her himself. Which wasn't going to be easy, considering her opinion of drifters in general, and him—a half-breed Comanche—in particular. His look was challenging as he asked, "What did you have in mind for me to do today?"

Honey had been watching Jesse's fingers trace the top rail of the wooden chair. There was a scar that ran across all four knuckles. She was wondering how he'd gotten it when his fist suddenly folded around the back of the chair. "I'm sorry—what did you say?"

"I asked what you wanted me to do today."

"There are some steers that need vaccinating, and the roof on the barn needs to be repaired. Some fence is down along the river and a few head of my stock have wandered onto the mohair goat ranch south of the Flying Diamond. I need to herd those strays back onto my land. Also—"

"That'll do for starters," Jesse interrupted. He rose and set his coffee cup on the table. "I'll start on the barn roof while you get dressed. Then we can vaccinate those steers together. How does that sound?"

Honey started to object to him taking charge of things, but she realized she was just being contrary. "Fine," she said. "I'll come to the barn when I'm dressed."

She waited for him to leave, but he just stood there looking at her. "What is it? Did I forget something?" she asked.

"No. I was admiring the view." He flashed a smile, then headed out the kitchen door.

Honey ran upstairs, not allowing herself time to contemplate the drifter's compliment. He probably didn't spend much time around respectable women. He probably didn't realize he shouldn't be blurting out what he was thinking that way. And she shouldn't be feeling so good about the fact the hired hand liked the way she looked.

She was grateful to discover that her mascara had been clumped, rather than smudged. She took the time to wash her face and reapply a layer of sun-sensitive makeup. It was a habit she'd gotten into and had nothing to do with the fact there was now a man around to see her. Honey dressed in record time in fitted Levi's, plaid western shirt, socks and boots.

Even so, by the time she reached the barn, Jesse was already on the roof, hammer in hand. He had his shirt off and she couldn't help looking.

Jesse had broad shoulders and a powerful chest, completely hairless except for a line of black down that ran from his navel into his form-fitting jeans. His nipples provided a dark contrast to his skin, which looked warm to the touch. She could see the definition of his ribs above a washboard belly. His arms were ropy with muscle and already glistened with sweat. Here was a man who had done his share of hard work. Which made her wonder why he had never settled down.

It dawned on her that the drifter had chosen the most dangerous job to do first. He was standing on the peaked barn roof without any kind of safety rope as though he were some kind of mountain goat. How could he be so idiotically unconscious of the danger!

She started up the ladder he had laid against the side of the barn and heard him call, ''No need for you to come up here.''

She looked up and found him hanging facedown over the edge of the roof. ''Be careful! You'll fall.''

''Not likely,'' he said with a grin. ''I grew up rambling around in high places.''

''I suppose you had the top bunk in an upstairs bedroom,'' she said with asperity.

Jesse thought of the high canyon walls he had scaled as a youth on his family's northwest Texas ranch and grinned. ''Let's just say I spent a lot of time climbing when I was a kid and leave it at that. By the way, I found the spot that needs to be patched. I brought the shingles up with me, but I didn't see hide nor hair of the roofing nails.''

''I put them away. I'll get them for you.'' Honey headed back down the ladder and into the barn. As she passed General's stall, she patted the bull on the forehead. She and Cale had raised him from birth, and though he had a ring in his nose, he would have followed her around without it.

''Hi, old fella. Just let me get these nails for Jesse and I'll let you out in the corral for a while.''

The barn was redolent with the odors of hay, leather and manure. Rather than hold her nose, Honey took a deep breath. There was nothing disagreeable to her about the smell of a ranch—or a hardworking man. Which made her think of the hired hand standing on the roof of her barn.

Honey didn't want to be charmed by Jesse Whitelaw, but there was no denying his charm. Maybe it was his crooked grin, or the way his eyes crinkled at the edges when he smiled, creating a sunburst of webbed lines. Or maybe it was the fact his dark eyes glowed with appreciation when he looked at her.

"Hey! Where are those nails?"

Honey jumped at the yell from above. "I'm getting them!" She grabbed the box of nails and headed back into the sunshine. Jesse had come to the edge of the roof and bent down to take the nails as she climbed the ladder and handed them up.

When he stood again, a trickle of sweat ran down the center of his chest. As Honey watched, it slid into his navel and back out again, down past the top button of his jeans. It was impossible to ignore the way the denim hugged his masculinity. It took a moment for Honey to realize he wasn't moving away. And another moment to realize he was aware of the direction of her gaze. Honey felt a single curl of desire in her belly and a weak feeling in her knees. Her fingers gripped the ladder to keep from falling. She was appalled at the realization that what she wanted to do was reach out and touch him. She froze, unable to move farther up the ladder or back down.

"Honey?"

Jesse's voice was gruff, and at the sound of it she raised her eyes to his face. His lids were lowered, his dark eyes inscrutable. She had no idea what he was thinking. His jaw was taut. So was his body. Honey was afraid to look down again, afraid of what she would find.

She felt her nipples pucker, felt the rush of heat to her loins. Her lips parted as her breathing became shallow. Honey knew the signs, knew what they meant. And tried desperately to deny what she was feeling.

"Honey?" he repeated in a raw voice.

Jesse hadn't moved, but if possible, his body had tautened. His nostrils flared. She saw the pulse throb at his temple. What did he want from her? What did he expect? He was a stranger. A drifter. A man who loved danger.

She wasn't going to get involved with him. Not this way. Not any way. Not now. Not ever.

"No!" Honey felt as though she were escaping some invisible bond as she skittered down the ladder, nearly falling in her haste.

"Honey!" he shouted after her. "Wait!"

Honey hadn't thought he could get off the roof so fast, but she had no intention of waiting around for him. She started for the house on the run. She was terrified, not of the drifter, but of her own feelings. If he touched her…

Honey was fast, but Jesse was faster. He caught her just as she was starting up the front steps and followed her onto the shaded porch. When Jesse grabbed her arm to stop her, momentum slammed her body back around and into his. He tightened his arms around her to keep them both from falling.

Honey would have protested, except she couldn't catch her breath. It was a mistake to look up, because the sight of his eyes, dark with desire, made her gasp. Jesse captured her mouth with his. His hand thrust into the curls at her nape and held her head so she couldn't escape his kiss.

Honey wished she could have said she fought him. But she didn't. Because from the instant his lips took possession of hers, she was lost. His mouth was hard at first, demanding, and only softened as she melted into his arms. By then he was biting at her lips, his tongue seeking entrance. He tasted like coffee, and something else, something distinctly male. His kiss thrilled her, and she wanted more.

It was only when Honey felt herself pushing against Jesse that she realized he had spread his legs and pulled her into the cradle of his thighs. She could feel his arousal, the hard bulge that had caught her unsuspecting attention so short a time ago. She heard a low, throaty groan and realized it had come from her.

Jesse's mouth mimicked the undulation of their bodies. Honey had never felt so alive. Her pulse thrummed, her body quickened. With excitement. With anticipation. *It had been so long.* She needed—craved—more. How could this stranger, this drifter, make her feel so much? Need so much?

At first Honey couldn't identify the shrill sound that interfered with her concentration.

Pleasure. Desire. Need.

The sound persisted, distracting her. Finally she realized it was the phone.

Honey hadn't been aware of her hands, but she discovered they were clutching handfuls of Jesse's black hair. His hat had fallen to the porch behind him. She stiffened. Slowly, she slid her hands away.

"The phone," she gasped, pushing now at his shoulders.

Honey felt Jesse's reluctance to release her. Whether he recognized the panic in her eyes, or the presumption of what he had done, he finally let her go. But he didn't step away. Honey had to do that herself.

"The phone," she repeated.

"You'd better answer it." It was clear he would rather she didn't. His body radiated tension.

Honey stood there another moment staring, her body alive with unmet needs, before she turned and raced inside the house. For a second she thought he would follow her, but from the corner of her eye she saw him whirl on his booted heel and head toward the barn.

She was panting by the time she snatched the phone from its cradle. "H-hello?"

"Honey? Why didn't you answer? Is everything all right?"

Dear Lord. It was Adam. Honey held her hand over the receiver and took several deep breaths, trying to regain her composure. There was nothing she could do about the pink spots on her cheeks except be grateful he wasn't there to see them.

At least there was one good thing that had come from the drifter's kiss. Honey knew now, without a doubt, that she could never marry Adam Philips. The sooner she told Adam, the better. Only she couldn't tell him over the phone. She owed him the courtesy of refusing him to his face.

"Honey, talk to me. What's going on?" Adam demanded.

"Everything's fine, Adam. I'm just a little breathless, that's all. I was outside when the phone started ringing," she explained.

"Oh. I called to see if your hired hand showed up."

"He's here."

There was a long pause. Honey wasn't about to volunteer any information about the man. If Adam was curious, he could ask.

"Oh," Adam said again.

To Honey's relief, it didn't appear he was going to pursue the subject.

"I know I said I wouldn't call until next week," he continued, "but an old school friend of mine in Amarillo called and asked me to come for a visit. His divorce is final and he needs some moral support. I'm leaving today and I don't know when I'll be back. I just wanted to let you know.''

Good old reliable Adam. Honey rubbed at the furrow on her brow. ''Adam, is there any chance you could come by here on your way out of town? I need to talk to you.''

''I wish I could, but I'm trying to catch a flight out of San Antonio and it's going to be close if I leave right now. Can you tell me over the phone?''

''Adam, I—''

Honey felt the hair prickle on the back of her neck. She turned and saw that Jesse had stepped inside the kitchen door.

She stared at him helplessly. She swallowed.

''Honey? Are you still there?'' Adam said.

''I'll see you when you get back, Adam. Have a good trip.''

Honey hung up the phone without waiting to hear Adam's reply. She stared at Jesse, unable to move. He had put his shirt back on, but left it unsnapped so a strip of sun-warmed skin glistened down the middle of his chest. He had retrieved his Stetson and it sat tipped back off his forehead. His thumbs were slung into the front of the beltless jeans. He had cocked a hip, but he looked anything but relaxed.

''The repairs on the roof are done,'' he said. ''I wanted to make sure it's all right with you if I saddle up that black stud to round up those steers that need vaccinating.''

''Night Wind was Cale's horse,'' Honey said. ''He hasn't been ridden much since—''

Naturally Jesse would want to ride the wildest, most dangerous horse in the stable. And why not? The man and the stallion were well matched.

''Of course, you can take Night Wind,'' she said. ''If you wait a minute, I'll come with you.''

''I don't think that's a good idea.''

She didn't ask why not. He could use the distance and so could she. ''All right,'' she said. ''The steers that need to be vaccinated are in the west pasture. Come get me when you've got them herded into the corral next to the barn.''

He tipped his hat, angled his mouth in that crooked smile and left.

Honey stared at the spot where he had been. She closed her eyes to shut out the vision of Jesse Whitelaw in her kitchen. It was plain as a white picket fence that she wasn't going to be able to forget the man anytime soon.

At least she had a respite for a couple of hours. She realized suddenly that because of Jesse's interruption she hadn't been able to refuse Adam's offer of marriage.

Horsefeathers!

She should never have kissed Jesse. Not that she had made any commitment to Adam, but she owed it to him to decline his offer before he found her in a compromising position with some other man. And not that she intended to get involved with Jesse Whitelaw, but so far, where that drifter was concerned, she hadn't felt as though things were under control. The smart move was to keep her distance from the man.

That shouldn't be a problem. No problem at all.

Three

The black stud had more than a little buck in him, which suited Jesse just fine. He was in the mood for a fight, and the stud gave it to him. By the time the horse had settled down, Jesse had covered most of the rolling prairie that led to the west pasture. It wouldn't take long to herd the steers back to the chutes at the barn where they would be vaccinated. Only he had some business to conduct first.

Jesse searched the horizon and found what he was looking for. The copse of pecan trees stood along the far western border of the Flying Diamond. He rode toward the trees hoping that his contact would be there waiting for him. He spotted the glint of sun off cold steel and headed toward it.

''Kind of risky carrying a rifle around these parts with everyone looking out for badmen, don't you think?'' Jesse said. He tipped his hat back slowly, careful to keep his hands in plain sight all the time.

''Don't know who you can trust nowadays,'' the other cowboy answered. ''Your name Whitelaw?''

Jesse nodded. ''From the description I got, you'd be Mort Barnes.''

The cowboy had been easy to identify because he had a deep scar through his right eyebrow that made it look as if he had come close to losing his eye. In fact, the eye was clouded over and Jesse doubted whether Mort had any sight in it. The other eye was almost yellow with a black rim around it. Mort more than made up for the missing eye with the glare from his good one. Black hair sprouted beneath a battered straw cowboy hat and a stubble of black beard covered his cheeks and chin.

Jesse evaluated the other man physically and realized if he had to fight him, it was going to be a tooth and claw affair. The cowboy was lean and rangy from a life spent on horseback. He looked tough as rawhide.

"Tell your boss I got the job," Jesse said.

Mort smiled, revealing broken teeth. The man was a fighter, all right. "Yeah, I'll do that," Mort said. "How soon you figure you can get your hands on that prize bull of hers?"

"Depends. She keeps him in the barn. He's almost a pet. It won't be easy stealing him."

"The Boss wants—"

"I don't care what your boss wants. I do things my way, or he can forget about my help."

Mort scowled. "You work for the Boss, you take orders from him."

"I don't take orders from anybody. I promised I'd steal the bull for him and I will. But I do it my way, understand?" Jesse stared until Mort's one yellow eye glanced away.

"I'll tell the Boss what you said. But he ain't gonna like it," the cowboy muttered.

"If he doesn't like the way I do things he can tell me so himself," Jesse said. "Meanwhile, I don't want any more cattle stolen from the Flying Diamond."

The look in Mort's eye was purely malicious. "The Boss don't like bein' told what to do."

"If he wants that bull, he'll stay away from here. And tell him the next time one of his henchmen shows up around here he'd better not be carrying a gun."

Mort raised the rifle defensively. "I ain't ridin' around here without protection."

Jesse worked hard not to smile. It was pretty funny when the badman thought he needed a gun to protect himself from the good guys.

"Don't bring a gun onto the Flying Diamond again," Jesse said. "I won't tell you twice."

It was plain Mort didn't like being threatened, but short of shooting Jesse there wasn't much he could do. The outlaw had kept a constant lookout, so he spotted the rider approaching from the direction of the ranch house when there was no more than a speck of movement in the distance.

''You expectin' company?'' Mort asked, gesturing toward the rider with his gun.

Jesse glanced over his shoulder and knew immediately who it was. ''Dammit. I told her I'd come get her,'' he muttered. ''It looks like Mrs. Farrell. Get the hell out of here and get now!''

Mort grinned. ''Got plans of your own for the Missus, huh? Can't say as I blame you. Mighty fine lookin' woman.''

Jesse grabbed hold of Mort's shirt at the throat and half pulled the man out of the saddle. The look in Jesse's eyes had Mort quailing even though the outlaw was the one with the gun. ''That's no way to talk about a lady, Mort.''

The outlaw swallowed hard. ''Didn't mean nothin' by it.''

Jesse released the man's shirt. He straightened it with both hands, carefully reining his temper. ''Back up slow and easy and keep that rifle out of the sunlight. No sense me having to make explanations to Mrs. Farrell about what you're doing here.''

Mort wasn't stupid. What Jesse said made sense. Besides, the Boss would skin him alive if he got caught anywhere near Mrs. Farrell. ''I'm skedaddlin','' he said.

Without another word, Mort backed his horse into the copse of pecans and out of sight. Jesse whirled the stud and galloped toward Honey to keep her from coming any closer before Mort made good his escape.

Why hadn't she waited for him at the ranch, as he'd asked? Damned woman was going to be more trouble than he'd thought. But she was sure a sight for sore eyes.

Her hair hung in frothy golden curls that whipped around her head and shoulders as she cantered her bay gelding toward him. She ought to be wearing a hat, he thought. As light-skinned as she was, the sun would burn her in no time at all. He remembered how her pale hand had looked in his bronzed one, how soft it had felt between his callused fingers and thumb. Never had he been more conscious of who and what he was.

Jesse hadn't known at first what it meant to be part Indian. He had learned. *Breed. Half-breed. Dirty Injun.* He had heard them all. What made it so ironic was the fact that neither of his two older brothers, Garth and Faron, nor his younger sister, Tate, looked Indian at all. He was the only one who had taken after their Comanche ancestors.

His brothers hadn't understood his bitterness at being different. They hadn't understood the cause for his bloody knuckles and blackened eyes. Surprisingly, it was his half-English, half-Irish father who had made him proud he was descended from a warrior people, the savage Comanche.

That knowledge had shaped his whole life.

Jesse had often wondered what would have happened if he had been born a hundred years earlier; he often felt as barbaric as any Comanche. He had not been able to settle in one place, but needed to wander as his forebears had. While it was still a ruthless world he lived in, the conventions of society had glossed over the ugliness so it was not as apparent. Except, he had chosen a life that brought him into daily contact with what was cruel and sordid in the modern world. And forced him daily to confront his own feral nature.

Jesse no longer apologized for who and what he was. He had not tied himself to any one place, or any one person. He had never minded being alone or even considered the loneliness and isolation caused by his way of life. Until he had met the woman riding toward him now.

His eyes narrowed on Honey Farrell. He wished he could tell her about himself. Wished he could explain how she made him feel, but he couldn't even tell her who he really was. Nevertheless, he had no intention of letting the circumstances keep them apart. It wasn't honorable to keep the truth from her, but he consoled himself with the thought that when this was all over, he would more than make it up to her.

It was unfortunate she didn't—couldn't—know the truth about him, but he convinced himself that it wouldn't matter to her. He would make her understand that they belonged together. And who—and what—he was would make no difference.

"Hello, there!" Honey called as she rode up to Jesse. "There was a phone call for you after you left."

Jesse took off his hat, thrust his hand through his too-long black hair and resettled the Stetson. "Can't imagine who'd call me," he said. His family had no idea where he was—and hadn't known for years.

"It was Dallas."

Jesse frowned. "Any particular reason for the call?"

"He invited you to dinner tonight." Honey didn't mention that Dallas had invited her to dinner as well. She had tried to refuse, but Dallas had put Angel on the phone, and Honey had succumbed to the other woman's plea for company.

Honey felt that same inexplicable tension she always felt around Jesse. Her gelding sidestepped and their knees brushed. That simple touch produced goose bumps on her arms. She was grateful for the long-sleeved Western shirt that hid her reaction. She stared off toward the copse of pecans in the distance, avoiding Jesse's startled glance.

And spotted a glint of sunlight off metal.

"There's someone in the trees behind you," Honey said in a quiet voice. "I think he has a gun."

Jesse said a few pithy words under his breath. "Don't let him know you see him. Help me get these steers moving toward the barn."

"Do you think it might be one of the rustlers?" Honey asked as she loosened the rope from her saddle.

"Don't know and don't care," Jesse said. "That's a matter for the police. Best thing for us to do is get ourselves and these cattle out of here."

There was no discussion as they used whistles and an occasional slap with a lasso to herd the steers back toward the barn. When they were a safe distance away, Honey kneed her gelding over to join Jesse.

"I've lost a lot of stock to rustlers since Cale died," Honey said. "I suppose they don't believe I'm any threat to them. But I didn't think they'd dare let themselves be seen in broad daylight. I'll call the police when we get back to the house and—"

Jesse interrupted. "There's no need for that. I'll tell Dallas about it when I call to accept his dinner invitation."

Honey frowned. "I guess that'll be okay. Uh...I suppose I should have mentioned I've also been invited to dinner. Would you mind if I got a ride with you?"

Jesse kept the dismay he felt from his face. He had hoped to use the time he was away from the ranch to do some other business without

Honey being any the wiser. Having her along meant he would have to curtail his plans. But he couldn't think of a good reason to refuse her a ride that wouldn't raise suspicion. "Sure," he said at last. "Why not? What time do you want to leave?"

"Around six, I suppose. That'll give me time after we finish with the vaccinating to get cleaned up and make some supper for Jack and Jonathan."

"That sounds fine. Meanwhile, until those rustlers are caught you'd better stay close to home."

Honey glanced at Jesse to see if he was serious. He was. "I have a ranch to run," she said.

"I'm here now. If there's work that needs to be done away from the house, I can do it."

"You're being ridiculous. I don't think—"

"No, you aren't thinking!" Jesse interrupted in a harsh voice. "What's going to happen if you chance onto those rustlers at the wrong time? They've killed before and—"

"Killed! Who? When?"

Jesse swore again. He hadn't meant to alarm her, just keep her safe. "A rancher near Laredo was found shot to death last month."

"Oh, my God," Honey whispered. "Surely it wasn't the same rustlers who took my cattle!"

"What if it is? Better safe than sorry. You stay around the ranch house." It came out sounding like the order it was.

Honey bristled. "I'm in charge here. And I'll do as I please!"

"Just try leaving," he said. "And we'll see."

"Why, of all the high-handed, macho cowboy talk I ever heard—"

Jesse grabbed the reins and pulled her gelding to a halt. "These guys aren't fooling around, Honey. They've killed once. They've got nothing to lose if they kill again. I wouldn't want anything to happen to you."

The back of his gloved hand brushed against her cheek. "I don't intend to lose you."

Honey's heart missed a beat. He was high-handed, all right, but when he spoke to her in that low raspy voice and looked at her with those dark mysterious eyes, she found herself ready to listen. Which made no sense at all.

''How does a drifter like you know so much about all this?'' she asked.

''Dallas filled me in,'' he said. When she still looked doubtful, he said, ''Ask him yourself at dinner tonight.''

''Maybe I will.''

The entire time they vaccinated bawling cattle, Honey said nothing more about the dinner at Dallas Masterson's house. She was thinking about it, though, because she realized Jesse would have to use the upstairs bathroom to clean up. She had yet to explain to him that she planned for him to sleep in a room in the barn that hired hands had used in the past.

She decided to confront him before the boys got home from school, in case he decided to argue. They were both hot and sweaty from the work they'd been doing, so it was easy to say, ''I could use some iced tea. Would you like some?''

''Sounds good,'' he replied. ''I'll be up to the house in a minute. I have a few things to put away here first.''

Honey was glad for the few moments the delay gave her to think about how to phrase what she wanted to say. She took her time in the kitchen, filling two glasses with ice and sun-brewed tea. She wasn't ready when he appeared at the screen door, hat in hand.

''May I come in?''

His request reminded her that she had met Jesse Whitelaw less than twenty-four hours earlier. It seemed like a lot longer. Like maybe she had known the cowboy all her life. It left her feeling apprehensive. She avoided his eyes as she pushed the screen door wide and said, ''Sure. I've made tea for both of us.''

He moved immediately to the glass of tea on the table and lifted it to his lips. She watched as he tipped the glass and emptied it a swallow at a time. Rivulets of sweat streamed down his temples, and his hair was slick against his head where his hat had matted it down. He smelled of hardworking man, and she was all too aware of how he filled the space in her kitchen.

Jesse sighed with satisfaction as he set the empty glass on the table. The sound of the ice settling was loud in the silence that followed as his eyes found hers and held.

''I think I have time to look at whatever fence you have down before

I have to get ready for supper,'' Jesse said. ''If you'll just head me in the right direction.''

''Certainly. There are a few things we need to discuss first.'' Honey threaded her fingers so she wouldn't fidget. ''When I offered you room and board I wasn't thinking about where I'd put you. There's a room at the rear of the barn I can fix up for you, but you'll have to use the bathroom in the house.''

Jesse worked to keep the grimace off his face. It would be a lot more difficult explaining how her prize bull had been stolen from the barn if he was sleeping there. ''Are you sure there isn't somewhere in the house I could sleep? I don't need much.''

Honey chewed on her lower lip. ''There is a small room off the kitchen.'' She pointed out the closed door to him. ''It's awfully tiny. I've started using it for a pantry. I don't think—''

Jesse opened the door and stepped inside. The room was long and narrow. Wooden shelves along one wall were filled with glass jars of preserves, most likely from the small garden he had seen behind the house. An iron bed with a bare mattress stood along the opposite wall under a gingham-curtained window. A simple wooden chest held a brass lamp and an old-fashioned pitcher and bowl for water.

''This'll do fine,'' he said.

''But—''

He turned and she was aware of how small the room was, or rather, how he filled it. She took a step back, away from the very strong attraction she felt. ''The room in the barn is bigger,'' she argued. ''You'd have more privacy.''

He grinned. ''I suppose that's true, if you don't count the livestock.''

''I have to come in here sometimes to get food from the shelves,'' she explained.

''You could knock.''

''Yes, I suppose I could.'' It was hard to argue with logic. Yet Honey didn't want to concede defeat. Otherwise, she was going to find herself with the hired hand constantly underfoot. She made a last effort to convince him the barn was a better choice. ''The boys sometimes make a lot of noise. Morning and evening. You won't get much peace and quiet if you stay here.''

"I expect I'll be going to bed later and getting up earlier than they will," he replied.

Honey sighed. This wasn't working out as she had planned at all. Somehow she had ended up with this part-savage stranger, this drifter, living under her roof. She wasn't exactly frightened of him, but she was uneasy. After all, what did she really know about him?

He seemed to sense her hesitation and said, "If you don't feel comfortable with me in the house, of course I'll sleep in the barn."

There it was, her chance to avoid coping with his presence in the house. She opened her mouth to say "Please do" and instead said, "That won't be necessary. I'm sure this will work out fine."

At that moment the kitchen screen door slammed open and Jonathan came racing through. "Hi, Mom! Hi, Jesse! I'm missing cartoons!" He was through the kitchen and gone before Honey could even gasp a hello.

A few moments later Jack appeared at the door. He didn't greet his mother or the hired man, simply dropped his books on the kitchen table and headed straight for the cookie jar on the counter. He reached inside and found it empty. "Hey! I thought you were going to bake some cookies today."

"I didn't have time," Honey apologized.

He opened a cupboard, looking for something else to eat.

Honey saw Jesse's jaw tighten, as though he wanted to say something but was biting his tongue. Perhaps Jack wasn't as courteous as he could have been, but from what Honey had gathered from the mothers of Jack's friends, it was typical teenage behavior. She was used to it. Apparently Jesse wasn't.

Jack seemed oblivious to them as he hauled bread, peanut butter and jelly out onto the counter and made himself a sandwich.

Honey watched Jesse's expression harden. She wasn't sure whether to be more vexed and annoyed by Jack's conduct, or Jesse's reaction to it.

Jack picked up his sandwich, took a bite that encompassed nearly half of it, and headed out the kitchen door toward the den and the television.

"Do you have any homework?" Honey asked.

''Just studying for tests,'' Jack said through a mouthful of peanut butter. ''I'll do it later.''

Honey hadn't realized Jesse could move so fast. Before Jack reached the kitchen door, the hired hand blocked his way.

''Just a minute, son.''

Jack stiffened. ''You're in my way.''

''That was the general idea.''

Jack turned to his mother, clearly expecting her to resolve the situation.

Honey wasn't sure what Jesse intended, let alone whether she could thwart that intention. For her son's sake, she had to try. ''Jesse—''

''This is between me and Jack,'' Jesse said.

''I don't have anything to say to you,'' Jack retorted.

''Maybe not. But I've got a few things to say to you.''

Jack balled his fist, turning the sandwich into a squashed mess. ''You've got no right—''

''First off, a gentleman greets a lady when he comes into the room. Second, he doesn't complain about the vittles. Third, he asks for what he needs from a lady's kitchen, he doesn't just take it. Fourth, he inquires whether chores need to be done before he heads for the bunkhouse. And finally, he doesn't talk with his mouth full.''

Jack swallowed. The soft bread felt like spiny tumbleweed as it grated over the constriction in his throat. This was the kind of dressing-down his father might have given him. The kind of talking-to he hadn't had for more than a year, since his father's death. He resented it. Even though he knew deep down that the hired hand was right.

Jack angled his face to his mom, to see what she was going to do about the drifter's interference. He felt sick in the pit of his stomach when he saw how pale her face was. Jack turned from his mother and confronted the hired hand. He let the hostility he was feeling show in his eyes, but for his mother's sake, struggled to keep it out of his voice. ''Maybe I was wrong,'' he conceded.

Jesse continued to stare at the boy and was pleased when the gangly teenager turned to his mother and gritted out, ''Hello, Mom. Thanks for the sandwich.''

Jack looked down at the mess in his hand and grimaced.

''You can wash your hands in the sink,'' Honey said.

Jesse stepped aside to allow the boy to pass and in doing so, glanced at Honey. Her dark blue eyes were afire with emotion, but it wasn't gratitude he saw there. Obviously he had stepped amiss. He clenched his teeth over the explanation for his actions that sprang to mind. She didn't look as though she wanted to hear reason.

Jesse and Honey stared at each other while Jack washed his hands. He turned from the sink, still drying his hands with a dish towel, and asked his mother, "Are there any chores that need to be done before supper?"

Since Cale's death, Honey had taken the responsibility for almost all the ranch chores her husband had done in the evening. When Jack offered, she realized there was work that still needed to be done in the barn that she would appreciate having Jack's help completing. "You can feed the stock," she said. "Also, I let General out into the corral. Would you bring him back inside the barn for the night?"

"Sure, Mom. Anything else?"

"That's all I can think of now."

Without looking at Jesse again, Jack pushed his way out the screen door and let it slam behind him.

The tension was palpable once the two adults were alone.

Jesse started to apologize for interfering, then bit his tongue. He had been hard on the boy, but no more so than his father had been with him. A tree grew as the sapling began. Now was the time for Jack to learn courtesy and responsibility.

"I don't quite know what to say," Honey began. "I don't agree with your methods, but I can't argue with the results. Maybe I've been too lax with Jack the past few months, but he took Cale's death so hard, I..."

Jesse heard the tremor in her voice and took a step toward her. As soon as he did, she squared her shoulders and lifted her chin.

"It hasn't been easy for any of us," she said in a firmer voice. "But we've managed to get along."

Jesse heard "without your help" even though she didn't say the words. So be it. This was the last time he would get involved. If she wanted to let the boy walk all over her, that was her business. It was just fine with him.

Like hell it was.

"Look," he said. "I can't promise I won't say anything more to the boy. We have to work together, after all. But I'll try not to step on any toes in the future. How does that sound?"

"Like the best compromise I'm going to get," Honey replied with a rueful smile.

"Guess I'll go work on that fence."

"I'll take my bath early," she said. "That way the bathroom will be free when you get back."

"Fine."

He had to walk by her to get to the door. Honey marveled at how small any room got with the two of them in it. She stepped back until she pressed against the counter, but their bodies still brushed. Jesse hesitated just an instant before he continued past her. He didn't look back as he pushed his way out the screen door. But she noticed he caught the door and kept it from slamming on his way out.

Honey heaved a sigh—of relief?—when she had the kitchen to herself again. She wished she didn't need Jesse's help so much on the ranch, because she wasn't at all sure she could handle having him around. His presence was already changing everything. She was beginning to feel things that she hadn't ever expected to feel again.

Nothing could come of her attraction to Jesse. He was a drifter. Sticking around wasn't in his nature. When the mood struck him, he would be moving on. And she would be left alone. Again.

She had best remember that when the yearning rose to let him get close.

Four

Honey scooted down, settled her nape on the edge of the free-standing, claw-footed bathtub and closed her eyes. Her entire body was submerged and steam rose from water that lapped at the top edge of the tub. There was no shower in the house, only this aged white porcelain tub. She smiled when she imagined what Jesse's reaction was going to be when he confronted this monstrosity.

It was easy to blame the absence of a modern shower on the lack of extra money over the years she and Cale had been married. But the truth was, Honey loved the old-fashioned deep-bellied tub, with its brass fixtures and lion's paw legs. Instead of putting in a shower, she and Cale had expanded the capacity of the water heater so it was possible to fill the giant tub with steaming hot water all the way to the top.

Honey had laced the scalding water with scented bath oil, and the room reeked of honeysuckle. She was reminded of hot baths she and Cale had taken together. Honey crossed her arms and caressed her shoulders, smoothing in the bath oil. And imagined how it would feel if Jesse…

Abruptly Honey sat up, sloshing water over the edge of the tub. Her eyes flew open and she looked around her. Her daydreams had seemed so real. For a moment it had seemed as though that man was here. In her tub. With her. His hands—never mind where his hands had been!

And his mouth— Honey shivered in reaction to the vivid pictures her mind had painted.

"Horsefeathers!" she muttered.

Honey lunged up, splashing water on the floor, and grabbed for a terry cloth towel. She wrapped herself in it, then reached down to pull the plug. And felt a spurt of guilt. The water heater would fill the tub once—but not twice. Her remorse didn't last long, and a smile slowly appeared on her face. Jesse Whitelaw could stand to cool off a little. A nice cold bath ought to help him along.

Honey was in her bedroom and had almost finished dressing when Jesse knocked at her door.

"Hey, there's no shower in that bathroom," he said.

"I know." Honey tried to keep the grin out of her voice.

He muttered something crude under his breath, then said, "Where are the towels?"

"The linens on the rack in the bathroom are yours to use."

Honey heard the water run for a short while, then stop. She left her bedroom and stood outside the bathroom door listening. There was a long silence, followed by a male yelp and frantic splashing. "This water's like ice!" he bellowed.

"I know," she said loud enough to be heard through the door. By now her grin was huge.

Jesse muttered again.

"I'm going downstairs to fix some dinner for Jack and Jonathan. Enjoy your bath."

Her laughter followed her down the stairs.

Jesse shivered, but not from the cold. It was the first time he'd heard Honey laugh, and the sound skittered down his spine. His lips curled ruefully. At least now he knew she had a sense of humor.

He soaped a rag and washed himself vigorously, as though that could obliterate his thoughts of her. But Honey Farrell had gotten under his skin. Every breath he took filled his lungs with the honeysuckle scent she had bathed in. Everywhere he looked there were reminders that he had invaded her feminine domain.

The pedestal sink was cluttered on top with all sorts of female paraphernalia—powder and lipstick and deodorant and suchlike—except where she had cleared a tiny space for his things.

Jesse cursed a blue streak as he rinsed himself with the icy water, then grabbed a towel and stepped out onto the deepest pile rug he had ever felt beneath his feet. It was decorated with whimsical daisies—as was the towel he had wrapped around his hips. If his brothers could see him now, they would rib him up one side and down the other.

He quickly pulled on clean briefs and jeans, then slung the towel around his neck while he shaved. He debated whether to leave his straight edge razor and strop in the bathroom, then decided that as long as she had left the space for him, he might as well use it. When he saw his things beside hers, he pursed his lips thoughtfully. It was as though an unfinished picture had been completed.

He spread the damp towel over the rack and put on the shirt he had brought into the bathroom with him. He had hoped the steam from a hot shower would ease some of the wrinkles out of it. Since he'd ended up taking a cold bath, he had no choice except to shrug into the wrinkled shirt.

Jesse started to borrow Honey's hairbrush but changed his mind and finger-combed his hair instead. It would hang straight once it dried no matter what he did with it now.

Jesse came down the stairs quietly and stood at the kitchen door undetected by the trio at the table. Honey was serving up her younger son's dinner. Her face was rosy, probably from all that hot water she'd bathed in, he thought with a silent chuckle. He was glad to see she wasn't wearing black again, but he thought the pale green was wrong for her.

She ought to be wearing vivid colors—reds and royal blues—that were as full of life as she was. He liked the way the dress clung to her figure, outlining her breasts and defining her slim waist and hips. She looked very much like a woman, and he felt the blood surge in his loins at the sight of her.

He watched unnoticed as Honey brushed a lock of hair off Jonathan's forehead. She put a hand on Jack's shoulder as she set the salt and pepper before him. Then she found another reason to touch Jonathan. Jesse wondered if Honey had any idea what she was doing. He felt his body tauten with the thought of her touching him like that.

Jesse's family members were fiercely loyal to each other, but they weren't much for touching. He could count on one hand the number of times his mother had caressed him in any way. He hadn't realized until now just how needful he was of Honey's touch and the feel of her hands on his body.

"Oh, there you are!" Honey froze with her hand outstretched for the butter dish. She wondered how long Jesse had been standing there. He had a way of watching her that she found totally unnerving. His dark, hooded gaze revealed a hunger that took her breath away, but there was a yearning, almost wistful expression in his eyes as well.

"Are you ready to go?" he asked.

Honey took a good look at what the hired hand was wearing and frowned. She wondered what kind of life Jesse Whitelaw had led when this was all he had to wear to dinner. His jeans were clean but worn white at the stress points and seams. The faded western shirt was frayed at collar and cuffs and badly creased. His leather belt was dark with age and had a shiny silver buckle she felt sure he had earned as a prize at some rodeo. He wore the same tooled black leather boots he had worn all day; the scuff marks showed the hard use they'd had.

She almost offered to iron his shirt, then changed her mind. Somehow she knew he wouldn't appreciate the suggestion. Besides, if he had really been concerned about his appearance, he could have asked for the iron himself. "I'm ready anytime you are," she said.

The ride to Dallas's place in Jesse's pickup truck—which was barely two years old and in surprisingly good shape compared to his clothing—took barely an hour. Because of the long, uncomfortable silences between inane bits of conversation, it felt a lot longer.

Even in the modern West, a man was still entitled to his privacy. Thus Honey didn't feel she could ask Jesse about himself. That left a myriad of other subjects, not one of which came readily to mind.

The silence was deafening by the time Jesse said, "How long have you known Dallas and Angel?"

Honey grabbed at the conversational gambit like a gambler for a deck of cards. "I met Dallas about four years ago when he and Cale started working together on assignments for the Texas Rangers. Dallas introduced me to Angel a little over a year ago, about the same time she and Dallas met each other."

"How did the two of them meet?" Jesse asked.

"You know, they never said. Every time I asked, Angel blushed and Dallas laughed and said, 'You wouldn't believe me if I told you.'"

"How did you and that Philips guy meet?" Jesse asked.

That was more personal ground. Honey hesitated, then grinned and admitted, "Dallas invited me on a double date with Adam and Angel. By the end of the day, Dallas ended up with Angel, and Adam and I were a couple."

"How serious are things between you and Philips?"

Honey shot a quick look at Jesse, but his expression was bland. "I don't think that's any of your business."

"I think maybe it is."

"I can't imagine why—"

"Can't you?" His piercing gaze riveted her for a moment before he had to look at the road again.

Honey's pulse began to speed. She grasped at the opportunity to put the hired hand in his place once and for all. "Adam has asked me to marry him," she said.

A muscle jerked in Jesse's cheek. "You don't love him," he said curtly.

"You can't possibly know whether I love him or not."

He cocked a brow and his lips drew up cynically. "Can't I?"

Honey turned to stare out the window, avoiding his searching look.

"Are you going to marry him?"

"I—" Honey considered lying. Perhaps if she told Jesse she was committed to another man, he would leave her alone. But she couldn't use Adam like that—simply to keep another man at arm's length. "No," she admitted.

"Good."

Nothing else passed between them for the few minutes it took to traverse the length of the road from the cattle guard at the entrance to Dallas's ranch to the Victorian ranch house. At least, nothing in words. But Honey was aware of the portal the drifter had forced open between them.

"I won't ever hurt you," Jesse said in a quiet voice.

"You can, you know," she said in an equally quiet voice.

His lips flattened. "I don't want you to be afraid of me."

"Then leave me alone."

"I can't do that."

"Jesse..."

The Mastersons' porch light was on, and Jesse pulled the truck up well within its glow. He killed the engine and turned to look at Honey. "Is it your husband?" he asked bluntly.

Honey felt the pain that always came with memories of Cale. "Cale is dead."

"I know that. Do you?"

Honey gasped and turned to stare at Jesse. "What do you want from me?"

"More than it seems you're willing to give."

Jesse's sharp voice cut through her pain, and Honey realized she was angry. "You can hardly blame me," she said. "I'm not in a hurry to get my heart torn out again."

"Who says you have to?"

Honey snorted inelegantly. "That sounds pretty funny coming from a man like you. How many women have you loved and left, Jesse? How long should I plan on you hanging around? And what am I supposed to do when you're gone? I'd have to be a fool to get involved with you. And whatever else I might be, I'm no fool. I—"

Honey broke off when she saw Angel come running out onto the porch to greet them. She flashed Jesse a look of frustration and quickly stepped out of the truck and headed up the porch steps.

"It's good to see you again, Honey," Angel said as the two women hugged. She didn't offer her hand to the drifter and kept her distance. "Dallas is putting the baby to bed. He'll be down in a minute. Won't you both come inside?"

She stepped away from Jesse and held the door. Honey saw the other woman actually shiver as Jesse passed by her. Honey wondered what it was about the drifter that caused Angel to shy away from him. Was it possible that Dallas had told her something about Jesse? Something sinister?

Honey shook her head and dismissed the possibility. She didn't know much about Jesse, but she didn't see him as a villainous figure. Probably there was something in Angel's own past that was causing her to react so strangely to Dallas's friend.

Dallas had none of his wife's reservations. He greeted Jesse warmly and shook his hand. ''I'm glad you could come on such short notice,'' Dallas said. ''I thought maybe we could talk about old times, maybe get reacquainted. How are your brothers and your sister?''

Honey's eyes widened and she stared at Jesse as though she had never seen him before. ''You have a family?''

Jesse grinned. ''Two older brothers and a younger sister.''

''Where?'' Honey asked.

''At the family ranch, Hawk's Way, in northwest Texas near Palo Duro Canyon.''

So, Jesse wasn't as much of a footloose drifter as he had led her to believe. He had some roots after all.

''Would anyone like something to drink?'' Angel asked.

''Whiskey and water,'' Jesse said.

''Iced tea for me,'' Honey said.

''Dallas?''

''I'll join Jesse and have a whiskey, but without the water, Angel.''

Honey sat on the Victorian sofa and Dallas took the leather chair that was obviously his favorite spot in the living room. Jesse joined Honey on the narrow sofa. It barely held the two of them, and Jesse's jean-clad leg brushed against her as he sat down.

Honey jerked away, then looked up to see if Dallas had noticed her reaction. He had. He looked concerned, but Honey wasn't about to explain the sexually fraught situation to him. Honey grimaced and folded her hands together in her lap. It was going to be a long evening.

Or it might have been if Angel hadn't been there. Honey had always liked Angel and had an affinity with the other woman that she couldn't explain. She did her best throughout the spicy Mexican meal to focus her attention on Angel and ignore Jesse Whitelaw. She wasn't totally successful.

It bothered Honey that Angel never got over her odd behavior around Jesse. Angel never quite relaxed, and her eyes were wary every time she looked at him. In fact, it bothered Honey enough that she mentioned it when she and Angel went upstairs to check on the baby after supper, leaving the men to stack the dishes in the dishwasher.

''You don't seem to like Jesse Whitelaw,'' Honey said bluntly.

Angel refused to meet her gaze, focusing instead on the baby sleeping in the crib. ''It's not that I don't like him, it's just...''

"Just what? Has Dallas told you something about him? Something I should know?"

"Oh, no!" Angel reassured her. "It's nothing like that. It's just..."

Honey waited while Angel searched for the words to explain her aversion to the drifter.

"When I was much younger, I had a bad experience with some Indians." What Angel wasn't able to tell Honey was that she had seen the tortured remains of a Comanche raid in 1857. But no one except Dallas knew Angel had traveled through time to reach this century. So Angel was forced to explain how she felt without being able to give specific details.

"Whenever I look at Jesse," she said, "I see something in those dark eyes of his, something so savage, so feral, it reminds me of that time long ago. He terrifies me." Angel visibly shivered. "Aren't you afraid of him?"

"Sometimes," Honey admitted reluctantly. "But not in the way you are." Honey felt certain Jesse posed no physical threat to her. The wild, savage looks that frightened Angel only served to make Jesse more intriguing to her. "I find him attractive," she confessed. And that was more frightening than anything else about the drifter that she might have admitted.

Their talking woke the baby, but Honey couldn't be sorry because she had been dying for a chance to hold the little boy.

"Aren't you a handsome boy, Rhett," Honey cooed as Angel laid the baby in her arms. "Can we take him downstairs?"

Angel seemed hesitant, but Honey urged, "Please?"

"All right." Angel had to face the fact that her fears of Jesse were misplaced in time. She might as well start now.

Dallas and Jesse stopped talking abruptly when the women came downstairs with the baby.

"Look," Honey said, holding Rhett so Jesse could see his face. "Isn't he something?"

Jesse wasn't looking at the child, he was looking at the glow on Honey's face. It was something, all right! She looked radiant and happier than he had ever seen her. He couldn't help imagining how she would look holding their child in her arms.

He frowned, wondering where that idea had come from. He wanted

Honey, but babies had a way of tying a man down. Still, he considered the idea and felt things he hadn't anticipated. Pride. Protectiveness. And fear.

Was Honey still young enough to carry a child without any danger to her health? She didn't look over thirty, but he knew she had to be older because Jack was thirteen.

''How old were you when Jack was born?'' Jesse asked.

Honey was surprised by the question. ''Eighteen. Cale and I married right out of high school.''

That made her thirty-two. Three years younger than he was. Maybe the better question was whether he was too old to be a father. He hadn't realized until just now how much he wanted a child of his own someday. Maybe he'd better not put it off too much longer.

''Do you wish you had more children?'' he asked Honey.

She never took her eyes off the baby's face. Jesse watched her fingers smooth over the tiny eyebrows, the plump cheeks, the rosy mouth and then touch the tiny fingertips that gripped her little finger. ''Oh, yes,'' she breathed.

She looked up at him and his heart leapt to his throat. Her eyes were liquid with feeling. Suddenly he wanted to be gone from here, to be alone with her.

Honey saw the fierce light in Jesse's eyes but knew she had nothing to fear. The fierceness thrilled her. The light drew her in and warmed her. Jesse Whitelaw was a danger to her, all right. But only because he had the power to steal her heart.

Honey was never sure later how they managed to take their leave so quickly, but she was grateful to be on her way home. In the darkness of the pickup cab she could hug her thoughts to herself. It was only after they had gone several miles that she thought to ask, ''Did you tell Dallas about that suspicious man I saw on my property today?''

There was only the slightest hesitation before Jesse replied, ''Yes. He said he'd look into it.''

''Did you have a good time tonight?''

''I had forgotten how much Dallas and I have in common,'' he said.

''Oh?'' She hadn't thought the two of them were much alike at all. ''Like what?''

Jesse was quiet so long Honey didn't think he was going to answer.

At last he said, "I can't think of any one thing. Just a feeling I had." He couldn't say more to Honey without raising questions that he wasn't prepared to answer.

"How did you like Angel?"

"Fine." *When she wasn't cringing from me.* He couldn't say that to Honey, either. He wasn't sure what it was about him that frightened Angel Masterson. He only knew she was terrified of him. His lip curled in disgust. She had probably heard stories about the savage Comanche. A hundred years ago his forebears had been savage. Perhaps Angel had been a victim of Comanches in another life.

Jesse shrugged off the uncomfortable feeling he got when he remembered Angel's fear of him. There was something about her that bothered him as much as he bothered her. If he stuck around long enough, maybe someday he would find out what it was.

"Jesse? Is something wrong?"

He hadn't realized he was frowning until Honey spoke. He wiped the expression off his face and said, "No. I'm okay."

"Can I ask you something?"

"Anything."

"Why didn't you tell me you have a family?"

Jesse shrugged. "It didn't seem important."

Family not important? Honey shook her head in despair. Everything she learned about Jesse confirmed him as a loner. She had to stay away from him if she wanted to survive his eventual leave-taking heart-whole.

"Now I want to ask a question?" Jesse said.

"What?"

"Why did you marry so young?"

"I was in love." She paused. "And pregnant."

That wasn't the answer he had been expecting, but it didn't really surprise him. He could imagine her youthful passion. He had tasted a little of it himself.

"Were you ever sorry?"

How could she answer that? Maybe she regretted losing some of her choices. But she didn't regret having Jack. As for having to marry…

"I met Cale when I was fourteen years old and fell in love with him at first sight,'' she said. ''I never wanted to be anything but Cale's wife, the mother of his children, and to work by his side on the Flying Diamond.''

Honey had never put her feelings into words, but it made her loss seem even greater when she realized that her whole life had been focused on Cale. Now that Cale was gone, she was forced to admit that they had never had the partnership she had imagined when she married him. Those youthful dreams were gone. The children were only hers to love for a little while before they grew up and left her. All she would have in the end was the Flying Diamond. Except now the Flying Diamond was being threatened as well.

''I wish someone would catch those rustlers,'' she said, expressing her fears aloud. ''About the only thing that's keeping the ranch afloat with the losses I've had is the service fees I get for General. I sure can't afford to lose any more stock.''

He thought of the devastation she would feel when the bull was stolen, but pushed it from his mind. ''You won't be losing any more cattle,'' Jesse said and then could have bitten his tongue.

''How can you be so sure?''

He shrugged. ''Just a feeling I have.''

One of those uncomfortable silences fell between them. Honey chewed her lower lip, wondering whether she ought to ask a question that had been on her mind lately. She saw the two-story ranch house come into sight and realized she would lose the opportunity to speak if she didn't do it now.

''Were you ever married?'' she asked.

Jesse's brow rose at the personal nature of the question. ''No.''

''Why not?''

His dark eyes glittered in the light from the dashboard as he turned to her and said, ''Never found the right woman.''

Honey shivered at the intensity of the look he gave her. On a subconscious level she was aware they had arrived at the house, that he had turned off the car engine, and that this time he had parked the truck in the shadows away from the front porch light.

''Honey?''

His voice rasped over her like a rough caress. She felt his need but wasn't sure what to do. She leaned toward him only a fraction of an inch. It was all the invitation he needed.

Jesse's hand threaded into her hair and tugged her closer. Their mouths were a breath apart but he didn't close the distance.

"Honey?"

He was forcing her to make a choice.

Honey drew back abruptly at a loud tapping on the window.

"Hey, Mom! You guys coming inside or what?" Jack shouted through the glass.

Honey closed her eyes and took a deep breath. Oh Lord. She had forgotten about her overprotective teenage son. He hadn't done anything quite this blatant with Adam, but apparently he recognized Jesse as a greater threat. He wasn't far wrong. She didn't understand the strength of her attraction to the hired hand, but she realized now she would be a fool to underestimate it.

She glanced at Jesse to see how he was handling the interruption and was surprised to see a smile on his face.

"I'm glad you're finding this so amusing," she said.

"If what I suspect is true, Jack hasn't allowed you much privacy with Philips. I have to be eternally grateful to him for that."

"You don't seem too worried that he's going to get in your way."

Jesse grinned. "Nope."

"Why not?"

"Because I don't intend to let him."

Right there, with Jack staring aghast through the window, Jesse took her in his arms and kissed her soundly. Then he reached across her and opened the truck door on her side, gently nudging Jack out of the way.

"Why don't you escort your mom inside, Jack. I've got some things I have to do."

Honey stepped out of the truck without thinking and stood with Jack as Jesse backed the truck and headed down the road that led off Flying Diamond property.

When the truck was gone, Jack confronted his mother in the faint light from the porch.

"Why'd you let him kiss you, Mom?"

"Jack, I—" Honey didn't know what to say.

''You're not gonna marry him or anything, are you?''

That she could answer more easily. ''No, I'm not going to marry him.'' He wasn't going to be around long enough for that.

''Then why'd you kiss him?'' Jack persisted.

''I like Jesse a lot, Jack. When two adults like each other, kissing is a way of expressing that feeling. When you're a little older, you'll understand.''

''Well, I don't like it,'' Jack said. ''And I don't like him, either.''

Honey thought of how hard it was for her son to accept another man in Cale's place, and to share his mother, whom he'd had to himself for the past year. ''You know, Jack, just because I kissed another man doesn't mean I'll ever love your father any less. Or you and Jonathan, either.''

''Oh, yeah? Well, Dad wouldn't like it.''

''Dad would understand,'' Honey said quietly. ''He wouldn't want us to stop living because he's not here with us. You're going to keep growing, Jack, and changing. Dad wouldn't have wanted you to stay a little boy. He'd want you to grow into the man you're destined to be.

''And I don't think he would necessarily want me to spend the rest of my life alone, without ever loving another man.''

Jack jumped on the one word that stuck out in all she'd said. ''Are you saying you're in *love* with that drifter?''

''No.'' *But I could be.*

Honey put her hand on Jack's shoulder, but he shrugged away from her. She ignored the snub as they headed up the porch steps and into the house. ''Let's just take each day one at a time, shall we? I hope you'll give Jesse the benefit of the doubt. I don't love him, but I do like him, Jack. I'd appreciate it if you could try to get along with him.''

''I'll try,'' Jack said. ''But I'm not promising you anything.''

''That's all I can ask,'' Honey said.

After she had sent Jack to bed, Honey stood at the lace-curtained window in her bedroom and looked out into the dark.

Where are you Jesse Whitelaw? What brought you here? And what do you want from me?

It was three in the morning before Honey heard the front door open and close. Jesse was back. She sat up, thinking to confront him about where he had been. Then she lay back down.

He wasn't her husband. He wasn't accountable to her. And it was none of her business what he had been doing. Or with whom.

Honey closed her eyes. When Cale died she had made up her mind never to let another man break her heart. She lay on her side and pulled the covers up over her shoulder. She was going to put that drifting man out of her mind once and for all.

Maybe Jack was right. From now on, she would keep a little more distance between herself and the hired hand.

Five

Jesse had known he was heading into deep water the first time he touched Honey Farrell. But it had been impossible to ignore the woman. There was something about her that called to him. He had no business getting involved with anyone, not with the life he led. Yet he hadn't been able to control the desire for her that rocked him whenever she was near. His attraction to her was as strong now, three weeks after he had first laid eyes on her, as it had been that first night. Once having tasted Honey, having touched her, it was an exercise of will to keep his distance from her.

He had been a fool to take that room off the kitchen. He could have found a way to steal General without arousing suspicion even if he were living in the barn. It was rough enough seeing Honey every morning for breakfast, without knowing that he didn't have the right to hold her the way he wanted.

As it turned out, he had ended up seeking out the room in the barn at odd times—like now—for the privacy it offered him. Jesse crossed his arms behind his head and lay back on the bunk. The room offered few amenities. The bed was hard and the walls were unadorned wooden slats. It smelled always of leather and hay. But at least here he could get away from her to think. Right now he had a lot to think about.

Something had happened this morning that he wasn't sure he wanted to remember, but he was quite sure he would never forget.

He had woken at the break of dawn, since he and Honey had agreed that he should have use of the bathroom first each morning. As he climbed the stairs wearing no more than jeans and socks, scratching his bare chest, he distinctly heard the water running. He had wondered what Honey was doing up so early. Over the past three weeks she had kept her bedroom door closed until he had bathed and shaved and headed back downstairs to make coffee. Then she would bathe and join him to finish making breakfast before the boys awoke.

Jesse had been curious enough about the change in routine to continue to the bathroom door. He knocked, but there was no answer.

"Honey?"

When she didn't respond, he tried the door. It wasn't locked, so he cautiously opened it. He wasn't sure what he expected, but what he found was disturbing.

Water was lapping at the edge of the tub, threatening to overflow. Honey was lying back with her nape against the edge of the tub. Her face was angled away from him. Her hair was wet and slicked back to reveal the plane of her jaw. In the steam-fogged room she provided an almost ethereal vision. He stood transfixed, staring at her.

"Honey?"

Concerned when there was still no response he stepped forward and knelt beside the tub. He gasped at his first glorious sight of her naked body. Before desire could take hold, he caught sight of her face, frozen in a mask of agony. Certain that something was seriously wrong, he rose to shut off the water and in the same deft move reached for a towel to wrap around her.

When he lifted her from the water, her eyes remained closed. Her face was frozen in a tragic pose like some marble statue. He picked her up in his arms and, rather than stay in the steamy room, headed for the open door down the hall that led to her bedroom. She offered no resistance, which made him even more concerned. Once inside, he shoved the door closed with his shoulder and carried her over to the canopied bed.

He wondered if her husband had slept with her in this frilly room, but decided she must have redone it since his death. It was a feminine place now, with the lace canopy overhead and lace curtains at the windows. It smelled of some flower, which he finally identified as the same honeysuckle scent he had breathed so often in the bathroom.

He tried to lay her on the bed but she grasped him around the neck, refusing to let go. He sat down on the bed and pulled her farther into his arms.

It was then that he realized she was crying. Sobbing, actually. Only there was no sound, just the heaving of her body and the closed, distorted features on her face.

''It's all right,'' he crooned. ''You're all right. I'm here now.''

Her grip tightened around his neck and her nose nuzzled against his throat. She moaned once, and the silent sobbing began again.

Jesse felt his throat swell with emotion. His arms tightened around her, as though he could protect her from whatever was causing her pain. Only he hadn't a clue as to why she was so distraught.

''It's all right, Honey. Nothing can hurt you. I'm here. You're fine.''

He meant what he said. He wouldn't allow anyone or anything to harm her. Jesse tightened his arms possessively, only to feel her struggle against his hold. Which reminded him he had no right to feel such feelings. They were virtual strangers. He knew little about her; and she knew nothing, really, about him.

He loosened his hold, caressing her bare shoulders in preparation for moving them apart. As soon as he tried to separate them, she clutched at him and buried her face even deeper against his chest. He was perfectly willing to hold her all day, if that was what she needed. He settled himself more comfortably, putting his stockinged feet on the bedspread, to wait out her tears.

She cried herself to sleep.

Jesse watched the sun rise with a sleeping woman in his arms. He had always wondered what it would be like to settle down, to have a woman of his own, to wake like this with her softness enfolded in his arms. His life hadn't allowed such a luxury. Lately he had begun to wonder whether he ought to think more seriously about finding a wife.

He had bitter experience already with one woman who hadn't been able to handle the kind of life he led. She had worried and begged and cried for him to change his ways. But he hadn't been able—or willing—to give up the life he had planned for himself. It had been a bitter separation, and he had learned that he could hurt, and be hurt.

That had been nearly ten years ago. He hadn't allowed himself to fall in love again. Or to dream about a permanent woman in his life.

Until he had met Honey.

Jesse brushed back a drying wisp of curl from Honey's brow. He had no idea what it was about this woman that made her different from every other. She was like the other half of him; with her he felt whole. He worried about what would happen when she knew the truth about him.

Maybe it wouldn't matter.

Jesse grimaced. It would matter.

At least the boys weren't around this morning. He shuddered to think what Jack would have said if he caught Jesse in Honey's bedroom—no matter how innocent the circumstances. Fortunately, since yesterday had been the last day of school, Jack had gone off to an end-of-school party and stayed the night with friends. Jonathan was spending the first six weeks of summer vacation with Honey's mother and father.

Jesse felt Honey stir in his arms and thought how well the name fit her, for she flowed around him, her softness conforming to all his hard planes. He smoothed the damp hair as best he could. "How are you feeling?"

She stiffened in his arms. "Jesse? What are you doing here?"

"You don't remember?"

She frowned. "No...yes...oh."

He watched an endearing pink blush begin at her neck and rise to her face as she realized she was naked under the towel. It had slipped some since he had carried her into the room. Now it exposed a rounded hip and teased him with the edge of one honey-brown nipple. He found the sight enchanting.

She tried to ease herself away.

"There's no sense worrying now," he said. "I've already seen everything there is to see. But I would like to hear what had you so upset."

Her shoulders sagged. For a moment he thought she wasn't going to tell him. When she did, he wished she hadn't.

"Yesterday would have been my fourteenth wedding anniversary. I couldn't get Cale out of my mind all night. I guess I was hoping to soak the memories out of my system—the sad ones, anyway."

"Did it work?"

Her face was surprisingly serene when she answered, "I think maybe it did. I feel better anyway. Thanks for being there. I hadn't realized how much I needed...someone...to hold me."

Once Jesse was reassured that Honey was no longer in pain, it left him free to acknowledge the other feelings that arose from holding her in his arms. And to pursue them.

"I wouldn't be honest if I didn't say I'm enjoying this," he said. "You're a beautiful woman, Honey." He felt his body tighten and knew she must feel the swell of arousal beneath her.

Honey tried to sit up, but Jesse kept her where she was. "No need trying to pretend you didn't hear what I said. I've kept my distance the past three weeks, but it hasn't been easy. I want you, Honey. I don't want to fight what I'm feeling anymore."

"How can you say something like that when you know I've spent the night crying over another man?"

"Cale is dead, Honey. You're entitled to your memories of him. But I won't let him come between us."

"There is no *us!*" Honey protested. "You're a drifter, Jesse. Here today and gone tomorrow. I can't—"

His voice was fierce because he feared she was right. "We have today," he said. "I can't offer you a tomorrow right now. Believe me, if I could, I would."

He could see that she wanted him, that she was tempted to take today and say to hell with tomorrow. He wished he could make promises, but a man in his line of work couldn't do that. So he held his tongue, his jaw taut as he waited to hear her answer.

"If it were only me," she began, "I might be willing to accept what you have to offer. But I have two sons. I have to think of them. You're a drifter, Jesse. You could never stay in one place long enough to be the father they need."

"What if I said I could?" She lifted her blue eyes to him and he saw they were filled with hope...and despair.

"I'd like to believe you. But I can't."

"So you're posting a No Trespass sign?" he asked.

"I didn't say that."

"Then what are you saying?"

"I have to think about it," she retorted. She looked up into Jesse's dark eyes seeking answers for her confused feelings. His gaze was intent, his lids hooded, his mouth rigid, tense with desire.

Suddenly she was aware again of her half-naked state and of the hard male body beneath her. Jesse put a hand on her bottom and shifted her so she was lying with the heart of her pressed to the heat of him.

She gasped. Honey had forgotten the pleasure of a man's hard body pressed against her softness.

"Ah, sweetheart, that feels so good," Jesse murmured.

She clutched at his shoulders, afraid to move lest she succumb to the pleasure or have to give it up. She closed her eyes and laid her head against his chest. He felt strong, and she felt secure in his arms, as though she could have no more worries if they faced the world together.

He was offering himself for a while. For the moment. Honey realized suddenly that she was seriously considering his offer. She didn't want to fall in love with him. That way lay disaster. When he left he would break her heart. But she couldn't deny that when she was with him she felt safe and, curiously, loved. It was a feeling she'd had with no other man since Cale's death.

She would be a fool to live for today; she would be a fool to give up today for the hope of tomorrow. But maybe the time had come for acting a little foolish. Knowing her decision was made, Honey relaxed and nuzzled her face against Jesse's throat.

He felt her acquiescence. Her body flowed once more like honey, hot and smooth. His blood began to thrum.

Honey suddenly felt herself being rolled over onto her back. Jesse lay on top of her, his hips pressed tightly into the cradle of her thighs, so there was no mistaking his intention. He levered himself onto his palms and she felt herself quivering as he took a long, lazy look at the breasts he had exposed.

"You're so beautiful," he rasped.

He lowered his mouth so slowly that Honey felt the curl of desire in her belly long before his mouth reached the tip of her breast. She anticipated his touch, but the reality was stunning. The warmth. The heat. The wetness of his tongue. The sharp pain as his teeth grazed the crest, and then the strong sucking as he took her breast into his mouth. It was almost more pleasure than she could bear.

Honey was frantic to touch his flesh, and her fingernails made distinct crescents in his back as his mouth captured hers and his tongue ravaged her.

Honey shuddered as his hand cupped her breast. He kneaded the tip between his callused finger and thumb, causing a feeling that was exquisite. There were too many sensations to cope with them all. The roughness of his hands, the wetness of his mouth, the heaviness of his lower body on hers. She was lost in sensation.

With Cale, they would have rushed to fulfillment. But when she reached for the metal buttons of Jesse's fly, his hand was there to stop her. It seemed he had not nearly had his fill of touching and tasting. He held her hand tight against the bulge in his jeans for a moment, then laid her palm against his cheek.

"Touch me, Honey. I need you to touch me."

And she did. Her fingertips roamed his face as though she were a blind woman trying to see him for the first time. She found the tiny scar in his hairline and the spiderweb of lines beside his eyes. The thickness of his brows. The petal softness of his eyelids and his feathery lashes.

She searched out the hollow beneath his cheekbone and the strength of his jaw. The long, straight nose and beneath it the twin lines that led to his lips, soft and damp and full.

He nipped her fingertips and made her laugh until his teeth caught the pad between her fingers and thumb. His love bite chased waves of feeling down her spine.

She used lips and teeth and tongue to trace the shell shape of his ear and was rewarded with a masculine groan that fought its way up through clenched teeth. She was lost in an adventure of discovery, so she wasn't aware, at first, of similar forays Jesse was making.

He nibbled at her neck and laved the love bites with his tongue. Honey felt her whole body clench in response. His hands entwined with hers, and he held them down on either side of her head so she couldn't interfere with his sensual exploration. His lips traced the length of her collarbone and slipped down to the tender skin beneath her arm. He bit and suckled until Honey was bucking beneath him.

"Jesse, please," she begged. She couldn't have said herself whether she wanted him to stop or go on.

Jesse certainly had no intention of stopping. He was fascinated by the woman under him. By her scents and textures and tastes. She smelled of honeysuckle, but her taste was distinct, a woman taste that was meant for him and him alone. Her skin was like satin, or maybe silk, smooth and alluring. He couldn't touch her enough, couldn't taste her enough.

His mouth found hers again, and he brought their bodies into alignment, feeling the moist heat of her through the denim that still separated them. He wanted her. How he wanted her!

He released her hands to reach down toward his Levi's, but her hand was there before him.

"Let me."

Her eyes were lambent, heavy-lidded, the blue almost violet with desire. His loins tightened. He couldn't speak, so he nodded curtly.

She took her own damn sweet time with it. A button at a time he felt himself come free until she was holding him, surrounding him with her hand.

He hissed out a breath. "Damn woman. You're going to kill me with kindness."

Honey smiled seductively. "Then you'll die smiling, cowboy."

The crooked grin flashed on his face and was gone an instant later as she led him toward the female portal that awaited him.

He paused long enough to rasp out, "Are you protected?"

She nodded at the same time he thrust himself inside her. *Hot. Wet. Tight.* The feelings were astounding, and he groaned as he seated himself deep within her body.

For a moment he didn't move, just enjoyed the feeling of being inside her, of having joined the two of them as one. *Right. It felt right. And good.*

"Honey, dammit, I—" He wanted to wait even longer, arouse her more, until she couldn't talk or even breathe. It was soon apparent she was as aroused as he. Her hands shoved his jeans down and she grasped his buttocks as her legs came up around him. He took his weight on his hands, leaving him free to caress her lips and breasts with his mouth.

Jesse felt a frenzy of uncontrollable need for this woman, at this moment in time. ''Honey, I can't—''

He needn't have worried that he was leaving her behind. He felt the convulsions deep inside her and knew she had reached the same pinnacle as he. He threw his head back, teeth clenched against the agony of pleasure that swelled through him as he spilled his seed. He was unaware of the exultant cry that escaped him at that ultimate moment.

Honey felt the tears steal into the corners of her eyes as Jesse slipped to her side and pulled her into his arms. She held on to him tightly, afraid to admit the awesomeness of what had just happened between them. It wasn't what she had expected. The pleasure, yes. But the feeling of belonging...That, she couldn't explain and didn't want to contemplate.

''Honey? Did I hurt you?''

She felt his lips at the corners of her eyes, kissing away the tears. ''No,'' she said. ''You didn't hurt me.''

''Then, why—?''

''I don't know,'' she admitted in a choked voice. Another tear fell.

He pulled her into his embrace. In a low voice, that rusty-gate voice, he said, ''It felt right, Honey. It felt good. Don't be sorry.''

''I'm not,'' she said. And realized she wasn't. Cale was dead; she was alive. She didn't fool herself. What she and Jesse had just experienced was rare. It hadn't even happened all the time with Cale. That must mean that she felt more for the drifter than even she had previously perceived. She wasn't ready yet to examine those feelings. She wasn't sure what she would find. She certainly wasn't ready to confront them head-on.

Honey changed the subject instead. ''Jack will be showing up soon,'' she whispered.

''Yeah. I'd better get out of here.'' He grinned and slicked his hand through hair damp with sweat. ''I could really use a bath.''

Honey arched a brow. ''Are you bragging or complaining?''

His eyes were suddenly serious as he said, ''I got exactly what I wanted. Are you saying you didn't want it, too?''

''No. I'm not saying that.''

He searched her eyes, trying to discern her feelings. First and foremost among them was confusion. Well, he could identify with that. Perhaps what they both needed now was time and distance. Especially since he could feel himself becoming aroused again simply by her nearness. ''I'd better get that bath.''

He pulled his Levi's back on and buttoned them partway, knowing he was just going to pull them off again down the hall, then turned back to look at Honey.

She had grabbed the towel and was using it to cover herself.

''I think I find you even more enticing half-clothed than when you're naked,'' he warned.

Honey clutched the towel closer, accidentally revealing even more skin. She was helpless to resist him if he touched her again.

Jesse considered making love to her again, but his common sense stopped him. Any moment Jack might return home. While he hadn't allowed her son's objections to prevent him from pursuing Honey, he didn't want to confront Jack coming from her bedroom, either. He didn't want the boy thinking any less of his mother because of her relationship with some drifter. When the time was right, he would tell them all the truth and let Honey decide whether she wanted anything more to do with him—or not.

He finished his bath and went downstairs to make coffee, as usual. Shortly thereafter he was joined by Honey, fresh from her bath and looking even more alluring with her hair curling in damp tendrils around her face. She was wearing the same man's robe she had worn the first day he had arrived. He wondered if she had done it on purpose, to remind him that she had belonged to another man. He wanted to cross the room and pull her into his arms, but the wary look on her face held him apart.

''I started coffee,'' he said, to break the uncertain silence.

''How about eggs and bacon this morning?'' she asked, heading for the refrigerator.

He let her pass by him without reaching out, but his nostrils flared as he caught the scent of honeysuckle from her hair. He watched her do all the normal things she had done for the past three weeks, as though nothing momentous had happened between them in the bed upstairs.

Then he saw her hands were trembling and realized she wasn't as calm as she wanted him to believe. He didn't think, just closed the distance between them. He had put his hands on her shoulders when a noise behind him froze them both.

''Hey, what's going on here?'' Jack said belligerently, shoving open the kitchen door and letting himself in.

Jesse turned to face Honey's older son, but he didn't take his hands from her shoulders. ''Your mom's making breakfast.''

''That's not what I mean and you know it,'' Jack retorted.

Jesse saw the tension in the boy's shoulders, the suspicion in his eyes. There was no purpose to be served by aggravating him. He let go of Honey's shoulders, picked up the pot of coffee from the stove and returned to the table to pour himself a cup.

Jack watched with hostile eyes from the doorway, then marched over to stand before the hired hand.

Jessie had been expecting Jack to confront him, but he wasn't prepared for the bluntness of the boy's attack.

''You stay away from my mother. She doesn't want anything to do with you.''

''That's her decision, isn't it?''

''I can take care of things around here now that school's out!'' the boy said. ''We don't need you.''

Jesse heard the pain beneath the defiant words. ''From what I've seen, your mother can use another helping hand.''

''You can never replace my father!'' Jack said. ''He was a Texas Ranger, a hero. You're nothing, just some drifter who rolled in like tumbleweed. Why don't you go back where you came from?''

''Jack!'' Honey was appalled at Jack's attack on Jesse. ''Apologize,'' she ordered.

''I won't!'' Jack said. ''I meant every word I said. We don't need him here.''

''But we do need him,'' Honey contradicted. ''I can't do it all, Jack. Even though you're a big help, there are jobs you can't do, either. We need a man's help. That's why Jesse is here.''

Honey realized immediately that she had used the wrong appeal with her son. He was a youth on the verge of manhood, and she had reminded him that despite the change in his voice and his tall lanky body, he was not yet a man.

"Fine!" he retorted. "Keep your hired hand. But don't expect me to like it!"

With that he shoved his way out the screen door and headed for the barn. Without breakfast. Which, knowing Jack's appetite, gave Honey some idea just how upset he was.

Honey felt the tears glaze her eyes. "I'm sorry that happened."

Jesse put his hands on her shoulders to comfort her. "He'll be all right."

"I wish I could be as sure of that as you seem to be."

"Don't worry, Honey. Everything will work out fine. You'll see."

But as he lay in the bunk in the barn, he felt a knot in his stomach at all the hurdles that would have to be crossed if he was ever to claim this woman as his own.

Six

Jesse found Jack in the barn brushing General. He stuck a boot on the bottom rail of the stall door and leaned his forearms on the top rail.

"You and that bull seem to be good friends," Jesse said.

The boy ignored him and continued brushing the bull's curly red coat.

Jesse tipped his hat back off his brow. "When I was a kid about your age my dad gave me a bull of my very own to raise."

"I was eight when Dad bought General," Jack said. "He wasn't much to look at then, but Dad thought he was something pretty special. He was right. General's always been a winner." Jack seemed embarrassed at having said so much and began brushing a little harder and faster.

"Sounds like your dad was something pretty special, too," Jesse said.

"You're nothing like him, that's for sure!"

"No, I expect not," Jesse agreed. "I do have one thing in common with your father."

Jesse waited for the boy's curiosity to force him to continue the conversation.

"What's that?" Jack asked.

"Feelings for your mother."

Jack glared at him. "Why can't you just leave her alone?"

How could he explain what he felt for Honey in words the boy would understand? Jesse wondered. What did one say to a thirteen-year-old boy to describe the relationship between a man and a woman? It would be easier if he could tell the boy he was committed in some way to Honey. But Jesse had never spoken of ''forever'' with Honey, and he wasn't free to do so until his business here was done.

''I wish I had an easy answer for your question,'' Jesse said quietly. ''But I don't. Will it help if I say I'll try my damnedest never to do anything that'll hurt your mom?''

Abruptly Jack stopped brushing the bull. ''She's never gonna love you like she loved Dad. You're crazy if you think she will. There's no sense in you hanging around. Now that school's out, I can handle things. Why don't you just leave?''

''I can't,'' Jesse said simply.

''Why not?''

''Your mother needs my help.'' *And I still have to steal this bull.*

Jack's body sagged like a balloon losing air. ''I wish Dad was still alive,'' he said in a quiet, solemn voice.

Jesse retrieved a piece of hay from the feed trough and began to shred it. ''My father died when I was twenty,'' he said. ''Bronc threw him and broke his neck. I didn't think anything could hurt so much as the grief I felt losing him. I missed him so much, I left home and started wandering. It took a few years before I realized he was still with me.''

The boy's brow furrowed, revealing the confusion caused by Jesse's last statement.

Jesse reached out to scratch behind the huge bull's ears. ''What I mean is, I'd catch myself doing something and remember how my dad had been the one to teach it to me. My father left me with the best part of himself—the memories I have of everything he said and did.''

Jack swallowed hard. His teeth gritted to stop the tremor in his chin.

''Your mom won't ever forget your dad, Jack. No more than you will. No matter who comes into her life, she'll always have her memories of him. And so will you.''

Jesse wasn't sure whether his words had caused any change in Jack's attitude toward him, but he didn't know what else to say.

The silence deepened and thickened until finally Jesse said, ''You're doing a fine job grooming General, boy. When you get done, I could use some help replacing a few rotted posts around the corral.''

Jesse turned and left the barn without waiting for a reply from Jack. Fifteen minutes later, Jack appeared at his side wearing work gloves and carrying a shovel. The two of them labored side by side digging out several rotten posts and replacing them with new ones.

Honey could hardly believe her eyes when she looked out the kitchen window. She forced herself to remain inside and give Jesse and Jack time alone together. When several hours had passed and they were still hard at work, she prepared a tray with two large glasses of iced tea and took it out to the corral.

''You both look thirsty,'' she said.

Jesse swiped at the dripping sweat on his neck and chest with a bandanna he had pulled from his back pocket. ''I am. How about you, Jack?''

Honey was amazed at the even, almost cordial sound of her son's voice as he said, ''I feel dry enough to swallow a river and come back for more.''

Both males made short work of the tall glasses of iced tea. Honey flushed when Jesse winked at her as he set his glass back on the tray. She looked quickly at Jack to see how he reacted to Jesse's flirtatious behavior. Her son shrugged...and grinned!

She turned and stared in amazement at Jesse. What on earth had he said to Jack to cause such a miraculous reversal in her son's attitude? Honey frowned as the two shared a look of male understanding. Whatever it was, she ought to feel grateful. And she did. Sort of.

Honey tried to pinpoint what it was that bothered her about Jack's acceptance of the drifter. Her forehead wrinkled in thought as she slowly made her way back to the house. She wasn't pleased with the conclusions she reached.

So long as Jack found the drifter a threat and an interloper, it had been easier for Honey to justify keeping Jesse at an emotional arm's length. She had realized there was no sense letting herself get attached to him if one of her children clearly abhorred him. Jack's sudden acceptance of Jesse left her without a piece of armor she had counted on. Now, with her defenses down, she was extremely vulnerable to the drifter's entreaties.

Halfway to the house, the phone started ringing. Honey was breathless from running when she finally answered it.

"Honey? Did I catch you outside again?"

"Oh, Adam. Uh, yes, you did. When are you coming home?"

"I am home. Are you free to go out tonight?"

Honey thought about it for a moment. Clearly she needed to be sure Jesse wasn't anywhere around when she told Adam she couldn't marry him. Going out was probably not a bad idea. "Sure," she said at last. "What time should I meet you and where?"

"I'll pick you up."

"That isn't necessary, Adam. I—"

"I insist."

It was clear he wouldn't take no for an answer. Rather than argue, she agreed. "All right."

"See you at eight, Honey."

Honey almost groaned aloud at Adam's purring tone of voice when he said her name. It was not going to be a pleasant evening. "At eight," she confirmed.

When Jesse and Jack came into the house for supper they found only two places set at the table. It was the most subtle way Honey could think of to say that she was going out for the evening. From the look in Jesse's eyes, subtlety wasn't going to help much.

It was Jack who asked, "Aren't you going to eat with us?"

"No. Adam is taking me out to supper."

Identical frowns settled on two male faces. It had apparently dawned on Jack that his mother had not one, but two suitors. Honey would have laughed at the chagrined expression on her son's face if the situation hadn't been so fraught with tension.

Jack looked warily at Jesse. "Uh...Adam is mom's...uh...friend," he said by way of explanation.

"That's what your mom said," Jesse agreed.

Jack relaxed when it appeared Jesse wasn't upset by the situation. He turned to his mother and asked, "Are you going to tell Adam tonight that you won't marry him?"

Honey clutched her hands together, frustrated by the situation Jack had put her in. The gleam of amusement in Jesse's dark eyes didn't help matters any. She simply said, ''Adam deserves an answer to his proposal. And yes, I intend to give it to him tonight.''

''And?'' Jack prompted.

''After I've given Adam my answer, I'll be glad to share it with you,'' she said to Jack. ''Until then, I think you should sit down and eat your supper.''

Honey escaped upstairs to dress, where she managed to consume most of the two hours until Adam's expected arrival at eight.

Shortly before Adam was due to arrive, Jack knocked on her door and asked if he could spend the night with a friend.

''What time will you be home tomorrow morning?'' Honey asked.

''Well, me and Reno were thinking maybe we'd go tubing tomorrow. I figured I'd stay and have lunch with him and spend the afternoon on the river.''

''Jack, I don't think—''

''It's the first Saturday of summer vacation, Mom! You aren't gonna make me come home and work, are you?''

Jack knew exactly what to say to push her maternal guilt buttons. ''All right,'' she relented. ''But I don't think you can make a habit of this. I'm depending on your help around the ranch this summer.''

''Believe me, Mom, it's just this once.''

Moments later Jack came by with his overnight bag thrown over his shoulder to give her a quick, hard hug. Then he scampered down the stairs and out through the kitchen. She heard the screen door slam behind him.

If Honey thought she had managed to avoid a confrontation with Jesse by staying in her room until the very last minute, she was disabused of that notion as soon as she descended the stairs. He was waiting for her at the bottom.

''You told me you aren't going to marry that Philips guy,'' Jesse said.

Honey postponed any response by heading for the living room. She brushed aside the lacy drapery on the front window and looked for the headlights of Adam's sports car in the distance. No rescue there. She turned and faced Jesse, who had followed her into the room and was standing behind the aged leather chair that had been Cale's favorite spot in the room.

''I've never given Adam an answer to his proposal,'' Honey said. ''He deserves to be told my decision face-to-face.''

''Tell him here. Don't go out with him.''

Honey felt a surge of anger. ''I may not be willing to marry Adam, but I care for him as a person. I agreed to go to dinner with him, and I'm going!''

She watched Jesse's eyes narrow, his nostrils flare, his lips flatten. His anger clearly matched her own. But he didn't argue further.

Neither did he leave the room. When Adam arrived five long minutes later, he found Jesse comfortably ensconced in Cale's favorite chair idly perusing a ranching magazine.

Jesse looked up assessingly when Adam entered the living room, but he didn't rise to greet the other man. He kept his left ankle hooked securely over his right knee and slouched a little more deeply into the chair, concentrating on the magazine.

''Don't be too late,'' he said as Adam slipped an arm around Honey to escort her out the door. Jesse smiled behind the magazine when the other man stiffened.

His smugness disappeared when Honey replied with a beatific smile, ''Don't wait up for me.''

Jesse would have been downright concerned if he could have heard what passed between Honey and Adam in the car on the way to the restaurant.

''That hired hand sure made himself at home in your living room,'' Adam complained before too many minutes had passed.

Honey sighed in exasperation. ''It wasn't what it looked like.''

''Oh?''

''He was trying to make you feel uncomfortable,'' Honey said.

''He succeeded. I wouldn't have been half as upset if it weren't for the things I know about him.''

''You've only seen him twice!'' Honey protested. ''You don't know anything about him.''

''Actually, I did some checking up on him.''

''Adam, that really wasn't necessary.'' Honey didn't bother to keep the irritation out of her voice. Men! Really!

''Maybe you'll change your mind when you hear what I have to say.''

Honey arched a brow and waited.

''Did you know he's got a criminal record?''

''What? *Jesse?*'' Honey felt breathless, as though someone had landed on her chest with both feet. ''Dallas vouched for him.''

''Dallas obviously covered for his friend. The man's been arrested, Honey.'' He paused significantly and added, ''For rustling cattle.''

Honey leapt on the only scrap of positive information Adam had given her. ''*Arrested.* Then he was never convicted?''

Adam released a gusty breath. ''Not as far as I could find out. Probably had a good lawyer. It was only by chance that there was any record of the arrest. Don't you see, Honey? He might even be one of the rustlers who've been stealing your stock. He probably moved in so he could look things over up close.''

''I lost stock long before Jesse showed up around here,'' Honey said coldly. ''I refuse to believe he's part of any gang of rustlers.''

But she couldn't help thinking about the night Jesse had been gone until three in the morning. Where had he been? What had he been doing? And Jesse hadn't wanted her to call the police when she had spotted someone suspicious on her property. He had said he would rather tell Dallas about it. Had he?

Adam had given her a lot to think about, and Honey was quiet for the rest of the journey to the restaurant in Hondo. Hermannson's Steak House was famous for its traditional Texas fare of chicken-fried steak and onion rings. A country band played later in the evening, and she and Adam danced the Texas two-step and the rousing and bawdy Cotton-eyed Joe.

Adam was always good company, and Honey couldn't help laughing at his anecdotes. But she was increasingly aware that the end of the evening was coming, when Adam would renew his proposal and she would have to give him her answer. She felt a somberness stealing over her. Finally Adam ceased trying to make her smile.

''Time to go?'' he asked.

''I think so.''

She tried several times in the car to get out the words *I can't marry you.* It wasn't as easy being candid as she wished it was.

Adam wasn't totally insensitive to her plight, she discovered. In fact he made it easy for her.

''It's all right,'' he said in a quiet voice. ''I guess I knew I was fooling myself. When you didn't say yes right away I figured you had some reservations about marrying me. I guess I hoped if I was persistent you'd change your mind.''

''I'm sorry,'' Honey said.

''So am I,'' Adam said with a wry twist of his mouth. ''I suppose it won't do any good to warn you again about that drifter you hired, either.''

''I'll think about what you said,'' Honey conceded. She just couldn't believe Jesse had come to the Flying Diamond to steal from her. She had to believe that or die from the pain she felt at the thought he had simply been using her all this time.

The inside of the house was dark when they drove up, but it was late. Honey was grateful that she wouldn't have to confront Jesse tonight about the things Adam had told her.

''Good night, Adam,'' Honey said. She felt awkward. Unsure whether he would want to kiss her and not willing to hurt him any more than she already had by refusing if he did.

Adam proved more of a gentleman than she had hoped. He took her hand in his and held it a moment. The look on his face was controlled, but she saw the pain in his eyes as he said, ''Goodbye, Honey.''

She swallowed over the lump in her throat. She hadn't meant to hurt him. ''I'm sorry,'' she said again.

''Don't be. I'll survive.'' Only he knew how deeply he had allowed himself to fall in love with her, and how hard it was to give up all hope of having her for his wife.

Slowly he let her hand slip through his fingers. He came around and opened the car door for her and walked her to the porch. As he left her, his last words were, ''Be careful, Honey. Don't trust that drifter too much.''

Then he was gone.

Honey let herself into the dark house and leaned back against the front door. Her whole body sagged in relief. She had hurt a good man without meaning to, though she didn't regret refusing his proposal.

''You were gone long enough!''

The accusation coming out of the dark startled Honey and she nearly jumped out of her shoes.

"You scared me to death!" she hissed. "What are you doing sitting here in the dark?"

"Waiting for you."

As her eyes adjusted to the scant light, she saw that Jesse was no longer sitting. He had risen and was closing the distance between them. Escape seemed like a good idea and she started for the stairs. She didn't get two steps before he grasped her by the shoulders.

"You didn't bring him inside with you. Does that mean you've told him things are over between you?"

"That's none of your—"

Jesse shook her hard. "Answer me!"

Honey was more furious than she could remember being at any time since Cale's death. How dare this man confront her! How dare he demand answers that were none of his business! "Yes!" she hissed. "Yes! Is that what you wanted to hear?"

Jesse answered her by capturing her mouth with his. It was a savage kiss, a kiss of claiming. His hands slid around her and he spread his legs and pulled her into the cradle of his thighs. He wasn't gentle, but Honey responded to the urgency she felt in everything he did. Against all reason, she felt a spark of passion ignite, and she began to return his fervent kisses.

"Honey, Honey," he murmured against her lips. "I need you. I want you."

Honey was nearly insensate with the feelings he was creating with his mouth and hands. He made her feel like a woman with his desire, his need. She shoved at his shoulders and whispered, "Jesse, we can't. Jack is—"

"Jack's spending the night with friends," he reminded her.

He grinned at the stunned look on her face as she realized that her youthful chaperon was not going to come to her rescue this time.

Without giving her a chance to object, Jesse swept her into his arms in a masterful imitation of Rhett and Scarlett and headed upstairs.

"What do you think you're doing?" Honey demanded.

"Taking you to bed where you belong," Jesse said.

"We can't do this," Honey protested.

Jesse stopped halfway up the stairs. "Why not?"

There was a long pause while Honey debated whether to confront him with the accusations Adam had made. "Because... You'd never lie to me, would you, Jesse?"

It was dark so she couldn't see his face, but being held in his arms the way she was, she felt the sudden tension in his body.

"I'd never do anything to hurt you, Honey."

"That isn't exactly the same thing, is it?"

There was enough light to see his smile appear. "That's one of the things I like about you, Honey. You don't pull any punches."

"I think you'd better put me down, Jesse," she said.

Slowly he released her legs so her body slid down across his. She was grateful for the way he held on to her, because her feet weren't quite steady under her. Her nipples puckered as he slowly rubbed their bodies together.

"You want me, Honey," he said in his rusty-gate voice.

"It would be hard to deny it without sounding like a fool," she said acerbically.

His mouth found the juncture between her neck and shoulder and blessed it with tantalizing kisses. Honey gripped his arms to keep from falling down the stairs as his mouth sought out the tender skin at her throat and followed it up to her ear. Her head fell back of its own volition, offering him better access. Her whole body quivered at the sensations he was evoking with mouth and teeth and tongue.

A hoarse, guttural sound forced its way past Honey's lips. "Jesse, please."

"What, Honey? What do you want?"

Honey groaned again, and it was as much a sound of pleasure as of despair. "You," she admitted in a harsh voice. "I want you."

Jesse lifted her into his arms and carried her the rest of the way upstairs.

Seven

Honey felt the heat of the man beside her and reached out to caress the muscular strength of a body she now knew as well as her own. When Jesse stirred, Honey withdrew her hand. She didn't want to awaken him. Last night had been magical. She didn't wish to rouse from the night's dream and face the reality of day.

Jesse looked younger in the soft dawn light, though still something of a rogue with the stubble of dark beard that shadowed his face. She rubbed her cheek against the pillow, noticing that her skin was tender where his beard had rubbed again—and again. As were her breasts, she realized with chagrin.

He hadn't been gentle, but then, neither had she. Their lovemaking had blazed with the feelings of desperation that had followed them upstairs to the bedroom.

Honey understood her own reasons for feeling that she had to reach for whatever memories she could make with Jesse before he was gone. She had no idea why Jesse had seemed equally desperate. Had he already made up his mind to leave her? Did he already know the day when their brief interlude would come to an end?

She touched her lower lip, which was tender from the kissing they had done, the love bites he had given her. She must have bitten him, as well. There was a purplish bruise on Jesse's neck, put there in a moment of passion, she supposed. She didn't remember doing it, and she was embarrassed to think what he was going to say when he saw it. She hadn't left such a mark on a man since she'd been a teenager, playing games with Cale.

Honey winced. She hadn't thought of Cale once last night. Jesse hadn't left room for thought. He had spread her legs and thrust inside her, claiming her like some warrior with the spoils of battle. And what had she done? She had allowed it. No, that wasn't precisely true. She had *reveled* in his domination of her. She had opened herself to Jesse and allowed him liberties that Cale had never enjoyed.

And she wasn't even sorry.

Honey had never needed a man so much, or felt so much with a man. She didn't understand it. What made Jesse so different from Adam? Why couldn't she have chosen a man who would give her the security she needed in her life? Why did she have to love—

Honey stopped her thoughts in midstream, appalled by the word that had come to mind. *Love.* Was that why the lovemaking had been so thrilling? Was she in love with Jesse Whitelaw?

It was unfair to be forced to evaluate her feelings when she was staring at the object of her desire. Because she loved the way Jesse's raven-black hair fell across his brow. She loved the way his dark lashes feathered onto bronze cheeks. She loved his mouth, with the narrow upper lip and the full lower one, that had brought her so much pleasure.

She loved the weight of his body on hers when they were caressing each other. She loved the feel of his skin, soft to the touch, and yet hard with corded muscle. She loved the way his flesh heated hers as his callused fingertips sought out her breasts and slid down her belly to the cleft between her thighs.

She loved the feel of their two bodies when they were joined together as a man and woman were meant to be. She loved his patience as he brought her to fulfillment. She loved the lazy-lidded satisfaction in his eyes when she cried out her pleasure. And she loved the agonized pleasure on his face as he followed her to the pinnacle of desire they had sought together.

Honey refused to contemplate the other facets of Jesse's character that appealed to her. They were many and varied. It was painful enough to know that she loved him this way. Because where there was love, there was hope. And Honey was afraid to hope that the drifter would be there in the days to come. She wasn't sure her memories would be enough when he was gone.

Honey knew she couldn't stay in bed any longer without turning to Jesse yet again. Rather than be thought a wanton, she slipped quietly from beneath the covers, grabbed a shirt, jeans, socks and boots and headed downstairs to dress in the kitchen.

She didn't make coffee, certain the smell would wake Jesse, and wanting more time alone. Honey headed outside to feed the stock. Maybe she could subdue her unruly libido with hard work. She entered the barn and was immediately assailed with familiar smells that comforted and calmed her. She headed for General's stall and stopped dead at the sight that greeted her. Or rather, didn't greet her.

At first Honey refused to believe her eyes. She gripped the stall where General was supposed to be with white-knuckled hands. Had she left General outside in the corral all night? She was appalled at her thoughtlessness.

Honey ran back outside, but the bull was nowhere to be seen. She hurried back to examine the stall, thinking he might have broken the latch. But it was still hooked.

Staring didn't make the bull appear. He was gone. *Stolen!*

Honey felt despair, followed by rage at the one suspect for the theft who was still within her reach. Purely by instinct, she grabbed two items from the barn as she raced back to the house. She made a brief stop in the kitchen before marching determinedly up the stairs.

Jesse came roaring to life, drenched by the bucket of icy water Honey had thrown on him. ''What the hell are you doing, woman?''

He leapt out of bed like a lion from its den, roaring with anger. He was naked, and she had never seen him look so powerful. Or so seductive to her senses.

He grabbed for her and she stepped out of his way. ''You bastard!'' she hissed.

''Honey, what the hell—''

''Don't come any closer.'' She held up the buggy whip she had found in the barn, a relic of days gone by. ''I'll use this,'' she threatened.

"What's going on here?" Jesse demanded. "It's a little late for outraged virtue."

"Outraged virtue! You low-down mealymouthed skunk!" she raged. "You stole my bull!"

She wanted him to deny it. With all her heart she yearned for him to say he was innocent. But the dark flush she could plainly see working its way up his naked flesh from his powerful shoulders, to his love-bruised neck, landing finally on his strong cheekbones, was as blatant a statement of guilt as she had ever heard.

"How could you?" she breathed, more hurt now than angry. "I trusted you." Then the anger was back, and she wielded the whip with all the fury of humiliation and pain she felt at his betrayal. "I trusted you!"

The whip landed once across his shoulders before he reached out and jerked it from her hands. He threw it across the room and pulled her into his arms.

Honey fought him, beating at him with her fists and kicking at him with her feet until he threw her down on the soaking-wet bed where he subdued her with his weight.

"Stop it, Honey! That's enough!"

"I hate you!" she cried. "I hate you! I hate you!"

She burst into gasping sobs and turned her head away so he wouldn't see the tears she cried over him. She lay still, emotionally devastated, as he kissed them away.

"Honey." His voice sounded like gravel. "I'm sorry."

"Where's—my—bull?" she gritted out between clenched teeth.

"In a safe place," he said.

Honey moaned. His words were final confirmation that he had used her, lied to her, stolen from her.

"It's not what you think," he began.

She turned to face him, eyes blazing. "Can you deny that you lied to me?"

"No, but—"

"That you stole General?"

"I did, but—"

She growled deep in her throat and bucked against him.

"If you know what's good for you, you'll lie still," Jesse warned.

Honey froze, suddenly aware of the fact he was naked, and they were in bed. "Don't you dare touch me. I'll fight you. I'll kick and scratch and—"

"If you'll just shut up for a minute, I can explain everything."

"I don't want to hear your excuses, you bastard. I—"

He kissed her to shut her up.

Honey felt the punishment in his kiss, and it was easy to fight his anger with her own, to arch her body against the weight of his, to grip the male fingers threaded through her own and struggle against his domination.

The more she fought, the more her body responded to the provocation of his. He insinuated his thigh between her legs knowing it would excite her. At the same time his mouth gentled and his lips and tongue came seeking the taste of her, dark like honey, rich and full. She fought his strength, but his hands held hers captive on either side of her head while he ravished her.

"Don't," she pleaded, aware she was succumbing to the desire that had never been far below the surface. "Don't."

She was helpless to deny him. He was stronger than she. To her surprise, he stopped kissing her and raised himself on his elbows so he could look at her.

"Are you ready to listen now?"

She turned her head away and closed her eyes.

He shoved one of her hands back behind her and held it there with the weight of his body while he grabbed her chin with his now-free hand and forced her to look at him.

"Open your eyes and look at me," he commanded.

When she didn't, his mouth came down hard on hers. "Open your eyes, Honey. I'm going to keep kissing you until you do."

Faced with that threat, her eyes flashed open and she glared at him.

His dark eyes burned with fury. His mouth was taut. A muscle jerked in his cheek. "There is an explanation for everything," he gritted out.

"I'll bet!" she retorted.

"Shut up and listen!"

She snorted. But she stayed mute.

He opened his mouth and closed it several times. *Searching for more lies,* Honey thought. He closed his eyes and when he opened them again, she saw regret.

"I don't know how to say this except to say it," he began.

She waited, wondering how she could bear to hear that the man she had spent the night making love to, the man she had begun to think herself in love with, was part of a gang of murdering rustlers.

He took a deep breath and said, "I'm a Texas Ranger. I'm working undercover to catch the leader of the gang of rustlers that's been stealing from ranches in this area."

Honey couldn't believe her ears. Her first reaction was relief. *Jesse wasn't a thief!* The very next was anger—make that fury. *He had lied to her!* It was a lie of omission, but a lie all the same to keep her ignorant of his true identity. Finally there was hopelessness. Which was foolish because she had never really had much hope that the drifter would settle down. Now that she knew Jesse was a Texas Ranger, the situation was clear. *He would leave her when his job was done.* Not that it really mattered. She would never repeat the mistake she had made with Cale.

"Honey? Say something?"

"Let me up."

"Not until I explain."

"You've said enough."

"I didn't want to lie to you, but Dallas—"

"Dallas was in on this? I'll kill him," Honey muttered.

Jesse was pleased by the fire in her eyes after the awful dullness he had seen when he had told her the truth. Or at least as much of the truth as he could tell her.

"Dallas was under orders, too," Jesse continued. "The Captain thought it would be better if you were kept in the dark. Because of..." His voice trailed off as he realized he couldn't tell her the rest of it. "I mean...I guess he thought you would understand, having been the wife of a Texas Ranger, why it was necessary."

"I understand, all right," Honey said heatedly. "You used me without a thought to the pain and anguish it would cause."

"How much of what you're feeling is the result of losing General and how much the result of my deceiving you?" Jesse asked in a quiet voice. "General would have been returned within a day or so at the most and no harm done. I hadn't counted on what happened between us, Honey.''

''You never should have touched me.''

''I know,'' he said.

''You should have left me completely alone.''

''I know,'' he said.

''Why didn't you?''

''Because I couldn't. I didn't know I would find the other half of myself here, now, under these circumstances.''

Honey swallowed over the lump that had suddenly risen in her throat. She closed her eyes to shut out the tenderness in his dark-eyed gaze.

''I love you, Honey.''

When her eyes opened they revealed an agony she hadn't ever wanted to feel again. ''Don't! Don't say things you don't mean!''

''I've never meant anything more in my life.''

''Well, I don't love you!'' she retorted.

''Who's lying now, Honey?''

''This can never work, Jesse. Even if you could settle down, and I'm not sure you can, you're a Texas Ranger.''

''What does that have to do with anything?''

''I don't want to spend my life worrying about whether you're going to come home to me at the end of the day. I had no choice with Cale. But I have one now. And I choose not to live my life like that.''

''I can't—won't—change my life for you,'' Jesse said, disturbed by the narrow lines she was drawing.

''I'm not asking you to,'' Honey said.

''Where does that leave us?''

''You've got a job to finish. I assume you're going to meet with the rustlers and exchange General for a great deal of money?''

He grinned crookedly. ''That was the plan.''

''Then I suggest you go to work.''

Jesse sobered for a moment. ''Things aren't over between us.''

She didn't argue with him. There was no sense in it. As soon as his job was done he would be leaving. She felt the pain of loss already. Even if he had been the drifter he first professed to be, he would have been moving on sooner or later. She had always known Jesse wouldn't be hanging around. Only now his leaving had a certainty that allowed her to begin accepting—and grieving—his loss.

She searched his features, absorbing them, cataloguing them so she would remember them. Her eyes skipped to the body she had adored last night, and she noticed a huge red welt on his right shoulder that had previously been hidden by the pillow.

"Oh, my God, Jesse. Look what I've done to you!"

Jesse gasped as she reached out and touched the spot where the horsewhip had cut into his flesh.

She pushed at his chest. "Let me up, Jesse. I need to get some salve for that before it gets any worse than it is."

Honey didn't know what she would have done if he hadn't let her up just then. She was feeling so many things—remorse and embarrassment and love. And the love seemed to be winning out. She didn't want to care for this man. It would only hurt worse when he left.

Jesse took advantage of the time Honey was out of the room to put on his pants and boots. When she came back he was sitting on the edge of the bed shirtless, waiting for her.

Honey laid the things she had brought back with her on the end table beside the bed, then sat down beside Jesse to minister to the wound.

He hissed in a breath of air when she began dabbing at the raw flesh with warm water. "I know this must hurt," she soothed.

As she worked, Jesse wasn't nearly so aware of the pain as he was of the care she was taking of him. It had been years and years since there had been a woman in his life to care for him. His mother had died when his sister, Tate, was born, leaving Tate to be raised by a father and three older brothers. He had been how old? No more than eleven or twelve.

He luxuriated in the concern Honey showed with every gesture, every touch. She cared for him. He felt sure of it. Even though she denied him in words, her gentleness, her obvious distress over his injury, gave her away. He meant to have her—despite the reservations she had voiced.

It had never occurred to him that she would demand that he leave the Rangers. He relished the danger and excitement of the job. There must be a way he could have Honey and the Texas Rangers, too. He would just have to find it.

"When are you going to meet with the rustlers?" Honey asked.

"Sometime tonight."

Honey bit her lip to keep from begging him not to go. She had learned her lessons with Cale. Her pleas would be useless. Instead she said, "Promise me you'll be careful."

He took her hand from his shoulder and held it between both of his. "Don't worry about me, Honey." He flashed her a grin. "I've been doing this a long time. I know how to take care of myself. Besides, I'm not about to get myself killed when I've got you to come back to."

"Jesse..."

He reached up and caught her chin in his fingertips, drawing her lips toward his. "Honey..."

Warm. Wet. Tender. His mouth seduced her to his will. His hand curled around her nape and slid up into her hair. Suddenly she was sitting in his lap, her hands circling his neck, and his mouth was nuzzling her throat.

"I can't get enough of you," he murmured. "Come back to bed with me, Honey."

She was tempted. Lord how she was tempted!

"Forget about General. Forget about the Texas Rangers. Don't think about—"

Honey tore herself from his grasp and stood facing him. Her breasts ached. Desire spiraled in her belly. It was hard to catch her breath. But catch it she did long enough to say, "No, Jesse. This has to stop. Right now. You can stay here long enough to finish your business. Until then...just leave me alone."

Jesse was equally aroused and frustrated by the interruption of their lovemaking. "You're being foolish, Honey."

"So now I'm a fool on top of everything else," she retorted. "You're making it very easy to get you out of my life, Jesse."

He thrust a hand through his hair, making it stand on end. "That came out wrong," he admitted. "You know what I mean."

He rose and paced the floor like a caged wolf. "We're meant to be together. I feel it *here*." He pounded his chest around the region of his heart. ''You're only fighting against the inevitable. We *will* spend our lives together.''

''Until you get shot?'' she retorted. ''Until I bury you like I buried Cale? No, Jesse. We aren't going to be together. I need someone I can rely on to be around for the long haul. You aren't that man.''

''That remains to be seen,'' he said through clenched teeth.

Jesse wasn't prepared for the tears that gathered in Honey's eyes. He watched her blink hard, valiantly fighting them. It was clearly a losing battle, and they spilled from the corners of her eyes.

''It's over, Jesse. I mean it.'' She dashed at the tears with the back of her hand. *''I won't cry for you.''*

He watched her eyes begin to blaze with anger as she battled against the strong emotions that gripped her—and won. The tears stopped, and only the damp streaks on her face remained to show the pain she was suffering.

He felt her retreating from him even though she hadn't moved a step. ''Don't go, Honey. I need you.'' He paused and added, ''I love you.''

''You lied to me. You used me. That's not the way people in love treat each other.'' She choked back the tears that threatened again and said, ''You should have told me the truth. You should have trusted me. You should have given me the choice of knowing who you really are before I got involved with you. That's what I can't forgive, Jesse.''

She turned and left the room, shoulders back, chin high, proud and unassailable. He had never wanted her more than he did in that moment, when he feared she was lost to him.

He sank down onto the bed and stared out through the lace-curtained window. He had to admit his excuse for keeping Honey in the dark about why he had come to the Flying Diamond had sounded feeble even to his ears. He could see why she was angry. He could see why she felt betrayed.

But there was no way he could have told her the real reason she hadn't been let in on his identity: every shred of evidence against the rustlers, every outlaw trail, led straight back to the Lazy S Ranch—and Adam Philips.

Eight

"Did you steal the bull?" Mort asked.

"Yes," Jesse replied.

"Then where is it?" the rustler demanded.

"In a safe place."

"The Boss is waiting for that bull," Mort said. "You were supposed to bring it here." Mort spat chewing tobacco toward the horse trailer he had brought to transport the bull, and which would apparently be leaving empty.

"Plans change," Jesse said.

Mort's eyes narrowed. "What's that supposed to mean?"

Jesse stared right back at the grizzle-faced cowboy. "I've decided to renegotiate the terms of our agreement."

"The Boss ain't gonna like that," Mort warned ominously.

"If he doesn't like it, I can find another buyer for the bull," Jesse said.

"Now hold on a minute," Mort sputtered. "You can't—"

"Tell your boss to be here at midnight tonight," Jesse interrupted. "I'll be waiting with the bull, but I'll only deal with him in person. Tell him the price is double what we agreed on. In cash—small bills."

Mort was clearly alarmed by Jesse's ultimatum. "You're making a big mistake."

"If he wants the bull, he'll come."

It wasn't a subtle method of getting to the top man, Jesse thought, but it inevitably worked. Greed was like that. Of course he would have to watch out for the also inevitable double-cross. There was always the chance that bullets would start flying. He hoped he'd have enough backup to ensure that the guys in the white hats won.

Mort drove away grumbling, and Jesse got into his pickup and headed in the opposite direction from the Flying Diamond. He felt confident that his business for the Rangers would soon be finished. Then he could concentrate on what really mattered—his relationship with Honey. First he had to see Dallas to confirm the details of their plan to capture the brains behind the brawn tonight.

Jesse might have had second thoughts about how soon things were going to be wrapped up if he had known that his visit with Mort Barnes had been observed by another very interested party.

Honey was sweeping off the front porch when Adam Philips drove up later that same afternoon. She felt a momentary pang of guilt, but it was quickly followed by relief that she had ended their relationship. Considering they were no longer romantically involved, she couldn't imagine why Adam had come calling.

Honey laid the broom against the wooden wall of the house—noticing that it badly needed another coat of white paint—and stepped over to the porch rail. She held a hand over her brow to keep the sun out of her eyes. "Hello, Adam," she greeted him cautiously. "What brings you out here today?"

It wasn't anything good, Honey surmised after one look at the grim line of Adam's mouth. His features only seemed to get more strained as he left the car and headed up the porch steps toward her.

"Have a seat," Honey said, gesturing toward the wooden swing that hung from the porch rafters. She set a hip on the porch rail, facing the swing.

Adam sat down but abruptly jumped up again and marched over to stand before Honey. "How much do you really know about that man you hired to help around here?"

"Not a lot," Honey admitted with a shrug. "He has a degree in ranch management and—"

"Did it ever occur to you to wonder why a man with a degree in ranch management is content to work as a mere hired hand?'' Adam demanded.

Honey stared at him. It hadn't, of course. She hadn't questioned anything about Jesse's story. Which was why his revelation that he was a Texas Ranger had caught her so much off guard. It was clear Adam was still suspicious of Jesse's motives. But there was no reason for him to be. ''You don't have to worry about Jesse,'' she said.

''What makes you so sure?''

''Because he's a Texas Ranger.''

''What?'' Adam looked stunned.

Honey grinned. ''He's working undercover to catch the rustlers who've been stealing cattle around here. I don't think he'll mind that I told you, but keep it under your hat, okay?''

Adam gave her a sharp look. ''Did you know all along that he was a Texas Ranger?''

''I only found out myself this morning,'' she admitted.

Adam stuck his thumbs into the pockets of his Levi's. He pursed his lips and shook his head ruefully. ''Looks like I've been a real fool. I thought that he— Never mind. I'll be going now. I've got some calls to make before dark.''

''Adam,'' Honey called after him.

He stopped and turned back to her. ''Yes, Honey?''

''Don't be a stranger.''

A pained expression passed fleetingly across his face. He managed a smile and said, ''All right. But don't look for me too soon, all right?''

''All right. Goodbye, Adam.''

Honey worked alone the rest of the afternoon. She was grateful for Jack's absence because it gave her time to come to terms with Jesse's revelation that he was a Texas Ranger. Equally fortunate, she was spared Jesse's presence as well. He had left earlier to run some errands and hadn't returned.

Maybe it was better that they didn't spend too much time alone. Last night had been a moment out of time, almost too good to be true. It had certainly been too perfect to expect it to last. If only…

Honey thought about what she would have to give up to have Jesse in her life. Having a partner to share the responsibility of the ranch and to be there when she needed him, for one thing. She had sworn when Cale died that she would never marry another man who didn't put her needs, and the needs of the Flying Diamond, at least on an equal footing with his profession.

Although Adam's work as a doctor would have taken him away on occasion, his free time would have been devoted to her. He was wealthy enough to have hired a local man, Chuck Loomis, whose ranch had gone bust, to manage the Lazy S. Honey knew Adam also would have hired the help necessary to take care of the Flying Diamond and preserve it as a heritage for her sons.

Over the past fourteen years, Honey had fought the steady demise of her ranch. But her efforts alone—while Cale had been off fighting badmen—hadn't been enough to make all the repairs needed. The Flying Diamond was a shabby shadow of what it had been in the years when Cale's father had devotedly nurtured it.

She owed it to her sons to marry someone who could help her bring the Flying Diamond back to its former glory. Jesse could help her make it happen if he devoted himself full-time to running the ranch. But Honey couldn't imagine him being willing to leave the Texas Rangers for any reason, least of all because she asked it of him.

Even if she swallowed her pride and shouldered all the burdens of the Flying Diamond, she would still have to face the constant fear of losing Jesse to an outlaw's bullet. She couldn't bear the constant strain of not knowing whether he would come home to her at the end of the day.

The case Jesse was working on right now was a good example of what she could expect if he didn't quit the Rangers. He had told her the men he was hunting weren't just rustlers, they were murderers. They had killed a rancher in Laredo. If they ever found out a Texas Ranger had insinuated himself in their organization...Honey shuddered at the thought of what would happen to Jesse.

She hadn't forgotten what it felt like when she'd heard that Cale had been killed in the line of duty. She didn't ever want to suffer through that kind of anguish again. In the few weeks he had been around, Jesse had made a place for himself in her life and in her heart. She didn't want to contemplate how she would suffer if something went wrong and he was killed.

"Penny for your thoughts?"

Honey nearly fell backward over the porch rail. Jesse reached out and caught her, pulling her into his embrace. Honey's arms circled his broad shoulders and she looked into his amused face.

"Nearly lost you," he said. "What were you daydreaming about?"

She wasn't about to admit she had been worrying about him. "I was just thinking what good weather Jack has for tubing on the river."

"You mean he's not home yet?"

"No," she said, embarrassed by how breathless her voice sounded. Honey flushed at the intent look on Jesse's face as it suddenly dawned on him that they had the place to themselves. She swallowed hard and said, "Where have you been all day?"

"Doing business for the Texas Rangers," he admitted. "But I'm all yours now."

The leer on his face made it plain what he hoped she would do with him.

Honey was tempted to start a fight, or do whatever else was necessary to make Jesse angry enough to leave her alone. On the other hand, she was also very much aware of the sensual lure he had thrown out to her. Their time together was coming to a close. It was hard to say no when he was here, wanting her, desiring her, with his eyes and his voice and his body.

He reached out and tugged on the waistband of her jeans. The top button popped free.

"Don't even think it," she warned.

"You can read my mind?"

"Enough to know you're crazy."

"Probably certifiable," he admitted. "But if you don't tell, I won't."

He made growling sounds and bit her neck, sending a frisson of fire through her veins.

She grabbed Jesse's face to try to make him stop whatever tantalizing thing he was doing to her throat with his tongue, but he caught her hands and forced them behind her. Twining their fingers together, he used them to pull her between his widespread legs where his arousal was evident.

"Jesse," she protested with a breathless laugh. "We can't. It's broad daylight."

"There's no one to see," he said, thrusting against her and causing her to groan as her body responded to the urgency of his.

She was running out of excuses for him not to do what she so desperately wanted him to do. "Jack might come home."

"Then we'll just have to go where he won't find us," Jesse murmured conspiratorially.

Honey thought he meant her bedroom, but he obviously had other ideas. She gasped when he threw her over his shoulder and headed for the barn.

"Not the barn!" she hooted.

"Why not the barn?" he said with a grin.

"Hay itches."

He stopped and rearranged her in his arms so he could see her face. "Sounds like you speak from experience."

The color rose on Honey's cheeks. When Jesse laughed she hid her face against his throat.

He murmured in her ear, "If you feel any itches anywhere I'll be glad to scratch them."

Honey giggled like a schoolgirl. She felt so carefree! If only it could always be like this, laughter and loving, with no thought of the future to spoil it. Honey nibbled on Jesse's ear and heard him hiss in a breath of air.

"Keep that up, woman, and we won't make it to the barn," he warned.

Honey was feeling in a dangerous mood. She teased his ear with her tongue, tracing the shell-like shape of it. She shrieked when Jesse teasingly threatened to drop her.

At the barn door he stopped and stood her before him so he could look at her.

When Honey caught sight of his face she knew she was playing with fire. His dark eyes were heavy-lidded, his features taut with desire. His nostrils flared and his hands tightened on her flesh. Her whole body tensed in response to his obvious sexual hunger.

Her fingertips caressed his cheekbones and slid up from his temple into the thick black hair at his nape. "I want you, Jesse."

Her words were like a match on tinder. Jesse's mouth came down on hers, his tongue thrusting in a mirror image of that age-old dance between men and women. Her fingers clutched at his hair, forcing his hat off his head. She grabbed hold of him as though to keep from flying off into the unknown. For nothing Jesse did to her from then on was like anything that had ever happened to her before.

His mouth found her nipple through her thin cotton shirt, rousing her to passion. His hand slid down the front of her jeans and cupped the heat and heart of her. He urged her hand down to the hard bulge that threatened the seams of his Levi's. He thrust against her, his desire a stronger aphrodisiac than any shaman's love potion.

They stood just inside the barn door, and Jesse molded them together belly to belly as he backed her out of the sunlight and into the shadows. "It's time you and I had a talk about what happens when you tease a man," Jesse rasped, pressing her up against the barn wall with his body.

He insinuated his thigh between her legs and lifted her so she could feel the heat and pressure of his flesh against that most sensitive of feminine places. Meanwhile he cupped a breast in one hand while the other captured her nape to hold her still for the onslaught of his mouth and the invasion of his tongue.

"Honey," he rasped. "I can't get enough of you, the feel of you, the taste of you."

Honey was overwhelmed. She couldn't breathe. She couldn't move. She could only respond to the sensations that assaulted her. Her knees collapsed and Jesse had to hold her upright.

Abruptly he left her and she leaned against the rough wooden walls, legs outstretched, while he grabbed a clean saddle blanket and spread it hurriedly over the fresh, crackling straw in an empty stall at the back of the barn.

She felt his urgency as he returned to lift her into his arms and carry her to the blanket, laying her down carefully before mantling her with his body.

Honey looked up into eyes that were narrowed in concentration on her, fierce, dark eyes that should have frightened her but only made her wild with anticipation.

Slowly, slowly, Jesse began unbuttoning her shirt. His mouth caressed her flesh as he exposed it, until he reached the button on her Levi's. The button hardly made a sound as it fell free, but her zipper grated noisily as he slid it down. His mouth followed where his hands had led and soon he was nuzzling at the very apex of her thighs.

Honey reached for whatever part of him she could grasp, but when he nipped her through her silken panties her nails curved into the muscles of his back.

''Jesse!''

He sat up to pull off her boots and then his own. She yanked off her socks and then his, grinning at the sight of his long naked feet. He started to unsnap his shirt, but she stopped him.

''Let me.''

She offered him the same enjoyment he had given her, exposing his bronze skin one snap at a time and caressing it with her lips and tongue. Intrigued by his distended nipples she forayed across his chest to nibble gently on one.

His whole body tensed, and he held himself motionless while she tested his control. He didn't last long. A moment later she found herself flat on her back, Jesse astride her.

''Play with fire and you can get burned, woman.''

He unsnapped the front clasp of her bra and brushed it aside as he took one of her nipples in his mouth to tease it with his tongue. Honey arched upward with her hips and encountered the hardness of his arousal.

She grasped his buttocks to pull him close and spread her legs to accommodate him more fully. Jesse returned the pressure as she gently rubbed herself against him.

Abruptly Jesse freed himself from her grasp and began stripping her. She was equally urgent in her efforts to undress him until moments later they stared at each other in the filtered sunlight.

''God, you're beautiful,'' he said reverently.

Honey felt herself flushing with pleasure at the compliment. She knew he wasn't merely mouthing the words. His delight was mirrored in his eyes.

''I'm glad I please you.''

The gentle touch of his mouth on hers was like a paean to a goddess. He honored her. He revered her. He desired her. His lips and mouth and tongue adored her. The kisses that began at her mouth continued downward to her throat, found their way to her breasts, then to her belly and beyond.

Honey stiffened and reached out a hand to grip his shoulder. She hadn't expected this. She wasn't sure whether she wanted it.

Jesse raised his eyes to hers. "I want to taste all of you," he said.

In all the years they had been married, Cale had never loved her this way. It was the most intimate of kisses. And it required complete trust. Jesse was aware of that, and he awaited her consent. Honey was wired as tight as a bowstring, anxious to please him, afraid she wouldn't, afraid of the unknown. Of that forbidden pleasure.

She had always wondered what it would feel like, always wondered whether it truly brought the immeasurable ecstasy that made it something to be whispered about. All she had to do was trust Jesse enough to allow him to love her as he so clearly wanted to do.

She opened her mouth to agree, but no sound came out. She swallowed hard and slowly nodded her head.

Jesse's quick grin surprised her. "You won't be sorry," he said. Just as quickly the grin disappeared. "You only have to say the word and I'll stop. This is supposed to please us both. All right?"

Honey nodded again.

She was surprised when he rose and kissed her on the mouth again. He took his time kissing his way back down her body, but she knew where he was heading. By the time he got there she was more aroused than she could ever remember being.

For Jesse had not relied on his mouth alone to make that journey. His callused hands had smoothed across her flesh, finding her breasts and teasing them, taunting her by rolling her nipples between fingers and thumb. He had caressed ribs and hipbones and the length of her back from her nape to the dimples at the curve of her spine. She was sure she would find impressions of his fingers on her buttocks where he had lazily learned the shape of them.

Finally he lifted her in his hands while his tongue teased her. She gasped as her body tautened. She grabbed handfuls of the wool blanket to keep from touching him, lest he think she wanted him to stop. For she didn't. Oh, no, she did not!

Honey felt the ripples building, felt her inner flesh clenching, felt the muscles in her thighs tighten until she could not move. And still he kissed her. Loved her. Teased her with his mouth and tongue.

She moaned and writhed in pleasure. Her body arched toward him and at last her hands reached for him, clutching at his shoulders as though he could save her from the cataclysmic—wondrous, astounding, remarkable—things her body threatened to do.

Honey did not want to let go of what little control she had left. There was no hiding the strong muscular contractions as she began climaxing beneath him. Excited, animal sounds came from her throat as she convulsed with pleasure.

Jesse met her eyes and watched the agony of ecstasy that she could not hide from him.

When it was over, she turned her face away from him. Her throat was swollen with emotion and tears stung her eyes.

''Honey?''

She heard the anxiety in his voice and tried to reassure him. But no sound would pass over the lump in her throat. She reached out and grasped his hand.

He lay down beside her and brushed a sweat-dampened lock of hair from her brow. ''Are you all right?''

She nodded jerkily.

''You're not acting all right,'' he said.

She hid her face in his throat and clutched him around the waist.

He continued smoothing her hair and rubbing her back gently. She couldn't see his face, but she could feel from the tension in his body that he was troubled. She wanted to reassure him that she was all right, but she was simply so *overwhelmed* by what had happened that words did not seem sufficient to explain how she felt.

Eventually her breathing calmed and her throat relaxed. ''It was so...''

Jesse put a finger under her chin and forced her eyes up to meet his. ''So what?''

''Beautiful,'' she whispered.

He hugged her hard then and rocked her back and forth. ''I'm glad,'' he said. ''I'm so glad. I was afraid—''

''It was wonderful,'' she said. Then, shyly, ''I only hope you're going to give me the pleasure of returning the favor.''

He grinned. ''Someday soon,'' he promised. ''Right now, there's something more I want from you.''

''What's that?''

''This.''

He nudged her knees apart and sheathed himself easily in her still half-aroused body.

When he kissed her again, Honey found the taste of herself still on his lips. She gave back to him that which he had given her. She was far beyond rational thought by that time, only wanting to join herself with him in any way she could.

Honey touched Jesse's body everywhere she could reach as he sought to bring her to a second pinnacle of pleasure. She wasn't really conscious of how she caressed him, but moved her hands in response to the way he arched his sinewy body beneath her, the way he moved toward her touch or away from it. By sheer luck she found a spot—the crease where belly met thigh—that made him shudder with pleasure.

Jesse did not allow her time to tarry. He lifted her legs up over his thighs and took them both on a journey of delight. After she had fallen off the world yet again, he poured his seed into her, his head arched back in ecstasy, every muscle taut with unspeakable pleasure.

Afterward, they both slept. It was nearly dark by the time Honey wakened. Jesse's head rested on his hand and he was staring down at her as though memorizing her features.

''It's late,'' she said.

''We'd better get dressed,'' he agreed.

Neither of them moved.

''After tonight, I'll be finished with my work here,'' Jesse said at last.

Honey closed her eyes to hide the myriad emotions vying for dominance. ''When will you be leaving?''

''Honey, I...''

She opened her eyes. ''I'll miss you,'' she admitted. She reached up to touch his mouth with a fingertip. Was she responsible for the sensuous look of his swollen lower lip?

He took her hand in his and kissed each finger. ''I love you, Honey. Will you marry me?''

Honey was so shocked her mouth fell open.

He nudged at her chin with a bent finger. "Catch a lot of flies that way," he teased in a husky voice.

But Honey saw how his hand trembled when he took it away. It was clear that despite his levity he cared a great deal about how she answered. She was so tempted to say yes! But it wasn't fair to marry Jesse without expressing the reservations she harbored.

"Are you willing to quit the Rangers?" she asked.

"Are you making that a condition of your acceptance?" he answered in a sharp voice.

Honey took a deep breath and said, "Yes, I think I am."

He was on his feet an instant later, pulling on his pants. "That's totally unreasonable, Honey, and you know it!" he ranted.

She was suddenly embarrassed to be naked when he was dressed. She grabbed at her shirt and stuck her arms into the sleeves. Honey searched for her panties and found them across the stall. She turned her back on Jesse to step into them and was conscious of the silence as she did. Over her shoulder she discovered him ogling her bottom.

She yanked her panties on and dragged her jeans over her legs. "I don't see what's so unreasonable about wanting a husband who'll be around to help run this ranch!"

"I'd be around!" he insisted.

"In between assignments," she retorted. "You forget, I've already been married to one Texas Ranger. You're as bad as Cale."

"Don't tar me with the same brush."

"How are you different?" she demanded. "You can't deny you take the same foolish, dangerous chances with your life that he did. And look what happened to him! I couldn't bear it if—"

Honey cut herself off and went searching for her socks.

Jesse grabbed her by the arms and forced her to face him. "I know you love me," he began.

"That isn't the point," Honey interrupted.

"Then you do love me?"

He stood there waiting for an answer. Honey grimaced and admitted, "I love you but—"

Jesse cut her off with a hard kiss. "Then all the rest is small stuff. We can work it out."

"You're not listening to me," Honey said, her voice rising as she felt control of the situation slipping away. "I won't marry you, Jesse. Not unless you're willing to give up the Rangers."

His mouth thinned in anger. "You're asking the impossible."

"Why is it impossible? There are other challenges in life besides hunting down outlaws."

"Like what?"

"Like raising kids. Like making a success of this ramshackle ranch. Like growing a garden. Like spending the afternoon making sweet, sweet love to your wife."

He captured her in his arms and nuzzled her throat. "The last part of that certainly sounds promising."

Honey remained stiff in his embrace, fighting the tears that threatened. *"Listen to me,"* she pleaded. "I'm fighting for our life together."

His head jerked up and he glared down at her. "So am I," he insisted. "You're asking me to give up what I *am.*"

Honey shook her head sadly. "No, Jesse. It's just a job. You can quit."

"And if I won't?"

She pushed at his shoulders, forcing him to release her. "Then I guess this is goodbye."

His lips flattened. "You don't mean that."

Her chin lifted and her shoulders squared. "Goodbye, Jesse."

She turned and marched barefoot from the barn, leaving Jesse to stare at her stiff back. "Damned fool woman," he muttered. "Can't expect me to give up everything for her. She's crazy if she thinks I will. No woman is worth that kind of sacrifice."

It was a sober and contemplative man who left the barn. The best thing to do was put the situation with Honey out of his mind and concentrate on his rendezvous with the rustlers. It wouldn't do to let himself get distracted. Honey was right about one thing. A Texas Ranger led a dangerous life. He had to pay attention to what he was doing tonight or he might end up getting himself killed. He snorted in disgust. He would hate like hell to prove Honey right about the dangers of his job.

Nine

Because of all she had been through with Jesse, Honey hadn't given Jack a thought for the past twenty-four hours. In fact, she had spent most of that time in a euphoric haze. Memories of Jesse's lovemaking had preoccupied her in the morning, and their interlude in the barn, his proposal and their subsequent quarrel had kept her agitated until well after dark. It wasn't until nearly nine o'clock Saturday evening that she realized how late Jack was in returning home and began making inquiries.

Honey was aghast when she discovered Jack had not spent the night with a friend—or even made plans to do so. He hadn't gone tubing on the Frio, either! Jack had never lied to her before. She couldn't imagine where he could have gone last night, unless…

The worst conclusion to be drawn from the facts came first: *Jack had run away from home.* Honey suddenly remembered how hard Jack had hugged her last night before he left the house, how intently he had looked into her eyes. She hadn't paid much attention to the hug except to be pleased by it because Jack so seldom indulged in such sentimentality these days. Now his hug took on ominous significance. *Jack had been saying goodbye!*

Honey's heart began thudding heavily. Her palms tingled. She felt light-headed. Her knees went weak and she had to sit down before she fell down.

Things had been rough for the past year since Cale's death, but surely not bad enough for her son to want to escape the situation. Jesse's appearance had injected a note of tension in the household, but Jack seemed to have made his peace with Jesse the day they worked together on the corral.

But maybe Jack had only been pretending things were all right. Maybe he had resented the hired hand much more than he had let on. Maybe having his mother courted by two men at the same time was more strain than he could handle. But he didn't have to run away!

To Honey's chagrin, the first person she thought of to help her hunt for Jack was Jesse Whitelaw. But shortly after their argument in the barn, Jesse had gotten into his pickup and driven away. Honey didn't know where. And she didn't care.

Honey snickered in disgust. Who was she trying to kid? She cared. She already missed Jesse and he hadn't even left the Flying Diamond. At least, she didn't think he was gone for good. His things were still in the small room off the kitchen. She knew because she had checked.

Honey shuddered to think that the man she loved had been in any way responsible for her son running away from home. What an awful mess her life had become!

Well, she would just have to straighten it out. Jack had to learn he couldn't run from his problems, that he had to confront them head-on and resolve them. And Jesse, well, he could stand to learn a lesson or two about not running from problems himself. She was just the woman to instruct them both!

Deciding she could use reinforcements, Honey picked up the phone and called Dallas Masterson. Angel answered.

"Is Dallas there?" Honey asked.

"I'm afraid he's gone for the evening. Some Ranger business," Angel said.

Honey had completely forgotten about General and the trap Jesse was supposedly laying for the rustlers. Was that where he was tonight? Was his life in danger even now?

"Honey, are you okay?" Angel asked, concerned by the long silence.

Honey sank back into a kitchen chair. "I don't think so."

"What's wrong? Can I help?"

"Jack's missing," Honey said. "And I don't have the first clue where to look for him."

"I'll be right over," Angel said.

"What about the baby?"

"I'll bring him. He'll be fine riding in the car while we look for Jack. Don't go anywhere till I get there. I won't be long."

"I'll use the time to call some more of Jack's friends. Maybe they'll have some idea where he is," Honey said.

Angel was as good as her word, and a short while later she drove into the yard. Honey came running out and jumped into the passenger's side of the car.

"Do you have any suggestions where we can start looking?" Angel asked.

"No," Honey said. She bit down on her lower lip to still its tremor. "We might as well start on the Flying Diamond. Maybe he—" Honey stopped herself from saying *had an accident;* it was a possibility she didn't want to consider. It was almost better believing he had run away.

They searched the Flying Diamond in vain. Jack was nowhere to be found. Honey was getting frantic. It was nearly midnight. *Where was her son?*

"I don't know where to look from here, except to check whether he might have gone to see Adam at the Lazy S," Honey said at last.

"Dallas told me to stay away from the Lazy S tonight. There's something going on at that corral where your boys practiced roping earlier this spring."

"As I recall, there's a pen for livestock," Honey said, thinking aloud. "So that's where Jesse hid General!"

"What are you talking about?" Angel asked.

"Last night Jesse stole General."

"What!"

"It's a long story. Anyway, he said he'd put him somewhere safe. I'm betting he meant the pen at that roundup corral on the southern border of the Lazy S. If Dallas told you to stay away from there tonight—"

"—because of Ranger business—"

"—then chances are that's where they both are right now." Honey hissed in a breath of air. "Jack couldn't have suspected...he wouldn't have gone...Jack just couldn't..."

"Jack couldn't what?" Angel asked.

Honey had a terrible feeling of foreboding. "We have to get to that corral," she said. "Hurry!"

"Dallas specifically said to stay away from there," Angel protested.

"Jack's there!" Honey said.

"How do you know?"

"Call it a mother's instinct if you like, but he's there, all right, and he's in trouble! Let's go!"

Jack hadn't liked lying to his mother, but sometimes there were things a man had to do. Protecting his mother was one of those things. So he had told her he was spending the night with a friend and asked if it was all right to spend the following day tubing on the Frio River. In reality, he planned to spend the entire time spying on Jesse Whitelaw.

Jack had grudgingly given Jesse the benefit of the doubt after their talk in the barn. By the end of a day spent working with the hired hand, he had felt a secret admiration for the cowboy. Then he had overheard Jesse on the phone after dinner, making plans to rent a stock trailer.

At first Jack supposed his mother had sold some cattle. When Jesse mentioned something about "restraints for the bull," Jack got suspicious. There was only one bull on the Flying Diamond, and General wasn't for sale. Jack felt sick.

He had secretly been dreaming about what it would be like if Jesse Whitelaw became his stepfather. He had imagined lots of days like the one they had spent together working to repair the corral. Jesse had treated him as an equal. He had respected him as a person. Working with Jesse hadn't been a chore, it had been fun.

Now Jack saw Jesse's behavior as a phony act to lull him and his mother into complacency, so they wouldn't interfere when Jesse stole the one thing of true value left on the Flying Diamond. Jack felt like a fool. The more he thought about it, the angrier he got, until there seemed only one course of action open to him. He would catch Jesse Whitelaw red-handed. He would put the deceitful drifter in jail where he would have plenty of time to regret having underestimated a gullible, trusting, thirteen-year-old boy.

Jack had packed an overnight bag and hugged his mom goodbye as though he were spending the night with friends. Instead, he had hidden himself where he could stand guard on the barn. Sure enough, about an hour after his mother left the house with Adam Philips, Jesse Whitelaw had backed a stock trailer up to the barn and let down the ramp.

At first Jack had been tempted to confront the drifter. But even at his age he knew discretion was the better part of valor. He thought about running to the house to call the police, but figured Jesse would be long gone before anyone could block the roads leading from the Flying Diamond.

So while Jesse was in the barn with the bull, Jack had snuck under a tarp lying in the back of the pickup truck pulling the stock trailer. It was all very easy, and Jack was pleased with how clever he had been. Surprisingly, Jesse had taken the bull to the roundup corral on the southern edge of the Lazy S.

Jack knew he ought to go right to his mother with what information he had, but he was afraid she would let Jesse go because of her soppy feelings for the drifter. So while Jesse was unloading the bull into one of the stock pens, Jack left the truck and hid inside a nearby tin-roofed shed, figuring he couldn't go wrong staying with General. Besides, if he left, the bull might be gone by the time he got back with the authorities.

Jack was nearly discovered when Jesse came inside the shed to get hay for the bull. Apparently the theft had been more well thought out than Jack had realized. To Jack's dismay, when Jesse left the shed he dropped a wooden bar across the door. *Jack was trapped!*

His first instinct was to call out. Fear kept him silent. There was no telling what the drifter would do if he knew he had been found out. Jack remained quiet as the truck drove away. Surely Jesse would return soon. All Jack had to do was wait and be sure he got out of the shed undetected when it was opened again.

Jack had spent a long, uncomfortable night on a pile of prickly hay. He had finally fallen asleep in the wee hours of the morning and only wakened when the sun was high in the sky. He was relieved to see through a knothole in the wooden-sided shed that General was still in the stock pen, but he was also confused. Surely someone should have come to collect the bull by now.

All day long, Jack waited expectantly for Jesse to return. It was late afternoon by the time he realized the exchange would likely be made after dark. He was hot and hungry and thirsty and dearly regretted not having called the police when he had first had an inkling of what Jesse intended.

Jack wondered whether his mother had checked up on him and uncovered his lies. He consoled himself with the thought that she wouldn't really start to worry until after dark. Only the sun had fallen hours ago. Where was she? Why hadn't anybody come looking for him? Where was Jesse? *Where was everybody?*

Jesse hunkered down in the ravine where Dallas was hidden so he wouldn't be spotted talking to the other Ranger. "Is everything set?" he asked.

"The local police have the entire area covered like a glove," Dallas reassured him.

"I just hope Adam steps into the trap," Jesse said.

Dallas shook his head. "He isn't going to be the one who shows up here tonight. You'll see. I'd stake my life on it."

Jesse arched a disbelieving brow. "You're still sticking by the man, even with all the evidence we have leading to the Lazy S? With all we've discovered about how his ranch has floundered lately? With everything we know about how bad Adam Philips's finances have gotten over the past year?"

Dallas nodded. "I know Adam. He just can't be involved in something like this. There's got to be another explanation."

"For your sake, I hope you're right," Jesse said. But he wouldn't mind if Adam Philips ended up being a villain in Honey's eyes. Maybe then she would start to see Jesse in a more positive light.

That woman was the most stubborn, bullheaded, downright maddening creature Jesse had ever known. How he had fallen so deeply in love with her was a mystery to him, but the fact was, he had. Now the fool woman was refusing to marry him unless he left the Rangers. Damn her willful hide!

He couldn't possibly give up an honor he had striven so hard to achieve. Why, the Rangers were an elite group of men. Independent. Fearless. Ruthless when necessary. He was proud to be part of such an historic organization. It was unfair of Honey to ask him to make such a sacrifice.

Yet he could see her side of the issue. Over the weeks he had worked on the Flying Diamond, he had gotten a glimmer of how little time Cale Farrell had devoted to the place. It wasn't just the roof that needed repair, or a few rotten corral posts that had to be replaced. The whole ranch showed signs of serious neglect.

It was apparent that because of Cale's commitment to the Rangers, the brunt of the ranch work must have fallen on Honey's shoulders. Not that they weren't lovely shoulders, but they weren't strong enough to support the entire weight of an outfit the size of the Flying Diamond.

Jesse had seen dozens of opportunities where better management—and plain hard work—would have improved the yield of the ranch. The Flying Diamond had land that could be put to use growing feed. Expanded, Honey's vegetable garden could easily provide for the needs of the ranch. And it wouldn't be a bad idea to invest in some mohair goats. The money from the mohair harvest could be applied to supporting the cattle end of the ranch.

If he stayed on as a Ranger, Jesse wouldn't have much time to invest in the ranch. He could expect to be called away on assignments often. Honey would be left to take care of things. As she must have been left for most of her married life, Jesse suddenly realized.

He had never heard Honey complain once about the burden she had carried all these years. And he was only thinking in terms of the ranch. Honey had probably borne most of the responsibility as a parent as well. She had done a good job. Jack and Jonathan were fine boys that any man would be proud to call sons.

Jesse felt a tightness in his chest when he remembered the look he and Jack had shared at the end of the day they had spent working together. Jesse had never known a stronger feeling of satisfaction. He had truly felt close to the boy. It was hard to imagine walking away from Jack and Jonathan. It was impossible to imagine walking away from Honey.

All his life Jesse had somehow managed to have his cake and eat it, too. Honey was asking him to make a choice. He just didn't know what it was going to be.

Jesse saw the truck lights in the distance and checked the revolver he had stuck in the back of his jeans. It wasn't particularly easy to get to, but then, he was hoping the show of force by the police would reduce the chance of gunplay. He stood by the corral waiting as the tractor-trailer truck pulled up. The engine remained running. It was Mort Barnes who stepped into the glare of the truck headlights.

Jesse stiffened. He saw his efforts to finally uncover the man in charge going up in smoke. "Where's your boss?" he demanded.

Mort grinned, though it looked more like a sneer. "I'm the boss."

"I don't believe you," Jesse said flatly.

Mort revealed the automatic weapon in his hand and said, "I'll take that bull."

Jesse didn't hesitate. He threw himself out of the light at the same instant Mort fired. Instead of running for cover, Jesse leapt toward the rustler. Blinded by the headlights, Mort didn't see Jesse until he had been knocked down and his gun kicked out of his hand, disappearing somewhere in the underbrush.

Moments later, Jesse straddled Mort on the ground, with a viselike grip on the rustler's throat and his gun aimed at the rustler's head. "I told you I'm only going to deal with your boss."

"Why you—" Mort rasped.

"You can release Mort," a voice said from the shadows on the other side of the truck, "and drop the gun. I'm here."

Jesse didn't recognize the man who stepped into view, his automatic weapon aimed at the center of Jesse's back. But it wasn't Adam Philips. Jesse dropped his gun. Then he released Mort and stood to face the newest threat. "Are you the boss of this outfit?"

"I am," the man said. "I can't say it's a pleasure to meet you, Mr. Whitelaw. Actually, you've thrown a bit of a corkscrew into my plans. If you'll just step over to that shed, we can finish our business."

"You brought the money?" Jesse asked.

"Oh, no. All deals are off. I'm simply offering you a chance to get out of this alive. Are you going to walk over there peacefully, or not? I've already killed once. I assure you I won't hesitate to do so again."

Jesse was pretty sure the Boss intended to kill him anyway, but he was counting on Dallas to make sure he got out of this alive. Meanwhile, he had best keep his wits about him. He took his time sliding away the board that held the shed door closed, giving Dallas plenty of time to get everybody into position. Once Jesse was inside the shed and, he hoped, before the Boss man shot him, Dallas would move and it would all be over.

The instant Jesse released the door, a blur of movement shot past him. The escaping body was caught by Mort. Jesse's blood froze when he saw the gangly teenager the rustler was wrestling into submission.

''What the hell are you doing here?'' Jesse rasped.

''Waiting for you!'' Jack retorted. ''You won't get away with this, you know. I'll tell them everything. They'll catch you, and you'll go to jail forever.''

''Dammit, Jack, I—''

''Hey!'' Jack was eyeing the man holding the gun on Jesse. ''I know you! You're the foreman of the Lazy S. What're you doing here, Mr. Loomis?''

''Dammit, Jack,'' Jesse muttered. Now the fat was in the fire.

''You got any more surprises hidden around here?'' Loomis asked Jesse.

''Look, the kid being here is as much a surprise to me as it is to you,'' Jesse said.

Jesse closely watched the man Jack had identified as Mr. Loomis and saw his mouth tighten, his eyes narrow. By identifying the Boss and making threats of going to the law, Jack had signed his own death warrant. Jesse forced himself not to glance out into the darkness. Adam's foreman was suspicious enough already. Dallas would realize that the boy's presence complicated things and make new plans accordingly.

''Both of you get into the shed,'' Loomis said, gesturing with the gun.

Jack spied the gun for the first time, and his eyes slid to Jesse's, wide with fright.

''It's all right,'' Jesse said in a voice intended to calm the youth. ''They're just going to lock us up in the shed.''

Jesse's last doubts that Loomis intended killing them both ended when Mort chuckled maliciously and said, ''Yeah, you two just mosey on inside.''

Jack struggled against Mort's hold, and the outlaw slapped him hard. ''Quit your bellyachin' and get movin'.''

Jesse had decided to use the distraction Jack was creating to make a lunge for Loomis's gun, when a pair of headlights appeared on the horizon.

''I knew it was a trap!'' the outlaw snarled. Loomis swung the gun around to aim it at Jack and fired just as Jesse grabbed at his hand, pulling it down.

Jesse grunted as the bullet plowed into his thigh, but he never let go of his hold on Loomis's wrist. He swung a fist at the foreman's face and heard a satisfying crunch as it connected with the man's hooked nose. Loomis managed to fire once more before Jesse wrenched the gun away, but the bullet drove harmlessly into the ground.

Moments later, the area was swarming with local police and Texas Rangers. It soon became apparent to Jack from the way Dallas Masterson greeted Jesse, that the drifter wasn't going to be arrested by the Texas Rangers *because he was one!*

''What idiot turned on those headlights?'' Jesse demanded. ''Damned near got us killed!''

Jesse's head jerked up when he heard the sound of a woman's voice beyond the arc of light provided by the semi's headlights. ''Who's that?''

Dallas grinned. ''The idiot who turned on the headlights.''

Jesse only had a second to brace himself before Honey threw herself into his arms. Her eyes were white around the rims with fright. Her whole body was shaking.

''I saw what happened. You saved Jack's life! I heard shots. Are you hurt?'' She pushed herself away to look at him and saw the dark shine of blood on his leg. ''My God! You've been shot!'' She turned to the crowd of men scattered over the area and shouted, ''Where's a doctor? Why haven't you taken this man to the hospital?''

Jesse pulled her back into his arms. ''It's all right, Honey. It's just a little flesh wound. I'll be fine.''

Jack stepped into the light and stood nearby, afraid to approach his mother and the drifter...who wasn't really a drifter after all.

Honey saw her son and reached out to pull him close. "Are you all right? You're not hurt?"

"I'm fine," Jack mumbled, feeling lower than a worm for having caused so much trouble.

"You're damned lucky not to be dead!" Jesse said.

Jack glared at Jesse. "If you'd just told me the truth in the first place, none of this would have happened. I spent a whole day in that stupid shed for nothing!" He turned to his mother and said, "I'm hungry. Is there anything at home to eat?"

Honey gaped at Jack and then laughed. If her son had started thinking about his stomach, he was going to be just fine.

Dallas had left briefly and now joined them again. "I've got a car to take you to the hospital, Jesse."

"I'll see you at home, Honey," Jesse said.

Now that she knew Jesse was all right, Honey forced herself to step away from him. If anything, this episode only proved what she had known all along. She didn't want to be married to a Texas Ranger. "I'll let you in to get your things," she said. "But I expect you to find somewhere else to spend what's left of the night."

Jesse didn't argue, just limped away toward the car Dallas had waiting.

But Jack wasn't about to let the subject alone. "He saved my life, Mom."

"I suppose he did."

"You can't just throw him out of the house like that."

"I can and I will."

"If you want my opinion, I think you're making a mistake," Jack said.

"I didn't ask for your opinion," Honey said. "Besides, you've got a lot to answer for yourself, young man."

Jack grimaced. "I can explain everything."

"This I've got to hear."

Angel interrupted to say, "I can give you both a ride home now."

"Let's go," Honey said. She put her arm around Jack and dared him to try to slip out from under it. ‘‘It’s been a hectic night. Let’s go home and get some sleep.’’

‘‘But I’m hungry!’’ Jack protested.

‘‘All right. First you eat. Then it’s bed for both of us.’’

But hours later—just before dawn—when Jesse Whitelaw returned, Honey was sitting in the kitchen, coffee cup in hand, waiting for him.

Ten

Honey didn't move when the kitchen door opened, just waited for Jesse to come to her. Her eyes drifted closed when his hands clasped her shoulders. She exhaled with a soughing sigh. He didn't give her a chance to object, just hauled her out of the chair, turned her into his arms and held her tight.

Honey's arms slipped around his waist and clutched his shirt. Her nose slipped into the hollow at his throat and she inhaled the sweaty man-scent that was his and his alone. She wanted to remember it when he was gone. And she *was* going to send him away.

"We have to talk," Jesse whispered in her ear.

Honey gripped him tighter, knowing she had to let him go. "I think I've said everything I have to say."

"I haven't." His lips twisted wryly. "I think this is where I'm supposed to sweep you into my arms and carry you off to the bedroom," he said. "But I don't think my leg could stand the strain."

Honey realized all at once how heavily he was leaning on her. "Come sit down," she said, urging him toward a kitchen chair.

"Let's find something a little more comfortable," he said. "Getting up and down is a pain. I'd like to find someplace I can stay awhile."

She slipped an arm around his waist to support him while he put an arm across her shoulders. Slowly they made their way to the living room, where he levered himself onto the brass-studded leather couch.

He winced as she helped him lift both legs and stretch out full-length. She knelt beside him on the polished hardwood floor.

Jesse took one of her hands in both of his and brought it to his lips. He kissed each fingertip and then the palm of her hand. He laid her hand against his cheek, bristly now with a day's growth of beard, and turned to gaze into her eyes.

"Let me stay here tonight," he said.

"Jesse, I don't think—"

"We have to talk, Honey, but I can barely keep my eyes open."

"You can't stay here," she said. If he did, she would be tempted to let him stay another night, and another. Before she knew it, he would be a permanent fixture. "You have to leave," she insisted.

He smiled wearily. "Sorry. I'm afraid that's out of the question. Can't seem to get a muscle to move anywhere." His eyes drifted closed. "I have some things to say..."

He was asleep.

Honey stared at the beloved face before her and felt her heart wrench in her breast. How could she let him stay? How could she make him go?

She sighed and rose to find a blanket. After all, it was only one night. She would be able to argue with him better once she had gotten some sleep herself.

The homemade quilt barely reached from one end to the other of the tall Ranger. Jesse's face was gentle in repose. There was no hint of the fierceness in battle she had seen, no hint of the savage passion she had experienced. He was only a man. There must be another—not a Ranger—who would suit her as well.

She leaned down slowly, carefully, and touched her lips to his. A goodbye kiss. She walked dry-eyed up the stairs to her bedroom. It looked so empty. It felt so forlorn. She lay down on the bed and stared at the canopy overhead. It was a long time before she finally found respite in sleep.

The sun woke Honey the next morning. It was brighter than bright, a golden Texas morning. Honey stretched and groaned at how stiff she felt. Then she froze. Where was Jesse now? Was he still downstairs sleeping? Had he packed and left? Was he dressed and waiting to confront her?

Honey scrambled off the bed and ran across the hall to the bathroom. She took one look at herself and groaned. Her face looked as if she'd slept in it. She started the water running in the tub as hot as she could get it and stripped off her clothes. There was barely an inch of liquid in the claw-footed tub by the time she stepped into it. She sank down, hissing as the water scalded her, then grabbed a cloth and began soaping herself clean.

It never occurred to her to lock the bathroom door. No one ever bothered her when she was in the bathroom. Her eyes widened in surprise when the door opened and Jesse sauntered in. He was shirtless, wearing a pair of jeans that threatened to fall off, revealing his navel and the beginning of his hipbones.

She held the washcloth in front of her, which didn't do much good, not to mention how silly it looked. ''What are you doing in here?'' she demanded indignantly.

''I thought I'd shave,'' Jesse said. ''We might as well get used to having to share the bathroom in the morning.'' He turned and grinned. ''That is, unless I can talk you into adding a second bathroom. One with a *shower?*''

''What's going on, Jesse?''

He soaped up his shaving brush and began applying the resulting foam to his beard. ''I'm shaving,'' he answered. ''Looks like you're taking a bath.'' He grinned.

Honey tried ignoring him. She turned her back on him and continued washing herself. She was feeling both angry and confused. *He has no right to be doing this! Why doesn't he just go?* If Jesse had changed his mind about leaving the Rangers he would have told her so last night. This was just another ploy to get his own way. She wasn't going to let him get away with it.

Honey covered herself with the washcloth as best she could while she reached for a towel. Just as she caught it with her fingertips, Jesse slipped it off the rack and settled it around his neck.

''I need that towel,'' she said through gritted teeth.

''I'll be done with it in a minute,'' he said. ''I need to wipe off the excess shaving cream.''

Honey was tempted to stand up and stroll past him naked, but she didn't have the nerve. What if Jack was out there? *Jack!*

"Where's Jack?" she asked.

"Sent him out to round up those steers we vaccinated and move them to another pasture."

"And he went?"

"Don't look so surprised. Jack's a hard worker."

Honey's brows rose. "I know that. I didn't think you did."

"Jack and I have an understanding," Jesse said.

"Oh?"

"I told him this morning that I was going to marry you and—"

"You what!" Honey rose from the water like Poseidon in a tempest. Water sluiced down her body, creating jeweled trails over breasts and belly.

Jesse didn't know when he had ever seen her looking more beautiful. Or more angry.

"Now, Honey—"

"Don't you 'Now, Honey' me, you rogue. How could you tell my son such a thing? How could you get his hopes up when you *know* I'm not going to marry you!"

"But you are," Jesse said.

Honey was shivering from cold and trembling with emotion. Jesse took the towel from around his neck and offered it to her. She yanked it out of his hand and wrapped it around herself.

"I'd like to play the gallant and carry you off to the bedroom to make my point, but—" He gestured to the wounded leg and shrugged. "Can't do it."

Honey made a growling sound low in her throat as she marched past Jesse to the bedroom. Actually she had to stop marching long enough to squeeze past him in the doorway, and she had to fight him for the tail end of the towel as she slid by.

"Just have one more little spot I need to wipe," he said, dabbing at his face.

"Let go!" she snapped. She yanked, he pulled, and the ancient terry cloth tore down the middle. "Now look what you've done!"

Tears sprang to Honey's eyes. "You're ruining everything!"

"It's just a towel, Honey," Jesse said, misunderstanding her tears. He tried to follow her into the bedroom, but she shut the door in his face. And locked it.

"Hey, unlock the door."

"Go away, Jesse."

"I thought we were going to talk."

"Go away, Jesse."

"I'm not going to leave, Honey. You might as well open the door."

"Go away, Jesse."

Jesse put a shoulder against the door, just to see how sturdy it was, and concluded that at least the house was well built. His bad leg wouldn't support him if he tried kicking it in. Which was just as well. Honey wasn't likely to be too impressed with that sort of melodrama.

"I'm leaving, Honey," he said.

No answer.

"I said I'm leaving."

Still no answer.

"Aren't you going to say goodbye?"

"Goodbye, Jesse," she sobbed.

"Jeez, Honey. This is stupid. Open the door so we can talk."

She sobbed again.

Jesse's throat constricted. She really sounded upset. Maybe this wasn't the best time to talk to her after all. He had some chores he could do that would keep him busy for a while. Surely she couldn't stay in there all day. He'd catch her when she came down for some coffee later.

Honey heard Jesse's halting step as he limped his way down the stairs. So, he was leaving after all. Honey got into bed and pulled the covers over her head. She didn't want to think about anything. She just wanted to wallow in misery. She should have taken the part of him she could get, the part left over after he'd done his duty to the Rangers. It would have been better than nothing, certainly better than the void he would leave when he was gone.

Then she thought of all the time she would have to spend alone, with no shoulder to share the burden, no lover's ear to hear how the day had gone and offer solace, and her backbone stiffened. She deserved more from a relationship than half measures. She had to accept the fact that Jesse had made his choice.

Honey didn't notice the sun creeping across the sky. She had no knowledge of the fading light at dusk. She never even noticed the sun setting to leave the world in darkness. Her whole life was dark. It couldn't get any blacker.

Meanwhile, Jesse had spent the day waiting patiently for Honey to come to her senses. At noon, he prepared some tomato soup and grilled cheese sandwiches, planning to surprise her with his culinary expertise. He ended up sharing his bounty with Jack, who ate all the sandwiches and dumped the soup with the comment, "Mom makes it better."

When Jesse had explained to Jack that he needed some time alone with Honey, Jack was more than willing to go spend the night with friends again. In fact, Jesse was embarrassed by the lurid grin on the teenager's face when he agreed not to come home too early the next morning.

"Does this mean Mom has agreed to marry you?" Jack asked.

"I haven't quite talked her into it yet," Jesse said.

"But you will."

"I'm sure going to try," Jesse said grimly.

"Don't worry," Jack said, slapping Jesse on the shoulder. "I think Mom loves you."

But as Jesse was discovering, the fact that Honey loved him might not be enough to induce her to marry him. Jack left late in the afternoon. Jesse tiptoed up the stairs and listened by Honey's bedroom door, but there was no sound coming from inside. He decided he was just going to have to outwait her.

It was nearly ten o'clock that evening before he finally decided she wasn't coming out anytime soon. He knocked hard on her bedroom door. "All right, Honey. Enough's enough. Come on out of there so we can talk."

He heard the sound of rustling sheets and then a muffled "Jesse?"

A moment later the door opened. Her hair looked as sleep-tousled as it had the first morning he had come to the Flying Diamond. Her blue eyes were unfocused, confused. She tightened the belt on the man's terry cloth robe she was wearing, then clutched at the top to hold it closed.

"Jesse?" she repeated. "Is that you?"

"Of course it's me. Who did you think it was?"

"I thought you left," she said.

‘‘Why the hell would I do that?’’ Jesse felt angry and irritable. While he’d been cooling his heels downstairs all day, she’d been up here *sleeping!* ‘‘If you’re through napping, maybe we could have that talk I mentioned earlier.’’

‘‘You want to talk?’’ Honey was still half-asleep.

‘‘Yes, by God, I want to talk! And you’re going to listen, do you hear me?’’ Jesse grabbed hold of her shoulders and shook her for good measure.

The moment Jesse touched her, Honey came instantly awake. This was no dream. This was no figment of her imagination. A furious Jesse Whitelaw was really shaking the daylights out of her.

‘‘All right, Jesse,’’ she said, putting her hands on his arms to calm him. ‘‘I’m ready to listen.’’

At that moment there was a knock on the kitchen door and a familiar voice called up the stairs, ‘‘Honey? Are you home?’’

Good old reliable Adam.

Honey ran past Jesse as though he wasn’t even there, scrambled down the stairs and met Adam at the door to the kitchen.

He looked tired and frazzled. Honey avoided meeting his eyes, because they still held too much pain.

‘‘I just wanted to let you know that I found some of your stolen cattle on my property,’’ he said. ‘‘I’ll have some of my cowhands drive them over here tomorrow.’’

Adam’s eyes flickered to a spot behind Honey. ‘‘It seems I misjudged you, Whitelaw,’’ Adam said. ‘‘I had no idea Chuck Loomis was using my ranch as a base for a statewide rustling operation. I owe you an apology and my thanks.’’ He stuck his hand out to Jesse, who slid a possessive hand around Honey’s waist before he reached out to shake it.

Honey felt the tension between the two men. They would never be close friends, but at least they wouldn’t be enemies, either.

‘‘I’ll be going now,’’ Adam said.

‘‘Are you sure you’re all right?’’ Honey asked.

‘‘My business affairs are in a shambles and I need a new ranch manager, but otherwise I’m fine,’’ Adam said with a self-deprecating smile.

''I'll let you out,'' Honey said. But when she tried to leave Jesse's side, he tightened his grasp.

Adam saw what was going on and said, ''I can see myself out. Goodbye, Honey.''

Honey saw from the look on Adam's face that he wouldn't be coming back anytime soon. She felt his sadness, his loneliness. Somewhere out there was a woman who could bring the sparkle back into Adam's life. All Honey had to do was keep her eyes open and help Adam find that special someone.

When the kitchen door closed behind Adam, Jesse took Honey's hand in his and ordered, ''Come with me.''

He limped his way back up the stairs, down the hall and into her room. Once inside, he turned and locked the door behind them. ''I've got something important to say to you, Honey, and it can't wait another minute.''

Honey could see Jesse was agitated. While he talked, she led him over to the bed and sat him down. She kneeled to pull off his boots, then lifted his feet up onto the rumpled sheets.

''Are you more comfortable?'' she asked.

''Yes. Don't change the subject.''

''What is the subject?'' Honey asked, climbing into the other side of the bed.

''You're going to marry me, Honey. No ifs, ands, or buts.''

''I know,'' she said.

''No more arguments, no more— What did you say?''

''I said I'll marry you, Jesse.''

''But—''

''I shouldn't have tried blackmailing you into quitting your job. I know how much being a Ranger means to you. It isn't fair to ask you to give that up.'' She smiled. ''I'll manage.''

Jesse couldn't have loved Honey more than he did in that instant. How brave she was! What strength she possessed! And how she must love him to be willing to make such a concession herself rather than force him to do it. What she couldn't know, what he hadn't realized himself until very recently, was that it was a sacrifice he was willing to make. He loved being a Ranger; he loved Honey more.

Jesse wanted the life she had offered him, a life working side by side with the woman he loved. Raising kids. Running the ranch. Loving Honey.

Jesse swallowed over the lump in his throat. It was hard to speak but he managed, "I love you, Honey." He gently touched her lips with his, revering her, honoring her.

She moved eagerly into his arms, but he held her away.

"There's something I have to tell you," he said.

He saw the anxiety flicker in her eyes and spoke quickly to quell it. "Before I came back here this morning, I resigned from the Texas Rangers."

Honey gasped. "You did? Really?"

"I did. Really."

Honey didn't know what she had done to be rewarded with her heart's desire, but she saw only rainbows on the horizon. Here was a man she could lean on in times of trouble, a man with whom she could share her life, the happiness and sorrow, the good times and the bad.

"I can't believe that this is really happening," Honey said. "Are you sure, Jesse?"

"Sure of what?"

"That you won't be sorry later. That you won't have regrets. That you won't change your mind and—"

"I won't change my mind. I won't have regrets or be sorry. Being a Ranger made it easy to avoid looking at my life as it really is. I've been drifting for years looking for something, Honey. I just didn't know what it was. I've found it here with you and Jack and Jonathan."

"What's that?"

"A place where I can put down roots. A place where my grandchildren can see the fruits of my labor. A home."

Honey didn't know what to say. She felt full. And happy. And by some act of providence she and the man she loved just happened to be in bed together.

"Where's Jack?" she asked.

Jesse grinned. "He's spending the night with a friend."

Honey arched a brow provocatively. "Then we have the whole house to ourselves?"

"Yes, ma'am. We sure do."

"Then I suggest we make use of it."

Jesse arched a questioning brow. ''The whole house?''

''Well, we can start in the bedroom. But the desk in the den is nice. There's the kitchen table. And the tub has definite possibilities.'' Honey laughed at the incredulous look on Jesse's face.

''You'll kill me,'' he muttered.

''Yeah, but what a way to go,'' Honey said.

Hours later, Jesse was leaning back in a tubful of steaming water, his nape comfortably settled on the edge of the claw-footed tub. Honey was curled against his chest, her body settled on his lap.

''I didn't think it could be done,'' he murmured.

''You're a man of many talents, Mr. Whitelaw.''

He grinned lazily. ''May I return the compliment?''

''Of course.'' Honey leaned over to lap a drop of water from Jesse's nipple. She felt him stiffen, and gently teased him until his flesh was taut with desire.

Jesse groaned, an animal sound that forced its way past his throat. ''Honey,'' he warned, ''you're playing with fire.''

She laughed, a sexy sound, and said, ''There's plenty of water here if I wanted to put it out...which I don't.''

A moment later he had turned her to face him, her legs straddling his thighs. He grasped her hips and slowly pulled her down, impaling her.

Honey gasped.

He held her still, trying to gain control of his desire, wanting the pleasure to last. She arched herself against him, forcing him deeper inside the cocoon of wetness and warmth.

''You feel so good, Honey. So damn good.''

''May I return the compliment?'' she said in a breathless voice. She grasped his shoulders to steady herself as she rocked back and forth, seeking to pleasure him and finding the pleasure given returned tenfold.

Jesse reached out to cup her breasts, to tease the nipples into peaks, to nip and lick and kiss her breasts until Honey was writhing in pleasure. He found the place where their bodies met and teased her until she ached with need. Their mouths joined as his body spilled its seed into hers.

Breathless, Honey sought the solace of his embrace. He held her close as the water lapped in waves against the edge of the tub.

''I can't believe it,'' she said as he pulled her close and tucked her head beneath his chin. ''Oh, the things we can do to improve the ranch! I have so many plans, so many ideas!''

Jesse chuckled. ''Whoa, there, woman. One thing at a time.''

She looked up at him and grinned. ''What shall we do first?''

''First I think we ought to do some planting.''

''What are we going to grow?''

''Some hay. Some vegetables. Some babies.''

Honey laughed with delight. ''Let's start with the babies.''

Jesse fell in love all over again. It was amazing how sheer happiness made Honey glow with beauty. His heart felt full. His chest was so tight with feelings it hurt to breathe. He didn't have to drift any longer. He had found his home. Where he would spend each night with his woman. Where he would plant seeds—of many kinds—and watch them grow.

* * * * *

THE COWBOY TAKES A WIFE

For my friend and fellow trail rider,
Priscilla Kelly.
May we have many more long, lazy rides
through orange groves on the ridge.
Ride him, Cowgirl!
Giddyap, Sadie!

One

Desiree Parrish had been secretly observing Carter Prescott throughout the Christmas pageant. So she saw the moment when his jaw tightened, when he closed his eyes and clenched his fists as though he were in pain. A bright sheen of tears glistened along his dark lashes. Moments later he rose from the back pew in which he sat and quietly, almost surreptitiously, left the church.

For a moment Desiree wasn't sure what to do. She didn't want to leave because her daughter, Nicole, hadn't yet performed her part as an angel in the pageant. Nicole *was* an angel, Desiree thought with a swell of maternal pride. But it was because of her five-year-old daughter that she needed Carter Prescott's help. Desiree had to speak privately with the cowboy, and she wasn't sure if she would get another opportunity like this one.

According to his grandmother, Madelyn Prescott, Carter had come to Wyoming from Texas looking for someplace to settle down. What if Carter moved on before she got a chance to make her offer to him? What if he decided to leave town tonight? Without giving herself more chance for thought, Desiree rose and headed for the nearest exit. She made a detour to grab her coat and wrap a scarf around her face to protect her from the frigid Wyoming weather.

Desiree was alarmed when she stepped outside to discover her quarry had disappeared into the night, hidden by the steady, gentle snowfall. She frantically searched the church parking lot, running through the fluffy snow in the direction his footprints led, afraid he would get away before she could make her proposition known to him.

She cried out in alarm when a tall, intimidating figure suddenly stepped from behind a pickup. She automatically put up a hand as though to ward off a blow. There was a moment of awful tension while she waited for the first lash of pain. In another instant she realized how foolish she had been.

She had found Carter Prescott. Or rather, he had found her.

"Are you all right?"

She heard the concern in his voice, yet when he reached out to touch her she took a reflexive step backward. It took all her courage to stand her ground. She had to get hold of herself. Her safety, and Nicole's, depended on what she did now.

Disconcerted by the growing scowl on Carter's face, she lowered her arm and threaded her fingers tightly together. "I'm fine," she murmured.

"Why did you follow me?" he demanded in a brusque voice.

"I..." Desiree couldn't get anything more past the sudden tightness in her throat. The cowboy looked sinister wrapped in a shearling coat with his Stetson pulled down low to keep out the bitter cold. He towered over her, and she had second thoughts about speaking her mind.

But she had no choice. It was two weeks until Christmas. She had to have a husband by the new year, and this cowboy from Texas was the most likely candidate she had found. She examined Carter closely in the stream of light glowing from the church steeple.

From the looks of his scuffed boots and ragged jeans, life hadn't been kind to him. His face was as weathered as the rest of him. He had wide-set, distrustful blue eyes and a hawkish nose. His jaw was shadowed with at least a day's growth of dark beard. His chin jutted—with arrogance or stubbornness, she wasn't sure which. From having seen it in church, she knew his hair was a rich, wavy chestnut brown. He had full lips, but right now they were flattened in irritation. Nonetheless, he was a handsome man. More good-looking than she deserved, everything considered.

"Look, lady, if you've got something to say, spit it out."

Desiree responded to the harsh voice with a shiver that she chose to blame on the cold. Plainly the cowboy wasn't going to stand there much longer. It was now or never.

Desiree spoke quickly, her breath creating a cloud of white around her. "My name is Desiree Parrish. I know from having spoken to your grandmother before the pageant this evening that you're looking for a place to set down some roots."

His scowl became a frown, but she hurried on without stopping. "I have a proposition to make to you."

She opened her mouth and then couldn't speak. What was she doing? Maybe this was only going to make things worse, not better. After all, what did she really know about Carter Prescott? The grown man standing before her was a stranger. She wondered whether he remembered the one time they had met. His eyes hadn't revealed whether he recognized her name when she had spoken it. But, maybe he had never known her name. After all, they had only spent fifteen minutes together twenty-three years ago, when she was a child of five and he was a lanky boy of ten.

It was spring, and Carter Prescott had come from King's Castle with his father to visit the Rimrock Ranch, since the two properties bordered each other. She would never even have met him if her kitten hadn't gotten stuck in a tree.

She had been trying to coax Boots down by talking to her, but the kitten had been afraid to move. The ten-year-old boy had heard Desiree's pleading cries and come to investigate. She thought now of all the reactions Carter could have had to the situation. He might have ignored her. Or come to see the problem but left her to solve it herself. He might have made fun of her or taunted her about the kitten's plight. After all, she was just a kid, and a girl at that.

Carter Prescott had done none of those things. He had patted her awkwardly on the shoulder and promised to get Boots down from the tree. He had climbed up into the willow and reached for the kitten. But Boots evaded his reach. He had finally lurched for the kitten and caught her, but cat and boy had come tumbling down in a heap on the ground.

Desiree had screamed in fright and hurried over to make sure Boots was all right. She found her kitten carefully cushioned in the boy's arms.

He had handed Boots to her with a grim smile. ''Here's your cat.''

She was too busy fussing over Boots to notice Carter's attempts to rise. It was his gasp of pain that caused her to look at him again. That was when she saw the bloody bone sticking out through his jeans above the knee.

Her second panicked scream brought their fathers on the run. Her father picked her up and hugged her tight, grateful she was all right. She babbled the problem out to him, her voice too hysterical at first for him to realize what had happened.

Carter's father bent down on one knee to his son. His lips had tightened ominously before he said, ''Your mother will give me hell for this.''

Carter hadn't made a sound when his father picked him up and carried him toward their pickup. His face had been white, his teeth clamped on his lips to stop any sound from escaping. Desiree had tried to follow him but her father had held her back.

''Let the boy be, Desiree,'' he'd said. ''He won't want to cry in front of you.''

''But Daddy, I have to see how he is,'' she protested. ''He saved Boots.''

Her father relented, and she ran after Carter and his father.

''I'm sorry,'' Desiree called up to Carter, her tiny legs rushing to keep pace.

''You ought to be,'' Carter's father said.

Stunned at the meanness in his voice, Desiree stopped in her tracks. But Carter turned to face her over his father's shoulder. He nodded and tried to smile, and she knew he had forgiven her.

But she and Carter had never crossed paths again. When she asked about him several days later, her father had told her that Carter had been visiting Wyoming for only a few days. His parents were divorced and Carter lived in Texas with his mother. He wouldn't be coming back.

Desiree had never seen Carter again, until he showed up at the Christmas pageant in Casper tonight. Was she willing to gamble her future on a man she had known for barely fifteen minutes twenty-three years ago? It seemed idiotic in the extreme.

Desiree wasn't an idiot. But she was in urgent need of a husband.

Carter might not be the same person now as he had been then. But she remembered vividly how he had cradled the kitten to keep it from harm at the expense of his own welfare. Surely he could not have grown up a cruel man. She was staking her life on it.

Carter was already turning to walk away, when she laid a slender hand on his arm. She tensed when she felt the steely muscle tighten even through the sheepskin coat.

''I need a husband,'' she said in a breathless voice.

Carter's head snapped back around. His icy blue eyes focused intently on her face.

''I'm willing to sign over half the Rimrock Ranch to you if you'll agree to marry me. Of course,'' she added hastily, ''it would be a marriage in name only.''

His eyes narrowed, and she found herself racing to get everything out before she lost her nerve. ''The Rimrock is the second largest outfit in the area, nearly as big as King's Castle, your father's place. It's got good water and lots of grass. The house was built by my great-great-grandfather. You'd be getting a good bargain. What do you say?''

Desiree gripped his arm tighter, as though she could hold him there until he responded in the way she wished him to answer. She chanced a look into his eyes and was surprised by the humor she saw there. His lips twisted in a mocking smile.

''Surely you could get a husband in a little more conventional way, Miss Parrish,'' he replied.

This wasn't a laughing matter. The sooner Carter Prescott realized that, the better. Desiree reached up and pulled aside the heavy wool scarf that was wrapped around her face.

''You're mistaken, Mr. Prescott.'' She angled her face so he could see the vivid scar that slanted across her right cheek from chin to temple. ''No man would willingly choose me for a bride.''

She raised wary brown eyes to the man before her and shuddered at the cold, hard look on his face. Her shoulders slumped. She should have known better. She should have known even the promise of the Rimrock wasn't enough to entice a man to face her over the breakfast table for the rest of his life.

Desiree hurriedly wrapped the scarf back around her face to hide the scar. ''This was a stupid idea,'' she muttered. ''Forget I mentioned it.''

Desiree quickly stumbled away, embarrassed by the stinging tears that had sprung to her eyes. It would have been humiliating enough to have him refuse her offer. She didn't want him to see how devastated she was by his reaction to the scar on her face. It had been so long since she had exposed herself to someone for the first time that she had forgotten the inevitable horror it caused.

She would have to find another way to save herself. But merciful Lord in heaven, what was she going to do?

Meanwhile, Carter had been so stunned by the entire incident that Desiree had nearly reached the door of the church before he recovered himself enough to speak. By then he was glad she was gone, because he wouldn't have known what to say. He stared after her, remembering the look of vulnerability in her deep brown eyes when she had exposed her face.

He was amazed even now at the strength of his reaction to the awful sight he had seen. He had felt fury at the destruction of something that had obviously once been quite beautiful. And pity for what it must be like to live with such a scar. And disgust that she had been reduced to begging for a spouse.

If he was honest, he also had to admit that his curiosity was piqued. How had she been wounded so horribly? Why was she so anxious to find a husband? And why had she singled him out?

Carter wondered if she remembered the one time they had met. It was a day he had never forgotten. He unconsciously rubbed his thigh. His thigh bone—the one he had broken saving her blasted cat—still ached when the weather was wet or cold. If he got tired enough, he sometimes limped. He never had liked cats much since.

For other reasons that day was etched in his memory like brutally carved glass. The scene between his mother and father when his mom had arrived at the emergency room of the hospital had been loud and vicious. It was easy to see why his parents hadn't stayed married. They had been in the process of a divorce when he was conceived, and he had been born before the divorce was final. His mother just hadn't seen fit to inform his father of that fact. She had only brought him to

Wyoming to meet his father because Wayne Prescott had accidentally found out about his son and demanded visitation rights.

The incident at the Rimrock Ranch had convinced his mother that his father was not a fit custodian. That day had been the first and last he had seen of Wayne Prescott. So Carter remembered well his first meeting with Desiree Parrish. It had been a dark day in his life.

Desiree was correct in her assumption that he wanted roots, but his wants and needs had culminated in a specific objective. He wanted the land that would have been his inheritance if his mother and father hadn't divorced. He wanted King's Castle.

Unfortunately, on his father's death the land had gone in equal shares to his father's very young widow, Belinda Prescott, and his father's bastard son, Faron Whitelaw. Carter had already made a generous offer to them for the land. They had promised him an answer tonight.

He felt queasy at the thought that they might refuse him. Where would he go if he couldn't stay at King's Castle? Where would he find the solace he so desperately needed from the memories that relentlessly trailed him wherever he went? He had been running for so long—six years—that he had begun to wonder if there would ever be an end to it.

As he stepped into the cab of his pickup and headed back to King's Castle, he couldn't help thinking about the offer Desiree Parrish had made to him. He remembered well the lush, grassy valleys to be found on the Rimrock. A river carved its way over the prairie, right through the ranch. The ranch house was a two-story, wooden-planked structure, simple but enduring. He had never seen the inside.

To tell the truth, before he had discovered King's Castle was on the market, he had inquired about purchasing the Rimrock. His agent had been told, in no uncertain terms, that the ranch was not for sale. So why had Desiree Parrish offered him half the place for his name on a marriage certificate? And how could she have believed that someone rich enough to buy the Rimrock, lock, stock and barrel, would bargain away his freedom for it?

Unless she doesn't know you're rich.

Carter found himself chuckling as he realized the image he must have presented to the young woman, unshaven, with his jeans frayed and his boots worn to a nub. Apparently his grandmother hadn't told Desiree his true circumstances. He sobered abruptly. He had learned, to his sorrow, that wealth couldn't buy happiness. In fact, it had been the source of great tragedy in his life.

Carter felt the tension pounding behind his eyes. He never should have given in to his grandmother's pleas for him to attend the Christmas pageant. Tonight the memories had come back to haunt him. Listening to those childish voices, seeing those angelic faces, had brought all the pain of betrayal and loss back into sharp focus. He wanted to forget the past, but he wasn't sure it was possible. Guilt rode heavy on his shoulders. And regret. And anger.

Carter stopped his truck in front of the ranch house at King's Castle, a three-story stone structure with turrets and crenels, which his father had called The Castle. It didn't fit this land anywhere near as well as the simple house on the Rimrock. He headed around back to the kitchen door, which he knew would be open. He found his way through the darkened house to the elegant parlor, where a fire still glowed in the grate. He stirred the ashes and added a log from the pile nearby. Finally, he poured himself a whiskey and settled into the chair near the fireplace, where he could empty his mind of the painful past and concentrate on the future.

It was Desiree Parrish who filled his thoughts. He remembered how tiny, almost delicate, she had seemed next to his great size, how the snowflakes had gathered on her dark hair and eyelashes. Those memories were overshadowed by the look of fear in her huge brown eyes when she had revealed her scar to him. And by the way she had braced herself for his revulsion.

It was true the scar was ugly, but Carter had shifted his gaze to her eyes, which had called out to him. He had seen a wounded spirit that was the equal of his own. It had taken a great deal of effort to resist reaching out to fold her protectively in his arms. Fortunately, she had run before he could do something so foolishly impulsive.

Carter didn't know how long he had been sitting there, when he heard Madelyn and Belinda Prescott and Faron Whitelaw returning. He felt his gut tighten, reminding him how much their answer mattered to him. He wanted this place; he *needed* this place, if he was ever to forget the past and go on with his life.

Madelyn entered the room scolding. ''What happened to you, young man? There were several more people I wanted you to meet, although I suppose we can have a party here and—''

He had risen the instant she came into the room and was already there to help her out of her coat. ''I'm not much interested in parties, Maddy.''

''You should be,'' she countered. ''Why, a handsome young man like you ought to be settled down now, with babies and—''

''I just want an answer from Belinda and Faron, one way or the other,'' he said sharply, cutting her off again. He laid her coat across the sofa, which gave him a chance to focus his attention anywhere except on Belinda and Faron. He was afraid he might see their answer to his offer on their faces. He was afraid that answer would be no.

At last, he forced himself to look at them. They were staring at each other, and he could feel the tension between them. His heart began to pound, sending blood rushing to his head, making him feel dizzy. He reached for his whiskey and swallowed a restoring gulp. He met his half brother's eyes and said, ''Well, what have you decided?''

''Give us another few minutes,'' Faron said. ''Belinda and I have some things we need to discuss before we can give you an answer.'' Faron quickly ushered Belinda out of the room and into the ranch office across the hall.

Carter crossed to the bar so he would have his back to his grandmother. He didn't want her to see the frustration—and fear—he felt. He poured a glass of port and turned to hand it to Madelyn. His casual calm was hard won. The hell of it was, he didn't think he was fooling Madelyn for a minute.

His grandmother settled herself on the sofa. Instead of launching into a thousand questions, she sipped her port and stared into the fire.

He was too nervous to sit and too proud to let Madelyn see him pacing anxiously. He hooked an arm over the mantel and focused on the map of King's Castle that hung above it. The boundaries had changed over the hundred-odd years the land had been owned by Prescotts, but even now it was an impressive spread. He froze when he heard the office door open.

''Maddy, can you come in here for a minute?'' Faron called.

"Excuse me, Carter," the old woman said. "I hate to leave you alone. I'm sure I won't be gone long."

He didn't look at her, afraid that his feelings were naked on his face. "Don't worry, Maddy. I'm used to being alone."

He could have bitten his tongue after he'd said the words, knowing how much he had revealed in that simple sentence. He felt more than saw, her hesitation. But he heard her set her glass down on the end table and leave the room.

He shook his head in disgust. How had he let possessing The Castle matter so much to him? He was only setting himself up for disappointment. He should have come sooner, when Wayne Prescott was still alive, and demanded his heritage. But he hadn't needed Wayne's land then. He hadn't yet experienced the tragedy that had left him rootless and alone.

"Carter?"

He forced all emotion from his face as he turned to face Faron, who was flanked by the two women. He knew the answer before Faron spoke.

"We've decided not to sell."

Two

Desiree concentrated on the road, which was slick with a layer of ice and difficult to see through the blowing snow. She had been among the last to leave the church, since she had helped with the cleanup. The storm had worsened in the past hour, and Desiree wished she had asked someone to follow her, at least until she got to the turnoff for the ranch. She didn't want to end up stuck on the road somewhere overnight, although if she ended up frozen to death that would solve the worry of finding a husband.

Beside her, Nicole chattered on happily about the Christmas pageant. Desiree responded to her daughter, but her thoughts were elsewhere. She was mentally kicking herself for being so foolish as to confront a perfect stranger with a proposal of marriage.

''Did you see me, Mommy? Was I a good angel?''

''You were wonderful, sweetheart. A perfect angel.''

Desiree worried her lower lip with her teeth. Why hadn't she stood firm until she had an answer from Carter Prescott? Because she was afraid, that's why! But although the ragtag cowboy's eyes had been cold, they hadn't been unkind. And while he had towered over her, she hadn't felt threatened. It had been the fear of rejection, not the fear of physical harm, that had sent her fleeing into the night.

''Did you see me fly, Mommy?''

Desiree smiled at the image of her daughter flapping her angel's wings. ''I certainly did.'' She had watched the finish of the Christmas pageant from the shadows along the side aisle of the church, her chest aching with love—and fear. She *must* find a husband before the new year. Her safety, and Nicole's, depended on having a man's presence in the house. If only she had been less fainthearted about confronting Carter Prescott!

"Look at me, Mommy. Look! I can fly even without my wings!"

"Nicole! Sit down, and put your seat belt back on this instant!"

Nicole quickly dropped down on the seat and began hunting for the end of the seatbelt in the darkened cab.

Desiree had taken her eyes off the road only for a second, but that was enough. She caught a patch of ice and felt the pickup begin to slide. She turned the wheel into the skid and resisted the urge to brake, knowing that would only make things worse. But she could already see the truck wasn't going to recover in time to stay on the road.

Nicole gave a cry of alarm as the pickup began to tilt. "Mommy! We're falling!"

"It's all right, Nicole. Sit still. Everything will be fine." Desiree's heart pounded as the pickup slid sideways off the road into a shallow gully.

The truck thumped to a stop at a sharp angle with the right wheels lodged in snow two feet deeper than the left ones. It took a second for Desiree to realize they really were all right. Nicole whimpered in fright.

Desiree reached over and grabbed Nicole and pulled her daughter into her lap, hugging her tight. "It's all right, sweetheart. We're fine. Everything's fine."

"We're going to fall, Mommy."

"No, we're not. The truck is stopped now. It's wedged in the snow. It won't tip any more." But she wasn't going to be able to drive out of this gulley. Which meant that unless she wanted to spend the night in the truck, she was going to have to walk back the two miles or so to the church and call for help.

"You'll have to wait here for me, Nicole, while I—"

"No, Mommy! Don't leave me! I'm scared!"

Despite her daughter's cries, Desiree shifted her onto the seat. "I won't be gone long."

"Don't leave! Please, Mommy." Nicole clambered back into Desiree's lap and twined her arms around her mother's neck.

Desiree hugged her daughter, fighting the tears that stung her nose and welled in her eyes.

She had been on her own for six years. She had gone through her pregnancy alone and had raised Nicole without help from anyone. Forced to cope with whatever life had thrown at her, somehow she had survived. She and Nicole were a family. Sliding off the road wasn't nearly the disaster that loomed on the horizon. Soon their very lives would be in danger.

So what if she was stuck miles from home in the middle of a snowstorm with her daughter clinging to her neck like a limpet? They, and the truck, had endured without a scratch. There was no reason to cry. But her throat had swollen so thick it hurt to swallow, and she could feel the heat of a tear on her cold cheek.

It wasn't the accident that was causing her distress, she conceded; it was the knowledge that she had so little control over her life.

Desiree took a deep breath and let it out. She had managed so far to keep things together. She just had to take one step at a time. She retrieved the blanket she kept in the well behind the seat and wrapped Nicole snugly in it.

"Mommy has to call a tow truck to haul us out of here," she explained to Nicole. "The closest phone is at the church. You need to wait right here for me until I get back. Don't leave the truck. If you wander off, you could get lost in all this snow. Okay, sweetheart?"

It was a sign of how much more quickly the child of a single parent had to grow up that Nicole sniffed back her tears and nodded reluctant agreement to her mother's order. There was a risk leaving Nicole alone, but there was even greater risk in taking her out walking in the bitter cold.

"I won't be gone long," Desiree promised as she closed the truck door behind her. Desiree wished she had a warmer coat to keep out the bitter wind, but at least she had warm boots. She would be cold when she arrived at the church, but anyone who lived in Wyoming was inured to the harsh weather.

To Desiree's amazement, she had been walking no more than two minutes, when she saw headlights through the snow. She was afraid she would be lost in the dark at the side of the road, so she stepped out onto the pavement and waved her arms. She knew the moment when the driver spotted her, because the pickup did a little slide to the side as it slowed.

As soon as the truck stopped, she raced to the driver's window. The door had already opened, and a tall man was stepping out.

"I need help! I—"

"What the hell are you doing out here walking on a night like this? Where's your car?"

Desiree felt her heart thump when she realized she was staring into the furious eyes of Carter Prescott. "My truck slid into a ditch. I was going back to the church to call for a tow. Can you give me a ride?"

"Get in," he said curtly.

Desiree raced around to the other side of the pickup before Carter could reach out to touch her.

As he pulled his door closed he said, "It's doubtful you'll get a tow truck to come out in this storm. I'll give you a ride home."

Desiree debated the wisdom of arguing with him. But she would rather have Nicole safe and warm at home than have to wait with her daughter in the cold until a tow truck arrived. "All right. But I left something in my truck that I need to pick up. It's only a little way ahead."

When Carter pulled up behind her truck he said, "Do you need any help?"

"I can handle it." Desiree was struggling with the door on Nicole's side of the truck, when it was pulled open from behind her. She whirled in fright—to find Carter standing right behind her.

"I figured you could use some help, after all."

Desiree took a deep breath. This man wasn't going to harm her. She had to stop acting so jumpy around him. "Thank you," she said.

The instant the truck door opened, Nicole came flying out. Desiree barely managed to catch her before she fell. In fact, she would have fallen if Carter hadn't put his arms around Desiree and supported both her and the child.

"This is the something you needed to pick up?" he asked.

Desiree heard the displeasure underlying his amazement and responded defensively, "This is my daughter, Nicole."

"You didn't say anything about a kid earlier this evening."

"It wasn't necessary that you know about her until we had reached some agreement."

"I don't think—"

Desiree cut him off. "I would rather not discuss this further until we're alone." Which was tantamount to a suggestion that they ought to have further discussion on the matter in private, Desiree realized too late.

"All right," he said.

"You can let go now. I've got her."

He was slow to remove his support, and Desiree was aware suddenly of how secure she had felt with his arms around her. And of being very much alone without them.

She carried Nicole the short distance to his truck. He held the passenger door open, but she found it awkward to step up into the truck with Nicole in her arms.

"Give her to me," Carter's tone of voice made it plain he would rather not have handled the child. Before either Desiree or Nicole could protest, he had the girl in his arms.

Desiree had barely settled herself in the truck when Carter dropped Nicole on her lap, shoved her thin wool coat inside and slammed the truck door closed.

"The turnoff for the Rimrock is about five miles ahead on the right," Desiree instructed.

"I know."

"How—"

"I drove by there on the way to my grandmother's. I haven't forgotten visiting your place when I was ten."

She watched him rub his thigh and wondered about the bone he had broken so many years ago. "Does it still bother you?"

"Sometimes."

"I'm sorry."

"No need to be. It was my own fault."

He looked sinister in the green light reflected off the dash, not at all like the savior she had sought out in the parking lot of the church.

"What's your name?" Nicole asked. "Do you know my mommy? I was an angel tonight. Do you want to see me fly?"

Carter's lips flattened in annoyance.

In the uncomfortable silence that followed her daughter's questions, a frown grew in the space between Desiree's brows. Carter's refusal to answer Nicole was rude—or at least, inconsiderate. Did Carter simply not like children? Or was it just Nicole's behavior he didn't approve of?

Carter's lack of response did nothing to curb Nicole's curiosity. "Are you coming to our house?"

"Yes," Carter replied sharply.

Desiree realized he had probably been curt in hopes of shutting her daughter up. But Nicole wasn't deterred by Carter's antagonism. The little girl had learned through dealing with a mother who was putty in her hands that persistence often won her what she wanted.

"Do you want to see my room?"

Carter sighed.

Desiree could see that he wanted to say no. He sought out her eyes, his lips pursed in displeasure. She decided to rescue him from her daughter's clutches.

"It's nearly bedtime, sweetheart. You'll have to wait to show Mr. Prescott your room until some other time." It was all she could do to keep her own displeasure at the cowboy's surliness out of her voice.

"Are you going to be my daddy?"

"Nicole!"

Desiree was mortified at the question because she had, in fact, proposed to the man sitting across from her, and because she hadn't realized Nicole was even aware that she was seeking a husband. The little girl's next words made it clear that she had thought of the idea all on her own.

"My friend Shirley has a daddy, but I don't. I asked Santa Claus for a daddy, but so far I haven't got one. Are you the daddy I asked for?"

"No," he said in a strangled voice.

"Oh. Well, it's not Christmas yet," Nicole said cheerfully. "Maybe Santa Claus will bring me a daddy."

Desiree was chagrined at her daughter's outspokenness. However, if she had anything to say about it, Nicole would get her wish, although

Carter's attitude toward Nicole was a matter that needed further exploration before their discussion of marriage continued.

Carter was pleased when they reached the Rimrock ranch house to discover it was just as he remembered it. The two-story frame structure had been built to last by people who cared. Someone had planted pines and spruce around the house, and with the drifting snow it was a scene worthy of a picture postcard.

"Follow the road around to the back," Desiree said.

Carter didn't volunteer to carry Nicole from the truck, and Desiree didn't ask. But halfway to the door, and though it made his stomach clench, he took the little girl in his arms to relieve Desiree of a burden that was obviously too heavy for her.

To his surprise, when he reached for the doorknob, he discovered that Desiree had locked the back door. Most ranches, even in this day and age, were left open, a vestige of range hospitality from a time when homesteads had been few and far between.

"Afraid of the bogeyman?" he asked with a wry grin.

Desiree didn't smile back. "I have to think of Nicole's safety." She stepped inside, turned on the light and held the door for him.

Carter immediately set the little girl down. His heart thudded painfully as he watched her race gleefully across the room, headed for the hall. She turned on the light and kept going. Carter could hear her running up the stairs.

"Make yourself comfortable while I put her to bed," Desiree said, following Nicole down the hallway that led to the rest of the house. "We'll talk as soon as I get her down. There's coffee on the stove or brandy in the living room. Help yourself." Then she was gone.

Carter hadn't been in the house before, but he knew the moment he crossed the threshold that this was a home. A band tightened around his chest, making it hard to breathe. This was what he had been seeking. There was warmth and comfort here, not only for the body, but also for the soul.

The kitchen was cluttered, but clean. There were crayon drawings taped to the refrigerator, and a crock full of wooden spoons and a stack of cookbooks sat on an oak chest in the corner. The red-and-white linoleum floor was worn down to black in front of the sink, and the wooden round-leg table and ladderback chairs were scarred antiques. An old-fashioned tin coffeepot sat on the stove. Carter decided he would rather have the brandy.

He followed where Desiree had gone, down a hallway, past a formal dining room, to a combination office and parlor, where a stone fireplace took up one wall and a large rolltop desk took up most of another. A picture window took up the third wall. The fire had burned down to glowing embers, and Carter took the poker and stirred the ashes before adding another log.

A spruce Christmas tree stood in the corner, decorated with handmade ornaments. Above the fireplace, a set of longhorn steer horns a good six feet from tip to tip had been mounted.

Carter looked longingly at an old sofa and chairs that invited him to sit down. He heard a *whoosh* from the vents as the furnace engaged. As he surveyed the room, he realized that the aged quality he had admired so much in the furniture was as much the result of poverty as posterity. Certainly there were heirlooms here. But there was a shabbiness to the furnishings that could only be the result of limited funds.

Carter felt sick to his stomach. Maybe Desiree Parrish knew more about him than he had thought. Maybe she had come after him because she knew he had the money to restore this ranch to its former glory. He had been married once for his money. It wasn't an experience he intended to repeat.

He spied the wet bar where he found the brandy and glasses. "Would you like me to pour one for you?" he called up the stairs.

"Please. I'll join you in a moment," Desiree called down to him.

Desiree took a deep breath and let it out. She had another chance to persuade Carter Prescott that he should marry her. She had to do everything in her power to convince him that she—and the Rimrock—were a bargain he couldn't refuse.

She leaned over and kissed Nicole good night. "Sleep tight, sweetheart." She left a small night-light burning. Not for Nicole. It was Desiree who feared the dark. She had made it a habit to leave a light so she could check on her daughter without the rush of terror that always caught her unaware when she entered a dark room.

Desiree closed her daughter's bedroom door behind her and hurried across the hall to her own room. She slipped out of her coat, which she hadn't even realized she was still wearing. But she had turned the heat down before she'd left for church to conserve energy, and it took time for the furnace to take the frost out of the air.

She crossed to the old oak dresser with the gold-framed mirror above it and checked her appearance. This was a heaven-sent second opportunity, and she wanted to look her best. It had become a habit to sit at an angle before the dresser, so only the good side of her face was reflected back to her. She forced herself to face forward, to see what Carter Prescott would see.

There was no way to disguise the scar. It was a white slash that ran from chin to temple on her right side. Plastic surgery would have corrected it, but she didn't have the money for what would be purely cosmetic work. She put another layer of mascara on her lashes and freshened her lipstick. And she let her hair down. It was the one vanity she had left. It spread like rich brown silk across her shoulders and down to her waist.

She smoothed her black knit dress across a body that was curved in all the right places, but which she knew had brought her husband no pleasure. Desiree forced her thoughts away from the sadness that threatened to overwhelm her whenever she looked at herself in a mirror. She had to focus on the future, not the past. This was her last chance to make a good impression on Carter Prescott. She couldn't afford to waste it.

But it took all her courage to open the bedroom door and walk down the stairs.

Carter controlled the impulse to gasp as Desiree entered the parlor. It was the first time he had seen her when she wasn't shrouded in that moth-eaten coat. She moved with grace, her body slim and supple. Her dress hugged her body, revealing curves that most women would have died for. His groin tightened with desire.

He thought maybe his hands could almost span her waist. There wasn't much bosom, but more than a handful was a waste. His blood quickened at the thought that if she were his wife, he would have the right to hold her, to touch her, to seek out the secrets of her body and make them his.

He wasn't aware he was avoiding her face until he finally looked at it. His eyes dropped immediately to the brandy in his hands. He forced himself to look again, but focused on her eyes. They were a rich, warm brown, with long lashes and finely arched brows. It was clear she had once been a very beautiful woman. Once, but no more. The scar ran through her mouth on one side, twisting it down slightly.

"Did you pour a brandy for me?" she asked.

Carter realized he was staring and flushed. He welcomed the excuse to turn away, and shook his head slightly, aware he ought to do a better job of hiding his feelings. She had to look at that scar every day. The least he could do was face her without showing the pity he felt. He turned back to her with the drink in his hand and realized she had turned herself in profile, so he only saw the good side of her face. Desire stabbed him again.

He wondered if she had done it on purpose or whether it was an unconscious device she used to protect herself when she was with other people. At any rate, he was grateful for the respite that allowed him to speak to her without having to guard his expression.

Desiree took the drink from him. "Why don't you sit down and make yourself comfortable?" She gestured to a chair near the fire and sat down across from him on the sofa so he saw only her good side. "I never gave you a chance earlier this evening to respond to my proposal."

"I was glad for the time to think about what you had to say." Carter took a sip of his brandy.

"And?" Desiree held her breath, determined to wait for his answer. Her nerves got the better of her. She couldn't help making one last pitch. "You can see the house is comfortable." She forced a smile. "And I'm a good cook."

"Tell me again why you want to get married," he said in a quiet voice.

Desiree debated the wisdom of telling Carter the real reason she needed a husband. She had always believed honesty was the best policy. When she opened her mouth to speak, what came out was, "I've been on my own for six years. Nicole needs a father. I...the winters are long when you're alone. And I could use a partner to help me do the heavy work on the ranch.

"As you've seen for yourself, my face makes it impossible for me to attract a husband in the conventional way. I decided to take matters into my own hands.''

''Why me?''

''Your grandmother speaks highly of you.'' She smiled. ''And I haven't forgotten how you saved Boots.''

''Boots?''

''My cat.''

He rubbed his thigh and grimaced. ''Right.''

So maybe she didn't know about his money, Carter thought. She wanted company. And a father for her child. And someone to do the heavy work on the ranch. That made sense. And he could understand why she didn't trust a man to see beyond the scar on her face. He was having trouble doing that himself, although his body had responded—was responding even now—to the thought of joining hers in bed. She had beautiful eyes. In profile, the scar didn't show at all. And in the dark…

He would be giving her something in return for something he wanted very badly. Carter knew he could put down roots here. This place felt like a real home. He wanted to make it his. Though Desiree apparently didn't know it, he had the money to restore the Rimrock to what it had once been, to make it even better.

He wanted to ask her when and where she had gotten the scar on her face, but he figured that could wait until they got to know each other better. Assuming they did.

''I have two problems with your proposal,'' he said.

Desiree had been certain he was going to say a flat no, so she welcomed the opportunity to overcome his objections. ''What problems?''

Carter's lips thinned. ''I hadn't counted on the girl. I'd want her kept out of my way.''

Desiree bristled. ''This is Nicole's home. I wouldn't think of confining her to any part of it to keep your paths from crossing. If you can't handle the fact that I have a daughter, this isn't going to work.''

Carter was amazed at how Desiree's eyes flashed like fire when she was angry. In that moment, her scar made her look like a fierce warrior. He nodded abruptly. ''All right.'' He supposed it wasn't necessary for her to keep the child out of his way; he would do whatever was necessary to keep his distance from the little girl.

"And the second problem?" Desiree asked.

"I can't agree to a marriage in name only."

Desiree paled. Her heart pounded, and her stomach rolled over so she felt like throwing up. She couldn't couple with any man, ever again. "Why not?" She forced out the words through stiff lips.

"I don't plan to spend the rest of my life as a monk. I'd expect my wife to provide the necessary comfort on cold winter nights."

Desiree flushed as his eyes boldly assessed her body. She found the man she had selected to be her husband quite handsome. But she had learned from bitter experience that a man became a beast when satisfying his sexual needs. She dreaded what he might expect of her. She was certain she had nothing to offer him.

But it would humiliate her to have her husband going to some other woman for his needs. In their small ranch community the talk would be bad enough if he married her. She didn't want to give her neighbors any more reason to gossip.

"I'm willing to compromise," she said at last.

"There is no compromise on this," he said. "Either you're willing to be my wife or you're not."

"I'm willing to be a real wife," she assured him. "But not until we know each other better."

Carter's lips twisted. "How long do you expect that to take?"

"I don't know." Desiree looked him in the eye and watched as he stared back, careful not to let his eyes drop to her scar.

"All right," he said at last. "I accept your proposal."

Three

They decided to be married a week later in a civil ceremony in Casper. Desiree offered Carter the guest bedroom, but he decided to stay in a hotel in town until the wedding so he could take care of some unfinished business.

"I'd like Nicole to be present at the wedding," Desiree said as she stood holding his shearling coat for him at the kitchen door.

"Is that really necessary?"

"Once we're married, you'll be her father. I think it would help her to adjust better if she saw us take our vows."

"From what I've heard, she'll probably think I'm a gift from Santa Claus," he muttered.

Desiree couldn't help smiling. Chances were, Nicole would.

The day of the wedding dawned clear and crisp. Most of the snow had blown away or into drifts, revealing a vast expanse of golden grass. Desiree woke with a feeling of trepidation. Was marriage the right solution to her problem? Would she and Nicole achieve safety by bringing Carter Prescott into the house? Was that alone enough? She considered buying a gun to protect them, but realized that she wouldn't be able to use it, so it would only become one more danger.

Desiree was still snuggled under the warm covers when she heard the patter of bare feet on the hardwood floor. Her door opened and Nicole came trotting over to the four-poster.

''Where are your slippers, young lady?'' Desiree chastised as she hauled Nicole up and under the covers with her.

Nicole promptly put her icy feet on Desiree's thigh.

''Your feet are freezing!''

Nicole giggled.

Desiree took her daughter's feet in her hands and rubbed them to warm them up. ''Today's the day Mr. Carter and I are getting married,'' she reminded Nicole.

''Is he going to be my daddy now?''

''Uh-huh.'' Desiree hadn't asked how Carter felt about being called Daddy. Surely he wouldn't mind. After all, being called Daddy didn't require any effort on his part.

One of her major concerns over the past week had been how well Carter would get along with Nicole. During his visits he was brusque if forced to speak at all, but mostly he held himself aloof from Nicole. She supposed that was only natural for a man who apparently hadn't spent time around children. And a man his age—he must be thirty-three or thirty-four—probably didn't remember what it was like to be a child. Obviously he would need a little time to adjust.

Desiree glanced at the clock and realized that by the time she put a roast in the oven for their post-wedding dinner, she would barely have enough time to dress herself and Nicole and get into Casper before they were due in the judge's chambers. ''We'd better get moving, or we're going to be late.''

Desiree took a deep breath and let it out. For better or worse, her decision had been made. Whatever price she had to pay for her own and her daughter's safety was worth it. Marriage, even the duty of the marriage bed, was not too great a sacrifice.

Carter was having second thoughts of his own. He paced the empty hallway of the courthouse in Casper, waiting for his bride. The sound of his bootsteps on the marble floors echoed off the high ceilings. The loneliness of the years he had spent wandering kept him from bolting. *Roots.* Finally he had found a place where he could belong. He would settle down on the Rimrock and be a husband and father. Again.

He paused in midstep. The sudden tightness in his chest, the breathlessness he felt, made him angry. He should have put the past behind him long ago. Beginning today he would. He wouldn't think about it anymore. He wouldn't let it hurt him anymore. It was over and done.

He looked up, and there she was.

"Hello. I'm sorry I'm late," Desiree said.

His gaze shifted quickly from the scar that twisted her smile to the first place he could think to look—his watch. "You're right on time."

"I didn't think I'd make it. We were late getting up and—"

"Are you going to be my daddy?"

"Nicole!" Desiree clapped a hand over her daughter's mouth. "She's a little excited."

"So am I," Carter admitted with a wry smile. "Shall we get on with it?" He snagged Desiree by the elbow and headed in the direction of the judge's chambers. She was wearing that moth-eaten coat again. He wondered what she had on under it. He didn't have to wait long to satisfy his curiosity. The judge's chambers were uncomfortably warm, and Desiree slipped the black wool off her shoulders and laid it over the back of a brass-studded maroon leather chair.

She smiled at Carter again, and he forced his eyes down over the flowered dress she was wearing. It was obviously the best she had, but wrong for the season, and it showed years of wear. He felt a spurt of guilt for not offering her the money for a new dress. But since she apparently didn't know about his wealth, he preferred to keep it that way. Then, if feelings developed between them, he would be sure they weren't motivated by the fact he had a deep pocket.

Desiree couldn't take her eyes off Carter. She was stunned by his appearance. In the first place, he had shaved off the shadow of beard. His blunt jaw and sharp, high cheekbones gave his face an almost savage look. His tailored Western suit should have made him look civilized, but instead it emphasized the power in his broad shoulders and his over-six-foot height. "You look…wonderful," she said.

For some reason, Carter appeared distressed by the compliment. Then she realized he hadn't said anything about how she looked. It didn't take much imagination to figure out why. She had done nothing to hide the scar on her face. She had seen how his eyes skipped away from it. But he was still here. And apparently ready to go through with the wedding.

The judge entered his chambers in a flurry of black robes. ''I've only got a few minutes,'' he said. ''Are you two ready?''

''There are three of us, Judge Carmichael,'' Carter said, nodding in Nicole's direction.

''So there are,'' the judge said. He peered over the top of his black-rimmed bifocals at the little girl. ''Hello there. What's your name?''

Nicole retreated behind her mother's skirts.

''Her name is Nicole,'' Desiree said.

''All right, Nicole. Let's get your mommy married, shall we? Why don't the two of you stand together in front of my desk?'' the judge instructed Carter and Desiree. He called his secretary and the court bailiff to act as witnesses.

Desiree suddenly felt as shy as her daughter and wished there were a skirt she could retreat behind. Carter reached out to draw her to his side, but she quickly scooted around him so the unblemished part of her face would be toward him while they said their vows. She wished she could have been beautiful for him. It would have made all this so much easier. But she wouldn't have needed a husband if things had been different.

''Are we all ready?'' the judge asked.

''Just a minute.'' Carter searched the room for a moment. ''There they are.'' He crossed to a bookshelf and picked up a small bouquet of flowers. ''When I arrived your secretary offered to put these in here for me.''

Desiree stared at the bouquet of wildflowers garnished with beautiful white silk ribbons that Carter was holding out to her. A flush skated across her cheekbones. The thoughtfulness of his gesture made her feel more like a bride. It made everything seem more real. Her heart thumped a mile a minute, and she put a hand up as though to slow it down.

She stared at Carter, seeing wariness—not warmth—in his green eyes as she reached out to take the flowers. ''Thank you, Carter.''

His features relaxed and the wariness fled, replaced by what looked suspiciously like relief. Unfortunately, Carter's trek for the flowers had taken him across the room, and when he returned he ended up on her right side, the side with the scar. She hid her dismay, but lowered her chin so her hair fell across her face.

''Now are we ready?'' the judge asked impatiently.

Desiree nodded slightly. She felt Carter's fingertips on her chin. He tipped her face upward until he was looking her in the eye.

''Are you sure you want to do this?''

''Yes,'' she croaked.

''Keep your chin up,'' he murmured. He turned to the judge and said, ''We're ready.''

Desiree appreciated Carter's encouraging words but had no idea how to tell him so. She heard very little of what the judge said. She was too conscious of the man standing beside her. She could smell a masculine cologne and feel the heat of him along her right side. On her other side, she was aware of Nicole's death grip on her hand.

''The ring?'' the judge asked.

''Here.'' Carter produced a simple gold band, which he slipped on Desiree's left hand.

He turned back to the judge, who was about to continue the ceremony when Desiree said, ''I have a ring for you, too.''

She saw the surprise on Carter's face, but he didn't object. She fumbled in the pocket of her skirt until she found the gold band she had so painstakingly selected. She was aware of the calluses on Carter's palm and fingertips as she held his hand to slip on the ring. Desiree dared a glance at Carter's face when she saw how well it fit.

He smiled at her, and she felt her heart skip a beat. She turned to face the judge, feeling confused and flustered.

Carter took her hand in his and waited for the judge to continue. It wasn't long before he said, ''I now pronounce you man and wife.''

To Desiree, the wedding ceremony was over too quickly, and it didn't feel ''finished.'' She realized the judge hadn't suggested that Carter kiss his bride. She waited, every muscle tensed, wondering if he would act on his own. A second ticked past, another, and another.

Which was when Nicole said, ''Are you going to kiss Mommy now?''

''Nicole!''

Desiree's face reddened with embarrassment. She couldn't bear to look at Carter, afraid of what she would see.

The sound of a masculine chuckle was followed by the feel of Carter's hand on her unblemished cheek. She closed her eyes, flinching when she felt his moist breath against her face. She heard him make a sound of displeasure in his throat and felt his hesitation.

Desiree forced herself to stand still, waiting for the touch of his lips against hers, but her body stiffened, rejecting before it came, this sign of masculine possession.

Soft. So soft. And gentle.

Desiree's eyes flickered open, and she stared wide-eyed at the man who had just become her husband. Her breathing was erratic, and her heart was bumping madly. It hadn't been a painful kiss. Quite the contrary. Her lips had…tingled. She raised her hand toward her mouth in wonder.

Carter was staring at her, the expression on his face inscrutable. She had no idea what he was thinking.

She had married a stranger.

It was a terrifying thought, and Desiree felt the panic welling up inside her. Carter must have sensed her feelings, because he quickly thanked the judge, shook Carmichael's hand, watched as the witnesses signed the marriage certificate, in which Desiree had once again given up her maiden name of Parrish, and hustled her and Nicole out of the courthouse.

"I've made reservations for lunch at Benham's," Carter said, naming one of the fanciest restaurants in Casper.

Desiree put a hand to her queasy stomach. The last thing she wanted right now was food.

"I'm starving," Nicole piped up.

"I guess that's settled," Carter said. "Let's go eat."

"Not in a restaurant," Desiree protested. "I put a roast in the oven before I left the ranch. Please, let's go home."

"Home," Carter said. It had a wonderful sound. "All right, then. Home. I'll follow you in my pickup."

Desiree welcomed the brief respite before they sat down to their first meal as husband and wife. Once in the truck, Nicole focused her attention on Desiree's wedding bouquet, which left Desiree free to mentally compare this wedding with her first one.

She had been only eighteen years old and desperately in love with Burley Kelton. Burley had come to work as a cowhand for her father, and she had fallen hard for his broad shoulders and his rakish smile.

After a whirlwind romance they had married in the First Presbyterian Church. She had worn her mother's antique-lace wedding gown and carried a pungent bouquet of gardenias.

Desiree had been a total innocent on her wedding night, naive and frightened, but so in love with Burley that she would have done anything he asked.

Only Burley hadn't asked for anything. He had taken what he wanted. Brutally. Horribly. Painfully. She didn't dare cry out for fear her parents would hear her in their room down the hall from her bedroom. So she bore her wedding night stoically. She survived, to endure even worse in the next weeks and months of her marriage.

They lived with her parents, and Burley continued working for her father. She kept up a front, refusing to let her parents know how bad things were. Then her mom and dad were killed in a freak one-car accident, and she was left alone with Burley. It was a ghastly end to what she now realized were girlish dreams of romance.

Burley told her the pain she felt when he exercised his husbandly rights was her fault. He had to work hard to find any pleasure in her, because she was frigid. He should have married a woman who had more experience, one who knew how to satisfy a man.

Even though Burley found her wanting in bed, he was insanely jealous if she so much as said hello to another man. When she suggested they might be better off apart, he became enraged and said he had taken his vows "Till death do us part!" and that he had meant them.

It had almost come to that.

Desiree stole a glance at Carter in the rearview mirror. At least she would be spared her wifely duties for a time. Maybe if she explained that he would find no joy in her, Carter might even change his mind about wanting to take her to bed.

Carter was having similar, but contrary, thoughts. In fact, he was wondering how long it would be before his wife became his wife—in the biblical sense. He had stood next to her during the short ceremony and felt her heat, smelled the soft floral fragrance that clung to her hair and clothes and felt himself forcing back the feelings of want and need that rose within him.

He had seen her flinch when he tried to kiss her after the ceremony.

It wasn't the first time she had recoiled from him, either. She must have been badly treated by some man, somewhere along the line. Her father? Her husband? So what were the chances she was going to let him get anywhere near her, anytime soon? Not good, he admitted. She had said they would have to wait until they knew each other better, and she had no idea when that would be. He was willing to be patient—for a while. He couldn't help comparing this wedding with his first one.

Carter hadn't been able to keep his hands off Jeanine, and she had been equally enamored of him. They had anticipated their wedding night by about a year, and knowing what he could expect in bed had kept him aroused through most of the ceremony and reception. He had been so much in love with Jeanine that it had been difficult to force the vows past his constricted throat. Knowing the reason they were marrying had been an extra bonus as far as he was concerned.

Looking back, he realized that the tears in Jeanine's eyes hadn't been tears of joy, as she had professed. His trembling bride had been trembling for entirely different reasons than the ones he had supposed. Now he knew why she had been so miserable. If only…

Carter swore under his breath. Wishing wouldn't change the past. He was crazy to be reliving that nightmare, especially when he had just promised himself he wouldn't look back anymore. He would do better to look forward to the future with Desiree Parrish—no, now Desiree Prescott.

Carter quashed the awful thought that arose like a many-headed hydra: *This woman can't betray me. Her scarred face will keep her from tempting another man.* It wasn't the first time he had thought it, and he couldn't truly say whether the scar on her face had been a consideration when he agreed to marry her. But he was ashamed for what he was thinking and grateful that Desiree couldn't read his mind. She deserved better from the man who had just become her husband.

Carter pulled his truck up beside Desiree's pickup in back of the house. His wife and new daughter were already inside the house before he could catch up to them. If he hadn't known better, he would have said Desiree was fleeing from him. If she was, she was wasting her time. Now that they were married, there was no place for her to run.

Desiree hurried to make herself busy before Carter came inside. She turned up the furnace and slipped off her coat and Nicole's and sent her daughter upstairs to play.

Then she returned to the kitchen and waited beside the stove, her arms crossed over her chest. Carter didn't bother to knock before he opened the door and stepped inside. He didn't bother to close the door, either, just headed straight for her, his stride determined. A moment later he had swept her off her feet and into his arms.

Desiree grabbed hold of his neck, afraid for a moment he might drop her. His arms tightened around her, and she knew there was no danger of that. He headed right back outside.

"What are you doing?" she asked breathlessly, her eyes wide with trepidation.

"There's a tradition that hasn't been observed."

"What's that?"

Once he was outside, he paused long enough to glare down at her. Through clenched teeth he said, "Carrying the bride over the threshold." He turned around and marched right back into the kitchen.

Desiree was too astonished to protest. She stared up at his rigid jaw and realized again how little they knew of each other. "I'm sorry," she said. "I didn't know you felt so strongly about it, or I would have waited. But we never discussed—"

"There are a lot of things we haven't discussed. I guess it's going to take a while for us to adjust to each other."

He was still holding her in his arms. Desiree became increasingly uncomfortable, as another kind of tension began to grow between them. She recognized the signs on Carter's face. The drooping eyelids, the nostrils flared for the scent of her, the jumping pulse at his throat. She began to struggle for freedom.

"Let me go. Let me down. Now!"

His hold tightened. "What the hell's the matter with you?"

"Let me go!" she shrieked.

A moment later she was on her feet. She retreated from him several paces, until her back was against the wall. She stared at him, eyes wide, blood racing. "We agreed we would wait!" she accused.

"I only wanted a kiss," he said.

She shook her head. "No kissing, no touching, nothing until we know each other," she insisted.

Desiree watched a muscle jerk in his jaw. She knew he could force her. Burley had. She reached behind her surreptitiously with one hand, searching for a weapon on the counter. But there was nothing close by.

"What did he do to you?" Carter asked in a quiet voice.

"What makes you think—"

"Every time I move too fast you flinch like a horse that's been whipped. You're trembling like a beaten animal right now. And the look in your eyes… I've seen men facing a nest of rattlers who've looked less terrified. It doesn't take a scientist to figure out you've been mistreated. Do you want to tell me about it?"

Desiree couldn't get an answer past the lump in her throat. She lowered her eyes to avoid his searching gaze. She couldn't help jerking when he reached out a hand to her.

Carter swore under his breath. "I'm not going to hurt you," he repeated through clenched teeth.

Desiree forced herself to remain still as he reached out again for her chin and tipped it up so they were staring into each other's eyes.

"You're my wife. We'll be spending the rest of our lives together. I'm willing to wait as long as it takes for you to accept me in your bed."

"No kissing, no—"

He shook his head. "There'll be kissing, and hugging and touching. Even friends do that much."

"But—"

He cut her off by putting his lips against hers. Desiree fought the panic, reminding herself that his first kiss had been gentle. This one was no less so, just the barest touch of lips, but she felt a shock clear to her toes. It wasn't a bad feeling. Oh, no, it wasn't bad at all.

Luckily, his lips left hers just at the moment when she felt herself ready to struggle in earnest. When she opened her eyes, she saw that he hadn't retreated very far.

"Desiree?"

"Carter, I…I'm scared," she admitted in a whisper.

He drew her slowly into his arms. As his strength enfolded her she forced herself to relax. It wasn't easy. Burley had sometimes begun gently, only to lose control later.

Carter's arms remained loose around her. In a few minutes she realized she was no longer trembling, that she was almost relaxed in his embrace.

"This is nice," he murmured in her ear. "You feel good against me."

Desiree stiffened. She knew he felt her withdrawal when he said, "It's all right, Desiree. It's just a hug, nothing more. Relax, sweetheart."

He cajoled her much as he might a reluctant mare, and she found herself responding to his warm baritone voice. She laid her head against his chest and tentatively put her hands at his trim waist.

Just as she made those gestures of concession, he stepped back from her. She raised her eyes to his in confusion. She hadn't expected him to stop. But she was glad he had.

"How soon will lunch be ready?" he asked.

Desiree turned quickly to the oven. She had completely forgotten about the roast beef during the past tension-filled minutes. "It should be done shortly."

"Anything I can do to help?"

Desiree raised startled eyes to study Carter's face. "You're willing to help in the kitchen?"

"Why not?"

Burley never had. Burley had said the kitchen was woman's work. "You could set the table if you'd like."

Carter took the initiative and started hunting through cabinets for what he wanted. "Best way to find out where everything is," he explained with a cheeky grin.

"You're probably right." Desiree found herself smiling back, even though it was unsettling to see a stranger going through everything as though he had the right.

He has the right. He's your husband.

As she peeled potatoes and put vegetables in a pot on the stove, Desiree realized she had been extraordinarily lucky in her second choice of husband. Carter wasn't like Burley. He could control his passions. It was too bad he was getting such a bad bargain. She couldn't be the wife he obviously wanted and needed. She was too bruised in spirit to respond as he wished.

Desiree had planned this dinner at home because she had feared that conversation between them would be stilted, and it would be embarrassing to sit across from each other in a restaurant in total silence. However, when the three of them sat down together, things didn't turn out at all as she had expected. Carter, bless him, wasn't the least bit taciturn. He even condescended to answer several of Nicole's questions. However, when Nicole finished eating and approached Carter, Desiree realized there were limits to his tolerance.

''Can I sit on your lap?'' Nicole asked.

''You're a big girl,'' Carter replied.

''Not too big,'' Nicole said, sidling up next to him. ''My friend Shirley sits in her daddy's lap.''

''I'm not your—''

Desiree cut him off before he could deny any relationship to her daughter. ''Carter has a full stomach right now. Why don't you go upstairs to your room and play,'' she said.

Nicole gave Carter a look from beneath lowered lashes. ''Is your stomach really full?'' she demanded suspiciously.

Desiree saw the war Carter waged, the way his hands fisted. ''Nicole! Go play.''

Nicole's lower lip stuck out, but she knew better than to argue when her mother used that tone of voice.

The little girl had already turned to leave when Carter grabbed her under the arms and hefted her into his lap. ''I suppose you can sit here for a minute,'' he said grudgingly.

But Desiree caught the brief, awful look of anguish in Carter's eyes as his arms closed around the little girl.

Nicole settled back against Carter's chest and chattered happily, oblivious to the undercurrents.

Over the next five minutes, Carter's face looked more and more strained, and his jaw tightened. Desiree realized there was something very wrong.

''That's enough for now, Nicole,'' Desiree said. ''It's time for you to go upstairs and choose a book for me to read before your nap.''

Carter sighed as though relieved of a great burden as he lifted Nicole from his lap and set her on her feet.

Nicole ran upstairs without a backward glance, leaving them alone at the table. Desiree waited for Carter to explain himself. To her amazement, he pretended as though nothing out of the ordinary had happened.

"If I'd know how good you can cook, I'd have jumped at that first proposal," he said.

Desiree didn't press the issue. And she chose to accept the compliment, rather than be put off by the fact Carter hadn't wanted to marry her at first. "Thank you."

"Maybe you could give me a tour of the ranch this afternoon," Carter suggested.

"Nicole usually takes a nap after lunch. I should be up there getting her settled right now. You're welcome to take a look on your own."

Carter saw the relief in Desiree's eyes at the thought they wouldn't have to spend the rest of the day together. He could see she was going to use the child as an excuse to keep them apart. It was funny, because he had planned to use ranch business with her as a way to avoid the child.

"I can wait until Nicole wakes up. We'll go then," he said.

"She'll have to come with us."

As a chaperon, Carter thought wryly. But the little girl obviously couldn't be left alone, and there was no one else around to take care of her. One or the other of them would always have to be with her. Which led him to ask, "How on earth have you managed to do the chores around the ranch and take care of Nicole at the same time?"

"Sometimes it isn't easy," Desiree admitted.

Carter thought that was probably the understatement of the century. "All right," he said. "While Nicole's napping you can show me around the house."

She gave him a disconcerted look. Was he looking for an opportunity to get her alone in the bedroom? "There isn't much to see."

"You can show me what needs fixing. I couldn't help noticing that the faucet drips in the kitchen, and the newel post on the stairs wobbles."

Two pink spots of color appeared on her cheeks. She was thinking of bed, while he was thinking of dripping faucets! It would be funny if it weren't so humilating. "I didn't marry you to get a handyman."

He grinned. ''But isn't it lucky that I am one? Come on, Desiree, every house needs a few repairs now and then.''

Her lips flattened grimly. ''I'm afraid this one needs more than that.''

''Oh?''

She recited a long list of problems with the house that ended, ''And I'm not sure the furnace will make it through the winter.''

He stared at her, stunned by the enormity of what she had been coping with on her own. No wonder she had wanted—needed—a husband. Strange as it seemed, he felt better knowing how much work the ranch needed. It was a rational explanation for why she had married him, even if she had done it in a damned havy cavy way.

He could have used his money and had repairmen do everything that needed to be done in a matter of weeks. But he didn't want her to know yet about his wealth. He wanted a chance to be needed—loved?—for himself alone. Later would be soon enough to reveal the rest.

''I guess I'll start on those repairs while Nicole is napping,'' he conceded finally.

''I usually do something quiet, so I won't disturb her.''

''And repairing the newel post is hardly quiet.'' He said it as a statement, not a question.

She shook her head. He was pleased to see just the hint of a smile tease the corners of her mouth. The scar didn't pucker so badly with the smaller smile. He forced his eyes away from the mark on her face.

''All right,'' he said with a gusty sigh. ''You can show me the ranch books this afternoon. If you don't think that would be too noisy a proposition?''

Desiree giggled. She didn't know where the sound had come from, and it certainly wasn't anything she could remember doing recently. But the look of surrender to the inevitable on Carter's face struck her as funny.

''Just let me get Nicole settled, and I'll be back to do the dishes.''

''I'll do them,'' Carter volunteered.

''That's not necessary, I—''

''The sooner the dishes are done, the sooner we can get to those ranch books.''

What Desiree heard in his voice, what she saw in his eyes was *The sooner we can be alone.*

"Maybe you'd rather take that tour of the ranch," she suggested.

Carter shook his head no. "I'd rather wait and go with you."

Desiree stood rooted where she was, pierced by a look in his blue eyes that held a wealth of promises. She wanted to warn him that she couldn't fulfill those promises. But something kept her silent. The longer it took him to figure out the truth about her sexually, the better. She dreaded the disgust she was sure would be her lot when he realized what a failure she was in bed.

Desiree took one last look over her shoulder at Carter before she left the kitchen. He was already clearing the table. Her grandmother's silver-rimmed china looked fragile in his big hands, but he moved with easy grace between the table and sink. The thought of Nicole waiting anxiously for her upstairs pulled her from the mesmerizing sight of her husband doing the dishes on their wedding day.

To Nicole's delight, Desiree read two stories. The first because she always did, the second because she was putting off the moment when she would have to rejoin Carter in the parlor, which also served as the ranch office.

When Nicole's eyelids drifted shut and her tiny rosebud mouth fell slack, Desiree realized the inevitable could be avoided no longer.

She rose and squared her shoulders like an aristocrat headed for the guillotine. It was time to begin the process of becoming a wife and partner to the stranger downstairs.

Desiree felt her legs trembling and told herself she was being foolish. There was no need to fear Carter. He was not like Burley.

Not yet. But what happens when you disappoint him in bed?

That won't be for a while yet. Carter promised— *You saw the look in his eyes when he carried you over the threshold. Was that the look of a patient man?*

So he desires me. That isn't a bad thing. Especially since we're married.

Are you ready to submit to him? To trust him with the secrets of your body?

Desiree shuddered. Not yet. *Not yet.* She ignored her trembling limbs and headed downstairs to join her husband. She would just have to be firm with Carter.

Sex would have to wait.

Four

Desiree walked down the stairs, knees trembling—and found Carter sound asleep on the couch. An awkward feeling of tenderness washed over her as she stared at the sleeping man. Apparently he had needed a nap as much as Nicole. She sat down across from him in the comfortable arm chair that faced the fireplace in the parlor and searched his features.

The rugged planes of his face were less fearsome in repose. The blue shadows under his eyes suggested that he had put in some long hours the week before they were married. What had he been doing? The fact that she had no idea pointed to how much a stranger he was to her. A boyish lock of chestnut hair fell across his forehead, and she had to resist the urge to reach over and brush it back into place.

Desiree breathed a sigh of relief that her fears about confronting Carter hadn't been realized. At least, not yet. She knew she ought to get up and go do some chores, but the fire made the room seem so cozy that she settled deeper into the overstuffed chair. The house was quiet, with only the sound of the furnace doing its level best to keep up with the cold. She scooched down in the chair, put her feet up on an equally overstuffed footstool, and let her eyelids droop closed.

Desiree wasn't sure what woke her, but she had the distinct feeling she was being watched. It was a feeling she recognized, and one that caused her heart to pound so hard she could almost hear it. She took a deep breath and let it out, forcing herself to relax. Then she opened her eyes.

Carter was sitting on the couch, staring at her. At some point while she was asleep, he had changed his clothes and was now wearing jeans and a red and blue plaid shirt with his work boots.

She watched him through wary eyes without moving.

''I didn't mean to wake you,'' he said.

She sat up carefully. ''You didn't.''

''If you say so.'' He yawned and stretched. She was impressed again by the breadth of his chest, by the play of muscles in his shoulders and arms. He caught her looking at him and grinned. ''I had hoped we'd spend some part of the day sleeping together, but I had something a little different in mind.''

Desiree tensed, waiting for him to make some move to close the distance between them. But he relaxed with one arm settled along the back of the couch and hung one booted ankle across the opposite knee.

''I don't suppose we'll have time now to look at the books before Nicole is awake.''

Desiree looked at her watch. ''We've slept away the afternoon!''

Carter thrust all ten fingers through his hair, leaving it standing in all directions. ''I guess I was more tired than I thought. It's been a tough week.''

''Oh?'' Desiree arched a questioning brow. ''What kept you so busy?''

Carter cleared his throat. ''Just some business I needed to clear up before the wedding. Nothing worth mentioning.''

He was lying. Desiree didn't know why she was so sure about it, except that one moment he had been looking at her—well, not at her face, but in her direction—and the next, his gaze was focused intently on the leafy design sewn into his worn leather boots. She didn't believe in keeping secrets. It spawned distrust. But considering the fact she hadn't been totally honest with Carter, Desiree could hardly challenge him on the matter.

''What shall we do with the time until supper?'' Carter asked.

Desiree was thinking in terms of chores that could be finished, when Carter suggested, ''Why don't you tell me a little bit about what you've been doing in the years since we last met?''

"I wouldn't know where to start. Besides, what matters is the present and the future, not the past."

Carter pursed his lips and muttered, "If only that were true."

Desiree met Carter's gaze. His eyes held the same despairing look she had seen when he held Nicole at the dinner table. What had happened, she wondered, that had caused him so much pain? "Are you all right?"

The vulnerability in his eyes was gone as quickly as it had appeared, replaced by icy orbs that didn't invite questioning. Desiree welcomed the sight of her daughter in the doorway. "Did you have a good nap, sweetheart?"

"Uh-huh. Are we going for a ride now?" Nicole bounced over to Carter and laid her hands on his thigh, as though she had known him forever.

Desiree held her breath waiting for his reaction. It came in the form of a puff of breath Carter expelled so softly it could barely be heard. He stared at the spot where Nicole's tiny hands rested so confidently against him. He stood without touching her, and her hands of necessity fell away.

Nicole reached up to tug on the sleeve of his flannel shirt. "Can we go see Matilda first?"

"Who's Matilda?" Carter asked.

"She's my calf. She's black."

"Matilda's mother didn't survive the birth," Desiree explained quietly. "I've been keeping the calf in the barn and feeding her by hand." Desiree saw the look of incredulity on Carter's face and hurried to explain, "I—we—can't afford to lose a single head of stock."

"I had no idea things were so bad," Carter said.

"There's no danger of losing the ranch," she reassured him. "I've just been extra busy because my hired hand broke his leg and has been out of commission for nearly two months."

For reasons Desiree didn't want to explain to Carter, she hadn't been able to bring herself to hire a stranger to work for her. Which made no sense at all, considering the fact she had married one.

Nicole grabbed Carter's hand and began tugging him from the room. Desiree watched to see if he would free himself. He did, quickly shoving his hands in his back pockets. But he followed where Nicole led.

She trailed the two of them from the parlor through the house to the kitchen, where they retrieved their coats, hats and gloves and headed out the kitchen door.

As usual in Wyoming, the wind was blowing. Desiree hurried to catch up to Nicole so she could pull her daughter's parka hood up over her head. Before she reached Nicole, Carter did it for her.

Desiree found his behavior with Nicole confusing, to say the least. He clearly didn't want anything to do with the little girl, but he stopped short of ignoring her. What had him so leery of children?

Desiree heard Nicole chattering and hurried to catch up. Carter had been doing fine tolerating the five-year-old, but she saw no reason to test his patience.

Thanks to the body heat of the animals inside, the barn felt almost warm in comparison with the frigid outdoors. Nicole let go of Carter's hand and raced to a stall halfway down the barn. She unlatched it and stepped inside. The tiny Black Angus calf made a bleating sound of welcome and hurried up to her.

"Matilda is hungry, Mommy," Nicole said.

"I'll fix her something right now." Desiree went to the refrigerator, where she kept the milk for the calf. She poured some out into a nursing bottle and set it in a pot of water on a hot plate nearby to warm. When she returned to the stall she found Carter down on one knee beside the calf.

"Matilda's mommy is dead," Nicole explained. "So Mommy and I have to take care of her."

"It looks like you're doing a fine job," Carter conceded gruffly.

The calf bawled piteously, and Nicole circled the calf's neck with her arms to calm it. "Mommy's getting your bottle, Matilda. Moooommy!" she yelled. "Matilda's starving!"

Desiree hustled back to the hot plate, unplugged it and retrieved the bottle. A moment later she dropped onto her knees beside the calf. Nicole took the heavy bottle from her mother and held it while the calf sucked loudly and hungrily.

Desiree met Carter's eyes over the calf's head. There was a smile on his face that had made its way to his eyes.

"This is turning out to be a great honeymoon," he said with a chuckle.

Desiree laughed. ''I suppose it is a little unconventional.''

''That's putting it mildly.''

There was a warmth in his eyes that said he would be happy to put the train back on the rails. Desiree was amazed to find herself relaxed in his presence. However, her feelings for Carter were anything but comfortable. Her fear of men hadn't disappeared. Yet she was forced to admit that Carter evoked more than fear in her breast. She hadn't expected to be physically attracted to him. She hadn't expected to want to touch him and to want him to touch her. She hadn't expected to regret her inability to respond to him—or any man—as a woman.

Her expression sobered.

''What's wrong?'' Carter asked.

She wondered how he could be so perceptive. ''What makes you think anything's wrong?''

He reached out a hand and smoothed the furrows on her brow. His callused fingertips slid across her unmarked cheek and along the line of her jaw.

Desiree edged away from his touch. Her heart had slipped up to lodge in her throat, making speech impossible.

''Matilda is done, Mommy,'' Nicole said as she extended the empty bottle toward her mother.

Desiree lurched to her feet. ''That's—'' She cleared her throat and tried again. ''That's good, darling.'' She took the bottle and Nicole's hand and hurried out of the stall. She headed for the sink in the barn and rinsed out the bottle.

Carter had started after her, but when she turned around she realized he had stopped at the stall and was examining the hinges.

''This is hanging lopsided. Do you have a pair of pliers?''

Desiree would rather have headed right back to the house, but forced herself to respond naturally. ''Sure. Let me get them.''

Desiree watched as Carter made a few adjustments to the stall door, tightening the bolts that held the frame in place.

''That ought to do it.''

Desiree thought of the months the door had been hanging like that, when neither she nor her hired hand, Sandy, had taken the time to fix it. In a matter of minutes Carter had resolved the problem.

''Thanks,'' she said.

''No need to thank me. It was my pleasure.''

Desiree searched his face and saw the look of satisfaction there. He was telling the truth. He had enjoyed himself. ''Fortunately for you there are lots of things that need fixing around here,'' she said sardonically.

He headed down the aisle of the barn to return the pliers to the tool box. ''I think that's enough for today, though. After all, I am still on my honeymoon.''

''What's a honeymoon?'' Nicole asked.

Desiree saw the smirk that came and went on Carter's face. She found the question embarrassing, especially with Carter listening to everything she was about to say. But she had made it a habit to answer any question Nicole asked as honestly as possible.

''It's the time a husband and wife spend together getting to know each other when they're first married,'' Desiree explained.

''Like you and Mr. Prescott,'' Nicole said.

Desiree brushed Nicole's bangs out of her eyes. ''Yes.'' Desiree looked up and found Carter watching her, his eyes hooded with desire. A glance downward showed her he was hard and ready. A frisson of alarm skittered down her spine. She rose abruptly and took her daughter's hand. ''I'm going to start supper,'' she said.

''I'll be in shortly,'' Carter replied in a raspy voice. ''I see a few more things I can do out here, after all.''

The atmosphere at supper was strained. Not that she and Carter conversed much more or less than at lunchtime, but Nicole never stopped chattering. Carter never initiated contact with Nicole, but he didn't rebuff her when she climbed into his lap after supper. If the threat of danger hadn't been hanging over her, she might actually have let herself feel optimistic about the future.

She and Carter did the dishes together, while Nicole colored with crayons at the kitchen table. It was so much a picture of a natural, normal family that Desiree wanted to cry. Her feelings of guilt for marrying Carter without telling him the whole truth forced her to excuse herself and take Nicole up to bed early the night of her wedding.

''I'll see you in the morning,'' she said to Carter.

She didn't know what to make of the look on his face—part desire, part regret, part something else she couldn't identify—but fled upstairs as quickly as she could.

Once in bed, she couldn't sleep. She heard Carter come upstairs, heard the shower, heard him brush his teeth, heard the toilet flush. His footsteps were soft in the hall, so she supposed he must be barefoot. She knew how cold the floor was, even with the worn runner, and wondered if his feet would end up as icy as Nicole's always did. She hoped she wouldn't be finding out too soon. As far as she was concerned, the longer it took Carter to end up in her bed, the better. Because he wasn't going to be happy with what he discovered when he got there.

Then there was silence. Desiree heard the house creak as it settled. The wind howled and whistled and rattled her windowpanes. The furnace kicked on. She closed her eyes and willed herself to sleep.

Two sleepless hours later Desiree sat bolt upright, shoved the covers off and lowered her feet over the side of the bed, searching for her slippers in the glow from the tiny night-light that burned beside her bed.

"Damn!" she muttered. "Damn!"

She had spent two hours lying there pretending to sleep. Maybe a cup of hot chocolate would help. She opened the door to her bedroom and swore again. Apparently Carter had turned off the light she always left burning in the living room. It was her own fault, because she hadn't told him to leave it on. But that meant she either had to brave the dark or turn on a light upstairs in order to see and take the risk of waking Carter.

Frankly, the darkness was less terrifying than the thought of facing a rudely awakened Carter when she was wearing a frayed silk nightgown, a chenille robe and tufted terry-cloth slippers. Desiree knew her naturally curly hair was a tumble of gnarled tresses worthy of a Medusa, and since she had washed off her makeup, her scar would be even more vivid.

She knew the spots on the stairs that would groan when stepped on. She had learned them as a child so she wouldn't awaken her parents when she snuck down to shake her Christmas presents and try to determine what they were. She slid her hand down the smooth banister, walking quietly, carefully. When she reached the bottom of the stairs, she turned on the tiny light that was usually always lit.

With the light, it was easy to make her way to the kitchen. The old refrigerator hummed as she opened it, and there was a slight clink as the bottles of ketchup and pickles on the door shifted. Even though she was careful, the copper-bottomed pot she planned to use to heat the milk clanked as she freed it from the stack in the cabinet beside the sink.

She was standing at the stove with her back to the kitchen door, when she heard footsteps in the hallway.

Someone was in the house!

Her heart galloped as she searched frantically for somewhere to hide, a place to escape. Then she realized Nicole was trapped upstairs. In order to get to her daughter she would have to confront whoever was in the house. She was halfway to the kitchen threshold, when she halted. Her hand gripped her robe and pulled it closed at the neck. She stared, wild-eyed, at the man in the doorway.

When she realized it was only Carter, bare-chested, barefoot, wearing a half-buttoned pair of frayed jeans that hung low on his hips, she almost sobbed with relief.

''Desiree? It's the middle of the night. What are you doing down here? Are you all right?''

''I couldn't sleep. I—''

He didn't wait for her explanation, just crossed the distance between them and enfolded her in his arms.

Desiree stood rigid. She was aware of the heat of him, the male scent of him. She was appalled by the way her nipples peaked when they came in contact with his naked chest. She became certain that he must be able to feel her arousal, even through the layers of cloth that covered her, when she felt the hard ridge growing in his low-slung jeans.

''Desiree,'' he murmured.

As his arms tightened around her, memories of the past rose up to choke her. And she panicked.

''No! Don't touch me! Let me go!'' Desiree struggled to be free of Carter's constraining hold. She slapped at his face, beat at him with her fists, shoved and writhed to be free. But his hold, although gentle, was inexorable.

Desiree didn't scream. She had learned not to scream. There was no one who would come to her rescue; she would have to save herself. She continued fighting until she finally realized through her panic that although he refused to release her, Carter wasn't hurting her. At last, exhausted, she stood quivering in his arms, like a wild animal caught in a trap it realizes it cannot escape.

''There, now. That's better,'' Carter crooned. ''Easy now. Everything's gonna be all right now. You're fine. You're just fine.''

As Desiree recovered from her dazed state, she became aware that Carter was speaking in a low, husky voice. She was being held loosely in his arms, and his hands were rubbing her back as though she were a small child. She looked up and saw the beginning of a bruise on his chin and the bloody scratches on his face and froze.

''I hurt you,'' she said.

''You've got a wicked right,'' he agreed with a smile. He winced as the smile teased a small cut in his lip.

''I'm so sorry.''

He looked at her warily. ''Would you like to explain what that commotion was all about?''

''No.''

His blue eyes narrowed. ''No?''

''No.'' For a moment she thought he wasn't going to let her evade his question.

Then he sniffed and said, ''Something's burning.''

''My hot chocolate!'' When she pulled away, he let her go. Desiree hurried to the stove, where the milk had burned black in the bottom of the pan. ''Oh, no. Look at this mess!'' She retrieved a pot holder and lifted the pot off the stove and settled it in the sink.

''You can make some more.''

''I don't think I could sleep now if I drank a dozen cups of hot chocolate,'' Desiree said in disgust.

''I heard a noise, and I came down to check it out,'' Carter said in a crisp voice. ''You're the one who went crazy.''

''I didn't—'' Desiree cut herself off. Although she didn't like the description, it fit her irrational behavior. She shoved a hand through her long brown hair and crossed the room to slump into one of the kitchen chairs. "Good Lord! I can't imagine what you must think of me."

Carter joined her at the table, turning a chair around and straddling it so he was facing her. "Do you think it would help to talk about it?"

Desiree wondered how much she should tell him. And how little he would settle for knowing. "My first marriage was a disappointment," she admitted.

"I guessed something of the sort. How long were you married?"

"Two years. Then we divorced."

"I was married for five years."

"You were married?" Desiree didn't know why she was so surprised. But she was. Suddenly she had a thought. Perhaps there was a good reason, after all, for Carter's strange, distant behavior toward Nicole.

"Do you have children?"

"I have...had a five-year-old daughter. She died along with my wife in a car accident six years ago."

"I'm so sorry." No wonder he didn't want to be around Nicole! Her daughter must be an awful reminder of his loss. Desiree knew there really was no comfort she could offer, except to share with him her own grievous loss. "My parents died the same way."

"I'm sorry," he said.

A tense silence fell between them. Both wanted to ask more questions. But to ask questions was to suggest a willingness to answer them in return. And neither was ready to share with the other the secrets of their past.

It was Carter who finally broke the silence between them, his voice quiet, his tone as gentle as Desiree had ever heard it.

"If I'm going to get anything accomplished tomorrow I ought to get some sleep. But I don't feel comfortable leaving you down here alone. Is there any chance you could sleep now?"

Quite honestly, Desiree thought she would spend the rest of the night staring at the ceiling. But she could see that Carter wasn't going to go back to bed until she was settled. "I guess I am a little tired."

"I'll follow you upstairs," he said.

Desiree rose and headed for the kitchen door. Before she had taken two steps, Carter blocked her way.

"I don't know what to do to make you believe that I'd never hurt you," he said.

"I...I believe you."

Nevertheless, she flinched as he raised a hand to brush the hair away from her face.

His lips flattened. "Yeah. Sure."

Desiree cringed at the sarcasm in his voice and fled up the stairs as fast as she could. Behind her she heard the steady barefoot tread of her husband. She hurried into her bedroom and shut the door behind her. She leaned back against the door and covered her face with her hands.

I hate you, Burley. I hate what you did to me. I hate the way you made me feel. And I hate the fact that I can never be a woman to the man I married today.

Hating didn't help. Desiree had learned that lesson over the six long years since she had divorced Burley and gone on with her life. But she hadn't been able to let go of the hate—or the fear.

Because she knew that when he got out of prison in two weeks, Burley would be coming back.

Five

Christmas was a bittersweet event. They went to the candlelight service on Christmas Eve as a family and received the warm wishes and congratulations of the congregation on their marriage. Some of the women with whom Desiree had worked on the Christmas pageant over the past couple of years knew that Burley was due to be released from prison soon. Desiree saw the knowledge in their eyes of why she had so hurriedly married a man she barely knew. She was grateful that none of them mentioned the fact to Carter.

Nicole fell asleep on the ride home, and Desiree carried her right upstairs to bed. Carter didn't offer to help her, and Desiree didn't bother to ask. She had seen how uncomfortable he was in church, and from the moment they left the service he had been uncommonly silent. She knew he must be remembering his family—his first wife and his daughter.

While she dressed Nicole for bed and slipped her daughter under the covers, Desiree debated whether to join Carter downstairs. She pictured his face as it had looked when lit solely by candlelight during the church service. He must have loved his wife very much to still be so sad six years after her death. Of course, Desiree could identify with his despair at the loss of his daughter. After all, hadn't she been willing to make any sacrifice to ensure Nicole's safety?

By the time she had finished her musings she was already at the bottom of the stairs. She took the few steps farther to the parlor, where the wonderful-smelling spruce Christmas tree forced an acknowledgment of the season, expecting to see Carter there. But the room was empty.

Desiree went in search of her husband. It amazed her to realize that she had been so wrapped up in her own agony over the past six years that she hadn't focused on the fact that there must be others in similar straits. In fact, she had seen with her own eyes that Carter Prescott was fighting demons of the past equally as ferocious as her own. Her heart went out to him. Comfort was something she could offer in repayment for the security she hoped this marriage would provide for her and her daughter.

She found Carter in the kitchen. Desiree couldn't help the bubble of laughter that escaped when she realized he was fixing the dripping faucet.

"What's so funny?" Carter demanded.

"You. It's Christmas Eve. What on earth are you doing?"

"Fixing the faucet."

"I can see that," Desiree said as she approached him. "What I want to know is why now?"

Carter shrugged. "You were busy. There was nothing else to do."

"You could have sat down in the living room and relaxed."

"I don't like sitting still. It leaves me with too much time to think."

"About your wife and daughter?" When Desiree saw the way his shoulders stiffened she wished she had kept her thoughts to herself.

"They were killed on Christmas Eve," Carter said in a quiet voice. "They were on the way to church. I...I wasn't with them. I was at my office when I heard what had happened." He gave a shuddering sigh. "I don't think I'll ever forget that night."

Desiree followed the impulse to comfort that had brought her seeking Carter in the first place. She put a hand on his arm and felt the muscles tighten beneath her fingertips. "I don't know what to say."

He threw the wrench he was using on the counter and turned to face her. "I'd rather not talk about it," he said brusquely.

"You aren't the first man to put business before family," she replied. "It wasn't your fault the accident happened."

"I said I don't want to talk about it."

His voice was harsh and his face savage. Instead of fleeing him,

Desiree stepped forward and circled his waist with her arms. She laid her head against his chest, where she could hear the furious pounding of his heart. ''I'm glad you came to Wyoming,'' she said. ''I'm glad you agreed to marry me. I'm glad you're here.''

She could feel his hesitation and knew he was trying to decide whether to thrust her away or accept the comfort she was offering. She had her answer when his arms circled her shoulders, and he pulled her snug against him.

Desiree forced herself to relax. There was nothing loverlike in his demeanor or in hers. She was simply one human being offering comfort on Christmas Eve to another.

Only it wasn't that simple.

She should have known it wouldn't be. He was a man. She was a woman. As much as she tried to ignore the fact, as much as she was appalled by it, her body responded to the closeness of his.

Desiree had believed, after her experience with Burley, that there was something wrong with her, that she was defective somehow, that she didn't have whatever was necessary to make her physically responsive to a man. But ever since she had met Carter, she had been discovering that her body was more than responsive. Her blood pumped, her body ached deep inside, her breasts felt heavy and her nipples peaked whenever she was close to him. All the signs of arousal were there.

She was simply too terrified of what might—or might not—happen to allow anything to go forward. What if she was wrong? What if she couldn't respond?

''Thank you, Desiree,'' Carter murmured. ''I didn't know how much I needed a hug.''

The feel of his warm breath in her ear made her shiver. ''I guess I know a little of what you're feeling,'' she murmured back.

He chuckled. ''If you knew what I'm feeling right now you'd run up those stairs and lock your bedroom door behind you.''

Desiree took a tremulous breath. ''Carter?''

''What?''

''You can kiss me, if you want.''

She heard him catch his breath, felt the tenseness in the muscles of his back where her hands rested. He lifted his head to look at her, but she lowered her gaze so he couldn't see that there was as much fear as anticipation lurking in her brown eyes.

"What brought this on?"

"I don't know," she mumbled. "I just thought—"

"I guess I shouldn't look a gift horse in the mouth."

Before Desiree had a chance to change her mind, his fingertip caught her chin and tipped her mouth up so it could meet his.

As with each of their two previous kisses, his mouth was gentle on hers. He cherished her with his touch. There was none of the pain she had come to expect from Burley.

"Desiree?"

She looked up at him through lids that were heavy with desire. "Yes, Carter?"

He smiled. "I keep waiting for the scratching tiger to show her claws. Are you sure you want to do this?"

"Could we just kiss, Carter? Without the touching, without anything else? I think I would like that."

She could see the rigid control in his body as he considered the scrap she had offered him in place of a Christmas feast. She wanted to offer more, but it was taking every ounce of courage she had to stand still within his embrace.

"All right, Desiree. Just kisses."

She expected him to focus on her mouth, but his lips dropped to her throat, instead.

"Ohhh." She shivered at the warmth and wetness of his lips and tongue against the tender flesh beneath her ear. He sucked just a little, and she felt her insides draw up tight. "Ohhh."

He chuckled as his mouth wandered up the slender column of her throat toward her ears. "You sound so surprised. What were you expecting?"

"Nothing like this," Desiree assured him with a gasp. "It feels…I never…"

She felt him pause. She was afraid her confession might make him stop, so she quickly said, "I like what you're doing. Very much."

His teeth caught the lobe of her ear and nibbled gently.

Desiree thought her knees were going to buckle right then and there. She laughed in delight and grabbed handfuls of Carter's shirt. One of his arms slipped around her waist and tightened, while the other remained around her shoulders. Instead of feeling imprisoned, she merely felt supported.

Now his tongue was tracing the shell of her ear, then dipping inside, before his teeth found her earlobe again. She shivered once more and realized it was becoming harder to catch her breath.

"Shouldn't I be kissing you, too?" she asked.

"In a minute," Carter rasped.

Desiree wanted to reciprocate in some way, and if he wasn't going to let her kiss him back, that left her with the option of caressing him with her hands. She felt at a distinct disadvantage. Burley hadn't been much interested in foreplay, so she didn't have any experience in arousing her partner. She wasn't sure what would please Carter. If she'd had more nerve, she would have asked him. But that was more than she could handle. She decided to experiment.

Desiree began by letting her hands slide up his back, feeling the play of muscle and sinew as she went. The sound of pleasure he made deep in his throat was all she needed to assure her that he enjoyed her touch. To her relief, although his grip on her tightened, his hands remained where they were.

His lips kissed their way across her unblemished cheek toward her mouth. He kissed one edge, then the other, then pressed his mouth lightly against hers. His tongue slid along the crease, which tickled and tingled at the same time.

"Desiree, open your mouth for me."

She felt his lips moving against hers as he spoke. She opened her mouth to answer him, but he must have thought she was responding to his request, because the instant her lips parted, his tongue slipped inside.

Desiree jerked her head away. She was panting, as though she had run a long race. And ashamed, because she had let her past fears rule once again. When Burley had kissed her like that, his tongue had thrust so hard and deep into her mouth that it had nearly gagged her.

Because she still had her hands on Carter's waist, she could feel the rigid displeasure in his body at her retreat. "I...I don't like to be kissed like that," she explained.

"What is it you don't like?"

Desiree's eyes flashed to his. She hadn't expected to be asked for details. It was too humiliating to tell the truth. ''I...I just don't like it.''

''All right,'' Carter said. ''I can accept that you don't like being kissed openmouthed.''

Desiree sagged with relief in his arms.

That is, until he continued, ''But I do like it. So, if I can't kiss you like that, you'll have to kiss me.''

''Like that?'' Desiree asked. ''You mean putting my tongue in your mouth?''

He laugh ruefully. ''Not all at once. A little bit at a time.''

Desiree cocked her head skeptically. ''Are you sure you'll like it?''

His husky laugh was infectious. ''I'm sure.''

''What if I do it wrong?''

''There isn't any right or wrong. Just what feels good to you.''

''If I just concentrate on my own feelings, how will I know you're enjoying yourself?'' she asked with asperity.

''Don't worry,'' he assured her. ''I'm sure I'll manage fine.''

Desiree knew there was a catch somewhere in his reasoning, but she was so intrigued by the idea of being the one in control of the kiss that she was willing to go along with his plan. Her hand crept up to circle his neck and angle his head down for her kiss. He bent to her, and she pressed her lips against his. To her surprise, he kept his lips sealed.

She settled back on her heels and looked at him in consternation. ''I thought you wanted me to kiss you.''

''I do.''

''Then why didn't you open your mouth?''

''You didn't open yours.''

''How do you know that?''

''Well, did you?''

She grimaced. ''All right. Let's try this again.'' Desiree put her hands flat against Carter's chest and rose on her toes to reach his mouth, careful to keep her lips parted. When they touched, she let her tongue slip into his mouth. A shiver shot down her spine. She retreated and looked up at him through lowered lashes. His lips were damp where they had kissed.

''Again?'' she asked.

He nodded.

This time, she leaned her body into his so her breasts brushed against his chest. She threaded both hands into his hair and used her hold to tug his head down so she could reach his mouth. His lips were sealed again. She ran her tongue along the seam of his lips, as he had done with her. His lips parted. Tentatively she slipped her tongue into his mouth.

He groaned, a purely male sound of satisfaction.

She waited for him to take control of the kiss from her, to thrust his tongue in her mouth. But he held himself still. He left the seduction to her.

Heady with a sense of feminine power, she used her tongue to taste him, to feel his teeth and the roof of his mouth and his rough tongue. She heard his ragged breathing and knew he was aroused by what she was doing to him. What amazed her was the fact that she was equally aroused by the intimate kisses.

She withdrew her tongue and nibbled on his lower lip. His hands clutched her more tightly, but he didn't make a move toward her breasts or bottom. He exercised a rigid control on himself that gave her the confidence to continue her experiment.

''Desiree.''

''What, Carter?''

''You're killing me.''

''You want me to stop?''

''Hell, no! But let me kiss you back. Please.''

Desiree thought about it a moment. ''No. Not yet.''

She watched his Adam's apple bob as he swallowed hard.

''All right,'' he said. ''I'm putty in your hands.''

Desiree grinned. The rock hard muscles in his shoulders were anything but malleable. But his mouth, as she touched it with her own, was as soft as she could wish.

As she practiced kissing him, using her tongue to tease and taste him, she was able to think less about what she was doing and more about what she was feeling. Soon her breathing was as ragged as his, her body hot and achy with need. She had kept herself separated from Carter from the waist down, not wishing to incite him to anything more than the kisses she had promised. But the instinctive need to arch her body into his became too hard to resist.

She knew the instant her belly brushed against the ridge in his jeans that she had made a mistake. The harsh, ragged sound he made was as wild as anything she had ever heard. She knew she should withdraw, but the teasing heat of him drew her back, and she rubbed herself against him, liking the feeling that streaked from her belly to her breasts to her brain.

It took her a moment to realize that his tongue was in her mouth. And that she craved having it there. He withdrew and penetrated again, mimicking the sexual act with his mouth and tongue.

Desiree had never felt anything so erotic in her entire life. She heard a guttural sound and realized it had come from her own throat. It was a sound of primitive animal need. It scared the hell out of her.

She tore herself from Carter's arms and stumbled back a step or two. She stared at him wide-eyed, panting to catch her breath, her body shuddering with unfulfilled need, her breasts swollen and aching to be touched.

''Desiree?''

Just that one word, said in a voice that demanded her attention like pebbles thrown at a windowpane. It was a plea. It was a prayer. It was an invitation she found hard to resist.

She knew, deep in her soul, that with Carter things were going to be different. After all, she had never felt anything with Burley like she had just experienced with Carter. But what if, when he bedded her, she stiffened and froze? What if she was dry inside as she had been with Burley? What if sex with Carter hurt her and disappointed him?

The risks were too great, and the rewards too uncertain. She had offered a kiss, and he had accepted. It wasn't her fault things had gotten out of hand. Well, not *all* her fault.

''I think that's enough for now.'' She waited with her weight balanced on the balls of her feet, her hands clenched into fists, ready to flee—or fight—if he sought more from her.

''All right, Desiree. I guess I'll be heading off to bed. It's bound to be an early morning if Nicole is anything like…''

''Like your daughter?''

He swallowed hard and nodded.

''Good night, Carter.''

He didn't say anything more, just whirled on his bootheels and left the kitchen. She heard his heavy tread on the stairs and his muffled steps as he headed down the carpeted hall to his bedroom.

Desiree heaved a sigh of relief, followed by a groan of dissatisfaction. If only she had been able to follow through on what she had started, she might be lying in Carter's arms right now. She was certain the experience would be nothing like it had been with Burley. The little bit of kissing she had done with Carter had been a mistake, because now she would want more. And so would he.

She didn't want to admit it, but anything that tied her more closely to Carter was important because of the confrontation she knew was coming. That might mean swallowing her fear and submitting to Carter's desire—although even that thought did not seem so horrid as it once had.

It took Desiree a long time to fall asleep that night. Her dreams were all of a chestnut-haired man with broad shoulders and narrow hips who held her close and made tempestuous, passionate—but always gentle—love to her.

Desiree was still half-aroused when she awoke to the sound of her daughter's laughter drifting up the stairs. It was followed by a masculine rumble. She hurried to throw on her robe and stuff her feet into her slippers. She practically ran down the stairs and moments later entered the parlor, where she found Carter and Nicole sitting cross-legged beside the Christmas tree.

A fire crackled in the fireplace, and snowflakes drifted lazily down outside the picture window. The decorative lights on the tree sparkled, and there were dozens of presents under the tree—many more than had been there when she had gone to bed last night.

''Mommy! Santa Claus came!'' Nicole scrambled up and headed toward her on the run.

Desiree caught her daughter and swung her up into her arms. She carried Nicole back to where Carter still sat beside the tree. ''Where did all these presents come from?''

''Santa Claus!'' Nicole said. ''He came! He came!''

Desiree tried to get Carter to meet her gaze, but he was already reaching for a present. Nicole struggled to be put down, and Desiree slid her down until her feet hit the floor. Nicole reached Carter in three hops and bounced down into his lap.

Desiree saw him stiffen only slightly before he accepted Nicole's closeness.

"Can we open presents now, Mommy?"

"I guess so."

Desiree started to sit on the couch, but Carter patted the braided rug beside him and said, "You don't want to be way over there. Come sit beside us."

"Yeah, Mommy. Come sit beside us."

Desiree raised a brow at the "us" but couldn't resist the invitation. "Sure." She settled cross-legged beside them and waited with as much excitement as Nicole while her daughter picked up one of the presents that had miraculously appeared under the tree overnight and shook it.

"Legos, Mommy! Legos!"

"How do you know?" Desiree asked with a grin.

By then Nicole had torn the paper off, revealing the Legos she had identified by sound.

While Nicole oohed and aahed over her present, Carter handed Desiree a box with a big red bow. "Here's one for you."

"Look at all these presents! Carter, you shouldn't have!"

"What shouldn't Carter have done, Mommy?" Nicole asked.

Desiree had maintained the illusion of Santa Claus for her daughter because she believed it was a harmless fiction. So she hesitated before chastising Carter for buying so many gifts that as far as her daughter knew had all come from Santa Claus. Carter must have spent a fortune! Desiree was certain it was money he didn't have, which made his gesture all the more touching.

"Uh...Carter shouldn't have given me a present to open before you finished opening yours," Desiree said, improvising.

"I'm done now, Mommy. Open yours!"

From the look on his face, Carter was enjoying himself. After the things he had told her about his daughter, Desiree was glad he was able to bring himself to share this Christmas morning with them. It would be churlish for her to diminish what he had done by making an issue of the money he must have spent. She gave Carter a timid smile and began ripping the paper off her gift.

Her mouth split wide in a grin of delight. ''How did you know I wanted this?'' She held up the bulky knit sweater against herself and ran her hands over the sections of the bodice where different textures—leather and fur and feathers—had been woven into the sandy beige garment to give it an earthy look.

''I have to confess I asked my grandmother.''

''How did Maddy know? I'm sure I never said anything to her about this sweater.''

''I believe she heard about it from one of the ladies at church.''

''Thank you,'' Desiree said with a shy smile.

Nicole had already helped herself to another present. ''Look, Mommy!'' It was a furry stuffed animal, a black cat with white paws that looked remarkably like Boots. ''My very own kitten.''

Nicole hugged the cat. ''You open one, Daddy.''

The color bleached from Carter's face. His smile disappeared, and a muscle jerked in his cheek as he clenched his teeth.

''Daddy?''

Desiree quickly scooped Nicole out of Carter's lap and into hers. She wasn't sure what to say. Apparently Nicole's innocent slip had reminded him of his child. She recognized his distress but was helpless to ease it.

''Carter?''

An instant later he was on his feet. ''I need a cup of coffee. You two go on without me.'' He was gone from the room before Desiree had a chance to ask him to stay.

''What's the matter with Daddy?'' Nicole asked.

Trust the child to know that all wasn't as it should be. Desiree was left with the unpleasant task of providing an answer that would appease her daughter. ''I guess he just needs a cup of coffee.''

''But we're opening presents!'' Nicole protested. ''He should be here.'' She rose with the evident intent of following Carter into the kitchen. Before she got very far they heard the back door open and close. Nicole ran into the kitchen. Desiree followed her.

''Where is Daddy going?'' Nicole asked.

''I don't know, darling.''

''When is he coming back?''

''I don't know.''

"I want to open my presents," Nicole said. "Do we have to wait for Daddy to come back?"

Desiree felt a surge of anger that Carter should have left so abruptly without a word of explanation, and on Christmas morning! Running away wouldn't ease his pain, only postpone it. She and Nicole would still be here when he came back. If he came back. Desiree shoved a hand through her hair in frustration. She had been as much caught off guard as Carter was by Nicole's ready acceptance of him as her father. They should have realized what Nicole's reaction was likely to be. Nicole knew nothing about Burley, so there was no male figure to whom she had previously given her affection.

And after all, Nicole *had* asked for a daddy for Christmas, and Carter *had* conveniently appeared.

Nicole tugged at her sleeve. "Mommy?"

"I don't think Carter will mind if we go ahead without him. We can show him all our gifts when he comes back. How does that sound?"

"Okay!" Nicole said. She raced back to the parlor.

Desiree stared out the kitchen window and saw the tread marks left in the snow by Carter's pickup. "He will come back," she murmured to herself.

Meanwhile, Carter had driven hell-for-leather several miles from the ranch before he calmed down enough to realize how badly he had acted. He pulled to the side of the road and stopped the truck. His head fell forward to the steering wheel, and he groaned.

"What have I done? What am I doing here?"

He had only been fooling himself to think he would be able to ignore having a five-year-old child in the house. From the very first day, Nicole had made it plain she expected him to be a father to her.

What amazed and appalled him was how quickly she had slipped past the walls he had set up to keep himself from caring—to keep himself from being hurt again. When Nicole had called him "Daddy," it had set off all those painful memories of Christmases with his daughter, along with a feeling of bitter regret that his child was dead. Far worse, it had brought a lump of feeling to his throat to find himself adopted by the fatherless little girl in his arms.

He had glanced at Desiree and seen the pity—and sympathy—in

her eyes. And felt ashamed that he wasn't able to handle the situation better. After all, she was willing to try marriage—and intimacy—again even though it was clear she had suffered at her husband's hands. She was dealing with her demons. Could he do less?

His feelings were complicated by the fact he had always wanted children, and Nicole was an adorable child. Nevertheless, it wouldn't be easy to play the role of father. He grimaced. It was no more difficult for him to be a father, than for Desiree to play the role of wife.

Carter didn't choose to examine his feelings for Desiree too closely. For now it was enough that he desired her, that he admired her courage and that she was the mother of the child who wanted him to be her father. Putting down roots meant having a family. He had the start of that family with Desiree and Nicole. He would be a fool not to embrace them both.

He twisted the key and turned the truck around.

They were still opening presents twenty minutes later when Carter reappeared. He stood in the parlor doorway with what could only be described as a sheepish look on his face.

"Did I miss anything?"

Desiree was too astonished that he had returned so quickly to speak. Nicole more than made up for her silence.

"Daddy! Daddy! Look what I got!"

Desiree thought for a moment he was going to run again. Though his face blanched and his jaw tightened, he stood his ground as Nicole came barreling toward him. He scooped her up and balanced her in the crook of his arm as she babbled on about the Raggedy Ann doll and the Teenage Mutant Ninja Turtle puzzle and the game of Chutes and Ladders she had gotten from Santa Claus.

"You'll never guess what Santa Claus brought Mommy!" she exclaimed.

"What?" Carter asked.

"A teeny tiny nightgown! And you can see right through it!"

Carter grinned. "You don't say!"

Desiree felt herself flush to the roots of her hair. She hadn't realized how revealing the negligee was until she held it up to look at it. She had quickly stuffed it back into the box, but not before Nicole had gotten a look at it.

''Are you going to open your presents now, Daddy?''

Desiree saw the mixed feelings that flashed across his face.

''There are presents for me?''

''Uh-huh.'' Nicole held up three fingers, then put one down. ''Two of them.''

''Guess I'd better open them and see what I got.''

He carried Nicole back over to the tree. He held on to her when he sat down cross-legged, so she was once more sitting in his lap. Desiree couldn't help but wonder what had caused Carter's acceptance of a situation she knew was painful for him.

She watched with bated breath as Carter opened the present she had bought for him. She breathed a sigh of relief when she saw the pleasure on his face as he caught sight of the Western leather boots.

''These are beautiful,'' he said as he reverently ran his fingers across the tooled brown leather. ''You shouldn't have. I can imagine these set you back a pretty penny.''

''I wanted to get them for you,'' Desiree said to keep him from focusing on the cost of the boots. They were expensive, but she had seen how the heels and toes, not to mention the soles, were worn on his boots. If he could have afforded to replace them, she knew he would have. She didn't want him focusing on the difference in their financial situations. She knew he hadn't married her for her money. Her land, yes. But not her money.

''Open the other one,'' Nicole urged as she handed it to him. ''This one's from me,'' she confided. ''For my new daddy.''

Desiree saw Carter's hesitation. He slowly unwrapped the gift.

Before he had the paper half off Nicole blurted, ''It's a book. So you can read stories to me at bedtime.''

Carter finished upwrapping the present and fingered the embossed illustration on the cover. ''It's a wonderful gift, Nicky.''

''My name isn't Nicky. It's Nicole.''

''Would you mind if I shortened it, sort of like a special nickname?'' Carter asked.

Nicole wrinkled her nose, then eyed Carter sideways. ''Will that make me your little girl for real and always?''

A sudden thickness appeared in Desiree's throat. Tears blurred her eyes and made her nose burn. She waited to hear what Carter would answer.

"It makes you mine, Nicky. Now and always."

"All right," Nicole said. "You can call me Nicky." She turned to her mother. "Daddy's going to call me Nicky. You can call me Nicky, too."

"All right, Nico—Nicky. If that's what you want." Desiree fought back the sudden spurt of jealousy she felt. She had wanted Nicole to have a father, but she hadn't realized at the time what that would mean. She no longer had her daughter all to herself.

Nicole was looking at Carter with what could only be described as worship. It remained to be seen how long her daughter's adoration would last.

Desiree stood and reached over to grasp Nicole's hands and pull her to her feet. "Now that all the presents are opened, I'd like some time to talk to Carter alone. Why don't you take a few of your things upstairs and play for a while?"

"All right, Mommy. Will you come read to me later, Daddy?"

"Sure, Nicky."

When the little girl was gone, Desiree paced away from Carter to stare out the window at the snow, which was now blowing sideways. "Where did you go?"

She was startled when his voice came from right behind her.

"Five miles down the road. It took me that long to realize it was foolish to run away from what I've been searching for all my life."

Desiree whirled to face him. She probed his blue eyes, looking for some kind of proof that she and Nicole were that important to him. "I know it must have been hard to have Nicole call you Daddy."

He nodded.

"Thank you for giving her the chance to have a father."

"I want us to be a family," Carter said in a fierce voice. "I want us to be happy together. I want to forget the past."

But it was clear from the agitation in his voice that though he might choose not to remember the past, he hadn't forgotten it. Not by a long shot.

Desiree knew she ought to take advantage of this moment to tell him the secret she had been keeping from him. But she didn't want to spoil the moment. He was offering to start over with her. She so much wanted this marriage to work!

"I want what you want, Carter," she admitted.

But her arms remained folded defensively across her chest.

He reached for her wrists and pulled her arms around his waist. He circled her shoulders so she found herself captured in his strong embrace. She waited for the fear to rise. It was marvelously absent. But she wasn't entirely comfortable, either. There was a tension, an expectation, an awareness that arced between them. She waited for Carter to act on it, to make a sexual overture.

Instead he stepped back from her and took her hands in his. She looked up at him and found his lips curled into a smile, his blue eyes twinkling with amusement.

"So you can see right through that nightgown. I can hardly wait!"

Desiree yanked her hands from his and perched them on her hips. "How could you give me a gift like that and not warn me about it? I was never so embarrassed in my life as when Nicole started asking me questions about it."

"What did you tell her, I wonder?" Carter said as his smile broadened to a grin.

Desiree felt the heat in her face. "That it was meant to be worn with a robe," she snapped.

Carter laughed, a sound that came up from his belly and rumbled past his chest. "When am I going to get to see it?"

"In your dreams, Prescott," she said. "In your dreams!"

"I'm sure they'll be sweet ones," he called to her retreating back.

Six

"Do you want to go?" Carter asked.

"I'm not sure we can," Desiree replied across the breakfast table. "I don't know whether I can get a baby-sitter on such short notice. Especially when tonight is New Year's Eve."

Desiree knew she was being contrary, but she couldn't help it. Ever since Carter had walked out on Christmas morning, she had worried that he would do it again. Even though he had returned, the trust she had been willing to give him without question when they married was qualified now. Her anxiety wasn't unjustified.

Carter hadn't disappeared without a word over the past week, but he had begun making forays around the ranch by himself, getting the lay of the land and looking the place over. He hadn't reissued the invitation he had made the day they were married to survey the ranch together.

Desiree suspected he needed the time alone to come to terms with his new responsibilities as husband and father—although they were more *father* than *husband* so far. To her chagrin, Desiree realized she very much wanted to make the effort to become Carter's wife in every sense of the word. Only she wasn't sure how to let him know.

Attending a New Year's Eve party at Faron and Belinda Whitelaw's home would be their first outing as husband and wife. The truth was, she wanted to go. But she was worried about leaving Nicole home alone with a baby-sitter. Burley was due to be released from prison today. There was no reason to believe he would head straight for Casper—except the threats he had made six years ago.

I'm coming back, Desiree. Then I'll finish what I started.

Desiree felt cold all over. She hadn't forgotten the last night she had spent with Burley in this house. It was something she had been trying to forget. Maybe it wasn't such a bad idea to be gone from here tonight. But she wanted Nicole where she could keep an eye on her.

"I suppose we could take Nicole with us," Desiree mused. "She could sleep upstairs at The Castle. I've done that in the past when I couldn't find a sitter."

"Great!" Carter said.

"Why are you so anxious to go to this party?" Desiree asked.

"I thought it was about time we did some socializing with our neighbors. Besides, it's a wedding celebration for my half brother, Faron. He and Belinda were married at home on Christmas, with just their families present."

"You're family. Why weren't you invited to the wedding?"

He shrugged. "I was, but I decided not to go."

"Were you worried that they might be upset at how quickly you married me?"

"Not at all. It's just that Faron and I may be related, but really, we don't know each other."

Desiree's lips curled into a wry smile. "The same thing could be said about us."

"Yeah, but I'm planning to spend the rest of my life with you."

Desiree hoped so. But she had her doubts about what Carter would do when he knew the truth about why she had married him.

When she had ruthlessly sought out a man to marry, she had done so because when Burley got out of prison and came hunting her she wanted her ex-husband to see that she had committed herself to someone else, that there was no sense in his pursuing her any longer. Now she admitted to herself that she had expected to get something else out of the bargain: actual physical protection if Burley got violent.

Desiree could see how her fear and desperation had led her to expect unrealistic things from marriage to Carter. Instead of being put off by the presence of another man, Burley was just as likely to become insanely jealous. It had happened before. And she knew that instead of being around to protect her, Carter might very well be off on one of his lonely jaunts around the ranch.

Which meant she had to be ready to protect herself and her daughter. She couldn't get a protective order to keep Burley away from her until he had actually done something that constituted a crime under the law. She would have to wait for Burley to make the first move. And hope she was still alive to apply to the court for succor.

There was another option.

She could confess the whole situation to Carter and ask for his help in confronting Burley when he showed up. She felt certain Carter would offer his assistance if he knew the situation she was in. But she had her own reasons for wanting to keep her secret as long as she could.

Ever since Christmas Eve, when she had stood in Carter's arms kissing him, the belief had been growing that maybe she wasn't as frigid as Burley had always accused her of being. She had thought and thought about her reaction to Carter's kisses, about her feelings when kissing him, and she had come to the conclusion that however much a failure she had been with Burley in bed, the same thing wouldn't happen with Carter.

Desiree wasn't sure what made the difference with Carter. She didn't think it was a simple matter of her feelings toward the two men. After all, she had been head over heels in love with Burley and sex with him had been a disaster. She wasn't sure exactly what she felt for Carter, but she knew it couldn't be love. Respect, maybe, and liking, but no more than that. After all, they were still virtual strangers.

Once the idea of making love to Carter caught hold, however, she couldn't let it go. She fantasized about what it would be like to touch him, to have him touch her, for the two of them to be joined as one. Since she couldn't be sure what Carter's reaction would be when he found out the truth about why she had married him, she had to act soon or perhaps lose the chance of knowing what it meant to make love to a man.

Maybe it wasn't fair to use Carter like that, but Desiree had gotten the distinct impression that he wouldn't find making love to her a hardship. They would both benefit, and she couldn't see the harm to either of them in her plan.

Only…time was running out. If she was going to seduce Carter, there could be no better opportunity than after the party tonight. It would be the beginning of a new year, a nostalgic time, to say the least. She would make sure Carter had a drink or two to relax him and would stay very close when they danced. And she would wear the silky black negligee he had given her for Christmas. Further than that, her thoughts would not go.

''So we're agreed?'' Carter said. ''We'll go to the party?''

Desiree nodded. ''I'll call Belinda so she can arrange a guest bedroom for Nicole.''

Desiree wasn't sure what to expect from her friends and neighbors at the Whitelaws' New Year's Eve party, but she was pleased by how cordially they greeted Carter when she introduced him as her husband.

Carter's grandmother, Madelyn, made a special point of introducing one young woman to Carter. ''This is Belinda's sister, Fiona Conner,'' she said. ''I'm disappointed you two didn't get a chance to meet sooner.''

Unspoken were the words *Before you married Desiree.*

Desiree felt an unwelcome stab of jealousy as the petite blond gave Carter an assessing look. She immediately forgave Fiona when the young woman grinned at her and said, ''Maddy tells me she had Carter all picked out for me, so I'm glad you two found each other. You've saved me from Maddy's matchmaking.''

''It was my pleasure,'' Desiree said, linking her arm possessively through Carter's. She was aware of how lovely the young woman was. There was no scar to mar her beautiful face.

Carter put his hand over hers where it rested on his arm. ''I'm happy with the choice I made,'' he told his grandmother. ''Although I can't say that if things had turned out differently, I wouldn't have enjoyed getting a chance to know you,'' he gallantly said to Fiona.

''It wouldn't have worked out between you and Fiona, anyway,'' Madelyn said with a sigh.

''Why not?'' Desiree asked, her curiosity piqued.

''Fiona has a cat.''

Desiree exchanged a look with Carter, and they burst out laughing.

''If you ladies will excuse us, I'd like to dance with my wife,''

Carter said. ''I'm not bad at matchmaking myself,'' he said with a wink at Madelyn.

Desiree was flustered but pleased by Carter's obvious preference for her company. She was delighted to be dancing with him because it fit into her plans of seduction so well.

A half hour later, Desiree wondered who was seducing whom. She had started by letting her fingers thread into the curls at Carter's nape and gotten all the response she could have hoped for when he drew her closer into his arms. He had let his hand drift down past her waist to the dimpled area above her buttocks and slipped his leg between hers, so she could feel his arousal. It was enough to make her weak in the knees.

His cheek was pressed close to hers—the unblemished one, of course—and his teeth nibbled on her earlobe.

''I've had a wonderful time meeting all your neighbors,'' he said as he backed away to look at her.

''They like you,'' she replied.

Desiree was warmed by the desire in Carter's eyes—even though his gaze avoided her scar. She could forgive him that. It wasn't easy to face herself in the mirror each morning, so she knew what it must be like for him. At least there was no obvious distaste apparent on his face when he looked at her.

She mentally pledged to be a good wife to Carter, to trust him, and—after the night was through—to reveal the secret she had kept from him.

''Listen up, everybody!'' Faron said. When those gathered for the party were quiet, he said, ''It's time to count down the last seconds to the new year. Ten. Nine. Eight.''

''Seven. Six. Five,'' everyone chanted.

Desiree looked into Carter's eyes as she counted with him, ''Four. Three. Two.''

''One,'' Carter said. ''Happy New Year, Desiree.''

''Happy New Year, Carter.''

''I think this is where we're supposed to kiss,'' he said as he looked around the room at the couples caught up in the celebration of the moment.

''I guess it is. Shall we join them?''

Apparently her invitation was the only thing holding Carter back, because he tightened his arms around her and sought out her lips with his. She felt the pressure of his mouth against hers and realized it wasn't enough. Her tongue slipped out and teased the seam of his lips. She felt his smile as he opened his mouth to her. Then she was opening her mouth to him, and the thrust and parry that followed was as erotic a dance as anything Salome might have managed with all her seven veils.

When they broke the kiss at last, they stared, stunned, into each other's eyes.

He was panting.

So was she.

"Let's go home," Carter said. "I'd like to start the new year together—with you in my bed."

Desiree blushed at his forthrightness. But his wishes were very much in accord with her own. "I'll go upstairs and get Nicole."

He put out a hand to stop her. "I asked Maddy if she would keep Nicky overnight. She told me Nicky had stayed with her before, and that she'd be glad to have her."

"But—"

"I told her I'd have to check with you first to make sure it was all right."

Desiree debated only a second before she said, "Tell Maddy I'm thankful for the offer. I'd like to check on Nicole before we go."

"I'll wait down here for you," Carter said.

During the ride home, Desiree chattered like Nicole, talking about how much fun the party had been and how she hoped they could invite some of their neighbors over for supper soon. Carter was silent except for a grunt of assent every so often to let her know he was listening.

Deep down, Desiree harbored the fear that Burley might somehow have already made his way to the Rimrock. So it was with a tremendous sense of relief that she observed when they entered the house that everything appeared untouched. She toed off her fur-lined boots and left them in the pantry along with her coat. Then she stepped into the terry-cloth slippers she had left there when she put on her boots. Carter followed suit, leaving his boots and shearling coat beside hers and heading upstairs in his stocking feet.

''Everything looks exactly as we left it,'' she said as they passed through the kitchen and into the hall.

Carter gave her a look askance. ''You were expecting Santa's elves to come through and change things around?''

Desiree laughed nervously. ''Of course not. I just... Never mind.''

Carter grasped her hand and started upstairs with her. ''Let's go to bed.''

There was a wealth of meaning in those words. He stopped upstairs outside her closed bedroom door. ''Your room or mine?''

''Yours,'' Desiree said. Her bedroom held too many awful memories.

Once she arrived at Carter's door she stopped. Even though she had made up her mind to make love to him, she couldn't help feeling afraid.

It was a sign of how attuned Carter was to her in just the little time they had been married that he asked, ''Are you sure you want to go through with this?''

''Yes,'' Desiree said. But the word came out as a hoarse croak. She stared into Carter's eyes, warmed by the glow of desire burning there. In the next instant, he had swept her off her feet and into his arms. She laughed nervously.

''You're safe with me, Desiree,'' he said as he stepped through the doorway and into his bedroom.

Desiree couldn't have asked for more than that.

Carter had left the lamp burning beside the bed, and it cast the room in shadows. He had already shoved the door closed behind them with his foot, when she realized she had forgotten something. ''I wanted to wear my new negligee for you.''

Carter grinned. ''I'm not saying I don't want to see you in it sometime, but I think it would be wasted tonight.''

Desiree stood uncomfortably by the door where he had set her down, as he left her and crossed to the bed to pull down the quilt and sheet. Then he crossed back to stand before her.

''Does this feel as awkward to you as it does to me?'' Desiree asked with a shy smile.

''I don't know how you feel,'' Carter replied, ''but this has been the longest three weeks of my life.''

Desiree gave a startled laugh. "We've only been married for two."

"I've wanted you since the night I met you, since the moment you came downstairs and I saw you for the first time without that awful moth-eaten coat."

"But my face—"

"Has a terrible scar. I know." He gently removed her hand from where it had crept to cover her cheek. "There's more to you than your face, Desiree. You're a beautiful woman."

But even as he said the words, he was avoiding her scar with his eyes.

Desiree noticed there had been no words of love spoken. But, then, she hadn't expected them. They had met and married under unusual circumstances and had known each other too briefly for stronger feelings to grow between them. The desires of the flesh did not need love or commitment to flourish. The animal instinct to couple and reproduce was bred deep. They could want without loving.

And she did want Carter. Her need grew as his fingertips followed where his eyes led, across the shoulders of her knit dress and lower where the flesh was exposed along her collarbone, then down along the line of buttons between her breasts to her belly, before they fanned out to circle her hips.

"Come here," he murmured as he pulled her toward him. A moment later their bodies were flush from waist to thigh.

Desiree stiffened reflexively at the intimate contact. She closed her eyes, caught her lower lip in her teeth and forced herself to relax. This wasn't Burley. This was Carter. When she opened her eyes, Carter was staring down at her.

Carter realized suddenly how important it was for him to keep a firm grip on his desire. He didn't want to frighten Desiree. And yet he did not feel in control when he was near her. The scent of her, the taste of her, had him hard and ready. He took a deep breath and slowly let it out in an attempt to steady his pounding pulse.

"I can stop anytime you want," he said. "Anytime."

Desiree lifted a disbelieving brow. "Anytime?"

"Anytime. There's no such thing as a point of no return," Carter said. "That's an old wives' tale. A man can stop. It might not be pleasant. But he can stop."

Desiree felt tears welling in her eyes. ''I wish—''

''Shh.'' He put a callused fingertip to her lips. ''No looking backward. There's only tonight. Just you and me. I don't want anyone else in this bedroom with us.''

She nodded.

He kissed her eyes closed, then let his lips drift downward toward her mouth. Desiree could feel the tension in his back and arms, the raging passion leashed by consideration for her fear. It wasn't fair, Desiree thought, that the man she had loved should have been so brutal, and this stranger so tender.

''Desiree?''

''Don't stop,'' she whispered.

Slowly, one at a time, he undid the buttons of her navy knit dress. She heard his murmur of approval as he revealed the black lace camisole she had worn, contemplating just such a moment. He slid the dress over her shoulders and freed her arms before shoving it down over her hips until it landed in a circle around her feet. She was left wearing only her camisole and tap pants.

Goose bumps rose on her skin.

''You're cold,'' he said as he enfolded her in his arms.

''You have on too many clothes,'' she replied, forcing him away far enough that she could reach the buttons on his shirt. Her hands were trembling, but it wasn't from the cold. Carter smiled and made short work of his buttons, letting the shirt slide down his arms. She pushed his long john shirt up and he pulled it off over his head.

At the sight of his bare chest she paused. He was so different from Burley. There was a small triangle of black curls at the center of his chest and a thin line of black down that headed past his navel. He took her hands and laid them on his chest.

''Touch me, Desiree.''

It was easier than she had thought it would be to let her hands roam at will over the firm muscles of his chest. To her amazement, his nipples hardened into peaks as her fingertips brushed across them.

Carter's hands were moving in a mirror image of her own and she felt a corresponding response in her body.

''That feels wonderful,'' Desiree said breathlessly.

''You can say that again,'' Carter muttered as Desiree's hands tensed down across his belly. He slid his hands down to cup the warmth between her legs.

"That feels wonderful." Desiree was in a state of euphoria, reveling in the powerful feelings he evoked.

Carter lowered the straps on the camisole. It caught for an instant on the tips of her breasts before slipping to her waist. He shoved it down along with her tap pants.

She immediately crossed her arms over her breasts and belly to cover her nakedness.

He laughed. "What are you hiding?"

She resisted momentarily when he grasped her wrists to remove her hands, but realized she was only postponing the inevitable.

He gasped when he saw what she had been trying to conceal from him. "What the hell?"

His eyes sought hers, asking questions, demanding answers. "I wasn't going to ask how your face got cut," he said in a voice roughened by emotion. "But I don't think I can keep quiet about the rest of these scars."

She flinched when his hand reached out to the faint, criss-cross scars on her breasts. She hissed in a breath as his fingertips followed the long slash that arced down her belly.

"I was attacked," she said.

"By a man," he concluded. "Which explains why you jump every time I come up behind you. Lord, Desiree, why didn't you tell me?"

She hung her head, knowing she should tell him now about Burley. He had given her the perfect opening to do so. But she couldn't. He would be disgusted with her. And this evening would be at an end. If it wasn't already.

"I know they're ugly to look at," she began.

"Nothing about you is ugly," Carter retorted fiercely.

Not even my face? she wanted to ask. She looked up to find out whether he was telling the truth. His eyes touched her body like hands, searching out her secrets. She kept waiting for his disgust—or her fear—to rise and spoil what was happening between them, but it never came. All she saw in his eyes was admiration, adoration.

"Come to bed, Desiree." Carter took her hand and drew her toward the bed. She knew he could feel her reluctance, because he paused.

"Have you changed your mind?"

She shook her head. "Unless you have."

He shook his head. "Is there something else you need?"

"I want to leave the light on." That would mean he would have to face her scars, but she hoped maybe she wouldn't encounter so many demons of the past if she kept the dark at bay.

He smiled. "That's fine with me."

Carter picked her up again and laid her on the bed, then rid himself of his trousers, long underwear and socks and joined her there. Desiree had already pulled the sheets up to her neck because she felt so self-conscious about her scars.

Carter slipped right under the covers with her and drew her into his arms so their bodies were aligned. They fit as though they were meant to be together, breast and thigh and belly. She could feel his heat and the hardness of his shaft against her thigh.

Her greatest fear was that now that they were in bed together he would satisfy his need and leave her wanting, as Burley had done so often.

She couldn't have been more wrong.

He went back to kissing her, concentrating on her mouth and neck and shoulders until she was undulating beneath him. His hands sought out places on her body she hadn't guessed could be so sensitive, making her arch toward his touch.

But she knew it was taking too long for her to become aroused. She could feel the rigid tension in his shoulders, the hard muscles of his thighs. She knew he was ready. He must be impatient to get it over with.

"I...I'm ready now," she told him. She wanted to please him. She wanted him to want to do this again. So she was willing to end her own pleasure so he could find his.

Carter's hand slid down her belly to the nest of curls between her legs. He slid a finger inside, but it didn't penetrate easily.

"I don't think so," he said. "I think maybe you need some more of this." His mouth slid down from her shoulder to her breast, where he circled her nipple with his tongue.

Desiree gasped. "What are you doing?"

"Kissing you."

"There?"

She saw the moment of shock on his face before he asked, "Your husband never kissed your breasts?"

Desiree was totally mortified. Her face turned pink. She shook her head. "No," she breathed. "He...he couldn't wait for...for the other."

Carter swore under his breath.

She shrank back against the bedding.

"Desiree, honey, I'm not angry with you. Honey, please...let me love you."

Desiree eyed him warily. "You...you want to kiss my breasts?"

A roguish grin tilted his lips. "Uh-huh."

"It did feel...kind of nice," she admitted shyly. She lay back against the pillow, but her whole body was tensed.

"Relax," he crooned. His mouth caught hers in a swift kiss, and while she was still enjoying its effects, he swept lower and captured her nipple with his mouth. He teased, he sucked, he nipped. Desiree felt things she hadn't even imagined were possible.

"I feel...I feel..."

"What do you feel?" Carter rasped.

"Everything. I can feel *everything!*" Desiree exulted. She wasn't even close to frigid. Far from it. With Carter, her whole body was burning with sensual desire.

Carter's tenderness soon gave way to ardor and became an unquenchable hunger.

"Carter," she begged. "Now!"

Once again, his hand slid down her belly, into the nest of curls, finding another spot she hadn't even been aware existed.

"Oh! Oh, my!" The pleasure was so intense she felt the urge to escape as much as the urge to lie still so he could keep on with whatever it was he was doing. She had done some reading since her divorce from Burley, but words in a book couldn't do justice to what she was experiencing.

"So you think you're ready now," he said in a husky voice.

"Yesss," she hissed.

He pressed a finger inside her, and it slid easily into the moist passage. She recognized the difference between this time and the last, and realized Carter had taken the time to be sure she was aroused.

She knew he had recognized her readiness when he used his knees to spread her legs and placed himself above her. She put her hands at his waist and looked into his eyes.

"It's all right, Desiree. We have all the time in the world."

She clenched her muscles in readiness for the pain she expected. But Carter didn't thrust himself inside her as Burley had. Instead he probed slowly at the entrance to her womb, pushing a little way inside her and then backing off before intruding again. Until finally, without any pain to her—and with a great deal of self-control on his part—he was fully inside her.

It didn't hurt at all! In fact, it felt decidedly good. Her body instinctively arched upward into his.

Carter gave a grunt of pleasure.

Desiree lowered her bottom and thrust again.

Carter groaned.

"Am I hurting you, Carter?"

"You're killing me," Carter said with a husky laugh. "Just please don't stop!"

Desiree was delighted with the reversal of roles, but it wasn't long before Carter was doing his part to help.

With the joining of their bodies, Desiree found herself reaching out to Carter with body and soul, seeking the satisfaction that she had been denied for so long. When it happened, when her body violently convulsed, she tried to fight it.

"Come with me, love. Ride it out. Let it happen," Carter urged.

She looked up and saw the sheen of sweat that beaded his brow, the hank of damp hair that hung over his forehead, the light burning fiercely in his eyes. She could see the leashed passion waiting to erupt, held on a fraying tether. He was keeping his promise to her. Even now, she was in control.

That knowledge freed her to give rein to the passions that threatened to overwhelm her. Her body spasmed, her muscles tightening in exquisite pleasure as a groan forced its way past her throat. Carter thrust once more, arching his head back as he spilled his seed.

The best was yet to come. When they were both sated, instead of abandoning her, Carter reached out to pull her snugly into his arms, with one of his legs thrown over hers in a continuing embrace.

Desiree was breathless, embarrassed and exhilarated all at once. ''That was...wonderful,'' she said with a shaky laugh.

''That word seems to be getting a lot of use tonight,'' Carter said with chuckle.

''I don't think anything else quite describes how I'm feeling right now,'' she admitted.

She was afraid to ask him how he felt, but she didn't believe he was dissatisfied, and certainly not disgusted. She didn't want to do anything to spoil the mood. It was hard to believe this sort of ecstasy could be repeated again and again all the years of their married life.

Desiree found solace for her bruised heart in Carter's arms. All the loving, all the gentle care she would have given to Burley, she bestowed on Carter. Tonight held a promise of the future, a hope for the new year. They would be good partners—in bed and out. Unfortunately, the depth of her feelings for Carter were too treacherous to admit or even to acknowledge.

Suddenly Desiree had to escape. The embrace that had felt so comforting now made her feel captive.

''I want to get up,'' she said in a harsh voice.

Carter was already half-asleep. ''What? What's going on?'' He was irritable at being woken. ''Lie down.''

''I'm going back to my own room.''

He came fully awake and stared into her eyes. She knew the fear was back, but couldn't explain that this was different from her fear of physical harm. Burley had only beaten and terrified and humiliated her. She had given Carter the power to destroy her heart and soul.

''I need to be alone,'' she offered by way of explanation.

Carter's lips curled in disgust. ''I'm not going to turn into some kind of beast in the middle of the night. But if you want to go, go.''

Desiree yanked on a flannel shirt that Carter had left tossed over a ladderback chair and fled the room.

Carter slumped back against the pillow, then smacked it with his fist. All the love he would have given to Jeanine he had bequeathed to the woman he had lain with tonight. The emotions he had experienced as Desiree climaxed beneath him were too dangerous to explore.

He hadn't been ready to let her go when she abandoned him. He felt…a loss. But what could he have done to stop her? After all, it wasn't as though they were in love. They were only married lovers.

He reached over to turn out the light. He hoped she spent a miserable night alone. He hoped she tossed and turned the way he was sure he would himself. He hoped she had bags under her eyes in the morning the size of suitcases. He hoped—

Desiree screamed. "Carter! Come Quick!"

Carter's blood ran cold at the terror in her voice. A second later he was on his way to her.

Seven

Carter grabbed a pair of jeans, stuck his legs in them and dragged them on as he headed on the run toward Desiree. He found her standing in the doorway to her room, her eyes so wide he could see the whites of them, the back of her hand across her mouth to stifle the awful, tearing sobs that erupted from her throat.

"Desiree, are you all right? Are you hurt? What happened?"

At the sound of his voice she turned and flung herself into his arms, which tightened around her. Over the top of her head he had a view of the chaos in her bedroom.

It had been ransacked. There wasn't an object left upright or unbroken. There were feathers everywhere from the destruction of the pillows, and even her mattress had been slashed. This wasn't the work of a thief. It was the devastation of a psychopath.

"This is crazy," Carter muttered. "Why so much destruction? And why only your bedroom?"

Desiree sobbed harder in his arms. He felt a fierce need to protect her, to crush the fiend who had threatened the woman he held so tightly.

"I'll call the police."

She grabbed him around the neck. "No!"

"Why not? They'll want to investigate. Anybody crazy enough to do something like this belongs in a cage where he can't hurt people. They'll want to find him fast."

Desiree dragged herself free of his embrace. "I know who did this," she said. "But it won't do any good to confront him. He'll just deny everything. Unless I can catch him in the act, they can't do a thing. I have to have evidence," she said bitterly, "before they'll interfere."

Carter felt his stomach turn over. "Who did this, Desiree?"

Her shoulders slumped, and she turned to lean her forehead against the cool wood framing the door. "He said he would come back."

"Who said he would come back?" Carter demanded, his voice laced with the irritation he was feeling at his helplessness.

"Burley Kelton." Desiree turned to look Carter in the eye. "My former husband. I should have told you," she said in an anguished voice. "He's been in prison for attempting to murder me, but he got out today. He warned me he was coming back. I hoped—"

"You hoped that if you had a husband he would keep his distance," Carter said in a voice like a rusty gate.

What a fool he had been! She had used him.

And weren't you using her to get the roots you wanted?

That was different.

How? You both wanted something from each other. So she wasn't totally honest about her motives. Have you been totally honest with her?

The truth was, he had married for his own reasons, not thinking much about hers. The band around his chest loosened enough that he could breathe again.

"Stay here while I check the house to make sure he's gone," Carter said.

Desiree's eyes rounded again in fear. "You don't believe he could still be here, do you?"

"I'm going to find out." Carter ushered her back to his bedroom door. He turned on the light and drew her inside. "Stay here. Close the door behind me and lock it."

Carter had no weapon handy, and wondered what he would do if he encountered the other man armed with a knife. Or a gun.

But the house had an empty feeling. A quiet, thorough search revealed no signs of an intruder. The broken lock on the front door explained how Burley had gotten in.

When Carter returned to his room he knocked and said, ''It's me. Let me in.''

Desiree stood hesitantly across from him until he opened his arms. Then she flew into them once more.

''Did you find anything?'' she asked.

''Nothing. Except a broken lock on the front door.''

She gave a shuddering sigh. ''Oh, Carter. What am I going to do?''

''You mean, what are *we* going to do? First, we're going to call the police.'' Before she could protest, he added, ''He might have left some fingerprints or some other evidence.''

''Do we have to do it now?''

Carter grimaced. ''I suppose tomorrow morning is soon enough.''

''I'm so sorry I got you involved in all this,'' she said, her cheek against his chest. ''I thought if he knew I was married again, he would leave me alone.''

''I guess not,'' Carter muttered. ''So Burley is the one who mistreated you?''

She nodded. She tried to talk but couldn't manage any sound past the knot in her throat.

Carter put an arm around her shoulders and walked over to the bed with her. He sat down with his back against the headboard and pulled her onto his lap. ''I want to hear about it,'' he said.

Desiree realized Carter was almost quivering with fury. But it was all directed at the man who had harmed her.

''I was too young when I married him, and very naive. I...I put up with...everything...as long as I could. While my parents were alive, it wasn't so bad. After they were gone, his abuse got worse.

''That explains all that flinching around me, I suppose.''

She nodded, her hair tickling his chin.

''One night after dinner, I got up the courage to ask him for a divorce. He went crazy. He accused me of seeing another man. He told me he'd make sure no other man would want to have anything to do with me. He told me he'd married me 'till death do us part,' and if he couldn't have me no one could.

''We were in the kitchen, and he grabbed a butcher knife. He cut my face first.'' Her hand protectively covered the scar. ''Then he raped me.''

''Desiree—''

''Let me finish!'' she said. ''He laughed while he was carving designs on my breasts. Said he was branding me so any other man I tried to sleep with would know I belonged to him. The wound in the belly came when I told him I would never belong to him, that I was going to leave him if it was the last thing I ever did. He assured me that leaving him would be the end of me.

''If one of the ranch hands hadn't heard my screams and come running, Burley would have killed me. As it was, he escaped the house and ran. Before he left, he promised me he would come back some dark night and finish what he had started. It took six weeks before he was caught. During that time I lived in fear for my life. I left the lights on because I was afraid of the dark. I still am,'' she admitted in a whisper.

''Desiree—''

''Nine months after he raped me, Nicole was born.''

''Oh, my God,'' Carter said. ''Does Burley know about the child?''

Desiree shook her head. ''I don't know if he'll figure it out. But he has friends who could tell him I've been living here alone until recently.'' Desiree's hands snuck up around Carter's neck, where she clung for support. ''I've been so afraid he'll do something to hurt Nicole. I know I've been dishonest with you. All I can say is, I'm sorry.''

In that instant, Carter was tempted to tell her the truth about himself, that he had also married under false pretenses. But he knew now that his money wasn't what Desiree had been after when she married him. Unfortunately, over the past three weeks he had discovered that he wanted—needed—much more from her than the pleasure to be had from her body. Telling her the truth would only complicate matters right now.

''He'll be back,'' Desiree said in a whisper.

''How can you be so sure?''

''I've been through this before,'' she said. ''I was in the hospital for a short while following Burley's attack. After I came home, in the six weeks before Burley was caught, he used to leave signs that he had been around—to terrorize me, I think. Or he would call me on the phone and just breathe. He was always careful not to leave anything that could be used as evidence against him in court.''

''The police can question Burley—''

''The police have to catch Burley before they can question him,'' Desiree said with asperity. ''Burley knows this place like the back of his hand, where to hide, all the back roads.''

''So you're just going to sit here and wait for him to finish what he's started?'' Carter demanded.

''What do you suggest?'' Desiree retorted.

''Do you have a gun?''

''No! And I don't intend to get one.''

''Then how do you propose to protect yourself?''

There was a pause before she replied, ''I was counting on you for that.''

There was another pause before he answered, ''What, exactly, did you have in mind?''

''There's the chance that your presence here will be enough to deter anything like this from happening again.''

''Do you really believe that?''

''I believe Burley will keep his distance so long as you're around.'' Burley only preyed on things weaker than himself.

''That's going to make it a little difficult for things to get done around here—I mean, if we have to do everything in tandem. And what about Nicole?''

''She would have to be with us, too.''

Carter shook his head. ''It won't work.''

Desire gripped his shoulders. ''It could. What other choice do we have?''

Carter tried to come up with some other solution to the problem. But until Burley made a move, there was nothing he could do. ''All right,'' he said. ''We'll call the police and report this intrusion tomorrow morning. If they don't find anything—''

''They won't.''

''I'll go along with your plan.''

She hesitated only an instant before she said, ''Thanks, Carter. I won't be a burden, I promise.''

Nevertheless, Carter felt a tremendous burden of responsibility. She had put her safety, and Nicole's, in his hands. Once before a woman had asked him to protect her. And he had failed her…and their daughter.

''You can sleep here,'' Carter said. ''I'll be comfortable on the couch.''

''Or we could sleep here together,'' Desiree suggested tentatively.

''You sure?'' Carter asked.

''As long as I can have the right side of the bed,'' she said with a shy smile.

Carter laughed. ''Fine.''

Desiree settled on her side of the bed as Carter turned out the light. She tossed and turned for several minutes trying to get comfortable. At last, he couldn't stand it any longer. He put an arm around her waist and dragged her back against him, so her bottom spooned into his groin and his knees were tucked behind hers. Her head fit just under his chin, and her flyaway hair tickled his nose.

''Go to sleep,'' he said gruffly.

He didn't know whether it was because he ordered it or because she was comfortable at last, but the sound of her steady breathing told him sometime later that she was asleep.

Meanwhile, he lay for hours staring into the darkness, confronting the memories he had been running from for six long years.

He had thought himself the happiest of men when he married Jeanine. He was in love, and they had a child on the way. Only years later had he discovered that things were not as they had seemed. By the time Jeanine had come to him with the truth, a tragedy had already been set in motion.

Carter had greeted his wife with surprise and pleasure when she appeared at his forty-third-floor corporate office in downtown Denver. ''What are you doing here, Jeanine?''

''We have to talk, Carter.''

''I was just going out to lunch,'' he said. ''Join me.''

''I think it would be best if we spoke here. In private.''

It was then he had noticed the redness around her eyes and the bruise on her cheek, barely hidden by makeup.

He led her over to the black leather sofa in the steel-and-glass office. ''Sit down,'' he said. ''Tell me what's going on.''

She fidgeted with the gold chain on her purse, refusing to meet his gaze. ''I have a confession to make.''

Carter's heart was in his throat. There was only one kind of confession a woman made to a man. She was having an affair. He felt a murderous rage toward the unknown man who had seduced his wife.

''I had an affair.''

Even though he had been expecting it, hearing the words was like getting punched in the gut. All the air whooshed out of his lungs.

She looked up at him, her gray eyes liquid, as beautiful as she had ever been. ''It was while we were engaged.''

Furrows appeared on his brow. ''That was years ago. Why are you telling me about it now?''

She left her purse on the couch and paced across the plush carpeting. ''Because he won't leave me alone!''

Carter rose and followed her to the window overlooking the street below. He actually felt the hairs bristling on his neck when he asked, ''Is he the one responsible for that bruise on your cheek?''

She lifted her hand to the revealing mark and winced in pain at even that slight touch. ''Yes.''

His hands fisted. ''I'll take care of it. Tell me where to find him.''

''It isn't that simple,'' she said. The tears began to fall, leaving tracks across her perfect makeup. ''You see, he's Alisa's father.''

Carter's heart skipped a beat. His face blanched. He couldn't have heard what he had thought he'd heard. ''Some other man is the father of my child?''

She nodded.

''Alisa isn't mine?''

''No, she's not.''

Carter's stomach churned. His heart was pounding so hard it felt as though he had been running a race. A race he was losing. ''Why are you telling me this now?'' he asked in a harsh voice.

''Because I need your help,'' she said. ''I realized my affair with Jack—''

''Is that his name?''

''Yes. Jack Taggert. I realized my affair with him was a mistake, but by then I was pregnant. I told him it was over, but he wouldn't take no for an answer. Business took him overseas for five years after you and I were married, but now he's back. He wants to pick up where we left off. And he wants to see Alisa."

"How the hell does he know Alisa is his?" Carter demanded.

"She has a birthmark. It's something all the Taggerts have. He saw it, and he knew."

"Dammit, Jeanine, why the hell didn't you tell me about this *before* we were married?"

"Because I was afraid you wouldn't understand."

"You're damn right I don't!" He paced angrily away from her. "Now what?" he demanded.

"I love you, Carter."

"Sure you do!" he said sarcastically. "That's why you've been passing off some other man's kid as mine!"

"Carter, I—"

"I don't want to hear any more of your lies, Jeanine. Just get the hell out of here."

"Carter, I'm afraid of Jack. He's—"

"He's your problem, not mine," Carter said ruthlessly. "You deal with him."

"You don't understand."

"I sure as hell don't! Why did you marry me, Jeanine? Why didn't you marry the father of your child?"

"You had more money," she snapped back at him.

Carter's lips flattened. "Thanks for that bit of honesty."

"I was being sarcastic!" she cried. "I love you, Carter. I need your help. Please!"

He went to the door and held it open for her. "I need to think, Jeanine. Go home."

"You don't seem to understand," she said as she stood on the threshold. "Jack has been stalking me, Carter. He's threatened to kill me if I don't come back to him."

"You expect me to believe that?" he said with a sneer.

"It's the truth."

"I'll call you when I make up my mind what I'm going to do," he said. "Don't let that bastard near Alisa until you hear from me."

He had closed the door quietly behind her, then sunk down along the wall and dropped his head onto his knees. His whole world had been ripped apart. He was furious with his wife for betraying him, hated her for lying to him. It had been a crushing blow to learn that the woman he had loved, and whom he believed had loved him, had really married him because he had more money than the man who had fathered her child.

But most of all, he was devastated by the discovery that his daughter was not his daughter. Alisa, the delight of his life, was not even his own flesh and blood!

Carter thought of the doll he had bought Alisa for Christmas, the one that could talk and drink and wet. Alisa had sat in his lap and played with his tie and told him all about it. He had brushed the blond hair from her eyes and told her she should be sure to write Santa and ask for one. Then he had rushed right out to buy one for her.

Later that fateful day he had asked his secretary to call his wife and tell her he was going on a business trip that would take him out of town for a week. Maybe by the end of that time he could figure out what he was going to do with his life.

But he hadn't been given a week. Three days later, on Christmas Eve, his wife and daughter had been on the way to the Christmas pageant, when they were run off the road in a fiery crash that had completely destroyed both cars. The police had identified the driver of the second vehicle as Jack Taggert.

It wasn't until he heard that his wife and daughter were dead that Carter realized the mistake he had made. Biology wasn't what had made Alisa his daughter. And even if Jeanine had not loved him, he had loved her. As his wife, he had owed her his trust and his protection. He had betrayed her every bit as badly as she had betrayed him. Only he was never going to get the chance to make things right.

Here in Wyoming he had found another daughter who was not his own, another woman who was threatened by a man from her past.

This time he wouldn't fail them.

Carter tightened his hold on Desiree, which was when he realized she wasn't asleep, after all.

"What are you thinking?" she whispered in the dark.

"How did you know I was thinking?"

"You kept making little noises in your throat."

Carter made a little sound in his throat.

''Just like that,'' she said as she snuggled back into the curve of his hips. ''What were you thinking about, Carter?''

''About my wife and daughter.'' He felt her stiffen.

''About how much you miss them?''

''My wife was being stalked by an old boyfriend when she was killed along with our daughter,'' Carter said. ''She asked me to protect her, but I didn't. I didn't realize how serious the danger was. And we had fought....''

Desiree reached for the light on her side of the bed and turned it on. She saw the pain of his loss etched in his blunt features. She reached out a hand to cradle his bristly cheek. ''How awful,'' she said in a quiet voice. ''Why didn't you tell me about this before?''

Carter lifted himself up on his elbow. ''It isn't something I'm very proud about. In fact, I've felt guilty about it for years.''

''And now you have a chance to atone,'' Desiree said as she brushed her thumb across his cheek, ''by taking care of me and Nicole.''

''Something like that,'' Carter admitted.

Desiree dropped her hand, then reached over and turned out the light. She lay down on the edge of the bed with her back to him and remained very still.

After a few minutes, Carter asked, ''What are you thinking, Desiree?''

''How do you know I'm thinking?''

''Because you're so quiet.''

At first he thought she wasn't going to answer him. Then she said, ''I'm not sure marrying you was the right thing to do.''

''Oh?''

''I had hoped that if I was married, Burley would accept the fact that I'm not ever going to let him back into my life. What happened tonight proves that either he hasn't seen you, or he doesn't care. I'm sorry for using you like that, Carter. But I was desperate.''

''Why didn't you just sell the Rimrock and go somewhere Burley would never find you?''

''This house was built generations ago by my forebears. Do you understand what I'm saying?''

''Yes. I think so. You have deep roots that tie you to the land.'' Like the roots he was beginning to grow himself.

"Besides," she said, "if I had run away, Burley would only have followed me. I'd rather stand and fight."

"You didn't do so well the last time you tangled with Burley."

"Last time I didn't have you on my side."

Carter grunted an acknowledgment of her point. Apparently, she thought his presence was going to make a difference. He hoped she was right.

"I'm glad I found you, Carter."

"I'm glad you found me, too. I promise I'll take care of you, Desiree. You and Nicky both."

"Thanks, Carter. I'm kind of tired. I think I'll go to sleep now."

She was curled up on the edge of the bed, as far as she could get from him. He could have left her there. It was clear that after his confession she was having second thoughts about her marriage to him. But Carter didn't want them to start the new year on opposite sides of the bed.

He scooted over to the middle of the bed, reached for Desiree and dragged her back against him.

"Carter—"

"I need you close to me, Desiree."

She lay stiff in his arms a moment longer, then pressed herself close to him. "Happy New Year, Carter."

"Happy New Year, Desiree."

Eight

Desiree knew Carter meant the promise he had made to protect her. But it was depressing to think that the care he took of her over the next weeks and months was motivated by guilt, rather than feelings of love. She wanted more. She wanted him to love her. Because, God help her, she had fallen in love with him. However, she wasn't about to tell him how she felt, because that wasn't part of their bargain. A marriage of convenience shouldn't have emotional strings attached.

Their call to the police on the morning after Burley's rampage through her bedroom had yielded exactly the result Desiree had expected. There were no fingerprints, no solid evidence to connect Burley to the crime. The officers were sorry, they would keep a lookout, but unless they had some proof that Burley was the culprit, there was nothing they could do.

Carter hadn't been satisfied with that. ''I'm going to hire a couple of extra hands to help out around here,'' he said.

''I—we—can't afford it.''

''I've seen the books,'' Carter said. ''We can afford it if we cut costs somewhere else. I want some people here, so I'll know you're safe if I'm not around.''

''But—''

''No buts.''

She had given in. Not graciously. She had argued for a day and a half. But she had seen he was determined, so she had agreed.

Gradually winter had loosened its grip on the land. The buffalo grass and wheatgrass and grama grass had put up sprouts of green. Desiree spent more and more time outside with Nicole, working in her vegetable garden behind the house. She always had one eye on the rolling prairie, waiting for Burley to show up. But he seemed to have disappeared.

Ordinarily she stayed close to the house. But on one unusually warm and beautiful March day, when Nicole was with Carter in the barn, her eyes strayed to the horizon. She caught sight of a patch of colorful wildflowers on the hillside that begged to be picked.

Even though the flowers were within easy calling distance of the house and barn, she debated the wisdom of leaving the area of the house to go pick them. As she dug with her trowel, weeding the carrots and squash and watermelon, she got angrier and angrier over the fact that Burley had made her so much a prisoner that she couldn't even walk a couple of hundred yards to pick wildflowers.

She dropped her trowel, yanked off her gloves and started marching up the hill. She picked wildflowers almost defiantly, breaking the stems and dropping them into her shirt, which she held out like a basket. Once she had picked the patch she had seen from the garden, she whirled to return to the house, which was when she spied another, even more beautiful, patch.

She looked around her, and there was nothing visible in any direction. She wasn't far from the house, still within easy shouting distance.

"He's *not* going to make me a prisoner," she said aloud. She started marching toward the next hill. She did that twice more, and was startled, when she glanced up, to realize she could no longer see the house.

He appeared out of nowhere.

Desiree realized she had been lured into a false sense of security by the extra men Carter had hired, and by the fact Burley hadn't shown his face in the twelve weeks since he had ransacked her bedroom.

"What are you doing here?" she demanded when he rose up to block her way.

"I was just taking a little look around the place. You've made some improvements while I've been away, Ice."

Desiree shuddered at the name he called her. It had hurt when he used it before, because she had believed it was true. Thanks to Carter, the word had lost its power to wound her. If she had ever been like ice in bed, that was no longer true. She lifted her chin and stared into Burley's dark brown eyes.

She wondered what she had found so attractive about him once upon a time. He wore his long hair combed back in front, in an old-fashioned bouffant that reminded her of Elvis. He had gained a bit of weight in prison, so now he was not only tall, but heavyset. A grizzled black stubble coated his cheeks and chin. The twinkling brown eyes that had courted her, that had flirted with lazy winks, were puffy, the color of dull brown mud.

His clothes were dirty and wrinkled, as though he had been sleeping in them. She realized it was entirely possible that he was camped somewhere on the Rimrock.

"You'd better leave," she said. "Or I'll call the police and have you arrested for trespassing."

"Oooh, I'm scared," he said in a singsong voice. "Where did you find the man?"

"What man?"

He grabbed her arms in a grip so tight she knew there would be bruises there tomorrow.

"Don't play games," he snarled.

"His name is Carter Prescott. He's my husband."

"I heard something like that," Burley said. "You can kiss him goodbye. Better yet, kiss me hello."

Desiree kept her teeth clenched as Burley forced a kiss on her. His breath was fetid, and she gagged.

"You've gotten awful high and mighty since I've been gone," he said, angrily shoving her an arm's distance away.

"Carter will kill you," she retorted.

"Not if I kill him first."

Desiree gasped at his threat. "I don't love you anymore, Burley. I don't want to be with you. I want you to leave me alone. And I want you to leave Carter alone."

"What about the kid?"

Desiree's heart missed a beat. "What about her?"

"Who's her father, Desiree?"

"Carter Prescott."

He shook his head. ''Uh-uh. Prescott didn't show his face around here till this past Christmas. The kid is what? Five? Six? She's mine, isn't she?''

''No. There was another man—''

''I want to see her,'' Burley interrupted.

Desiree felt panic clawing at her insides, but she kept her voice calm and firm. ''No.''

''I'll bet one of those new-fangled blood tests would prove she's mine,'' Burley said in a silky voice. ''Then I could get a court to let me see her, don't you think?''

''Don't do this, Burley. You never wanted children. You told me so every time we—'' Desiree cut herself off. She couldn't bring herself to identify intercourse with Burley as making love, not after she had experienced what lovemaking really was.

''I'd be willing to forget about the kid if you paid a little attention to me.''

Desiree gritted her teeth to keep the disgust she felt from showing on her face. She should have known Burley was only using Nicole to blackmail her. She was determined not to be a victim again. She decided to promise him anything now. And make sure she was never anywhere he could catch her alone again.

At the sound of approaching hoofbeats, Burley jerked his head around and searched the hillside. ''You're expecting company?''

''Carter was planning to join me,'' Desiree lied.

Burley pulled out a switchblade and snapped it open. ''Don't go doing anything stupid,'' he said. ''I'll be back to see you another time. So long, Ice.''

Once he was gone, Desiree whirled and ran toward the man approaching on horseback. To her relief, it was Carter. He dismounted on the run, and she met him halfway, sobbing with relief by the time she threw herself into his arms.

''Are you all right?'' he asked, clutching her tightly against him.

''I'm fine. I wanted to pick some wildflowers, and I guess I wandered too far and got frightened.''

She saw him eyeing the wildflowers strewn carelessly across the ground, flowers she hadn't been holding when they had first spied each other.

''What happened here, Desiree?''

''Nothing.''

''Don't tell me that!'' Carter said in a harsh voice. ''He was here, wasn't he?''

Desiree nodded jerkily. She clung to Carter to keep him from going after Burley. ''He has a knife! Let him go.''

''How did he get here?''

They heard the roar of a motorcycle, which answered his question.

''I was so scared,'' Desiree said as she clutched Carter around the waist. ''I'm so glad you came. How did you know he was here?''

''I didn't,'' Carter admitted. ''I stepped out of the barn for a minute and looked for you in the garden. When I didn't see you, I thought…I thought maybe something had happened to you.'' His grip tightened so she could barely breathe. ''I don't know what I would do if anything happened to you.''

Desiree knew it wasn't love that made him say such things. It was guilt. Carter wouldn't be able to live with himself if he lost another wife to a stalker. Whatever the source, she was grateful for the concern that had sent him hunting for her.

She looked up into Carter's eyes, trusting him enough to let him see her desperation and her fear. ''Burley said he wants to see Nicole. He knows she's his.''

''Nicky isn't going anywhere with that man,'' Carter said. ''You don't have to worry about that.''

''He is her father.''

''Only biologically. I'm Nicky's father now.''

Desiree stared up at Carter in surprise. Even though Nicky had been referring to Carter as her daddy for the past three months, it was the first time he had acknowledged himself in that role.

''You want to adopt her?'' Desiree asked.

Now it was Carter who looked surprised. ''I hadn't thought that far ahead, but I suppose so. Yes.''

Desiree laid her head on his shoulder. ''Thank you, Carter.''

''This time we've got that bastard cold,'' he said. ''He was trespassing on Rimrock land.''

''Did you actually see him?''

''No. But I know he was here.''

She shook her head, her brown hair whipping her cheeks. ''It wouldn't do any good. It's his word against mine.''

''Dammit, Desiree! That man should be put away in a cage where he can't hurt you or Nicky.''

''I won't go beyond sight of the house again unless someone is with me,'' she promised. ''He won't come near the house as long as there are people around.'' Her lips twisted ruefully. ''He's too smart—and too much of a coward—for that.''

''I hate living like this,'' Carter said.

''And you think I don't?'' Desiree responded tartly. ''But there's nothing either of us can do about it.''

''There's something I can do,'' Carter said.

Desiree framed his beard-roughened cheeks with her palms and forced him to look at her. ''You aren't going to confront him, are you? Because all that would accomplish would be to get one or the other of you killed. I don't want to lose you, Carter. Promise me you'll stay away from him.''

His lids dropped to conceal the feral look in his blue eyes. His lashes fanned out like coal crescents across his weathered face. When he opened his eyes again, he had hidden his feelings behind a wall of inscrutability. ''I'll stay away from him. But I'm not making any guarantees if he comes back to the Rimrock.''

''All right.'' She let her hands drop to her sides, but kept her eyes on Carter. Now that her fear had dissipated, there was another kind of tension building. She couldn't be around Carter without feeling it. The need. The desire. This time she was the one who let her lids drop to hide her avid expression.

''Desiree?''

Her body trembled at the sound of her name in that husky voice he used when he wanted her. His body almost quivered with animal excitement. The blunt ridge in his jeans was proof of his need. The wind carried with it the musky scent of aroused male. Desiree lifted her lids and stared up into blue eyes lambent with passion.

It was a sign of how far they had come over the past three months that there was no longer any question whether she was ready for him. She was always as ready for him as he was for her. What was more, she trusted him not to hurt her—no matter how uninhibited their love-making became.

So when he grabbed the front of her blouse and jerked, sending buttons flying, she responded by pulling the snaps free on his shirt and forcing it down off his shoulders. His mouth clamped onto her breast and sucked through the lace bra she was wearing. She followed him down onto the soft shoots of new grass, their tangled bodies rolling once or twice until they came to rest with her beneath him.

While he unsnapped her jeans and pulled down the zipper, she did the same to him. He shoved her jeans down, while she released him from his. With a single thrust he was inside her. Carter claimed her as she claimed him, their bodies moving urgently, seeking satisfaction.

"You're mine," Carter said as he climaxed within her.

"Yours," Desiree confirmed. "Only yours."

When it was over, they lay beside each other in the cool grass, staring up into a sky as wide and blue as any on earth.

"Do you ever wonder where you would be now if I hadn't proposed to you in the church parking lot?" Desiree asked.

Carter pulled up some clover and twirled it between his fingers. He leaned over to hold it under Desiree's nose so she could smell the sweet scent. "I'd still be looking, I guess."

"For a wife?"

"For a place to settle down."

"Are you happy, Carter?"

"Are you?" he countered.

Desiree thought about it a moment. "Most of the time."

"And the rest of the time?" She hedged against admitting that what would make her really happy was to know that he loved her. Instead she said, "I don't think we've seen the last of Burley."

"If he comes back, I'll be ready for him."

As the days turned to weeks, and the weeks to a month, Desiree began wishing that Burley would just return so they could get the confrontation over with. The waiting was driving her crazy. Especially since there were signs—ominous things, but nothing she ever dared mention to Carter—that he hadn't gone away.

She found the laundry she had hung on the line in the backyard pulled down into the dirt. The heads of her marigolds were all cut off.

A birdhouse was destroyed. And Nicole's Black Angus calf, which had never been sick, not even when it was first born, mysteriously died.

Desiree had been with Nicole when they found the calf. Nicole had let herself into the stall and dropped to her knees beside the calf, which was lying on its side with its tongue hanging out.

"Mommy, what's wrong with Matilda? She isn't moving."

Desiree entered the stall and lowered herself to the hay beside Nicole. "Let's see what the problem is."

She knew the instant she touched the stiff, cold body that the calf was dead. One of the basic laws of farm life was not to make pets of the animals. It was likely they would have to be sold, or killed and eaten. She had broken that rule when she had allowed Nicole to name the calf. Nicole would have to suffer now for her folly.

"Matilda's dead, Nicky," Desiree said.

Her daughter looked up at her in shock, then looked back at the motionless calf. She put a finger on its nose, seeking for breath that wasn't there, and felt the unnatural texture of its skin. Her face scrunched up and tears flowed freely down her cheeks.

Desiree enfolded her daughter in her arms and did her best to console the inconsolable child.

"What happened to him, Mommy? Why did he die?"

Until Nicole mentioned it, Desiree hadn't focused on what might have killed the calf. She looked around her suspiciously. "I don't know. Let's check and see if we can find out what happened."

Having something to do helped both of them. Desiree examined the calf, but there was no obvious wound. Nor was there anything in the feedbox that appeared different or unusual. Desiree did find a white dusting of powder that had sifted through the feed box onto the stall floor.

Poison. Strychnine or arsenic, most likely, she realized.

Which meant that Burley had been there. Desiree was furious that Burley had chosen to kill the calf. She was terrified at the thought that he had been so close, that if Nicole had come in here alone, her innocent daughter might have been confronted by a man fully capable of brutalizing her, perhaps even killing her. Suddenly Desiree no longer felt safe in the barn.

''Come on,'' she said to Nicole, ''let's go tell your daddy what happened.''

Grim-lipped, Carter listened to Nicole's tale of woe. He lifted her into his arms and carried her upstairs, where he sat with her until she fell asleep for her afternoon nap.

Desiree waited downstairs for the showdown she knew was coming. Carter didn't keep her waiting long.

''Burley did this.'' He said it as a fact, or rather, snarled it through his teeth.

''I found some white powder on the floor of the stall that I think might have been poison.''

''You don't expect me to keep this from the police, do you?'' he asked through tight jaws.

She sighed and lay back in the chair where she was ensconced. ''No. I think this should be reported. But I don't think you'll get any satisfaction.''

''I want it on the record that someone's been making mischief around here.''

''All right.''

''You aren't arguing with me.''

She sighed again. ''It isn't the first time Burley's come onto the Rimrock over the past month.''

''What?'' He crossed to her and stood with his legs spread and his hands fisted on his hips.

''I didn't want to worry you, but he's done a few things to let me know he's still around.''

''Like what?''

''Pulling down the laundry, trampling my flowers, wrecking the birdhouse. Stuff like that.''

''And you never said anything to me?''

Desiree could see that Carter was hurt, by the fact that she hadn't shared her problems with him. She shoved herself up out of the chair until she was sitting on the back with her feet on the seat. ''There was nothing you could do.''

''I could have shared what you were feeling.''

''I didn't know you wanted to,'' she said simply.

''We're husband and wife—''

''Because you wanted the Rimrock,'' Desiree said, being brutally frank.

She saw him open his mouth to deny it, then snap it shut again. She dropped her head into her hands. ''If I'd thought you could help, I would have said something,'' Desiree admitted. ''But there was no way any of those things that happened could be connected with Burley. It would have been a waste of time confronting him.''

And dangerous. But she wasn't going to say that to Carter. He was already too anxious to go hunting for Burley Kelton.

Abruptly Carter left the room.

Desiree felt a despair such as she hadn't experienced since the time she was married to Burley and had been bullied by him day and night. She was as much Burley's prisoner now as she had ever been as his wife. And it seemed there was no escape from her nightmare.

She had thought things couldn't get worse, but later that afternoon a police car drove up behind the house. Desiree was on her feet in an instant and running toward it. Carter had been gone all afternoon, and she was deathly afraid that something might have happened to him.

Something had.

When Carter stepped out of the backseat of the police car, Desiree barely recognized him. His face was a mass of cuts and bruises. Both his eyes were black and his lip was swollen. She didn't ask what had happened to him. She knew.

''The doc said to keep some ice on those bruises, Mizz Prescott,'' the young patrolman said. He turned to Carter and grinned. ''That's some right cross you've got. Never saw a man go down so hard as Burley did.''

Desiree stared in vexation as Carter tried to return the grin. His face was too battered to manage it.

''When you two are through exchanging compliments I'd like to follow the doctor's orders and put some ice on Carter's face,'' she said in a frigid voice.

The patrolman tipped his hat. ''Sure, Mizz Prescott. The judge'll be expecting you on Monday,'' he reminded Carter.

Desiree didn't wait to see if Carter followed her. She marched into the kitchen and began pulling ice from the freezer and wrapping it in a dish towel. When she turned, he was standing in the doorway.

''Sit down and shut the door,'' she snapped.

''He looks worse than I do,'' Carter said as he dropped with a groan into a kitchen chair.

''That's comforting,'' Desiree said sarcastically.

''It had to be done.''

''I don't know why men think everything can be settled with violence. What have you accomplished except to give Burley another reason to want revenge?''

''He won't be doing anything anytime soon,'' Carter said with satisfaction.

''Are you going to end up spending time in jail because of this?'' Desiree asked with asperity.

Carter started to grin again, put a hand to his puffy lip and thought better of it. ''You may not believe this, but Burley started it. I was only defending myself.''

''Where did you find him?'' Desiree asked.

''There's a bar in Casper where he hangs out.''

''Where's Burley now?''

''In jail. Or the hospital.''

''Oh, Carter,'' Desiree said as she eyed his battered face. ''You foolish, foolish man. You didn't have to do this for me.''

His features hardened, his eyes narrowed. ''I didn't do it for you,'' he said. ''I did it for Nicky.''

Desiree turned away so he wouldn't see how hurt she was. Carter didn't—couldn't—love her, but he had given his affection to her daughter. She tried to be happy that Nicky had found such a protector. It was hard not to wish that he could love her just a little bit, too.

''Desiree?''

Carter took her hand and pulled her onto his lap. She laid her head on his shoulder and felt him stroking her back, playing with her hair.

''I have a confession to make,'' he said in a quiet voice.

''What?''

''I've wanted to get my hands on Burley Kelton ever since I first realized he was responsible for the scar on your face.'' He paused and added. ''What he did to the calf...it was just an excuse to go after him.''

Desiree let her hands slip into the hair at Carter's nape. ''You foolish, foolish man,'' she whispered. ''I'd rather have a hundred scars than see one bruise on this face of yours.''

Carter's arms tightened around her. They sat there for a long time. Wishing things were different.

She wished that he loved her.

He wished that she could love him.

Neither spoke their wishes, both being too grown up to believe that dreams do come true.

Nine

As spring passed into summer, Burley kept his distance. Maybe Carter had beat some sense into him after all, Desiree mused. She began to hope that perhaps Burley had changed his mind about wanting her, that he had gotten over his unhealthy obsession. Maybe he had found someone else and that was why she hadn't seen hide nor hair of him—or any sign that he had been watching her. She began to relax her vigil, to make occasional forays from the house on her own.

Carter was not so sanguine about Burley's intentions. When he caught Desiree hunting for four-leaf clovers up in the hills behind the house one afternoon during Nicole's nap, he lashed into her. "Are you crazy?" he demanded. "Or do you have a death wish?"

"What's the matter with you?" Desiree demanded, her fists perched on her hips.

"I happen to care what happens to you," he retorted.

His comment smacked too much of the guilt she knew he felt, and not enough of the love she wished for in vain. "Don't worry," she snapped back at him. "I won't get myself murdered by a stalker. Lord knows how you would survive it a second time!"

His face bleached white and his mouth flattened into a thin line. "If you don't care whether you live or die, I don't suppose it makes much difference what I think."

Desiree was still too angry to be sorry for the wound she had inflicted on Carter. She had flung the accusation at him hoping he would deny that guilt was what motivated his care for her, hoping he would contradict her with protestations of love. Instead he had responded to her wound with a wound of his own.

"Faron has a bull I want to take a look at," Carter said through clenched teeth. "I was going to ask you to come with me, but I can see you've got other plans." He turned and marched down the hill.

She watched him speak to one of the men he had hired to watch over her. The two appeared to argue for a moment before Carter got into his pickup and gunned the engine, raising a cloud of dust as he peeled out of the backyard.

Desiree sank down onto her haunches and dropped her head on her knees. How could she expect Carter to mention love, when she was so careful not to speak the word herself? She couldn't go on this way. When Carter returned, she was going to have to tell him how she really felt. The mere fact he didn't love her back wasn't going to change anything.

Desiree wasn't aware how long she had been sitting there, until she realized she wasn't alone anymore.

"Carter?"

"Guess again."

A shiver of terror raced down Desiree's spine. She lurched to her feet and started to run. She didn't get far before Burley caught the tails of her shirt and hauled her to a stop.

She turned and fought him like a wildcat, her nails raking his face, her fists beating at him. She screamed, knowing there was help not far away.

"Don't waste your breath," Burley said with a laugh. "The man your husband left to watch over you drove away five minutes ago."

Desiree paused to stare in horror at Burley's malicious smile of triumph. "If you touch a hair on my head Carter will hunt you down," she threatened.

"Carter will be dead before you are," Burley retorted. "Come on." He began hauling her down the hill toward the house.

"Where are we going?"

"I want to see my kid," Burley said.

"No," Desiree begged. "Please, do whatever you want with me, but leave Nicky alone."

He ignored her, tightening his hold and yanking her after him.

Desiree kicked at him and caught him behind the knee, causing his leg to buckle. Instead of losing his hold, he dragged her down with him. Burley was good and angry by the time he got back on his feet. He slapped her once, hard enough to split her lip and make it bleed.

"Don't do that again, Ice," he warned. "Or I might have to get mean."

Desiree dug in her heels as Burley dragged her down the hill. She had no doubt of the fate that awaited her when they reached the house. What terrified her was the thought of what Burley might do to Nicole. She had to find some way to escape him, or to render him helpless. Carter was gone. She would have to protect Nicole herself.

Think, Desiree! Think!

By the time they reached the kitchen door, Desiree still had no idea how she was going to save herself and her daughter. By the time they reached the foot of the stairs, she was frantic.

Think, Desiree, think!

But her wits had been scattered by terror. No plan of action came to mind.

Fight, Desiree. Don't give up without a fight.

But he was so much stronger! If only words could kill, she thought. She knew they could wound. She had hurt Carter easily enough.

Words. Use words against Burley!

They had reached the top of the stairs and were heading down the hall to Nicole's room.

"You really ought to stop calling me Ice, you know," Desiree blurted.

"If the shoe fits," Burley said with a sneering glance.

"But it doesn't," she protested. "It wasn't me who had the problem in bed, Burley. It was you."

He stopped so abruptly she ran into his back. He whirled around to face her. "Who says?"

"I'm not cold in bed with Carter," she taunted. "I'm hot. Steamy. He's a better lover than you could ever think of being."

"We'll just see about that," Burley said.

Desiree had accomplished her purpose. Burley was no longer headed for Nicole's room. He was dragging her back down the hall in the other direction, toward her bedroom. She didn't want to imagine what was going to happen when they got there.

As they crossed the threshold into her bedroom, Desiree was very much afraid she might have jumped right from the frying pan into the fire. She only knew that she had to stay alive. For Carter's sake.

What on earth was she going to do now?

Carter was furious with Desiree and even angrier with himself. Why hadn't he just told her he was in love with her? So what if she hadn't even mentioned the word? So what if she had married him just to have someone to protect her from Burley Kelton? The fact he loved her wasn't going to change, even if she didn't love him back.

He wished he could be sure that hired man wouldn't take off before he got back. He had promised Jubal Friar that he could have the afternoon off, but that was when he thought he was going to have Desiree and Nicole with him. Jubal had been upset that Carter had gone back on the agreement. Carter had threatened that if Jubal didn't stay, he was fired.

He hadn't waited for an answer from Jubal before he had jumped into his pickup and taken off. What if Jubal had just walked away? That would mean Desiree and Nicole were alone on the Rimrock right now. Burley would find no one to say nay if he decided to go after the two people who meant everything to Carter.

Carter turned the wheel of the truck so sharply that it skidded as he made the U-turn to take him back to the Rimrock. He knew he was going to feel like a tomfool when he got back and found everything just as he had left it. But a gnawing in his gut told him he would be forever sorry if he didn't make sure.

His heart leaped to his throat when he drove up behind the house and realized Jubal's truck was gone.

"Damn him! And damn me for a stubborn fool!" he railed to himself.

He looked up on the hillside, but there was no sign of Desiree where he had left her. He checked the garden, but she wasn't there. He gave the barn a glance, but realized it was far more likely she was in the house. It wasn't long before Nicole would be up from her nap.

He entered the house quietly, listening for the voice of his wife, the laughter of his daughter. Everything was deathly silent. He was on the stairs when he heard the murmur of voices. A woman's. And a man's. Burley Kelton was upstairs! Judging from the sound, he was in Desiree's bedroom. And Desiree was in there with him.

Carter felt the contradictory urges to race up the stairs and to remain as silent as a shadow. He couldn't do both. He opted for silence. If he could surprise Burley, the situation might be resolved with a minimum of bloodshed. Not that he minded shedding Burley's blood. But he didn't want to see Desiree hurt. Not before he told her he loved her. Not before they had a chance to explore their feelings for each other.

He bit his lip to remain silent when he heard Desiree taunting Burley about his prowess as a man. Did the fool woman think she was invincible? By the time she was through pricking Burley's pride, the ex-convict was going to attack her like the maniac he was.

He could hear the snaps coming undone on Burley's shirt, the rasp of his zipper and the rustle of cloth as his jeans came off. One more second, another second and the man would be naked and vulnerable. Then Carter would attack.

It didn't take another second before he heard a scuffle in Desiree's room.

"Give me my knife, you bitch!" Burley shouted. "If I have to take it from you, I'll break your arm."

Carter's heart shot to his throat as he charged into the bedroom. When the door crashed open, he saw that Burley was still dressed in his long johns. The huge man wrenched the knife from Desiree's fist and backhanded her, sending her flying against the wall.

Carter saw red. "How would you like to try that on someone your own size?" he said with a low growl of menace.

Burley ignored Desiree and turned to face this new foe. "Well, well, well. If it isn't the husband. Desiree and I were just renewing our acquaintance, so to speak." He waved the knife in front of him. "Come on in and join the fun."

With his eyes, Carter warned Desiree to stay put. Then he gestured Burley forward with his hands. "Come on, big man. Let's finish this once and for all."

"Fine by me," Burley said.

Carter had taken a step toward Burley when he heard a small noise behind him. At the same instant he turned to investigate, Desiree screamed, "Nicole, call 911!" and Burley charged.

The little girl turned and fled downstairs.

"Carter!" Desiree cried. "Look out!"

Carter arched his body, so the knife that would have cut him deep merely left a bloody arc across his chest.

"I'm going to kill you," Burley said.

Carter said nothing, merely watched his adversary with intent blue eyes, waiting for the next attack, looking for any chance to get in under Burley's guard.

Both men had forgotten about Desiree, who hadn't been idle. The only thing she had found to use as a weapon was an antique pitcher and bowl that sat on her chest. She grabbed the pitcher and swung it at Burley.

Because he was so tall, the pitcher's effect was lessened. Instead of being knocked out by the blow, Burley was merely irritated and distracted by it.

Desiree's distraction was exactly what Carter had been waiting for. He shot forward and grabbed the wrist that held the knife and began applying pressure to make Burley release it.

Unfortunately, Desiree hadn't retreated quickly enough after hitting Burley, and he managed to grasp her hair and pull her toward him. When she was close enough, he caught her head in the crook of his other arm.

Burley smiled a feral grin and turned to Carter. "Let go of my wrist, or I'll crush her head like a walnut."

"Don't do it," Desiree said. "He'll only kill you, too, before he kills me."

Carter wavered, uncertain what he should do.

Desiree saw that Carter would let Burley kill him rather than watch her be killed before his eyes. She did the only thing she could think of to do.

She pretended to faint.

Unready for so much deadweight, Burley watched in dismay as Desiree slid through his arm and onto the floor at his feet. He tried to take a step forward, but stumbled over her. As he fell, the knife the two men had been struggling over imbedded itself deep in his chest.

Carter waited a moment to see whether the big man would get up. But the knife had done its work.

Carter went down on one knee and pulled Desiree into his arms. ''Desiree? Darling, are you all right? Are you hurt? Please say something!''

''I...I...'' Three simple words, *I love you,* and she didn't have the courage to say them. Desiree slowly opened her eyes and beheld the worried, beloved face hovering over her.

''What is it you're trying to say, darling?''

''Oh, Carter, I...I...I'm glad you're all right.''

He kissed her. A deep, possessive kiss, that claimed and captivated her. Then he lifted her into his arms, stepped over Burley and turned to pull the door closed behind him.

The sound of sirens in the distance announced that help was on the way. And reminded Desiree of her daughter. She struggled to be set down. Once on her feet, she clambered down the stairs, with Carter right behind her.

''Nicky? Where are you?''

She found her daughter sitting at the kitchen table, with the phone at her ear, still talking to the 911 operator. ''I have a mommy and a daddy,'' she was saying, ''just like my friend Shirley.''

Desiree picked up her daughter and hugged her tight, while Carter took the phone and explained to the operator that the situation was under control. When he hung up the phone he turned to embrace his wife and daughter.

''Who was that mean man, Mommy? Why did he want to hurt Daddy?''

Desiree met Carter's eyes and begged him for an explanation that a five-year-old could understand.

''He was just a man who got lost and scared,'' Carter said.

''Where is he now?'' Nicole asked.

''He's in your mother's room. He had an accident.''

''Is he all right?''

Carter reached out a hand to smooth Nicole's bangs from her eyes. ''No, Nicky. He's dead.''

''Oh. Can we still go see Maddy this afternoon?''

Carter and Desiree exchanged a look that expressed their gratefulness that Nicole was too young to understand the horror of what had happened.

"Maybe we'll have time to go see Maddy after the police are gone," Carter replied.

But it was well after dark before the police had finished their investigation, collected Burley's body and warned Carter not to leave the neighborhood. Desiree's room was cordoned off, and she had instructions to stay out of it until the police had another chance to look around in the morning.

Desiree had retreated to the kitchen and prepared a meal that she was loath to eat. She pushed the food around her plate, washed the dishes after dinner, then headed upstairs to bathe Nicole and put her to bed. She couldn't help shuddering as she passed the closed door to her bedroom.

It was over. The years of horror, of dread, were finished at last. She was free.

Carter joined her at Nicole's bedside and put his arm around her as she read her daughter a story from the book Nicole had given Carter for Christmas. It had only been a few short months, but it felt as though she had known the man sitting beside her for a lifetime.

When the story was done, Carter leaned over and kissed Nicole on the forehead. She threw her arms around him and hugged him. "I love you, Daddy," she said.

Desiree saw the moistness in Carter's eyes, and fought to keep from crying herself.

"I love you, too, Nicky," he said.

Abruptly Desiree rose and left the room, heading for the deep, comfortable chair in the parlor. She sank into it wearily and waited. It wasn't long before Carter joined her.

"We have to talk," she said as he sat down on the sofa across from her.

"Yes, we do," Carter agreed.

"The reason I married you no longer exists," she said tentatively. "As for the reasons you married me—"

"I married you to have a place where I belong. That holds as true now as it did the day we married."

Desiree felt her heart sink to her toes. She had known he only wanted roots. She had confirmation of it now. She couldn't bear staying married to him, when all he really wanted was the ranch. "Now that I'm no longer in danger, there's no reason for us to stay married. We could just be business partners," she suggested.

"Is that so?"

Carter realized that he had to reach for happiness with both hands, or he was going to lose it. "There are a few things you might like to know before we change things around here," he said.

Desiree cocked her head. "Such as?"

"I've found everything I've been searching for my whole life right here on the Rimrock," he said.

"You mean you've put down roots."

"Yes, I have. Only what I've discovered is that roots aren't a particular place or a thing that can be bought. All the money in the world—" He paused and flushed before he continued. "And I have quite a bit—won't buy roots."

"You're rich?"

He ignored her and went on, "Roots are a sense of belonging. Roots grow wherever the people you love are. This is where you are, Desiree. And Nicky. I could never give you up now."

Desiree lifted her eyes to meet Carter's intense gaze. She discovered that he was looking right back at her, and that his loving gaze didn't avoid the scar on her cheek, but encompassed it. She suddenly realized that her terrible scar no longer existed for him, except as a beloved part of her. Desiree launched herself from the chair into Carter's open arms.

"I love you, Carter. I have for so long!"

"I love you, too, Desiree, but I was too damned scared to admit it."

They headed upstairs together, smiling. Actually, they were grinning like idiots. Once in Carter's bedroom, they undressed each other slowly and carefully. His lips found the teardrops of joy at the corners of her eyes and followed them down her scarred cheek to her mouth, where his tongue joined hers in a passionate exchange.

They spent the night loving each other, reveling in the knowledge that their lovemaking was an extension of the feelings they had for each other. They were still twined in each other's arms the next morning—like the gnarled roots of a very old oak—when Nicole joined them there.

She climbed under the covers and stuck her feet on Desiree's thigh, only it turned out to be Carter's, instead.

Carter yelped. ''How can your feet be so cold in the middle of summer?'' He grabbed for them to warm them with his hands.

Nicole giggled as she snuggled down under the covers. ''My friend Shirley has a sister,'' she said. ''Do you think if I asked Santa, he would bring me a sister for Christmas?''

Carter chuckled.

Desiree laughed.

''It is entirely possible,'' Carter said.

''Entirely,'' Desiree agreed with a knowing smile.

Birds sang outside the window as the sun rose on a new day. They were a family, Carter thought, with roots and branches and little buds. It was a great beginning for a solid family tree.

* * * * *

THE TEMPORARY GROOM

This book is dedicated to Anne,
who learned to enjoy books at the age of 37
when she began reading romance novels,
and who has since decided to return to school
and continue her education.

One

Cherry Whitelaw was in trouble. Again. She simply couldn't live up to the high expectations of her adoptive parents, Zach and Rebecca Whitelaw. She had been a Whitelaw for three years, ever since her fifteenth birthday, and it was getting harder and harder to face the looks of disappointment on her parents' faces each time they learned of her latest escapade.

This time it was really serious. This was about the worst thing that could happen to a high school girl. Well, the second worst. At least she wasn't pregnant.

Cherry had been caught spiking the punch at the senior prom this evening by the principal, Mr. Cornwell, and expelled on the spot. The worst of it was, she wasn't even guilty! Not that anyone was going to believe her. Because most of the time she was.

Her best friend, Tessa Ramos, had brought the pint bottle of whiskey to the dance. Cherry had been trying to talk Tessa out of spiking the punch—had just taken the bottle from Tessa's hand—when Mr. Cornwell caught her with it.

He had snatched it away with a look of dismay and said, "I'm ashamed of you, young lady. It's bad enough when your behavior disrupts class. An irresponsible act like this has farther-reaching ramifications."

"But, Mr. Cornwell, I was only—"

"You're obviously incorrigible, Ms. Whitelaw."

Cherry hated being called that. *Incorrigible.* Being *incorrigible* meant no one wanted her because she was too much trouble. Except Zach and Rebecca had. They had loved her no matter what she did. They would believe in her this time, too. But that didn't change the fact she had let them down. Again.

''You're expelled,'' Mr. Cornwell had said, his rotund face nearly as red as Cherry's hair, but not quite, because nothing could ever be quite that red. ''You will leave this dance at once. I'll be in touch with your parents tomorrow.''

No amount of argument about her innocence had done any good, because she had been unwilling to name her best friend as the real culprit. She might be a troublemaker, but she was no rat.

Mr. Cornwell's pronouncement had been final. She was out. She wasn't going to graduate with the rest of her class. She would have to come back for summer school.

Rebecca was going to cry when she found out. And Zach was going to get that grim-lipped look that meant he was really upset.

Cherry felt a little like crying herself. She had no idea why she was so often driven to wild behavior. She only knew she couldn't seem to stop. And it wasn't going to do any good to protest her innocence this time. She had been guilty too often in the past.

''Hey, Cherry! You gonna sit there mopin' all night, or what?''

Cherry glanced at her prom date, Ray Estes. He lay sprawled on the grass beside her at the stock pond on the farthest edge of Hawk's Pride, her father's ranch, where she had retreated in defeat. Her full-length, pale green chiffon prom dress, which had made her feel like a fairy princess earlier in the evening, was stained with dirt and grass.

Ray's tuxedo was missing the jacket, bow tie, and cummerbund, and his shirt was unbuttoned halfway to his waist. He was guzzling the fourth can of a six-pack of beer he had been slowly but surely consuming since they had arrived at the pond an hour ago.

Cherry sat beside him holding the fifth can, but it was still nearly full. Somehow she didn't feel much like getting drunk. She had to face her parents sometime tonight, and that would only be adding insult to injury.

''C'mon, Cherry, give us a li'l kiss,'' Ray said, dragging himself upright with difficulty and leaning toward her.

She braced a palm in the smooth center of his chest to keep him from falling onto her. ''You're drunk, Ray.''

Ray grinned. ''Shhure am. How 'bout that kiss, Cher-ry?''

''No, Ray.''

''Awww, why not?''

''I got thrown out of school tonight, Ray. I don't feel like kissing anybody.''

''Not even me?'' Ray said.

Cherry laughed at the woeful, hangdog look on his face and shook her head. ''Not even you.'' Ray was good fun most of the time. He drank a little too much, and he drove a little too fast, and his grades hadn't been too good. But she hadn't been in a position to be too picky.

She had dreamed sometimes of what it might be like to be one of the ''good girls'' and have ''nice boys'' calling her up to ask for dates. It hadn't happened. She was the kind of trouble nice boys stayed away from.

''C'mon, Cher-ry,'' Ray said. ''Gimme li'l kiss.''

He teetered forward, and the sheer weight of him forced her backward so she was lying flat on the ground. Cherry was five-eleven in her stocking feet and could run fast enough to make the girls' track team—if she hadn't always been in too much trouble to qualify. But Ray was four inches taller and forty pounds heavier. She turned her head away to avoid his slobbery, seeking lips, which landed on her cheeks and chin.

''I said no, Ray. Get off!'' She shoved uselessly at his heavy body, a sense of panic growing inside her.

''Awww, Cher-ry,'' he slurred drunkenly. ''You know you want it.'' His hand closed around her breast.

''Ray! No!'' she cried. She grabbed his wrist and yanked it away and heard the chiffon rip as his grasping fingers held fast to the cloth. ''Ray, please!'' she pleaded.

Then she felt his hand on her bare flesh. ''No, Ray. No!''

''Gonna have you, Cher-ry,'' Ray muttered. ''Always wanted to. Know you want it, too.''

Cherry suddenly realized she might be in even worse trouble than she'd thought.

* * *

Billy Stonecreek was in trouble. Again. His former mother-in-law, Penelope Trask, was furious because he had gotten into a little fight in a bar in town and spent the night in jail—for the third time in a year.

He had a live-in housekeeper to stay with his daughters, so they were never alone. He figured he'd been a pretty damned good single parent to his six-year-old twins, Raejean and Annie, ever since their mother's death a year ago. But you'd never know it to hear Penelope talk.

Hell, a young man of twenty-five who worked hard on his ranch from dawn to dusk all week deserved to sow a few wild oats at week's end. His ears rang with the memory of their confrontation in his living room earlier that evening.

''You're a drunken half-breed,'' Penelope snapped, ''not fit to raise my grandchildren. And if I have anything to say about it, you won't have them for much longer!''

Billy felt a burning rage that Penelope should say such a thing while Raejean and Annie were standing right there listening. Especially since he hadn't been the least bit drunk. He'd been looking for a fight, all right, and he'd found it in a bar, but that was all.

There was no hope his daughters hadn't heard Penelope. Their Nintendo game continued on the living room TV, but both girls were staring wide-eyed at him. ''Raejean. Annie. Go upstairs while I talk to Nana.''

''But, Daddy—'' Raejean began. She was the twin who took control of every situation.

"Not a word,'' he said in a firm voice. "Go."

Annie's dark brown eyes welled with tears. She was the twin with the soft heart.

He wanted to pick them both up and hug them, but he forced himself to point an authoritative finger toward the doorway. ''Upstairs and get your baths and get ready for bed. Mrs. Motherwell will be up to help in a minute.'' He had hired the elderly woman on the spot when he heard her name. She had proven equal to it.

Raejean shot him a reproachful look, took Annie's hand, and stomped out of the room with Annie trailing behind her.

Once they were gone, Billy turned his attention back to his nemesis. ''What is it this time, Penelope?''

''This time! What is it every time? You drove my Laura to kill herself, and now you're neglecting my grandchildren. I've had it. I went to see a lawyer today. I've filed for custody of my granddaughters.''

A chill of foreboding crawled down Billy's spine. ''You've done what?''

''You heard me. I want custody of Raejean and Annie.''

''Those are my children you're talking about.''

''They'll have a better life with me than they will with a half-breed like you.''

''Being part Comanche isn't a crime, Penelope. Lots of people in America are part something. Hell, you're probably part Irish or English or French yourself.''

''Your kind has a reputation for not being able to hold their liquor. Obviously, it's a problem for you, too. I don't intend to let my grandchildren suffer for it.''

A flush rose on Billy's high, sharp cheekbones. He refused to defend himself. It was none of Penelope's business whether he drank or not. But he didn't. He went looking for a fight when the pain built up inside, and he needed a release for it. But he chose men able to defend themselves, he fought clean, and he willingly paid the damages afterward.

He hated the idea of kowtowing to Penelope, but he didn't want a court battle with her, either. She and her husband, Harvey Trask, were wealthy; he was not. In fact, the Trasks had given this ranch—an edge carved from the larger Trask ranching empire—as a wedding present to their daughter, Laura, thereby ensuring that the newlyweds would stay close to home.

He had resented their generosity at first, but he had grown to love the land, and now he was no more willing to give up the Stonecreek Ranch than he was to relinquish his children.

But his behavior over the past year couldn't stand much scrutiny. He supposed the reason he had started those few barroom brawls wouldn't matter to a judge. And he could never have revealed to anyone the personal pain that had led to such behavior. So he had no excuses to offer Penelope—or a family court judge, either.

"Look, Penelope, I'm sorry. What if I promise—"

"Don't waste your breath. I never wanted my daughter to marry a man like you in the first place. My granddaughters deserve to be raised in a wholesome household where they won't be exposed to your kind."

"What kind is that?" Billy asked pointedly.

"The kind that doesn't have any self-respect, and therefore can't pass it on to their children."

Billy felt his stomach roll. It was a toss-up whether he felt more humiliated or furious at her accusation. "I have plenty of self-respect."

"Could have fooled me!" Penelope retorted.

"I'm not letting you take my kids away from me."

"You can't stop me." She didn't argue with him further, simply headed for the front door—she never used the back, as most people in this part of Texas did. "I'll see you in court, Billy."

Then she was gone.

Billy stood in the middle of the toy-strewn living room, furnished with the formal satin-covered couches and chairs Laura had chosen, feeling helpless. Moments later he was headed for the back door. He paused long enough to yell up the stairs, "I'm going out, Mrs. Motherwell. Good night, Raejean. Good night, Annie."

"Good night, Daddy!" the two of them yelled back from the bathtub in unison.

Mrs. Motherwell appeared at the top of the stairs. "Don't forget this is my last week, Mr. Stonecreek. You'll need to find someone else starting Monday morning."

"I know, Mrs. Motherwell," Billy said with a sigh. He had Penelope to thank for that, too. She had filled Mrs. Motherwell's head with stories about him being a dangerous savage. His granite-hewn features, his untrimmed black hair, his broad shoulders and immense height, and a pair of dark, brooding eyes did nothing to dispel the image. But he couldn't help how he looked. "Don't worry, Mrs. Motherwell. I'll find someone to replace you."

He was the one who was worried. How was he going to find someone as capable as Mrs. Motherwell in a week? It had taken him a month to find her.

He let the kitchen screen door slam and gunned the engine in his black pickup as he drove away. But he couldn't escape his frenetic thoughts.

I'll be damned if I let Penelope take my kids away from me. Who does she think she is? How dare she threaten to steal my children!

He knew his girls needed a mother. Sometimes he missed Laura so much it made his gut ache. But no other woman could ever take her place. He had hired a series of good housekeeper/nannies one after another—it was hard to get help to stay at his isolated ranch—and he and his girls had managed fine.

Or they would, if Penelope and Harvey Trask would leave them alone.

Unfortunately, Penelope blamed him for Laura's death. She had been killed instantly in a car accident that had looked a whole lot like a suicide. Billy had tried telling Penelope that Laura hadn't killed herself, but his mother-in-law hadn't believed him. Penelope Trask had said she would see that he was punished for making Laura so miserable she had taken her own life. Now she was threatening to take his children from him.

He couldn't bear to lose Raejean and Annie. They were the light of his life and all he had left of Laura. God, how he had loved her!

Billy pounded his fist on the steering wheel of his pickup. How could he have been so stupid as to give Penelope the ammunition she needed to shoot him down in court?

It was too late to do anything about his wild reputation. But he could change his behavior. He could stop brawling in bars. If only there were some way he could show the judge he had turned over a new leaf....

Billy didn't drive in any particular direction, yet he eventually found himself at the stock pond he shared with Zach Whitelaw's ranch. The light from the rising moon and stars made a silvery reflection on the center of the pond and revealed the shadows of several pin oaks that surrounded it. He had always found the sounds of the bullfrogs and the crickets and the lapping water soothing to his inner turmoil. He had gone there often to think in the year since Laura had died.

His truck headlights revealed someone else had discovered his sanctuary. He smiled wistfully when he realized a couple was lying together on the grass. He felt a stab of envy. He and Laura had spent their share of stolen moments on the banks of this stock pond when the land had belonged to her father.

He almost turned the truck around, because he wanted to be alone, but there was something about the movements of the couple on the ground that struck him as odd. It took him a moment to realize they weren't struggling in the throes of passion. The woman was trying to fight the man off!

He hit the brakes, shoved open his truck door, and headed for them on the run. He hadn't quite reached the girl when he heard her scream of outrage.

He grabbed hold of the boy by his shoulders and yanked him upright. The tall, heavyset kid came around swinging.

That was a mistake.

Billy ducked and came up underneath with a hard fist to the belly that dropped the kid to his knees. A second later the boy toppled face-forward with a groan.

Billy made a sound of disgust that the kid hadn't put up more of a fight and hurried to help the girl. She had curled in on herself, her body rigid with tension. When he put a hand on her shoulder, she tried scrambling away.

"He's not going to hurt you anymore," he said in the calm, quiet voice he used when he was gentling horses. He turned her over so she could see she was safe from the boy, that he was there to help. Her torn bodice exposed half of a small, well-formed breast. He made himself look away, but his body tightened responsively. Her whole body began to tremble.

"Shh. It's all right. I'm here now."

She looked up at him with eyes full of pain.

"Are you hurt?" he asked, his hands doing a quick once-over for some sign of injury.

She slapped at him ineffectually with one hand while holding the torn chiffon against her nakedness with the other. "No. I'm fine. Just…just…"

Her eyes—he couldn't tell what color they were in the dark—filled with tears and, despite her desperate attempts to blink the moisture away, one sparkling teardrop spilled onto her cheek. It was then he realized the pain he had seen wasn't physical, but came from inside.

He understood that kind of pain all too well.

''Hey,'' he said gently. ''It's going to be all right.''

''Easy for you to say,'' she snapped, rubbing at the tears and swiping them across her cheeks. ''I—''

A car engine revved, and they both looked toward the sound in time to see a pair of headlights come on.

''Wait!'' the girl cried, surging to her feet.

The dress slipped, and Billy got an unwelcome look at a single, luscious breast. He swore under his breath as his body hardened.

The girl obviously wasn't used to long dresses, because the length of it caught under her knees and trapped her on the ground. By the time she made it to her feet, the car she had come in, and the boy she had come with, were gone.

He took one look at her face in the moonlight and saw a kind of desolation he hadn't often seen before.

Except perhaps in his own face in the mirror.

It made his throat ache. It might have brought him to tears, if he had been the kind of man who could cry. He wasn't. He thought maybe his Comanche heritage had something to do with it. Or maybe it was simply a lack of feeling in him. He didn't know. He didn't want to know.

As he watched, the girl sank to the ground and dropped her face into her hands. Her shoulders rocked with soundless, shuddering sobs.

He settled beside her, not speaking, not touching, merely a comforting presence, there if she needed him. Occasionally he heard a sniffling sound, but otherwise he was aware of the silence. And finally, the sounds he had come to hear. The bullfrogs. The crickets. The water lapping in the pond.

He didn't know how long he had been sitting beside her when she finally spoke.

''Thank you,'' she said.

Her voice was husky from crying, and rasped over him, raising the hairs on his neck. He looked at her again and saw liquid, shining eyes in a pretty face. He couldn't keep his gaze from dropping to the flesh revealed by her tightened grip on the torn fabric. Hell, he was a man, not a saint.

"Are you all right?" he asked.

She shook her head, gave a halfhearted laugh, and said, "Sure." The sarcasm in her voice made it plain she was anything but.

"Can I help?"

"I'd need a miracle to get me out of the mess I'm in." She shrugged, a surprisingly sad gesture. "I can't seem to stay out of trouble."

He smiled sympathetically. *I have the same problem.* He thought the words, but he didn't say them. He didn't want to frighten her. "Things happen," he said instead.

She reached out hesitantly to touch a recent cut above his eye. "Did Ray do this?"

He edged back from her touch. It felt too good. "No. That's from—" *Another fight.* He didn't finish that thought aloud, either. "Something else."

He had gotten a whiff of her perfume. Something light and flowery. Something definitely female. It reminded him he hadn't been with a woman since Laura's death. And that he found the young woman sitting beside him infinitely desirable.

He tamped down his raging hormones. She needed his help. She didn't need another male lusting after her.

She reached for an open can of beer sitting in the grass nearby and lifted it to her lips.

Before it got there, he took it from her. "Aren't you a little young for this?"

"What difference does it make now? My life is ruined."

He smiled indulgently. "Just because your boyfriend—"

"Ray's not my boyfriend. And he's the least of my problems."

He raised a questioning brow. "Oh?"

He watched her grasp her full lower lip in her teeth—and wished he were doing it himself. He forced his gaze upward to meet with hers.

"I'm a disappointment to my parents," she said in a whispery, haunted voice.

How could such a beautiful—he had been looking at her long

enough to realize she was more than pretty—young woman be a disappointment to anybody? ''Who are your parents?''

''I'm Cherry Whitelaw.''

She said it defiantly, defensively. And he knew why. She had been the talk of the neighborhood—the ''juvenile delinquent'' the Whitelaws had taken into their home four years ago, the most recently adopted child of their eight adopted children.

''If you're trying to scare me off, it won't work.'' He grinned and said, ''I'm Billy Stonecreek.''

The smile grew slowly on her face. He saw the moment when she relaxed and held out her hand. ''It's nice to meet you, Mr. Stonecreek. I used to see you in church with your—'' She cut herself off.

''It's all right to mention my wife,'' he said. But he knew why she had hesitated. Penelope's tongue had been wagging, telling anyone who would listen how he had caused Laura to kill herself. Cherry's lowered eyes made it obvious she had heard the stories. He didn't know why he felt the urge to defend himself to her when he hadn't to anyone else.

''I had nothing to do with Laura's death. It was simply a tragic accident.'' Then, before he could stop himself, ''I miss her.''

Cherry laid a hand on his forearm, and he felt the muscles tense beneath her soothing touch. She waited for him to look at her before she spoke. ''I'm sorry about your wife, Mr. Stonecreek. It must be awful to lose someone you love.''

''Call me Billy,'' he said, unsure how to handle her sympathy.

''Then you have to call me Cherry,'' she said with the beginnings of a smile. She held out her hand. ''Deal?''

''Deal.'' He took her hand and held it a moment too long. Long enough to realize he didn't want to let go. He forced himself to sit back. He raised the beer can he had taken from her to his lips, but she took it from him before he could tip it up.

''I don't think this will solve your problems, either,'' she said with a cheeky grin.

He laughed. ''You're right.''

They smiled at each other.

Until Billy realized he wanted to kiss her about as bad as he had ever wanted anything in his life. His smile faded. He saw the growing recognition in her eyes and turned away. He was there to rescue the girl, not to ravish her.

He picked a stem of sweet grass and twirled it between his fingertips. "Would you like to talk about what you've done that's going to disappoint your parents?"

She shrugged. "Hell. Why not?"

The profanity surprised him. Until he remembered she hadn't been a Whitelaw for very long. "I'm listening."

Her eyes remained focused on her tightly laced fingers. "I got expelled from high school tonight."

He let out a breath he hadn't realized he'd been holding. "That's pretty bad, all right. What did you do?"

"Nothing! Not that I'm innocent all that often, but this time I was. Just because I had a whiskey bottle in my hand doesn't mean I was going to pour it in the punch at the prom."

He raised a skeptical brow.

"I was keeping a friend of mine from pouring it in the punch," she explained. "Not that anyone will believe me."

"As alibis go, I've heard better," he said.

"Anyway, I've been expelled and I won't graduate with my class and I'll have to go to summer school to finish. I'd rather run away from home than face Zach and Rebecca and tell them what I've done. In fact, the more I think about it, the better that idea sounds. I won't go home. I'll…I'll…"

"Go where?"

"I don't know. Somewhere."

"Dressed like that?"

She looked down at herself and back up at him, her eyes brimming with tears. "My dress is ruined. Just like my life."

Billy didn't resist the urge to lift her into his lap, and for whatever reason, she didn't resist his efforts to comfort her. She wrapped her arms around his neck and clung to him.

"I feel so lost and alone," she said, her breath moist against his skin. "I don't belong anywhere."

Billy tightened his arms around her protectively, wishing there was something more he could do to help. He crooned to her in Comanche, telling her she was safe, that he would find a way to help her, that she wasn't alone.

"What am I going to do?" she murmured in an anguished voice. "Where can I go?"

Billy swallowed over the knot in his throat. "You're going to think I'm crazy," he said. "But I've got an idea if you'd like to hear it."

"What is it?" she asked.

"You could come and live with me."

Two

Cherry had felt safe and secure in Billy Stonecreek's arms, that is, until he made his insane suggestion. She lifted her head from Billy's shoulder and stared at him wide-eyed. ''What did you say?''

''Don't reject the idea before you hear me out.''

''I'm listening.'' In fact, Cherry was fascinated.

He focused his dark-eyed gaze on her, pinning her in place. ''The older lady who's been taking care of my kids is quitting on Monday. How would you like to work for me? The job comes with room and board.'' He smiled. ''In fact, I'm including room and board because I can't afford to pay much.''

''You're offering me a job?''

''And a place to live. I could be at home evenings to watch the girls while you go to night school over the summer and earn your high school diploma. What do you say?''

Cherry edged herself off Billy's lap, wondering how he had coaxed her into remaining there so long. Perversely, she missed the warmth of his embrace once it was gone. She pulled her knees up to her chest and wrapped her arms around the yards of pale green chiffon.

''Cherry?''

Her first reaction was to say yes. His offer was the simple solution to all her problems. She wouldn't have to go home. She wouldn't have to face her parents with the truth.

But she hadn't lived with Zach and Rebecca Whitelaw for four years and not learned how they felt about certain subjects. ''My dad would never allow it.''

''A minute ago you were going to run away from home. How is this different?''

''You obviously don't know Zach Whitelaw very well,'' she said with a rueful twist of her lips. ''If he knew I was working so close, he'd expect me to live at home.''

''Not if you were indispensible to me.''

''Would I be?'' she asked, intrigued.

''I can't manage the ranch and my six-year-old twin daughters all by myself. I'm up and working before dawn. Somebody has to make sure Annie and Raejean get dressed for school and feed them breakfast and be there when they get off the school bus in the afternoon.'' Billy shrugged. ''You need a place to stay. I need help in a hurry. It's a match made in heaven.''

Cherry shook her head. ''It wouldn't work.''

''Why not?''

''Can I be blunt?''

Billy smiled, and her stomach did a queer flip-flop. ''By all means,'' he said.

''It's bad enough that you're single—''

''I wouldn't need the help if I had a wife,'' Billy interrupted.

Cherry frowned him into silence. ''You're a widower. I'm only eighteen. It's a toss-up which of us has the worse reputation for getting into trouble. Can you imagine what people would say—about us—if I moved in with you?'' Cherry's lips curled in an impish grin. ''Eyebrows would hit hairlines all over the county.''

Billy shook his head and laughed. ''I hadn't thought about what people would think. We're two of a kind, all right.'' His features sobered. ''Just not the right kind.''

Cherry laid her hand on his arm in comfort. ''I know what you're feeling, Billy.''

''I doubt it.''

Cherry felt bereft as he pulled free. He was wrong. She understood exactly what he was feeling. The words spilled out before she could stop them.

''Nobody wants anything to do with you, because you're different,'' she said in a quiet voice that carried in the dark. ''To prove it doesn't matter what anyone else thinks, you break their rules. When they look down their noses at you, you spit in their eyes. And all the time, your heart is aching. Because you want them to like you. And respect you. But they don't.''

Billy eyed her speculatively. ''I guess you do understand.''

For a moment Cherry thought he was going to put his arm around her. But he didn't.

She turned to stare at the pond, so he wouldn't see how much she regretted his decision to keep his distance. ''I've always hated being different,'' she said. ''I was always taller than everyone else, thanks to my giant of a father, Big Mike Murphy.'' When she was a child, her father's size had always made her feel safe. But he hadn't kept her safe. He had let her be stolen away from him.

''And I don't know another person with hair as godawful fire-engine red as mine. I have Big Mike to thank for that, too.'' Cherry noticed Billy didn't contradict her evaluation of her hair.

''And your mother?'' Billy asked. ''What did you get from her?''

''Nothing, so far as I can tell,'' Cherry said curtly. ''She walked out on Big Mike when I was five. That's when he started drinking. Eventually someone reported to social services that he was leaving me alone at night. They took me away from him when I was eight. He fell from a high scaffolding at work the next week and was killed. I think he wanted to die. I was in and out of the system for six years before the Whitelaws took me in.''

''I'm sorry.''

''It doesn't matter now.''

''Doesn't it?'' Billy asked.

Cherry shrugged. ''It's in the past. You learn to protect yourself.''

''Yeah,'' Billy said. ''You do.''

Billy had inherited his six-foot-four height and dark brown eyes from his Scots father. His straight black hair and burnished skin came from his Comanche mother. They had been killed in a car wreck when he was ten. He had developed his rebellious streak in a series of foster homes that treated him like he was less than human because he wasn't all white.

He opened his mouth to share his common experiences with Cherry and closed it again. It was really none of her business.

"Too bad you aren't looking for a wife," Cherry mused. "That would solve your problem. But I guess after what happened, you don't want to get married again."

"No, I don't," Billy said flatly.

"I certainly wasn't volunteering for the job," Cherry retorted. Everyone knew Billy Stonecreek had made his first wife so unhappy she had killed herself. At least, that was the story Penelope Trask had been spreading. On the other hand, Billy Stonecreek had been nothing but nice to her. She couldn't help wondering whether Billy was really as villainous as his mother-in-law had painted him.

They sat in silence. Cherry wished there was some way she could have helped Billy. But she knew Zach Whitelaw too well to believe he would allow his daughter to move in with a single man—even if she was his housekeeper. Not that Zach could have stopped her if she wanted to do it. But knowing Zach, he would find a way to make sure Billy changed his mind about needing her. And she didn't want to cause that kind of trouble for anybody.

"Having you come to work for me wouldn't really solve my biggest problem, anyway," Billy said, picking up the beer can again.

Cherry took it out of his hand, set it down, and asked, "What problem is that?"

He hesitated so long she wasn't sure he was going to speak. At last he said, "My former mother-in-law is taking me to court to try and get custody of my daughters. Penelope says I'm not a fit parent. She's determined to take Raejean and Annie away from me."

"Oh, no!" It was Cherry's worst nightmare come to life. She had suffered terribly when she had been taken from her father as a child. "You can't let her do that! Kids belong with their parents."

Cherry was passionate about the subject. She had often wondered where her birth mother was and why she had walked away and left Cherry and Big Mike behind. Cherry had died inside when the social worker came to take her away, and she realized she was never going to see Big Mike again. It was outrageous to think someone could go to court and wrench two little girls away from their natural father.

"You've got to stop Mrs. Trask!" Cherry said. "You can't let her take your kids!"

"I'm not *letting* her do anything!" Billy cried in frustration. His hands clenched into fists. "But I'm not sure I can stop her. Over the past year I haven't exactly been a model citizen. And I haven't been able to keep a steady housekeeper. Especially once Penelope fills their ears with wild stories about me."

Billy made an angry sound in his throat. "If Laura hadn't died... Having a wife would certainly make my case as a responsible parent stronger in court."

"Isn't there somebody you could marry?"

"What woman would want a half-breed, with a ready-made family of half-breed kids?" Billy said bitterly.

Cherry gasped. "You talk like there's something wrong with you because you're part Comanche. I'm sure you have lots of redeeming qualities."

Billy eyed her sideways. "Like what?"

"I don't know. I'm sure there must be some." She paused and asked, "Aren't there?"

Billy snorted. "I've been in jail for fighting three times over the past year."

Cherry met his gaze evenly and said, "Nobody says you have to fight."

"True," Billy conceded. "But sometimes..."

"Sometimes you feel like if you don't hit something you'll explode?"

Billy nodded. "Yeah."

"I've felt that way sometimes myself."

"You're a girl," Billy protested. "Girls don't—"

"What makes you think girls don't get angry?" Cherry interrupted.

"I guess I never really thought much about it. What do you do when you feel like that?"

"Cause mischief," Cherry admitted with a grin. Her grin faded as she said, "Think, Billy. Isn't there some woman you could ask to marry you?"

Billy shook his head. "I haven't gone out much since Laura died. When I haven't been working on the ranch, I've spent my time with

Raejean and Annie. Besides, I don't know too many women around here who'd think I was much of a catch.''

Cherry sat silently beside Billy. Her heart went out to his two daughters. She knew what was coming for them. She felt genuinely sorry for them. For the first time in a long time she regretted her past behavior, because it meant she couldn't be a help to them.

''I wish we'd met sooner. And that I had less of a reputation for being a troublemaker,'' Cherry said. ''If things were different, I might volunteer to help you out. But I'm not the kind of person you'd want as a mother for your kids.''

Billy's head jerked around, and he stared intently at her.

Cherry was a little frightened by the fierce look on his face. ''Billy? What are you thinking?''

''Why not?'' he muttered. ''Why the hell not?''

''Why not what?''

''Why can't you marry me?'' Billy said.

Cherry clutched at her torn bodice as she surged to her feet. ''You can't be serious!''

Billy rose and grabbed her by the shoulders, which was all that kept her from running. ''More serious than I've ever been in my life. My kids' lives depend on me making the right choices now.''

''And you think marriage to me is the right choice?'' Cherry asked incredulously. ''We're practically strangers! I barely know you. You don't know me at all.''

''I know plenty about you. You understand what it feels like to be different. What it feels like to lose your parents. What it feels like to need a parent's love. You'd be good for my kids. And you could really help me out.''

''Why me?''

''I'm desperate,'' Billy said. ''I thought you were, too.''

Cherry grimaced. Why else would a man choose her except because he was desperate? And why else would a woman accept such a proposal, unless she were desperate, too?

''Are you ready to go home and face your parents and tell them you got expelled and that you aren't going to graduate?'' Billy demanded.

''When you put it that way, I... No. But marriage? That seems like such a big step. Make that a *huge* step.''

''It doesn't have to be a real marriage. It can be strictly a business arrangement. We can stay married long enough for you to finish the high school credits you need and maybe take some courses at the junior college. When you figure out what you want to do with the rest of your life, we could go our separate ways.''

''Couldn't I just be your housekeeper?''

Billy shook his head. ''You've said yourself why that wouldn't work.''

''But marriage is so...permanent.''

''It would be if it were for real. Ours wouldn't be.''

''Are you suggesting we tell people we're married but not really go through with it?''

He considered a moment. ''No, we'd have to get married, and as far as I'm concerned, the sooner the better.''

Cherry's heart bounced around inside her like a frightened rabbit. She pressed a fistful of chiffon hard against her chest, as though she could hold her heart still, but it kept right on jumping. ''You want to get married right away? This week?''

''As soon as we can. We could fly to Las Vegas tonight.''

''Fly?''

''I've got a pilot's license. We can charter a small private plane for the trip. Would you mind?''

''I guess not,'' Cherry said, overwhelmed by the speed at which things were moving.

''The more I think about it, the more I like the whole idea. Getting married would certainly spike Penelope's guns.''

Cherry gnawed on her lower lip. ''If you're looking for someone who'd be an asset in court, maybe you ought to reconsider taking me as your wife. My reputation's almost as bad as yours.''

''You're a Whitelaw,'' Billy said. ''That means something around this part of Texas.''

''An adopted Whitelaw,'' Cherry reminded him. ''And I'm not so sure my parents wouldn't change their minds if they had the chance.''

Billy smiled. ''I think we can make this arrangement work for both of us. How about it, Cherry? Will you marry me?''

If Cherry had been anybody except who she was, she would have said no. Any rational person would have. It didn't make sense to marry a virtual stranger, one who had reportedly made his previous wife miserable. But Cherry wasn't thinking about Billy or even about herself. She was thinking about his two innocent little girls. If marrying Billy would give them a better chance of staying with their father, she really didn't think she had any other choice.

"All right, Billy," she said. "I'll marry you."

Billy gave a whoop of joy, swept her up into his arms, and whirled her in a dizzying circle, sending chiffon flying around her.

"Put me down, Billy," she said, laughing.

He immediately set her on her feet. When she swayed dizzily, he reached out to steady her.

The feel of his strong, callused hands on her bare shoulders sent an unexpected quiver skittering down her spine. She knew she ought to step away, but Billy's dark eyes held her spellbound.

"Okay now?" he asked, his voice rasping over her.

"I'm fine." She shivered, belying her words.

"You must be getting chilly." He slipped an arm around her shoulder that was warm and supportive...and possessive.

She shivered again as he began walking her toward his pickup. Only this time she realized it had nothing to do with the cold.

As Billy held open the pickup door she said as casually as she could, "This will be a marriage in name only, right?"

He closed the door behind her, slid over the hood, got into the cab, and started the pickup before he answered, "That's right."

She gave a gusty sigh of relief as the engine roared to life. "Good."

"We don't even have to sleep in the same bed," Billy said as he headed back toward the main road. "You can have the room my housekeeper will be vacating. If I feel the urge for some feminine comfort, I can get what I need from a woman in town."

"Wait a minute," Cherry said. "I don't think I'm going to want my husband satisfying his lustful urges in town."

"I won't really be your husband," Billy reminded her.

"As far as my parents and neighbors and friends are concerned, you will be."

Billy eyed her cautiously. "What do you suggest?"

"Couldn't you just...not do it."

"I'm a man, not a monk," Billy said.

Cherry pursed her lips thoughtfully. "Then I suppose I'd rather you come to me than go to some other woman."

"This is starting to sound like a real marriage," Billy said suspiciously. "I was looking for a temporary solution to both our problems."

"Oh, you don't have to worry about me falling in love with you or anything," Cherry reassured him. "I don't believe in happily-ever-after."

"You don't?"

Cherry shook her head. "Except for the Whitelaws, I've never met any married couples who really loved each other. But I can see where it would be unfair to expect you to give up sex for who knows how long. Only, if you don't mind, I'd rather we had a chance to get to know each other a little better before...you know..."

"Maybe this marriage thing isn't such a good idea, after all," Billy said. "You're just a kid, and—"

"I may be only eighteen," Cherry interrupted, "but I've lived a lifetime since my father died. You don't have to worry about me. I've been in and out of a dozen foster homes. I've spent time in juvenile detention. I've survived the past four years in a house with seven other adopted brothers and sisters. I've come through it all with a pretty good idea of what I want from life. I'm plenty old enough to know exactly what I'm doing."

"I doubt that," Billy said. Maybe if he hadn't been so panicked at the thought of losing Annie and Raejean, he would have taken more time to think the matter over. But marriage to Cherry Whitelaw would solve so many problems all at once, he accepted her statement at face value.

"All right, Cherry. We'll do this your way. I won't go looking for comfort in town, and you'll provide for my needs at home."

"After we get to know one another," Cherry qualified.

"After we get to know one another," Billy agreed.

He turned onto the main highway and headed for the airport. "Will your parents worry if you don't show up at home tonight?"

"It's prom night. I was supposed to be staying out all night with some friends of mine and have breakfast with them tomorrow. In fact, if you'll stop by my friend's house, I've got an overnight bag there with a change of clothes."

"Good. That'll leave us about twelve hours to get to Las Vegas and tie the knot before we have to face your parents."

Cherry pictured that meeting in her mind. *Good grief,* she thought. *The fur is going to fly.*

Three

The wedding chapel in Las Vegas was brightly lit, even at 3:00 a.m. To Cherry's amazement, they weren't the only couple getting married at such an ungodly hour. She and Billy had to wait ten minutes for an elderly couple to complete their vows before it was their turn. The longer they waited, the more second thoughts she had. What had she been thinking? Zach was going to be furious. Rebecca was going to cry.

The image she conjured of two identical cherubic six-year-old faces was all that kept her from running for a phone to call Zach and Rebecca to come get her. She tried to recall what Billy's twins looked like from the last time she had seen them at church. All she could remember were large dark eyes—like Billy's, she realized now—in small, round faces.

What qualities had they gotten from their mother? Cherry tried to remember how Laura Trask had looked the few times she had seen her. Did the twins have delicate noses like hers? Determined chins? Bowed lips? Had they remained petite like their mother, or become tall and raw-boned like their father?

"If you keep chewing on your lip like that, you're going to gnaw it right off."

Startled, Cherry let go of her lower lip and turned to find Billy behind her.

"Here," he said, handing her a bouquet of gardenias. "I got them from a vendor out in front of the chapel. I thought you might like to carry some flowers.''

''Thank you, Billy.'' Cherry took the bouquet with a hand that shook. ''I guess I'm a little nervous.''

''Me, too,'' he admitted.

Cherry wished he would smile. He didn't.

''The bouquet was a lovely thought.'' She raised it to her nose and sniffed. And sneezed. And sneezed again. ''I must be—*achoo!*''

''Allergic,'' Billy finished, the smile appearing as he retrieved the bouquet from her and set it on an empty folding chair. ''Forget the flowers. There are blooms enough in your cheeks for me.''

''You mean the freckles,'' Cherry said, covering her cheeks with her hands. ''I know they're awful, but—''

Billy took her hands in his and kissed her gently on each cheek. ''They're tasty bits of brown sugar. Didn't anyone ever tell you that?''

Cherry froze as a memory of long ago came to mind. She was sitting on Big Mike's lap at the supper table. He was alternately taking bites of vanilla ice cream and giving her ice-cold kisses across her nose and cheeks, making yummy sounds in his throat and saying, ''Your freckles sure taste sweet, baby.''

Her throat tightened with emotion, and she looked up, half expecting to see Big Mike standing in front of her.

But it was Billy, his brow furrowed as his dark eyes took in the pallor beneath her freckles. ''Are you all right? You look like you're about to faint.''

Cherry stiffened knees that were threatening to buckle. ''I've never fainted in my life. I don't expect to start now.''

''Are you folks ready?'' the minister asked.

''Last chance to back out,'' Billy whispered to Cherry.

The sound tickled her ear, but she managed to stifle the inappropriate giggle that sought voice. This ridiculous wedding ceremony was serious business. ''I'm not backing out. But if you've changed your mind—''

''I haven't,'' Billy interrupted her.

He tightened his grip on one of her hands and released the other, leading her down the aisle to the makeshift pulpit at the front of the room.

Throughout the ceremony, Cherry kept repeating two things over and over.

Those little girls need me. And, *This is the last time I'll be disappointing Zach and Rebecca. Once I'm married, I won't be their responsibility anymore.*

She was concentrating so hard on convincing herself she was doing the right thing that she had to be prompted to respond when the time came.

"Cherry?"

She turned and found Billy's eyes on her. Worried again. *And I won't be a burden to Billy Stonecreek, either,* she added for good measure. "What is it, Billy?"

"Your turn to say I do."

Cherry gave Billy a tremulous smile and said, "I do." It was more of a croak, actually, but when Billy smiled back, she knew it was all right.

"Rings?" the minister asked.

"We don't have any," Billy replied.

The minister pulled open a drawer in a credenza behind him, and she heard a tinny clatter. To Cherry's amazement, the drawer was full of fake gold rings.

"Help yourself," the minister said.

Cherry watched Billy select a plain yellow band and try it on her finger. Too small. The next was too big. The third was also a little loose, but because she wanted the awkward moment over with she said, "This one's fine, Billy."

"That'll be ten dollars extra," the minister said.

She saw the annoyed look that crossed Billy's face and pulled the ring off. "I don't need a ring."

Billy caught it before it could drop into the drawer and put it back on her finger. He caught her chin and lifted it so she was forced to look at him. "I'm sorry, Cherry. I should have thought of getting you a ring. This is so..."

Cheap? Tawdry? Vulgar? Cherry knew what he was thinking, but couldn't bring herself to say it, either. "Don't worry about it, Billy. It doesn't matter."

"You deserve better."

"It's not a real marriage. I don't need a real ring," Cherry said quietly so the minister wouldn't overhear.

Billy let go of her chin. He opened his mouth as though to speak and closed it again. Finally he said, "I guess you're right. This one will have to do. Shall we get this over with?"

They turned back to the minister, and he finished the ceremony. "You may kiss the bride," the minister said at last.

It wasn't a real wedding, so Cherry wasn't expecting a real kiss. To her surprise, Billy put his hands on either side of her face and murmured, "The ring is phony, but at least this can be real."

Cherry had done her share of kissing. Experimenting with sex was an age-old method of teenage rebellion. She thought she knew everything there was to know about kissing and sex. It was no big deal. Boys seemed to like it a lot, but she didn't understand what all the fuss was about.

Something odd happened when Billy Stonecreek's lips feathered across hers. An unexpected curl of desire flitted across her belly and shot up to her breasts. Her hands clutched fistfuls of his Western shirt as his mouth settled firmly over hers. His tongue traced the seam of her closed lips, causing them to tingle. She opened her mouth, and his tongue slipped inside for a quick taste of her.

She made a sound in her throat somewhere between confusion and protest.

His hand slid around to capture her nape and keep her from escaping.

Cherry wasn't going anywhere. She was enthralled by what Billy was doing with his lips and teeth and tongue. She had never felt anything remotely like it. Before she was ready, the kiss ended.

She stared, bemused, into Billy's hooded eyes. His lips were still damp from hers, and she didn't resist the impulse to reach out and touch.

His hand clamped around her wrist like a vise as her fingertips caressed his lips. "Don't." His voice was harsh, and his lips pressed flat in irritation.

Cherry realized her reaction, her naive curiosity, must have embarrassed him. The kiss had merely been a token of thanks from Billy. He didn't want anything from her in return.

She had told him she didn't want to be touched until they knew each other better. But she had touched him. She had set the ground rules, and then she hadn't followed them.

It wasn't a real marriage. She had to remember that.

There were papers to sign and collect before they could leave. The minister was in a hurry, because two more couples had arrived and were awaiting their turns. Minutes after the ceremony ended, she and Billy were back in the rental car they had picked up at the airport.

Billy finally broke the uncomfortable silence that had fallen between them. "I don't know about you, but I could use a few hours of sleep before we fly back. We have the time. Your parents won't start missing you until noon."

"I must admit I feel exhausted," Cherry said. But she wasn't sure whether it was fatigue or a delayed reaction to their strange wedding. She had never wanted to get married, but that didn't mean she hadn't fantasized about having a grand wedding. She had imagined wearing a white satin gown with a train twenty feet long, having at least three bridesmaids, and hearing the wedding processional played on an immense pipe organ. This ceremony had fallen far short of the fantasy.

"Regrets?" Billy asked.

Cherry stared at him, surprised at his intuitiveness. "Were my thoughts that transparent?"

"I can't imagine any woman wanting to get married the way we did. But drastic situations sometimes require drastic solutions. In this case I believe the end—we're now legally husband and wife—justifies the means."

Cherry hoped Zach would see the logic in such an argument.

The hotel Billy chose was outlined in pink and white neon and advertised a honeymoon suite in the center of a pink neon heart. "At least we're sure they've got a honeymoon suite here," Billy said with a cheeky grin.

Cherry laughed breathlessly. "Why would we need a honeymoon suite?"

"It's probably going to have a bigger bed than the other rooms," Billy said. "It'll be more comfortable for someone my size."

"Oh," Cherry said.

"That almost sounded like disappointment," Billy said. "I agreed to wait until you're ready to make it a real marriage. Are you telling me you're ready?''

''No, Billy. I'm not.''

He didn't say anything.

''Are you disappointed?'' Cherry asked.

''I guess grooms have fantasies about their wedding nights the way brides have fantasies about their weddings,'' Billy conceded with a grin. ''Yeah. I suppose I am. But I'll survive.''

Cherry wondered if Billy was remembering his first wedding night. She knew she looked nothing like Laura Trask. She wasn't the least bit petite. Her hair wasn't golden blond, and she didn't move with stately grace. She had a million freckles that speckled her milk-white skin and frizzy hair that changed color depending on the way the sun struck it. She had a small bosom that had no freckles at all and absolutely no intention of letting the groom find that out for himself tonight. No, this was not a night for fulfilling fantasies.

She followed Billy inside the hotel with the overnight bag she had picked up at her friend's house, so they weren't entirely without luggage. She pressed the ring tight against her fourth finger with her thumb so it wouldn't slip off. She stood at Billy's shoulder while he registered and got a key card for the door.

They took the elevator to the top floor and found the honeymoon suite at the end of the hall. Billy used the key card to open the door.

Before she could say anything, Billy picked her up and carried her over the threshold. She was wearing the jeans and T-shirt she had put on to replace the torn chiffon dress and she could feel the heat of him everywhere his body touched hers.

Her arm automatically clutched at his shoulder to help him support her weight, but she realized when she felt the corded muscles there, that he didn't need any help. He carried her over to the bed and let her drop.

She bounced a couple of times and came to rest. ''Good grief,'' she said, staring at the heart-shaped bed. ''How do they expect two people to sleep on something shaped like this?''

He wiggled his eyebrows. ''I don't think they expect you to sleep, if you know what I mean.'' He dropped onto the bed beside her and stretched out on his back with his hands behind his head on one of the pillows. ‘‘It’s nowhere near as big as it looked in neon, either.’’

Cherry scooted as far from him as she could, but although there was plenty of room for two pillows at the top of the bed, the bottom narrowed so their feet ended up nearly touching.

Billy toed off one cowboy boot, then used his stockinged foot to shove off the other boot. He reached for the phone beside the bed. ‘‘I’ll ask for an eight o’clock wake-up call,’’ he said. ‘‘That’ll give us time to fly back before noon.’’

Cherry was wearing tennis shoes, and she reached down and tugged them off with her hands and dropped them on the floor. She lay back on the pillow with her legs as far on her side of the bed as she could get them, which was a few bare inches from Billy’s feet.

Billy reached over and turned out the lamp beside the bed. It should have been dark in the room, but the neon lights outside bathed the room in a romantic pink glow.

‘‘Do you want me to close the curtains?’’ Billy asked.

‘‘It’s kind of pretty.’’

Which might make a difference if they wanted to watch each other while they made love, Cherry thought, but wasn’t going to matter much when they closed their eyes to sleep. But she noticed Billy didn’t get up to close the curtains.

‘‘Good night, Cherry,’’ Billy said, turning on his side away from her. ‘‘Thanks again.’’

‘‘Good night, Billy,’’ Cherry said, turning on her side away from him. ‘‘You’re welcome.’’

She lay there in uncomfortable silence for perhaps five minutes before she whispered, ‘‘Are you asleep, Billy?’’

Cherry felt the bed dip as he turned back toward her.

‘‘I thought you were tired,’’ he said.

‘‘I am. But I’m too excited to sleep. It’s not every day a girl gets married.’’

She stiffened when she felt one of his hands touch her shoulder and slide down to the small of her back.

‘‘Don’t get skittish on me, woman. I’m just going to rub your back a little to help you relax.’’

His thumb hit her somewhere in the center of her back, and his hand wrapped around her side.

Cherry gave a luxuriant sigh as he massaged her tense muscles.

"Feel better?"

"Yes." She was impressed again by his strength. And his gentleness. And wondered how his hand would feel caressing other places on her body.

Cherry sought a subject they could discuss that would get her mind off the direction it seemed to be headed. "Could you tell me a little bit about your daughters?"

"Raejean and Annie are just finishing the first grade. Their teacher has had a devil of a time telling them apart."

"Do they look that much alike?" Cherry asked.

Billy chuckled. "Sometimes they try to fool me. But it isn't hard to tell them apart once you get to know them. Raejean carries herself differently, more confidently. She looks at you more directly and talks back more often. Annie is kinder, sweeter, more thoughtful. She follows Raejean's lead. When the two of them team up, they can be a handful."

"Have you had a lot of trouble with them?"

His hand paused for a moment, then resumed its disturbing massage. "A little. Just lately. I think they're missing Laura as much as I am."

He rubbed a little harder, as though he had admitted something he wished he hadn't.

"Were you expecting twins when they were born?"

Cherry felt his hand tighten uncomfortably on her flesh. She hissed in a breath, and his hand soothed the hurt.

"The twins were a complete surprise. They came early, and for a while it was touch and go whether Laura and the girls would all make it. They did, but there were complications. The doctor said Laura couldn't have any more children."

"You wanted more?"

"I didn't care one way or the other. But Laura did."

Abruptly his hand left her back, and he rolled away from her. "Go to sleep, Cherry."

Apparently their conversation was over, leaving her with a great deal of food for thought.

The twins missed their mother. Like he did.

Cherry could do something to replace the loss in the twins' lives. She could be a mother to Billy's little girls. Of more concern was the temptation she felt to ease Billy's sorrow. There were dangers in such an undertaking. She had to remember this was a temporary marriage. It was safer to let Billy cope with his loss on his own.

On the other hand, Cherry never had chosen the safe path. As she closed her eyes again, she saw the four of them smiling at one another…one happy family.

Billy stared at the neon outside the window, willing himself to sleep. But he couldn't stop thinking about his new wife.

The wedding kiss had surprised him. In the fluorescent light of the wedding chapel, Cherry Whitelaw had looked like anything but a radiant bride. Her blue eyes had been wide with fright and her skin pale beneath a mass of orange freckles. He'd had significant second thoughts about the marriage. And third and fourth thoughts, as well. All his thoughts came back to the same thing. She needed his help. And he needed hers.

He had been proud of her for getting through that awful ceremony—including the last-minute search for a ring that would fit—with so much dignity. That was why he had offered her the kiss, not because he had been wondering what her lips would taste like. When she had reached out to him afterward, he had stopped her because that wasn't part of their deal, not because he had been shocked at the way his body had gone rock-hard at her touch. Just thinking about it caused the same reaction all over again.

Billy swore.

"Billy? Is something wrong?"

"Nothing's wrong, Cherry. Go to sleep."

He closed his eyes, determined to get some rest, but a picture of her breast half revealed by the torn chiffon bodice appeared behind his eyelids.

He opened his eyes and stared at the neon again. Who would have thought he would find a freckle-faced redhead so erotically exciting? Or that his new wife would be off-limits for heaven knew how long?

Billy heaved a long-suffering sigh. It was going to be one hell of a marriage.

His eyes slid closed again as sleep claimed his exhausted body.

Billy was having a really spectacular dream. He had a handful of soft female breast, which just happened to belong to his new wife. Her eyes were closed in passion, and as he flicked his thumb across her nipple, he heard a moan that made his loins tighten. He lowered his head to take her nipple in his mouth. It was covered by a thin layer of cotton. He sucked on her through the damp cloth and felt her body arch toward him. Her hands threaded into his hair…and yanked on it—

Billy came awake with a jerk. ''What the hell?''

Cherry was sitting bolt upright in bed with her hands crossed defensively under her breasts. A damp spot on her T-shirt revealed that he hadn't been dreaming.

It shouldn't have surprised him. His last thoughts before drifting to sleep had been about Cherry. No wonder his body had been drawn to hers during the night. He shoved a hand through hair that was standing on end and groaned. ''God, Cherry, I'm sorry. I was dreaming.''

She eyed him suspiciously.

''I swear I didn't know what I was doing.''

That made her look crestfallen.

''Not that it isn't exactly what I'd like to be doing at this moment,'' he said.

She gave a hitching breath that was almost a sob. ''We agreed to wait.''

''Yeah, I know,'' Billy said. ''I don't suppose you've changed your mind.''

She hesitated so long he thought maybe she had. Until she shook her head no.

Billy looked at the clock. It was only six. But he didn't trust himself to lie back down beside her. ''I can't sleep anymore. How about if we head for the airport?''

''All right,'' she said.

He started pulling on his boots and felt her hand on his shoulder. He froze.

She cleared her throat and said, ''I liked what you were doing, Billy. It felt...good. I wanted you to know that. It's just...''

He shoved his foot down into the boot and stood. He had to get away from her or he was going to turn around and lay her flat on the bed and do something he would be sorry for later. ''I know,'' he said. ''We agreed to wait.''

She had a brave smile on her face. And looked every bit her youthful age.

What on earth had possessed him to marry her?

It was a silent flight from Las Vegas to the airport in Amarillo. And an even more silent truck ride to the Stonecreek Ranch. Billy pulled up to the back door of a large, two-story white clapboard house and killed the engine. The blue morning glories he had planted for Laura were soaking up the midday sun on a trellis along the eastern edge of the porch.

''We're home,'' Billy said. His throat tightened painfully. They were the same words he had spoken to Laura—how many years ago?—when they had moved into this house.

Suddenly he realized he couldn't go back into Laura's house right now with a new wife. It was still too full of Laura. He needed a little time to accept the fact that she really was gone forever.

''Look, why don't you go inside and introduce yourself to Mrs. Motherwell, my housekeeper. I just realized I was supposed to pick up a load of feed in town this morning. I'll be back in an hour or so.''

Cherry was staring at him as if he had grown a second head. ''You want me to go in there without you?'' she asked.

''Just tell Mrs. Motherwell you've come to replace her. I'll explain everything to the kids when I get back.'' When Cherry continued sitting there staring at him, he snapped, ''Changed your mind already?''

His new wife looked sober and thoughtful. There were shadows of fatigue beneath her eyes. ''No. I'm determined to see this through.'' She gave him one last anxious look before she left the truck. ''Don't be gone long.''

''I won't.''

Billy resisted the urge to gun the engine as he backed away from the house. Once he hit paved road he headed the truck toward town. He hadn't gone two miles when he saw flashing red and blue lights behind him. He glanced down at the speedometer and swore. He swerved off the road and braked hard enough to raise a cloud of dust.

He was out of the truck and reaching for his wallet to get his driver's license when he saw the highway patrolman had a gun in his hand that was pointed at him.

''Freeze, Stonecreek, or I'll blow your head off.''

Billy froze. ''What the hell's the matter with you?''

''Put your hands up. You're under arrest.''

''Arrest? For what?''

''Kidnapping.''

It took a full second for the charge to register. *Kidnapping?* Then he realized what must have happened and groaned. ''Look, Officer, I can explain everything.''

''You have the right to remain silent,'' the officer began.

Billy's lips pressed flat. He had married Cherry Whitelaw in the hope of solving his problems. Instead he had jumped right out of the frying pan into the fire.

Four

Cherry stared at the back door of Billy's house—now her home, too—trying to work up the courage to go inside, wondering, absurdly, if she should knock first.

She turned and stole a glance at Billy's rugged profile as he drove away, pondering what it was about him she had found so beguiling. He had rescued her, listened to her troubles, and shared his in return. She had felt his desperation and responded to it. Now he was her husband. She twisted the cheap gold ring that confirmed it wasn't all a dream, that she was, indeed, Mrs. Billy Stonecreek.

Good grief. What had she done?

Cherry had gone off half-cocked in the past, but the enormity of this escapade was finally sinking in. Surely it would have been better to face Zach and Rebecca and explain the truth of what had happened at the dance. How was she going to justify this latest lapse of common sense?

She felt a surge of anger at Billy for abandoning her at the door. It wouldn't have taken long to introduce her to Mrs. Motherwell and explain the situation. So why hadn't he done it?

Maybe because he's having the same second thoughts as you are. Maybe in the cold light of day he's thinking he made a bad bargain. Maybe he's trying to figure out a way right now to get out of it.

If the back door hadn't opened at that precise moment, Cherry would have turned and headed for Hawk's Pride.

But it did. And Cherry found herself face-to-face with Penelope Trask.

''I saw you standing out here,'' Mrs. Trask said. ''Is there something I can do for you?''

''I, uh… Is Mrs. Motherwell here?''

''She packed her bags and left this morning.''

Cherry stood with her jaw agape, speechless for perhaps the first time in her life. Had Mrs. Trask already managed to gain legal custody of Billy's children? Had their marriage been for naught? She wished Billy were here.

''Don't I know you? Aren't you one of those Whitelaw Bra—'' Mrs. Trask cut herself off.

Cherry knew what she had been about to say. The eight adopted Whitelaw kids were known around this part of Texas as the Whitelaw Brats, just like Zach and his siblings before them, and Grandpa Garth and his siblings before that. Cherry had done her share to help earn the nickname. She was proud to be one of them.

She met the older woman's disdainful look with defiance. ''Yes, I'm a Whitelaw Brat. You have a problem with that?''

''None at all. But if you're looking for your missing sister, she isn't here. I have no idea what my no-account excuse for a son-in-law has done with her.'' She started to close the door in Cherry's face.

Cherry stuck her foot in the door. ''Wait! What are you talking about?''

A flare of recognition lit Mrs. Trask's eyes. ''Oh, my God. You're the girl, aren't you? The one Billy kidnapped.'' She stuck her head out the screen door and looked around. ''Where is he? I have a few things to say to him.''

''Kidnapped?'' Cherry gasped. ''I wasn't kidnapped!''

''Your parents reported you missing late last night.''

''Why would they think I was with Billy?''

''Your date wrapped his car around a telephone pole, and when he kept mumbling your name the police called your parents, thinking maybe you'd been thrown from the car. At the hospital, the boy told your father that he'd left you at the stock pond with Billy, after my son-in-law ran him off with his fists.

''Your father couldn't find you at the stock pond, and when he came looking for you here in a rage, Mrs. Motherwell called me. Your father seemed bent on strangling someone before the night was out.''

Probably me, Cherry thought morosely.

''Of course I came right over,'' Mrs. Trask said. ''All I could tell your father was that I wouldn't put it past my reckless son-in-law to kidnap an innocent young woman.''

''Mrs. Trask, I wasn't kidnapped.''

''I suggest you go home and tell that to your father. He told the police Billy must have kidnapped you, because you'd never go off on your own like that.'' Mrs. Trask smirked. ''Of course, that was before he found out you'd been expelled from school earlier in the evening.''

Cherry groaned.

''You're in an awful lot of trouble, young lady. Where have you been? And where's Billy?''

Cherry put a hand to her throbbing temple. Zach and Rebecca must be frantic with worry. And disappointed beyond belief. She didn't want to think about how angry they were going to be when they heard what she had done.

''May I please use your phone?'' It was her phone now, so she shouldn't have to ask. Except, this didn't seem the right moment to announce that she and Billy had run off to Las Vegas to get married.

Mrs. Trask hesitated, then pushed the screen door open wide. ''Come on in, if you must.''

As soon as Cherry's eyes adjusted to the dim light in the kitchen, she saw Raejean and Annie standing together near the table.

They wore their straight black hair in adorable, beribboned pigtails, and stared at her with dark, serious brown eyes. Their noses were small and their chins dainty, like their mother, but they had high, sharp cheekbones that reminded her of Billy. They were tall for six-year-olds and dressed exactly alike in collared blouses tucked into denim coveralls and white tennis shoes.

''Hello, Raejean,'' she said, addressing the child who had her arm wrapped comfortingly around the other's shoulder.

The child's eyes widened in surprise at being recognized. Then she said, ''I'm not Raejean, I'm Annie.''

The other twin's mouth dropped open, and she glanced at her sister.

Then she turned to Cherry, pointed to her chest with her thumb, and said, ''I'm Raejean.''

''I see,'' Cherry said. They were both missing the exact same front tooth. No help there telling them apart. Billy had said Raejean was the confident one, so Cherry had assumed it was Raejean who was giving comfort to her sister. But maybe she had been wrong.

''I need to use your phone,'' she said, moving toward where it hung on the kitchen wall.

Cherry felt the girls watching her while she dialed.

''We don't need another housekeeper,'' the twin who had identified herself as Annie said. ''We're going to stay at Nana's house until Daddy gets home.''

Cherry felt her heart miss a beat. She turned to Mrs. Trask and said, ''Billy went into town for supplies. He should be back any time now. There's no need to take the girls anywhere.''

''I'll be the best judge of that,'' Mrs. Trask said. ''Go upstairs, girls, and finish packing.''

The twins turned and ran. Cherry heard their footsteps pounding on the stairs as the ringing phone was answered by her sister, Jewel. Of her seven Whitelaw siblings, Jewel was the sister closest to her in age. Jewel had been adopted by Zach and Rebecca when she was five—the first of the current generation of Whitelaw Brats.

It had taken Cherry a while to straighten them all out, but now she could recite their names and ages with ease. Rolleen was 21, Jewel was 19, she was 18, Avery was 17, Jake was 16, Frannie was 13, Rabbit was 12, and Colt was 11.

Of course Rabbit's name wasn't really Rabbit, it was Louis, but nobody called him that. Jewel had given him the nickname Rabbit when he was little, because he ate so many carrots, and the name had stuck. Colt was the only one of them who had been adopted as a baby. The rest of them had all known at least one other parent before being abandoned, orphaned, or fostered out.

''Is anybody there?'' Jewel asked breathlessly. ''If this is the kidnapper, we'll pay whatever you ask.''

''It's me, Jewel.''

''Cherry! Where are you? Are you all right? Are you hurt?''

''I'm fine. I'm at Billy Stonecreek's ranch.''

"So he did kidnap you! I'll send Daddy to get you right away."

"No! I mean..." Cherry had turned her back to Mrs. Trask and kept her voice low thus far, but she figured there was no sense postponing the inevitable. "Billy didn't kidnap me. Last night we flew to Las Vegas and got married."

She was met with stunned silence on the other end of the line. Which was a good thing, because Mrs. Trask gave an outraged shriek that brought the two little girls back downstairs on the run.

"Nana! Nana! What's wrong?"

"I have to go now, Jewel," Cherry said. "Tell Zach and Rebecca I'm okay, and that I'll come to see them soon and explain everything."

"Cherry, don't—"

Cherry hung up the phone in time to turn and greet the twins a second time. Again, she identified the twin taking the lead as Raejean, which meant the one standing slightly behind her was Annie. "Hello, Raejean. Hello, Annie."

"I'm Annie," Raejean contradicted.

Before Annie could misidentify herself as Raejean, Mrs. Trask snapped, "Don't bother trying to tell them apart. They're identical, you know."

"But—" From Billy's descriptions of them it was so obvious to her which twin was which. Couldn't Mrs. Trask see the difference?

"What's wrong, Nana?" Raejean asked. "Why did you scream?"

Mrs. Trask's face looked more like a beet or a turnip than a human head, she was so flushed. It was clear she wasn't sure exactly what to say.

"Your grandmother was just excited about some news she heard," Cherry said.

"What news?" Annie asked.

"It's a surprise I think your Daddy will want to tell you about himself when he gets home," Cherry said.

"We're not going to be here that long," Mrs. Trask retorted. "The girls and I are leaving."

"Not until Billy gets back," Cherry said firmly. "I'm sure Raejean and Annie want to wait and say goodbye to their father." Cherry turned to the girls and asked, "Don't you?"

Raejean eyed her consideringly, but Annie piped up, "I want to wait for Daddy."

Mrs. Trask made an angry sound in her throat. "I hope you're happy now," she said to Cherry. "My grandchildren have had a difficult enough time over the past year, without adding someone like you to the picture."

Cherry reminded herself that Mrs. Trask was always going to be Raejean and Annie's grandmother. Throwing barbs now, however satisfying it might be, would only cause problems later. Zach and Rebecca would have been astounded at her tact when she spoke.

"I'm sorry we surprised you like this, Mrs. Trask. I know Billy will want to explain everything to you himself. Won't you consider waiting until he returns before you leave?"

"No."

Of course, there were times when being blunt worked best. Cherry crossed to stand beside the twins. "I'm sorry you have to leave, Mrs. Trask. The girls and I will have Billy give you a call when he gets home."

Cherry saw the moment when Mrs. Trask realized that she had been outmaneuvered. She wasn't going to make a quick and easy escape with Billy's children. Cherry was there to stand in her way.

Billy chose that moment to pull open the screen door and step into the kitchen.

Annie and Raejean gave shrieks of joy and raced into his wide open arms. He lifted them both, one in each arm, and gave them each a smacking kiss. "How are my girls?" he asked.

Raejean answered for both of them.

"Some man got mad at Mrs. Motherwell because she didn't know where you were and Nana came and Mrs. Motherwell packed her bags and left and Nana said we should pack, too, and go live with her until you came back home, only this lady came a little while ago and said you were coming home really soon and we had to wait for you because you have a surprise for us. What's our surprise, Daddy? Can we have it now?"

Cherry had watched Billy's narrowed gaze flicker from his daughter to Mrs. Trask and back again as Raejean made her breathless recital.

When Raejean got to the part about a surprise, his gaze shot to her, and she thought she saw both panic and resignation.

''What are you doing back here so soon?'' Mrs. Trask said. ''I was told you were going into town for supplies.''

''I got stopped by the police long before I got there and arrested for kidnapping,'' Billy said.

''Then why aren't you in jail?'' Mrs. Trask demanded.

Billy's lips curled. ''I showed them my marriage license.''

''Who got kidnapped, Daddy?'' Annie asked.

''Nobody, sweetheart,'' Billy replied. ''It was all a big mistake.''

''Then, can we have our surprise now?'' Annie asked.

He knelt down and set them back on their feet. Keeping an arm around each of them, he said, ''The surprise is that you have a new mother.''

Annie's brow furrowed. ''A new mother?''

Raejean frowned. ''Our mother is in heaven.''

''I know that,'' Billy said in a sandpaper-rough voice that made Cherry's throat swell with emotion. ''I've married someone else who's going to be your mother from now on.''

Raejean and Annie looked at each other, then turned as one to stare with shocked, suspicious eyes at Cherry.

Raejean's head shot around to confront her father. ''Her?''

Billy nodded.

Raejean jerked free and shouted, ''I don't want another mother! Make her go away!'' Then she ran from the room.

Annie's eyes had filled with tears and one spilled over as she stared at Raejean's fleeing form. Cherry willed the softhearted child to accept her, but Annie paused only another moment before she turned and ran after her sister.

Cherry met Billy's stricken gaze. She felt sick to her stomach. The two charming and innocent little girls she had married Billy to save from harm, didn't want anything to do with her.

''You're a fool, Billy,'' Mrs. Trask said, grabbing her purse from the kitchen counter. ''I don't know what you hoped to accomplish with this charade, but it won't work. I'm more convinced than ever that my grandchildren belong with me.'' She gave Cherry a look down her nose. ''I'll see you both in court.''

She made a grand exit through the doorway that led to the front of the house. Cherry and Billy stood unmoving until they heard the front door slam behind her.

"She's right," Billy said. "I always intend to do the right thing, but somehow it turns out wrong."

"This wasn't wrong, Billy. If I hadn't gotten here when I did, Mrs. Trask would have taken the children and been gone before you returned. At least Raejean and Annie are still here."

"And angry and unhappy."

"We can change that with time."

"I hope so. It won't help much to argue in court that I've got a wife to take care of my children, if my children hate her guts."

"We have a more immediate problem," Cherry said.

"What's that?"

"Zach Whitelaw."

"What about him?"

"He's going to kill you on sight."

Billy gave a relieved laugh. "Is that all? I thought it was something serious."

"Don't joke," Cherry said. "This is serious. Three years ago a boy tried to force himself on Jewel at a Fourth of July picnic. I'll never forget the look in Zach's eyes when Jewel stood crying in his arms, her face bruised and her dress torn. He took a horsewhip to the boy and nearly flayed him alive. Both families kept it quiet, but you know how that sort of thing gets around. None of us girls has ever had any problems with boys since then.

"That's why it surprised me when Ray... If Ray hadn't been drunk, he would never have done what he did."

"And we wouldn't be where we are today," Billy said. "I won't let any man whip me, Cherry. If your father tries—"

"I'm only telling you all this so you'll understand why I have to go home and explain all of this to him by myself. Once he understands I was willing and—"

Billy shook his head. "We go together, or you don't go at all."

"Zach's going to be furious with me."

"All the more reason for us to go together. You may have been his daughter yesterday, but you're my wife today. No man is going to threaten my wife. Not even her father."

Cherry stared wide-eyed at Billy. She supposed she should have told him that no matter how angry Zach got with her, he would never raise a hand to her. In the past she had been sent to her room without supper, or been forced to spend a day alone thinking about the wisdom of a course of action. But the Whitelaws had always used reason, rather than force, to teach their children right from wrong.

Billy wouldn't have to defend her, but she reveled in the thought that he was willing to do so. Of more concern to her was the possibility that the two men might provoke one another to violence. She already knew that Billy liked to fight. Zach would be more than willing to give him one.

"I'll let you come with me on one condition," she said.

"What's that?"

"We bring the girls with us."

Billy frowned. "What purpose would that serve?"

"Zach won't be able to fight with you—or yell at me—if he's busy meeting his new grandchildren."

"Raejean and Annie don't even like you. What makes you think they'll take to your father?"

"Trust me. Zach Whitelaw could sell snow in Alaska. He'll have Raejean and Annie eating out of his hand in no time. Besides, we have no choice but to take them with us. Mrs. Motherwell is gone."

"I forgot about that," Billy said as he headed toward the door that led upstairs. "Damn. All right. Let me go get them. We might as well get this meeting over with."

"Billy," Cherry called after him. When he stopped and turned to her, she said, "We can still call the whole thing off."

He walked the few steps back to her and lifted her chin with his finger. "Buck up, kid. You're doing great."

Cherry felt tears prickle her eyes and blinked to keep them from forming.

Billy leaned down and kissed her mouth. His touch was gentle, intended to comfort. "I'm sorry, Cherry. I shouldn't have left you here alone and driven away. It's not easy to admit it, but I was scared."

Cherry searched his eyes. If he had once been afraid, the fear was gone now. If he had regrets, he wasn't letting her see them. She wished she knew him better as a person. Could she rely on him? Would he be there for her when the going got rough?

When he pulled her into his arms and hugged her, she felt safe and secure. She knew that was an illusion. Her father had made her feel safe, too. But they had been torn from each other. It was better not to try and make more of this relationship than it was.

Before she could edge herself away from Billy, the screen door was flung open. Billy threw her aside to confront whatever danger threatened them.

Zach Whitelaw stood in the doorway.

Five

''Daddy, don't!'' Cherry cried as Zach took a step toward Billy, his hands tightened into angry knots.

Zach froze, his eyes wide with shock.

It took Cherry a second to realize she had called him ''Daddy'' instead of ''Zach,'' something she had never done before. She felt confused, unsure why she had blurted it out like that, especially now, when she wasn't going to be his daughter anymore, but someone else's wife.

''Please don't fight,'' she said.

''Stay out of this, Cherry,'' Billy said, his hands curling into fists as menacing as Zach's.

''How did you get here so quickly?'' Cherry said to her father. ''I just got off the phone with Jewel.''

''The police called me when they picked up Billy. A phony marriage license isn't going to save you from me,'' he snarled at Billy.

''We really are married,'' Cherry said, taking a step to put herself between the two men. Temporarily, it kept them from throwing punches.

Zach snorted. ''In a Las Vegas ceremony? That's no kind of wedding.''

''It's legal,'' Billy said coldly.

There was nothing Zach could say to counter that except, ''Come home, Cherry. I know the situation last night must have upset you, but

Rebecca and I want you to know we're on your side. We believe there must be some reasonable explanation for what happened. We can fix this problem.''

''It's too late for that. Billy and I are married. I'm staying with him.''

Zach glared at Billy. ''You should be ashamed of yourself, taking advantage of a vulnerable child to—''

''She's no child,'' Billy said quietly. ''She's a woman. And my wife.'' His hands slid around Cherry's waist from behind, and he pulled her back against the length of his body.

Cherry saw the inference Zach drew from Billy's words and actions that the two of them had done what husbands and wives do on their wedding night. By the time her father's gaze skipped to her face, she bore a flush high on her cheekbones that seemed to confirm what he was thinking. There was no way she was going to admit the truth.

She saw the wounded look in Zach's eyes before he hid it behind lowered lids.

''I didn't meant to hurt you or Rebecca,'' she forced past the lump in her throat.

''Why, Cherry?'' he asked. ''Why couldn't you trust us to be on your side? I thought...''

They were good parents. They had done everything they could to make her feel loved and appreciated, safe and secure. But they expected her to believe parents could protect their children from the evils of the world. She knew from experience that simply wasn't true. She could never trust them completely. She would never trust anybody that much again.

''I'm sorry, Zach.'' She saw his gaze flicker at her reversion to the less familiar, less personal title. ''Please tell Rebecca—''

Zach cut her off. ''You explain this to your mother. I couldn't find the words.'' He turned and left as abruptly as he had come.

Cherry felt her nose burning, felt the tears threaten and fought them back. She had chosen to travel this road. She had no one to blame but herself for her predicament. Crying over spilled milk wasn't going to accomplish anything.

''Thanks for sticking by me,'' Billy said against her ear.

''I'm your wife.''

''Sometimes that doesn't mean much when parents enter the picture,'' Billy said bitterly.

Cherry turned in his embrace and put her arms around him to hug him, laying her cheek against his shoulder. ''I'll try to be a good wife, Billy.'' She raised her face to his, only to find herself unexpectedly kissed.

There was as much desperation as there was hunger in Billy's kiss. Something inside Cherry responded to both emotions, and she found herself kissing Billy back.

''Hey! What are you doing to my dad?''

Cherry pulled free of Billy's grasp and turned to the urchin who had spoken. Behind her stood the other twin, her face less belligerent, more perplexed.

''Uh...'' Cherry began. She had no idea where to go from there. She expected Billy to make some sort of explanation, but he gave her a helpless one-shouldered shrug. Cherry turned back to the twins and said to the one who had spoken, ''Your dad and I were kissing, Raejean. That's what married people do.''

''I'm Annie,'' Raejean said.

''I'm Raejean,'' Annie dutifully added.

''Hey, you two,'' Billy said. ''What's the big idea trying to fool Cherry?''

Raejean's chin jutted. ''I don't know why you're so mad, Daddy. She isn't fooled at all.'' She turned to Cherry, her brow furrowed. ''How do you do that, anyway? No one but Mommy and Daddy has ever been able to tell us apart.''

Cherry said, ''There's nothing magic about it. You're as different from your sister as night from day.''

''We're twins,'' Raejean protested. ''We're *exactly* alike.''

''You look alike on the outside,'' Cherry conceded, ''but inside here—'' Cherry touched her head. ''And here—'' She touched her heart. ''You're very different.''

''I'm glad you can tell us apart,'' Annie said. ''I don't like fooling people.''

''I don't care if you can tell us apart,'' Raejean said. ''I'm not going to like you.''

"Isn't it a little soon to make up your mind about that?" Cherry asked. "You hardly know me."

"I know you want to be my mother. I don't want another mother. My mother's in heaven!" Raejean turned and headed for the stairs. She hadn't gone very far before she realized Annie hadn't automatically followed her. She turned and said, "Come on, Annie."

Annie hesitated briefly before she turned and followed her sister.

Cherry whirled on Billy the instant they were gone. "I can't do this all by myself, Billy. You're going to have to help."

"You can't blame them for being confused, Cherry. After all, the only woman they've ever seen me kissing is their mother."

"Then maybe we shouldn't let the girls see us kissing. Maybe you should keep your distance when they're around."

Billy thought about it for a moment, then shook his head. "I don't want to do that for two reasons. Penelope would be sure to notice if we never touched each other. It would be a dead giveaway that there's something fishy about our marriage."

"And the second reason?"

"I don't want my daughters to see me ignoring the woman they believe is my wife. It would give them the wrong impression of what marriage is all about."

"I see." What she saw was that Billy had all sorts of reasons for kissing and hugging her that had nothing whatsoever to do with actually loving her. But loving hadn't been a part of their bargain. She had to remind herself of the rules of this game. *Help each other out. Don't get involved. Don't start to care.* That way lay heartache.

"All right, Billy," Cherry said. "I'll play along with you where the kissing and touching is concerned. So long as we both know it's only an act, I suppose neither of us can be hurt. Now that we have that settled, I believe you need to get to town for those supplies, and I'd better get some lunch started."

Cherry turned her back on Billy, but she hadn't taken two steps toward the sink before his arms slid around her from behind again, circling her waist. Her treacherous body melted against him. She forced herself to stiffen in his embrace. "Don't, Billy," she said in a quiet voice.

"You're my wife, Cherry."

"In name only," Cherry reminded him. "We can pretend for everybody else, but I think it's best if we're honest with each other. We aren't in love, Billy. We never will be."

Billy's hands dropped away, but he didn't move. She felt the heat of his body along the entire length of her back. Her eyes slid closed, and she held herself rigid to keep from leaning back into his fiery warmth.

"If we're being honest," Billy said in a husky voice, "I think you should know I'm more than a little attracted to you, Cherry. I have been since the moment I first laid eyes on you." Billy took her by the shoulders and turned her to face him. "That's the truth."

She lifted her eyes to meet his. "That's lust, Billy. Not love."

His dark eyes narrowed, and his hands dropped away from her shoulders. "There's nothing wrong with desiring your wife in bed."

"I'm not your wi—"

"Dammit, Cherry!"

When Billy took a step back and shoved his hands into his jeans pockets, Cherry had the distinct impression he did it to keep himself from reaching for her again.

"You *are* my wife," he said through gritted teeth. "Not forever. Not even for very long. But we most definitely are married. I suggest you start thinking that way!"

Before she could contradict him, he was gone, the screen door slamming behind him.

Billy couldn't remember a time when he had been more frustrated. Even when he had been arguing with Laura about whether or not she should try to get pregnant again when the doctor had advised her against it, he hadn't felt so much like he was butting his head against a stone wall. Deep down, he knew Cherry was right. It would be better for both of them if he kept his distance from her.

He had made up his mind to try.

Of course, that was before he stepped into Cherry's bedroom the morning after their wedding. He had expected her to be up and dressed, since he had helped her set the alarm for 5:30 a.m. the previous evening. Apparently, she had turned it off.

He found her sleeping beneath tousled sheets, one long, exquisite leg exposed all the way to her hip, one rosy nipple peeking at him, her lips slightly parted, her silky red curls spread across the pillow, waiting for a lover's hands to gather them up.

He cleared his throat noisily, hoping that would be enough to wake her. All she did was roll over, rearranging the sheet, exposing an entire milky white breast.

He swallowed hard and averted his eyes. He sat down beside her, thinking maybe the dip in the mattress would make her aware of his presence.

She slept on.

His gaze returned to rest on her face. Close as he was, he could see the dark shadows under her eyes. She must not have slept very well. He could understand that. He hadn't slept too well himself. He had resorted to a desperate act—marriage—to solve one problem and had created a host of others in the process. Not the least of which was the fact he wanted to have carnal knowledge of his new wife.

He debated whether he ought to kiss her awake. But he wasn't Prince Charming. And Sleeping Beauty had never had such a freckled face. Nevertheless, his body responded to the mere thought of pressing his lips against hers, of tasting the hot, sweet wetness of her mouth.

Billy swore viciously.

And Cherry woke with a start.

It took her a second to realize how exposed she was, and she grabbed at the sheet as she sat up and drew her knees to her chest. Her blue eyes were wide and wary. "What are you doing in here?"

"I came to wake you up. You overslept."

She glanced at the clock, then dropped her forehead to her knees and groaned. "I must have turned off the alarm."

"I figured as much when you didn't show up in the kitchen. I've already had my breakfast. I left some coffee perking for you. The kids'll be up in a little while. You probably have time for a quick shower."

Thinking about her naked in the shower had about the same effect as contemplating kissing her. Billy needed to leave, but he was too aware of what Cherry would see if he stood right now. So he went right on sitting where he was.

Unfortunately, she now had the sheet flattened against herself, and he could see the darker outline of her nipples beneath the soft cotton. He found that every bit as erotic as seeing her naked.

"Hell," Billy muttered, shifting uncomfortably on the edge of the bed.

"What's the matter?"

Billy's lip curled wryly. "I'm not used to looking at a woman in bed without being able to touch."

"Oh." She clutched the sheet tighter, exposing the fact that her nipples had become hard nubs.

Billy bolted to his feet and saw her gaze lock on the bulge beneath his zipper. He froze where he was, his body aching, his mouth dry.

He watched her until she lifted her eyes to his face. Her pupils were enormous, her lips full, as though he had been kissing her. She was aroused, and he hadn't even touched her.

"Tell me to go, Cherry." He wanted to consume her in a hurry, like ice cream on a hot day. He wanted to take his time and sip at her slow and easy, like a cool mint julep on a lazy summer afternoon.

She licked her lips, and he felt his body harden like stone.

"The girls will be up soon," Cherry reminded him. "I need to get dressed."

Heaven help him, he had forgotten all about his daughters. He shoved a distracted hand through his hair and huffed out a breath of air. "I'll be working on the range today. If you need anything..."

Cherry smiled. "Don't worry about us, Billy. We'll manage fine."

"All right. So long."

He was almost out the door when she called him back.

"Billy?"

He turned and found her standing beside the bed with the sheet draped around her in a way that revealed as much as it covered. "What?" he asked, his voice hoarse from the sudden rush of desire he felt.

"You didn't kiss me goodbye."

He shook his head. "I don't think that would be a good idea, Cherry."

Before he realized what she had in mind, she closed the few steps between them and lifted her face to him. "I thought a lot about our situation last night, when I couldn't sleep," she said earnestly. "And

I realized that if we're going to convince Mrs. Trask that this is a real marriage, we're going to have to act as much like a happily married couple as possible.

"Zach always gives Rebecca a kiss goodbye in the morning." She gave him a winsome smile. "So, pucker up, Mr. Stonecreek, and give me a kiss."

She didn't give him much of a choice. She raised herself on tiptoe and leaned forward and pressed her lips against his.

Billy gathered her in his arms and pulled her close as his mouth opened over hers, taking what he had denied himself only moments before. His hands slid down her naked back, shoving the sheet out of his way. Then he held her buttocks tight against his arousal with one hand while the other caught her nape and slid up to grasp a handful of her hair.

He took his time kissing her, his tongue thrusting hard and deep, and then slowing for several soft, probing forays, seeking the honey within. She made a moaning sound deep in her throat, and he gave an answering growl of passion.

When he let her go at last, she gave him a dazed look through half-closed lids, then grabbed at the sheet that had slid down to her waist and pulled it back up to cover herself. He grinned and said, "That was a good idea. I think we'll keep it up."

It took all the willpower he had to turn and walk out the bedroom door.

Cherry watched Billy go this time without calling him back. She was still quivering from his kiss. She forced her wobbly legs to take one step, and then another, as she headed for the bentwood rocker where she had thrown her robe. She slipped it on and let the sheet drop to the floor.

She was tying her terry-cloth robe closed when she heard a knock on the door. She hurried to open it and found Billy standing there with his hat on, his hip cocked, and his thumbs in his front pockets.

"Did you forget something?" she asked.

Not a thing, Billy realized. He remembered exactly how she had looked in bed. *And you look as delicious in that robe as you did in bed.* He couldn't very well tell her he had come back just to look at her again. So he said, ''I forgot to say good morning.'' He smiled and tipped his hat. ''Mornin', ma'am.''

Cherry laughed.

And then, because he was looking for an excuse to spend more time with her, he said, ''I wondered if you'd like to join me for a cup of coffee before I leave.''

''I should get dressed,'' Cherry said, tightening the belt on her robe. ''The girls will be up soon.''

''You're right about that.'' Billy searched for something else to say, because otherwise he would have no excuse to linger.

''By the way, I never got around to telling you, but you'll need to go grocery shopping today. The ranch has an account at the store in town. I think Harvey Mills already knows we're married—I doubt there's anyone in the county who doesn't know by now—but just in case, I'll give him a call and tell him to put your name on the account. Feel free to get anything you think we'll need.''

It was more than Cherry had heard Billy say at one time since she had met him at the pond. But the words had nothing to do with what he was saying with his eyes. His eyes were eating her alive. Her heart was pumping hard. Her breasts felt full. Her mouth felt dry.

She cleared her throat and said, ''Shopping. Got it. Anything else?''

''Not unless you'd like that cup of coffee.''

Cherry slowly shook her head. She had to send him away or she was going to invite him into her room. ''I need to shower and dress before the girls wake up. Have a nice day, Billy.''

''Yeah. I'll do that.''

When he didn't leave, she raised a brow and said, ''Is there something else, Billy?''

''If you want, I can go with you later today to see your family...to explain things.''

Cherry felt a sense of relief. ''Thanks, Billy. I'd like that.''

''Well. I guess I'd better get started.''

It took him another moment or two before he moved away from the door. She watched his sexy, loose-limbed amble until he was gone from sight, then scurried up the stairs to the shower.

However, when she reached the bathroom, it was locked. She would have to wait her turn. She leaned against the wall, a towel over her arm, one bare foot perched atop the other and waited. And waited. The door never opened.

She leaned her ear against the door, but there was no sound coming from inside. She knocked and said, ''Is someone in there?''

No answer.

''Raejean? Annie?''

Nothing.

She walked down the hall to the girls' bedroom. Their unmade twin beds were empty. She checked the other doors along the hall and found an office and Billy's bedroom, but no sign of the children.

''Raejean!'' she called loudly. ''Annie! If you're hiding somewhere up here, I want you to come out right now!''

Nothing.

She crossed back to the bathroom door and listened intently. She thought she heard whispers. She banged on the door. ''I know you two are in there. I want you to come out right now.''

Nothing.

She grabbed the doorknob and yanked on it, then slammed her shoulder against the door as though to break it open. ''Open up!''

Nothing.

Cherry leaned back against the wall and sighed heavily. She hadn't counted on this sort of misbehavior when she had nobly volunteered to rescue Billy's daughters from their grandmother's clutches. Right now, Mrs. Trask was more than welcome to the two of them!

Cherry smiled. Actually, she had pulled the same trick on one of her foster parents. She had spent almost two days in the bathroom before hunger finally forced her out. Which gave her an idea.

''All right, fine, stay in there. But you're going to get awfully hungry before the day is out. I'm going downstairs and make myself some blueberry pancakes with whipped cream on top and scrambled eggs and sausage and wash it all down with some hot chocolate with marshmallows.''

Loud, agitated whispers.

The bathroom door opened and one of the twins stuck her head out. ''Whipped cream on pancakes?''

Cherry nodded.

An identical face appeared and asked, ''Big marshmallows? Or little ones?''

''Which do you prefer?''

''Little ones. Mrs. Motherwell only bought the big ones.''

''Then we'll cut them into little pieces,'' Cherry suggested.

''All right.'' Annie shot out of the bathroom before Raejean could stop her and took Cherry by the hand. ''Let's go.''

Cherry waited to see what Raejean would do. The twin obviously wasn't happy to see rebellion in the ranks. She seemed unsure whether to stay where she was or abandon the fort. Her stomach growled and settled the matter. Raejean left the bathroom and headed down the hall toward the stairs, ignoring the hand Cherry held out to her.

Cherry realized as she followed Raejean down the stairs, Annie chattering excitedly beside her, that she might have won this battle, but the war had just begun.

Six

Breakfast was a huge success. Cherry sat at the kitchen table giving herself a pat on the back for having pleased both girls so well. Two plates had been licked clean. Annie must have eaten almost as many additional marshmallows as the two of them had cut up together for her hot chocolate. Raejean had devoured the entire batch of whipped cream. The kitchen was a mess, but Cherry would have time to clean it once the twins were at school.

''Uh-oh,'' Annie said.

''Daddy's going to be *really* mad,'' Raejean said.

Cherry followed the direction of the girls' gazes out the kitchen window and saw the school bus at the end of the lane. It paused momentarily, honked, and when no one appeared, continued on its way.

''Oh, no!'' Cherry raced to the back door, yanked it open and shouted to the bus driver. ''Wait!''

He didn't hear her, which was just as well, because when she turned back to the kitchen she realized the girls weren't dressed and their hair wasn't combed.

Billy hadn't asked much of her—only that she feed his children breakfast and get them to school and be there when they got home in the afternoon. She couldn't even manage that.

She looked at the clock. Seven-thirty in the morning and she was already a failure as a stepmother. Before despair could take hold, it dawned on her that elementary school surely couldn't start this early. Maybe she could still get the girls there on time.

"When do classes start?" she asked Raejean.

"Eight o'clock sharp," Raejean answered. "Mrs. Winslow gets *really* mad if we're late."

"You still have time to get there if we move like lightning," Cherry said.

She hurried the girls upstairs, but the more urgency she felt, the slower they both seemed to move. She ended up accidentally yanking Annie's hair as she shoved the hairbrush through a knot.

"Ouch!" Annie cried. "That hurt."

Cherry was instantly contrite. She had too much experience of her own with substitute parents who were in too much of a hurry to be gentle with her. She went down on one knee in the bathroom beside Annie and said, "I'm sorry, Annie. I should have been more careful. I guess I'm worried that I won't get you to school on time."

"Yeah. And Daddy will be *really* mad," Raejean reminded her through a mouthful of toothpaste.

"Spit and rinse," Cherry ordered Raejean as she finished putting Annie's hair into pigtails. "I'll get to you next."

For a moment Raejean seemed to consider putting up a fight, but she stood still while Cherry pulled the brush through her tangled hair.

"My mom always put ribbons in our hair," Raejean said.

Cherry heard the wistful longing in the complaint, but there wasn't time to fulfill any wishes this morning. "Tonight we'll see what we can find and have them ready for tomorrow morning," she promised.

It wasn't until she had dressed herself and was ushering the girls out the back door that she realized she had no idea what they were going to use for transportation. There had to be some vehicle available, because Billy had suggested she go shopping during the day. But the only thing on four wheels she saw was a rusted-out pickup near the barn.

A set of hooks inside the back door held a key attached to a rabbit's foot. She grabbed the key, shoved the girls out the door, and prayed the truck had an automatic transmission.

It didn't.

"Don't you know how to drive?" Annie asked, concern etched in her young brow.

"I can drive. I have the license to prove it."

"Then why aren't we moving?" Annie asked.

Cherry stared helplessly at the stick shift on the floor of the pickup. "I'm not sure how to get this thing into gear." She tried moving the stick, and it made an ominous grinding sound.

"If you break Daddy's truck, he's going to be *really* mad," Raejean said.

Cherry was getting the picture. If she didn't figure out something soon, she was going to be dealing with a seriously annoyed teacher when she got the girls to school and a fierce, wild-eyed beast of a man when Billy got home.

She crossed her arms on the steering wheel and leaned her head down to think. She could call her sister Jewel to come rescue her, but that was so mortifying a prospect she immediately rejected it. She felt a small hand tapping her shoulder.

"I can show you how to do it," Annie volunteered.

Cherry lifted her head and stared suspiciously at the six-year-old. "You know how to drive a stick shift?"

"Sure," Annie said. "Daddy lets us do it all the time."

Since there wasn't anyone else to show her how, Cherry said, "All right. Go ahead and show me what to do."

"Put your foot on that pedal down there first," Annie said. "Turn the key, and then move this thing here."

Cherry pushed down the clutch, turned on the ignition, and reached for the black gearshift knob. To her amazement the gearshift moved easily without making a sound. However, she ended up in third gear, didn't give the truck enough gas, and let the clutch go too fast. The pickup stalled.

"You have to follow the numbers," Raejean chided, pointing to the black gearshift knob. "See? One, two, three, four, and R."

"R isn't a number," Cherry pointed out.

"R is for reverse," Annie piped up.

Maybe Billy did let them drive, Cherry thought. At least they knew more about a stick shift than she did. "All right. Here goes."

It was touch and go at first, but she managed to get the truck into second gear, and they chugged down the lane headed for the highway. She stalled a couple of times and ground the gears more than once before she got the hang of it. But she felt proud of herself when she finally pulled into the school parking lot and killed the engine.

''We made it,'' she said, glancing at her wristwatch. ''With five minutes to spare.''

''You forgot our lunches,'' Raejean said.

''What lunches?''

''Mrs. Motherwell always made us a sack lunch. We're going to starve,'' Annie said.

''Daddy's going to be *really* mad,'' Raejean said.

''Maybe you could buy your lunches today,'' Cherry suggested.

''I guess we could,'' Raejean conceded.

Annie and Raejean held out their hands for money.

Cherry realized she hadn't brought her purse with her. She checked both her jeans pockets and came up empty. ''Look, I'll go home and make lunches for you and bring them back to school. How would that be?''

''Okay, I guess,'' Raejean said.

''I don't feel so good,'' Annie said, her hand on her stomach.

''Probably all the excitement this morning,'' Cherry said sympathetically. ''You'll feel better once you're settled in class. Have a nice day, Raejean. Enjoy yourself, Annie.''

She watched the two girls make their way inside, Raejean skipping and Annie holding on to her stomach.

To be honest, her own stomach was churning. It had been a hectic morning. And it wasn't over yet. She had to get home, make lunches and get back, then get the kitchen and the house cleaned up before the girls got home in the afternoon.

It was a lot of responsibility for someone whose biggest problem before today was whether she could figure out her calculus homework or get the formulas right in chemistry class. The entire responsibility for the house and two lively children now rested on her shoulders. It was an awesome burden.

She should have thought of that sooner. Now that she had made the commitment, she was determined to see it through. There were bound to be a few glitches at first. The important thing was to keep on trying until she succeeded.

Of course, she wasn't going anywhere until she figured out how to get the pickup into reverse. No matter how many times she put the gearshift where she thought R ought to be, she couldn't get the truck to back up. When the final tardy bell rang, she was still sitting there.

She was going to have to call Jewel after all.

"Hey, Cherry, what's the matter?"

Cherry looked up into the sapphire blue eyes of her eleven-year-old brother, Colt. A black curl had slipped from his ponytail and curled around his ear. He was wearing tight jeans instead of the frumpy ones currently in style, and a white T-shirt and cowboy boots reminiscent of James Dean. Colt truly was the rebel in the family. But he somehow convinced everybody that doing things his way was their idea.

Cherry glanced at the empty schoolyard and said, "You're late, Colt."

He grinned. "Yeah. Looks that way."

"You don't seem too concerned about it. Zach will be—" Cherry stopped herself when she realized she was about to echo Raejean and say "*really* mad."

"Dad knows I'm late," Colt said. "Things were a little crazy this morning because of you disappearing and all. You really did it this time, Cherry. Mom went ballistic when she heard what you did, and Dad hasn't come down off the ceiling since he got back from the Stonecreek Ranch. Are you really married to Billy Stonecreek?"

"Uh-huh."

"Neat. He really knows how to use his fists to defend himself." Colt shrugged his book bag off and did some shadow boxing. He was tall for his age, his body lean, his movements graceful. "Billy's been in three fights this year," he said. "Do you think he'd show me a few punches?"

"Absolutely not! And where did you find out all this information about Billy?" Cherry asked.

"I heard Mom and Dad talking. They're worried that Billy's a bad influence on you. They said he's gonna undo all the hard work they've done, and you're gonna end up back in trouble again."

Cherry felt her face heating. Not that she didn't appreciate what

Zach and Rebecca had done for her. But she had come a long way since the days when she had habitually cut school and been ready to fight the world.

''You'd better get inside,'' she told Colt.

''It's all right. Mom called and told them I'd be late,'' Colt replied. ''What are you doing here?''

''I drove Raejean and Annie Stonecreek to school.''

''Why didn't they take the bus?''

''They missed the bus.''

Colt grinned. ''Overslept, huh? You never were very good at getting up in the morning.''

''Not that it's any of your business, but I didn't oversleep. I merely lost track of the time.''

''Same difference,'' Colt said. ''So why aren't you headed back home?''

''I can't figure out how to get this damn truck into reverse.''

Colt laughed. ''It's easy. Press the stick down and over.''

''Press down? You have to press *down* on the stick before you move it?''

''Sure.''

Cherry tried it, gave the truck a little gas, and felt it move backward. ''Good grief,'' she muttered. ''Thanks, Colt. I owe you one.''

''Will you ask Billy if he'll show me a few punches?''

''I'll think about it,'' she replied as she backed out of the parking lot. ''Tell Rebecca I'll come see her tonight,'' she called out the window as she drove away.

It was the coward's way out to have Colt relay her message. She should have called Rebecca and told her she was coming. But she didn't want to be forced into explaining things to her mother over the phone, and she knew Rebecca must be anxious for some sort of explanation for what she had done. The truth was, she needed the rest of the day to think of one.

By the time she made it back to the ranch she was a pro at shifting gears. She parked the truck behind the house, stepped inside the kitchen, and realized it looked like a tornado had been through. What if Billy came back home for some reason and saw it looking like this?

But she didn't want to stop and clean it right now and take a chance on being late with the girls' lunches. The mess was even worse by the time she finished making sandwiches. She vowed to clean up the kitchen as soon as she returned. She was out the door half an hour later, sack lunches in hand.

When she arrived at the principal's office, Cherry was surprised to be told that Annie still wasn't feeling well. Her teacher had asked the office to call the house and have someone come and pick her up.

"I was concerned when I couldn't reach anyone at the ranch," the principal said, "so I called Mrs. Trask."

"Oh, no," Cherry groaned. "Call her back, please, and tell her it isn't necessary to come. I'll take Annie home."

"I'll try," the principal said. "But she's probably already on her way."

Cherry's only thought was to get Annie and leave as quickly as possible.

"I'm Cherry Whitelaw, Mrs. Winslow," she said when she arrived at Annie's classroom. Cherry flushed. "Except it's Stonecreek now. My name, I mean. I'm here for Annie."

"She's lying on a cot at the back of the room, Mrs. Stonecreek. Raejean insisted on sitting with her."

It felt strange to be called by her married name. Only she really was Mrs. Stonecreck, and responsible for the twins' welfare. She sat on a chair beside the cot and brushed the bangs away from Annie's forehead. "How are you, sweetheart?"

Annie moaned. "My stomach hurts."

"She ate too many marshmallows," Raejean said from her perch beside her sister.

"Marshmallows?" Mrs. Winslow asked.

"Annie had a few marshmallows with her hot chocolate this morning," Cherry said.

"How many is a few?" Mrs. Winslow asked.

Cherry hadn't counted. "Too many, I guess. Can you walk, Annie? Or do I need to carry you?"

Annie sat up, holding her stomach. "I don't feel so good."

Cherry picked her up in her arms.

"Where are you taking her?" Raejean demanded.

"Home," Cherry said.

''I'm going, too,'' Raejean said.

''There's no reason for you to miss a day of school,'' Cherry said reasonably. ''I'll take good care of Annie.''

''How do I know that?'' Raejean demanded. ''You're practically a stranger!''

''Raejean,'' Mrs. Winslow said. ''Mrs. Stonecreek is right. There's no reason for you to leave.''

''I'm going with Annie,'' Raejean said to Mrs. Winslow, her face flushed. ''I'm not staying here alone.''

''You won't be alone,'' Mrs. Winslow soothed. ''You'll—''

''I'm going with Annie!'' Raejean cried.

''Raejean—'' Cherry began.

''I'm going with Annie!'' she screeched hysterically.

Cherry knew the dangers of giving in to a tantrum. But in her mind's eye she saw Mrs. Trask arriving to find a scene like this and knew she was over a barrel. ''All right, Raejean, you can come. I'm sorry for the trouble, Mrs. Winslow.''

She turned and headed for the door with Annie in her arms and Raejean a half step behind her. She was almost out the door when Mrs. Trask showed up.

''What's the matter with my granddaughter? What have you done to her?'' she demanded.

''Annie is fine, Mrs. Trask.'' Cherry kept moving down the hall toward the front door of the school, still hoping to escape without a major confrontation.

''Annie's sick because she ate too many marshmallows,'' Raejean volunteered.

''Marshmallows?'' Mrs. Trask said as though what she was really saying was ''Poison?''

''Annie will be fine, Mrs. Trask.''

''I was afraid of something like this. You're not responsible enough to be left in charge of two little girls.''

Cherry didn't want to admit Mrs. Trask might be right. She had misjudged the situation this morning, but that didn't mean she couldn't do better. She would learn. After all, nobody had practice being a parent before they actually became one.

"Thank you for coming, Mrs. Trask, but as you can see, I have the situation well in hand."

"I'm coming home with you," Mrs. Trask said.

"I don't believe that's necessary," Cherry countered.

"I—"

"What's going on here?"

Cherry stopped in her tracks.

It was Billy. He didn't look *really* mad, as Raejean had promised. He looked frantic, his brow furrowed, his sweat-stained work shirt pulled out of his jeans and hanging open, revealing a hairy chest covered with a damp sheen of sweat. He was still wearing his buckskin work gloves, but he was missing his hat. He had obviously shoved an agitated hand through his dark hair more than once, leaving it awry. He looked virile and strong...and very worried.

"I stopped by the house for some tools and found you gone and a message on the answering machine that Annie wasn't feeling well. Is she all right?"

"I'm sick, Daddy," Annie cried.

For a moment Cherry thought Billy would take Annie from her. Instead he asked, "Do you need any help with her?"

"I can manage if you'll get the door to the pickup."

"I knew something like this would happen," Mrs. Trask said to Billy as they all headed outside to the rusted pickup.

"Something like what, Penelope?" Billy said.

"Something awful."

"Kids get stomachaches, Penelope," Billy said.

"Not if parents are careful and watch what they eat."

"Look, Penelope, I appreciate you coming, but Cherry and I can handle things now."

"How can you trust that woman—"

Billy turned on his former mother-in-law, and for the first time Cherry saw the anger Raejean had threatened. "*That woman* is my wife. And I have the utmost trust in her to take the very best care possible of Raejean and Annie."

"Well, I don't."

"You don't have anything to say about it, Penelope."

"We'll see about that! The day is coming—"

Billy cut her off again. ‘‘You’ll have your day in court, Penelope. Until then, I can manage my family just fine without any help from you.’’

Cherry was impressed by Billy’s support of her. She had done nothing to deserve his trust, and yet he had given it to her. She wanted very much to prove his faith in her was well-founded. She was simply going to have to try a little harder to be responsible.

‘‘I’ll follow you back to the house,’’ Billy said to her as he buckled Raejean into her seat belt. ‘‘Maybe we can figure out what made Annie sick.’’

‘‘She ate too many marshmallows,’’ Raejean volunteered.

‘‘What the hell was she doing eating marshmallows at breakfast?’’ Billy demanded of Cherry.

‘‘I gave them to her,’’ Cherry confessed. ‘‘With her hot chocolate. I guess I gave her a few too many.’’

Billy opened his mouth and snapped it shut on whatever criticism was caught in his throat. ‘‘We’ll discuss this when we get home.’’ He turned and marched to the other truck, a pickup in much better shape than the one she was driving.

The ride home was silent except for an occasional moan from Annie. When they arrived home, Billy carried Annie inside with Raejean trailing behind him. Billy breezed through the chaos in the kitchen without a pause and headed for the stairs. Cherry followed them, feeling as unwelcome as red ants at a picnic.

She stood at the bedroom door watching as Billy tucked Annie into bed and settled Raejean at a small desk with a coloring book and some crayons. She was amazed at his patience with his daughters. Amazed at his calm, quiet voice as he talked to them. The longer she watched, the worse she felt.

Billy had needed someone to help him out. All she had done was cause more trouble. Maybe he would want out of the marriage now. Maybe that’s what he wanted to discuss with her.

When he rose at last and came toward her, he indicated with a nod that she should precede him down the stairs. Cherry felt the tension mounting as she headed into the kitchen, where the peanut butter jar stood open and blobs of jelly lay smeared on the counter. A pan bearing the scraped remnants of scrambled eggs sat in the sink, along with one lined with scalded milk.

She turned to face Billy. ''I can explain everything,'' she said.

That was when he started laughing.

Seven

"What's so funny?" Cherry demanded.

"Annie eating all those marshmallows. She probably begged you for more."

"How did you know?"

"Laura and I let the twins eat too much ice cream the first time they tried it. It's hard to deny them anything when you see how much they're enjoying it. You'll learn." His expression sobered as he added, "That's what parents have to do, Cherry. They have to set limits and stand by them, for the sake of the kids."

"I'll try to do better, Billy," she replied.

Rather than say more, he merely scooped her into his arms, gave her a hug and said, "I've got to get back to mending fence. See you at supper."

It wasn't until he was out the door and gone that she realized he hadn't said a word about the sorry state of the kitchen. Cherry took a look around. There was no way he hadn't noticed. She blessed him for not criticizing, and decided to reward him with a sparkling kitchen when he next saw it.

Of course, that was before she knew what the afternoon held in store.

Grocery shopping was out of the question because Annie was in bed sick, so she took some hamburger out of the freezer to defrost for meatloaf while she cleaned up the kitchen. When she went to check on the twins, she found Annie sound asleep.

Raejean was gone.

She searched the entire house, high and low, without finding her. "She couldn't have left the house. I would have seen her," Cherry muttered to herself.

Unless she went out the front door.

Cherry found the front door open a crack.

"Oh, no, Raejean."

She was afraid to leave Annie alone in the house while she searched, but she knew she had to find Raejean before Billy came home. It was one thing to let a child overeat; it was quite another to lose one entirely. She had no choice but to call for help.

"Jewel, can you come over here?"

"What's wrong, Cherry? Should I get Mom and Dad?"

"No! I'm sure I can handle this. Would you please just come over?"

When she was home from college, Jewel helped run Camp Littlehawk, a retreat that Rebecca had started years ago at Hawk's Pride for kids with cancer. Summer sessions hadn't yet begun, so Jewel was free to come and go as she pleased.

"I'll be there in thirty minutes," Jewel said. "Is that soon enough?"

"No. But I guess it'll have to do."

"It sounds serious, Cherry. Are you sure—"

"I'm sure I can handle it with your help, Jewel. Please hurry."

The next thirty minutes were the longest of Cherry's life. Billy had shown a tremendous amount of trust in her, and she had already let him down once. She had to find Raejean before anything happened to her.

"How can I help?" Jewel asked the instant she came through the kitchen door.

With that single question, Jewel proved what a gem of a sister she was and why she was Cherry's favorite sibling. Jewel gave a thousand percent to whatever she did and never asked for anything in return.

She walked with a slight limp, a result of the car wreck that had orphaned her, and her face bore faint, criss-crossing scars from the same accident. She had mud-brown eyes and dishwater-blond curls, and looked so ordinary you wouldn't see her in a crowd. But she had a heart so big it made her an extraordinary human being.

"I'm in way over my head, Jewel," Cherry confessed. "I thought taking care of two little girls was going to be a breeze. It isn't."

"What's the problem?" Jewel asked.

"Annie's upstairs in bed sick, and Raejean's missing. I need you to watch Annie while I hunt for Raejean."

"I'll be glad to do that. Are you sure you don't want some more help hunting down Raejean?"

"I'd rather try to find her myself first. With any luck, she's hiding somewhere close to the house."

Cherry looked in the barn, which was the most obvious place for the little girl to hide. It was dark and cool and smelled of hay and leather and manure. A search of the stalls turned up two geldings and a litter of kittens, but no little girl.

She climbed the ladder that led to the loft and gave it a quick look, but there was nothing but hay bales and feed sacks, so she climbed down again. As she turned to leave the barn, she heard a sound in the loft. Several pieces of straw wafted through the air and landed on the cement floor in front of her.

"I know you're up there, Raejean," she said. "Please come down. I've been very worried about you."

Footsteps sounded on the wooden floor above her before Raejean said, "You have not! I'm not coming down till my Daddy gets home."

Cherry climbed the ladder to the loft and followed the sounds of a sobbing child to the feed sacks in the corner. Raejean was huddled there, her knees wrapped up in her arms, her stubborn jaw outthrust as she glared at her new stepmother.

Cherry sat on the scattered straw across from Raejean. "I know what it feels like to lose your mother, Raejean. I know what it feels like to have a stranger try to boss you around. I'm sorry your mother died. I'm sorry she isn't here right now. I know I can never replace her. But your Daddy asked me to take care of you and Annie for him while he works every day. Won't you let me help him?"

Raejean's tear-drenched eyes lowered as she picked at a loose thread on the knee of her coveralls. "I miss my mommy. I want my nana."

Cherry's heart climbed to her throat. She could understand Raejean's need for the familiar. In the ordinary course of things, it would have been wonderful to have the girls' grandmother take care of them temporarily. But Mrs. Trask wanted to wrench them away from their father permanently. Cherry wasn't willing to worry Raejean with that possibility, but she wasn't going to encourage Raejean's desire to run to her grandmother for solace, either.

''I'm sure your daddy will take you to visit your grandmother soon. Right now we need to go back inside and check on Annie. I invited my sister, Jewel, to stay with her while I looked for you, but I think Annie needs us.''

''She doesn't need you!'' Raejean retorted.

''Maybe not. But she needs you. Will you come back inside with me?''

Cherry's heart sank when the little girl said nothing. What was she supposed to do now? She couldn't very well drag Raejean down the ladder. And while she could probably let her sit up here until Billy came home, it wasn't a particularly safe place for a six-year-old.

She put a comforting hand on Raejean's shoulder, but the child shrugged it off. ''Please, Raejean? I need your help with Annie.''

''Oh, all right,'' Raejean said. ''But I'm coming inside for Annie. Not for you.''

Her face remained sullen as she followed Cherry inside, and she glowered when she discovered that Annie was still asleep.

''Maybe while Annie's sleeping you could help me make supper,'' Cherry cajoled.

''I don't know how to cook,'' Raejean said. ''Mrs. Motherwell wouldn't let us in the kitchen, and Nana has a lady to do all her cooking.''

''Would you like to learn?''

Reluctantly Raejean nodded her head.

''Let's give it a try, shall we?''

''If the emergency is over, I've got some chores I need to do this afternoon,'' Jewel said.

''I'll walk you to your car,'' Cherry said. ''I'll be back in a few minutes, Raejean. Then we can get started on supper.''

''When will I see you again?'' Jewel asked as they headed downstairs.

''I told Colt I was going to bring the girls and Billy to meet Zach and Rebecca this evening, but I think I'd better revise that plan. Will you tell Rebecca that Annie's not well, and that we'll come visit as soon as we can?''

''Why don't you call her yourself?'' Jewel urged as Cherry walked her out to her car. ''I know she wants to talk to you.''

''I can't face her, Jewel. Not after the way I disappointed her again.''

''You know Mom and Dad are proud of you.''

''Most of the time.''

''You're their daughter. They love you.''

''I don't know why,'' Cherry said with a sigh.

Jewel shook her head. ''There's no rhyme or reason to loving someone. You should know that by now.'' She gave Cherry a hug. ''Take care, Mrs. Stonecreek.''

''Please don't call me that, Jewel.''

''Why not? You're married, aren't you?''

''Yes.'' *Temporarily.* ''It feels strange, that's all. It's a marriage of convenience,'' she confessed. ''Billy needed someone to take care of his girls, and I—I couldn't face Zach and Rebecca after what happened at the prom.''

''I figured it might be something like that.''

Cherry could tell Jewel was curious, but Jewel didn't ask questions. She merely smiled and gave Cherry another hug. ''Call me if you need me, okay?''

As Jewel drove away, Cherry turned back to the house, to perhaps the biggest challenge of her life—being a mother to two little girls who didn't want one.

Billy entered the kitchen at dusk, after a long, discouraging day that had included a visit to a lawyer, to find utter chaos.

The open peanut butter and jelly jars were gone from the counter, replaced by catsup and a round container of oatmeal. Dirty dishes no longer sat in the sink; it was filled with potato peels. The kitchen smelled like something good was cooking in the oven. But instead of a table set for supper, he found three flour-dusted faces standing on a flour-dusted floor, laboring over a flour-dusted table.

''Hi, Daddy!'' Raejean's face bore perhaps the biggest smile Billy had seen there since Laura's death. She held a rolling pin in her small hands and was mashing it across some dough spread on the table. ''We're cooking.''

''Hi, Daddy!'' Annie's grin was equally large. She held up two flour-dusted hands, one of which held a hunk of half-eaten dough. ''We're making an apple pie for you, because it's your favorite!''

Billy finally let his gaze come to rest on Cherry. She had been in his thoughts too often during the day. She had a panicked look on her face as she glanced around at the mess in the kitchen. She pointed to the dough in Annie's hand and said, ''I only let her have this little bit. It's not enough to make her sick.''

''I see,'' Billy said.

What Billy saw was Cherry reassuring him that she had learned her lesson. That she was willing to take responsibility for being the adult when she was barely one herself.

''We're running a little late,'' Cherry said, rubbing her hands across the front of her jeans and leaving them flour-dusted, as well. ''After we got the meatloaf and mashed potatoes prepared, there was still time before we expected you back, so we decided to make a pie.''

''I see.''

What Billy saw was something he had never seen when Laura was alive, and likely never would have seen, even if she had lived. Laura had never learned to cook, and she didn't pretend to be any good at it or take any joy in it. The only apple pie she had ever made for him had come from a frozen food box. Culinary expertise hadn't been high on Billy's list of requirements for a wife, so he had never minded.

Now he realized what he had been missing. To see the three of them working together to make something especially for him touched a place deep inside of him. It fed a hunger for the sort of hearth and home that he imagined others experienced, but which had been lost to him since his parents' deaths. It was an added bonus to see Raejean and Annie so happy.

A different man might have seen only the mess and not the loving gesture that had been the source of it. Billy merely said, ''Would you mind if I take a quick shower before I join you? I'm a little rank after a day on the range.''

Cherry looked relieved. "That'll be fine. It'll give us time to finish up here."

He started for the hall but turned around before he got there and returned to the table. He saw the wariness in Cherry's eyes, the vulnerable look that said, "What have I done wrong now?"

He brushed a patch of flour from her cheek with his thumb before he lowered his mouth to touch hers. The shock was electric. When he could breathe again, he said, "Thanks, Cherry. Homemade apple pie will be a real treat."

"I helped," Raejean said.

"Me, too," Annie added.

Billy gave each of them a quick kiss on the nose. "I can tell," he said with a smile. "You two need a shower almost as bad as I do."

He made himself leave them and go shower, even though he was tempted to stay. He had to remind himself that Cherry was only there for a little while. Long enough to keep Penelope at bay. Long enough to make sure he kept custody of his kids.

By the time he got back downstairs, the pie was in the oven and the kitchen had undergone a partial transformation. The sink was stacked high with everything that had been on the table, but the floor was swept clear, and Cherry and his daughters no longer sported a liberal dusting of flour on their faces and clothes.

"I set the table," Raejean said proudly.

"It looks great," Billy said as he eyed the knife and fork on a folded paper napkin beside his plate.

"I picked the flowers," Annie said.

A collection of blue morning glories with tiny, half-inch stems floated in a bowl of water.

"They're beautiful," Billy said as he sat down and joined them at the kitchen table. "Your mother..." His throat closed suddenly. The swell of emotion surprised him. He had thought he had finished grieving. But the senseless tragedy of Laura's death was there with him again, as though it hadn't happened a full year in the past, but only yesterday.

The two girls looked at him expectantly, waiting for him to finish. He swallowed back the lump in his throat and managed to say, "Your mother would have loved to see them there."

''It was Cherry's idea,'' Annie volunteered. ''She said they would be pretty.''

''They are,'' Billy agreed softly. He let his gaze slip to Cherry for the first time since he had come to the table. ''Morning glories were Laura's favorite flower,'' he said.

''I didn't know,'' she replied. ''I can take them off the table, if you like.''

''No. Leave them there. It's all right.'' He had to keep on living. He had to go on despite the fact Laura was no longer with him. He fought back the anger at Laura for leaving him alone to raise their two girls. It didn't help to feel angry. Better not to feel anything.

Only, that wasn't possible anymore. Not with Cherry living in the same house. Just looking at her made him feel way too much. He wanted her. And felt guilty because of it, even though he knew that was foolish. He was still alive. He still had needs. And she was his wife.

Temporarily. And only as a matter of convenience.

That didn't seem to matter to his body. It thrummed with excitement every time he looked at her. He wondered how her breasts would feel in his hands. He wondered whether she had freckles everywhere. He wanted to see her blue eyes darken with passion for him.

He was damned glad she couldn't read his mind.

After supper, the two little girls who had enjoyed making pie were less willing to clean up the results of their handiwork.

''Mrs. Motherwell always did the dishes by herself,'' Raejean protested.

''Yeah,'' Annie added.

''Maybe so, but she isn't here anymore,'' Cherry said. ''Now everybody helps in the kitchen.''

Raejean's eyes narrowed as though gauging whether she had to obey this dictum. She glanced at her father, still sitting at the table finishing up his second slice of pie, and asked, ''Even Daddy?''

Billy had been listening to the byplay between Cherry and his daughters, a little surprised that she expected the twins to help. There was nothing wrong with them learning to do their share of the chores. Of course, he hadn't expected to be included. Dishes were women's work.

Now what, smart guy? Are you going to act like a male chauvinist pig? Or are you going to provide a good example to your children and pitch in to help?

Billy rose and carried his plate to the sink. ''All of us have to do our part,'' he said. ''Even me.''

It was fun.

He had never done dishes as a family project, but there were definite advantages to doing the work as a team. Like having the girls tease him with the sprayer in the sink as they stood on a chair and rinsed off the dishes before Cherry loaded them in the dishwasher. And tickling Cherry, who turned out to be the most ticklish person he had ever known.

In the past, jobs at the ranch had been divided into *his* and *hers.* Cherry made everything *ours.*

''Where did you learn all these communal work ethics?'' Billy asked as they each toweled off one of the twins after their bath.

''When there are eight kids in a household, everyone has to chip in and do their part,'' Cherry said. ''And knowing there was at least one extra pair of hands to help made every job easier.''

''And more fun,'' Billy said, as he picked up the twins, one in each arm, and headed toward their bedroom.

''And more fun,'' Cherry agreed as she turned down the twins' beds.

Billy set each twin on her bed and then sat down cross-legged on the floor between them. Cherry stood against the wall, her arms crossed around herself, watching them.

''Tell us a story,'' Raejean begged.

''Please, Daddy,'' Annie wheedled.

When the twins were younger and having children was still a novelty, Billy had often told them bedtime stories. As they had gotten older and his responsibilities on the ranch had become more pressing, Laura had been the one to put the girls to bed at night. He'd had to be satisfied with looking in on them after they were already asleep. Over the past year he had allowed a series of housekeepers to enjoy this precious time with his daughters.

Billy realized that he would probably be working on the bookkeeping right now if Cherry hadn't made everything so much fun that he had wanted to stay with them rather than retire to his office to work.

He was grateful to her, but he couldn't tell her why without admitting he had been lax as a parent.

It shocked him to realize that maybe Penelope was right about him. Maybe he hadn't been a very good parent for his daughters over the past year. Maybe it was time to acknowledge that being a father meant more than planting the seeds in a woman that grew into children and earning the money that put food in their mouths, a roof over their heads, and clothes on their backs.

When he finished the story and his giggling girls were tucked in and kissed on their noses, he turned at last to find Cherry and realized that sometime during the reading of the bedtime story she had left the room.

''Good night, girls,'' he said as he turned out the light. ''Sleep tight.''

''Don't let the bedbugs bite!'' they recited in chorus.

Billy headed downstairs in search of Cherry, anxious to thank her for making him aware of the priceless moments he had been missing with his daughters.

He knocked on the door to her room, but she wasn't there. He searched the house and finally found her sitting in one of the two rockers on the front porch. It was dark outside, and when he turned on the front porch light she said, ''Please leave it off.''

''All right,'' he said as he settled in the second rocker. ''What are you doing sitting out here in the dark?''

''Thinking.''

''About what?''

''About us. About why we got married.'' She pulled her feet up onto the rocker seat, circled her legs with her arms, and set her chin on her knees as she stared into the darkness. ''We shouldn't have done it, Billy,'' she said softly.

''I disagree, Cherry. Especially after today.''

She lifted her head and turned to stare at him. ''I would think, if anything, today proved what a rotten mother I am. I wasn't going to tell you, but Annie and Raejean missed the bus this morning, so I had to take them there and I didn't know how to drive a stick shift and I forgot to make them lunches and then I let Annie eat too many marshmallows and then Mrs. Trask showed up at school because I wasn't here to get the call from the principal, and then Raejean ran off and the kitchen was a mess and supper wasn't ready and—''

Billy stood abruptly and lifted her out of the rocker and settled her in his lap as he sat back down. He felt the tension in her body and wanted desperately to ease the misery he had heard in her voice.

''So maybe you don't have the mechanics down. But you know everything about being a mother that really counts.''

''Like what?'' she said, her voice muffled because she had her mouth pressed against his throat.

''Like wanting them to be happy. Like caring what happens to them. Teaching them to do their share. Showing them the pleasure of doing something nice for somebody else. And showing me how much I've been missing by letting someone else try to be both parents, instead of doing my part.''

He felt her relax against him, felt her hand curl up behind his neck and thread into his hair. He liked the feel of her in his arms, liked the way she leaned on him.

''Thanks, Billy,'' she murmured. ''I want to be a helpmate for you.''

She sounded tired, half asleep. After the day she had described to him, it was no wonder. ''You are, Cherry,'' he said, pulling her close. ''You are.''

He only meant to give her a kiss of comfort. His intent wasn't the least bit amorous. He tipped her chin up with his forefinger and pressed soothing kisses on her closed eyelids, her freckled cheeks, and her nose. And one last kiss on her mouth.

Only he let himself linger a bit too long.

And Cherry returned the kiss. Her tongue made a long, lazy foray into his mouth.

His body reacted instantly, turning rock-hard. He groaned, almost in pain. He wanted her. Desperately. But he had agreed to wait.

''Cherry, please,'' he begged.

She didn't answer him one way or the other. He had to touch her, needed to touch her. He slid his hand up under her T-shirt and let his fingertips roam the silky flesh across her belly. His thumb caught under her breast.

He reached for the center clasp of her bra, holding his breath, hoping she wouldn't ask him to stop. He felt the clasp come free and huffed out a breath all at the same time.

She made a carnal sound as his hand closed over the warmth of her breast and gasped as his thumb flicked across the rigid nipple.

His mouth covered hers, and his tongue mimicked the sexual act as his hand palmed her flesh and then slid down between her legs. He cupped her and felt the heat and heard her moan.

His mouth slid down to her throat, sucking hard at the flesh as his thumb caressed her through a thin layer of denim, making her writhe in his arms.

''Billy, no!''

He froze, his breath rasping out through his open mouth, his body aching. He didn't try to stop her when she stumbled from his lap and grabbed at one of the porch pillars to hold herself upright. Her whole body was trembling with desire—or fear, he wasn't sure which.

''I'm sorry,'' she said. ''I can't. I'm sorry.''

Then she was gone.

Eight

Cherry spent the first month of her marriage trying desperately to win Raejean's and Annie's trust. And trying desperately not to think about how close she had come those first few days to making love with Billy.

She had felt warm and safe and secure in his arms. She had felt desired and cherished. She had felt the beginnings of passion—and torn herself from his embrace.

It was fear that had kept her from surrendering. Fear that she would begin to care too much. Fear that what she felt for him was illusion. Fear that what he felt for her was too ephemeral to last. If she gave herself to him body and soul, she would be lost. And when the marriage was over, she would die inside.

It was safer to keep her distance. That was the hard lesson she had learned as a child. She knew better than to trust anyone with her heart. If she gave it up to Billy, he would only break it.

But she wasn't strong enough to deny herself his touch entirely. She liked his kisses. She liked his caresses. And they were a necessary part of the charade she and Billy were playing out for the benefit of Mrs. Trask.

Of course, Mrs. Trask wasn't there each morning when Billy slipped up behind her while she was making coffee and nuzzled her neck and said in a husky voice, "Good morning, Cherry."

Mrs. Trask wasn't there when she turned and pressed herself against him, sieved her fingers into his thick, silky hair, and waited for his morning kiss.

Mrs. Trask wasn't there when Billy lowered his head and took her lips in a kiss as tender as anything Cherry had ever experienced, or when that same kiss grew into something so terrifyingly overwhelming that it left her breathless.

If Billy had asked her to yield entirely, she would likely have stopped allowing the kisses. But he seemed to be satisfied with what she was willing to give him. It wasn't until a month had passed that it dawned on Cherry that each morning Billy asked for a little more. And each morning she gave it to him.

A hand cupping her breast. The feel of his arousal against her belly. Drugging kisses that left her knees ready to buckle. Her hand pressed to the front of his fly to feel the length and the hardness of him. His mouth on her throat. Her robe eased aside, and his mouth on her naked breast.

The feelings were exquisite. Irresistible. Like Billy himself.

If physical seduction had been his only allure, she might have resisted him more successfully. But not only was she attracted to Billy physically, she liked and admired him, as well. He was a good father, a hard worker, a considerate helpmate. Cherry knew she was sliding down a slippery slope. She was in serious danger of complete surrender.

She tried not to think about Billy during the day. It was easy for great stretches of time to involve herself with Raejean and Annie and housekeeping and the chores in the barn she had taken over for Billy. And she had started night school to earn her high school diploma, and there was always homework to be finished. Her life was full and busy, and she felt useful and satisfied.

Most of the time.

But she could feel Billy's eyes on her in the evening after supper when they spent time with the children and gave them their baths. Watching her. Waiting for her to want him the way he wanted her.

The sexual tension between them had grown palpable. Her skin tingled at the mere thought of him touching her. Her breasts ached for the feel of his callused hands. Her blood raced when she saw him come through the door each evening, his washboard belly visible through his open shirt, his sinewy arms bared by rolled-up shirtsleeves, his muscular body fatigued from a day of hard labor.

And her heart went out to him when she saw his face, his dark eyes haunted by the stress of an imminent showdown in court with Mrs. Trask. Was it any wonder she wanted to hold out her arms to him and offer comfort?

As he shoved open the kitchen screen door, her thoughts became reality. Their eyes met and held for an instant, and Cherry knew that tonight she would give herself to him. Tonight she would offer him solace, even if it meant giving up her own peace of mind.

''Hi, Daddy,'' Raejean said as Billy settled his Stetson on a hat rack by the kitchen door.

''Hi, Daddy,'' Annie echoed.

Cherry felt a tightness in her chest as she saw the smile form on his face when he lifted the girls up into his arms and gave each of them a kiss on the nose. He loved them so very much. And there was a very real danger that he would lose them.

''How are my girls?'' he asked. ''What are you doing to keep busy now that school's over?''

''Cherry made us work!'' Raejean said.

Billy raised his eyebrows. ''Oh?''

''We had to help dig a garden behind the house.''

''A garden?''

Cherry met Billy's surprised look and explained, ''I thought it would be nice to have some fresh vegetables.'' Then she realized how presumptuous it was to assume she would still be around in the fall to harvest them.

''We had to plant flowers around the edge of the garden when we were done digging,'' Annie said.

''What kind of flowers?'' Billy asked.

''Marigolds,'' Annie chirped. ''It was fun, Daddy.''

''Did you have fun, too, Raejean?'' Billy asked.

''Maybe,'' Raejean conceded. ''A little.''

Cherry knew it had been an adjustment for Raejean and Annie to find themselves suddenly responsible for chores appropriate to their ages. Before Laura's death they had been too young, and the series of housekeepers had found it easier to do the work themselves than to involve the children. Cherry had explained to Billy that she wasn't there as a housekeeper, she was there as a surrogate mother. And she could best teach the girls the things they would need to know to manage a ranching household by involving them in every aspect of what she did.

It wasn't until she had come to live with Rebecca and Zach that Cherry had been included in precisely that way in the running of a household. In previous foster homes she had been more like a maid-of-all-work. In the Whitelaw home she had been part of a family in which each member did his or her part. She had learned the satisfaction to be had from contributing her fair share.

The more she put to good use the lessons Rebecca had taught her, the more she realized how much she had learned from her, the more grateful she felt for having been adopted into the Whitelaw family, and the more guilty she felt for having run away and married Billy instead of coming home and facing Zach and Rebecca the night she had been expelled.

There was no doubt she had been a difficult child to parent. The longer she was a stepparent, the more understanding she had of the other side of the fence. And the more appreciation she had for Zach and Rebecca's endless patience and love.

She knew she ought to tell them so.

But she couldn't face them and say on the one hand how much she appreciated all the things they had taught her, while on the other she was perpetrating the deceit involved in her temporary marriage to Billy Stonecreek.

So she had found excuses to avoid visiting them and reasons to keep her family from visiting her. Except for Jewel, who knew everything, and was quick to point out that Cherry was acting like an idiot and should simply call Zach and Rebecca and confess everything.

"They'll understand," Jewel had said. "And they'll forgive. And they'll still love you as much as ever. That's what parents do."

Cherry was finding that out for herself. Raejean still resented her and complained about nearly everything Cherry asked her to do, although she would eventually do it. Annie hadn't surrendered her trust to Cherry in loyalty to Raejean.

If her marriage to Billy had been a permanent thing, Cherry would have said time was on her side. It had taken more than a year for her barriers to come down with Zach and Rebecca, but in the face of all that love, they *had* come down. She needed to win Raejean's and Annie's trust before the court hearing—a matter of weeks. A great deal depended on her finding a way to break through the little girls' stubborn resistance.

They had long since broken through hers. She loved them both dearly, enough to know it was going to hurt a great deal when she was no longer a part of their lives.

''You got a letter today,'' she told Billy as he set the girls back on their feet. ''It looks official.''

Billy's face was grim as he went to the kitchen counter where she always left the mail and sorted through it. He picked up the envelope, looked at it, and set it back down again. ''It can wait until after the kids are in bed.''

Cherry understood why he was postponing the inevitable. But she knew he was as aware of it sitting there all evening as she was.

He hugged the girls so hard at bedtime that Annie protested, ''I can't breathe, Daddy.''

She knew he was afraid of losing them. So was she.

She walked ahead of him down the stairs and instead of heading for the porch rockers to relax for a few minutes before going back to work, she headed for the kitchen. Billy followed her.

She went directly to the stack of mail, found the letter she wanted, and handed it to him. ''Read it.''

He tore it open viciously, his teeth clenched tight enough to make a muscle in his jaw jerk. He read silently. Without a word, he handed the official-looking letter to her. ''Read it.''

She read quickly. The court date had been set for July 15. Billy was asked to appear and explain certain accusations that had been made against him that he was not a fit custodian for his children.

''Three weeks,'' he said bitterly. ''Three lousy weeks before I have to appear in court and prove I'm a fit father. How the hell am I going to do that, Cherry? Tell me that? I can't make those nights in jail go away. And you can bet Penelope will make sure the judge knows that the mother I've provided for my children is an eighteen-year-old girl who used to be a juvenile delinquent.''

Cherry went white around the mouth. She hadn't expected his attack. It was useless to point out that he was the one who had suggested marriage. It didn't change the facts. "What do you want to do, Billy? Do you want to annul the marriage? Would that help, do you think?"

"Oh, God, no!" His arms closed tight around her. "I'm sorry, Cherry. I didn't mean to suggest that any of this is your fault, or that you aren't a wonderful mother. You are. Raejean and Annie are lucky to have you. Only..."

"Only I have been a juvenile delinquent."

"And I've spent a few nights in jail," Billy said. "Nobody's perfect, Cherry. We simply have to convince the judge that all that behavior is in the past. That right now we're the best possible parents for two little girls who've lost their mother, and whose grandmother is a bit misguided."

"Is that what she is?" Cherry asked, her lips twisting wryly.

"She misses her daughter, Cherry. She's still grieving. But that doesn't mean I'm going to give her my children to replace the one she lost," Billy said, his voice hard, his eyes flinty.

"Raejean still doesn't like me," Cherry pointed out. "What is the judge going to make of that?"

Billy's brow furrowed between his eyes. "I don't know, Cherry. He'll have to understand that we're all still making adjustments. He'll have to see that you're doing the best you can."

She took a deep breath and said, "I couldn't bear to see you lose them, Billy."

"I won't. I can't." He paused at the realization that the court had the power to take his children away from him before repeating, "I won't."

His arms tightened painfully around her, and she knew he was holding on to her because he was afraid of losing them. When his mouth came seeking hers—seeking solace, as she had known he would—she gave it to him.

"I need you," he said in a guttural voice. "I need you, Cherry."

"I'm yours, Billy," she answered him. "I'm all yours."

He picked her up and carried her to her room, shoving open the bedroom door with his hip and laying her on the bed. He turned on the bedside lamp and sat down beside her.

‘‘I want to see you. I want to feel your flesh against mine,’’ he said as he tore off her T-shirt and threw it across the room. He had her bra unclasped a second later and it was gone, leaving her bared to him from the waist up.

He stopped to look at what he had. ‘‘No freckles here,’’ he mused as a callused finger circled her breast. ‘‘Just this rosy crest,’’ he finished as his mouth closed on her.

Her hands tangled in his hair and held him as he suckled her. Her body arched with pleasure as his hand slipped down between her legs to hold the heat and the heart of her.

Cherry had endured weeks of teasing foreplay. Now she wanted what had been denied her. ‘‘Please, Billy. Please.’’ She shoved at his shirt, wanting to feel his flesh against her fingertips. She reached for his belt buckle and undid it with trembling fingers and then undid the button and slid down the zipper on his jeans. Billy copied everything she did.

When her hand slid beneath his briefs to reach for him, his did the same beneath her panties.

They stopped and looked at each other and grinned.

‘‘Gotcha,’’ Billy said as he slid a finger deep inside her. She was wet and slick, and he added another finger to the first.

Cherry groaned.

Her gaze trailed down to where her hand disappeared inside Billy’s briefs. She tightened her grasp and slid her hand up and down the hard length of him.

Billy groaned.

Their mouths merged, their tongues mimicking the sexual act as their hands kept up their teasing titillation.

Suddenly it wasn’t enough. Cherry wasn’t sure which of them shoved at the other’s jeans first, but it wasn’t long before both of them were naked. A moment after that, Billy was inside her.

They both went still.

It felt like she had found her other half. Now she was whole.

Cherry looked up into Billy’s dark eyes and saw a wealth of emotion. Too many feelings. More than were safe. She closed her eyes against them.

‘‘Look at me, Cherry,’’ Billy said.

She slowly raised her lids and gazed at him with wonder.

He loves me, she thought. *I never dreamed...I never imagined...*

She waited for the words, but he never said them.

And she knew why. She didn't love him back. She wouldn't allow herself to love him. He knew the rules. It was to be a safe, temporary marriage.

Her eyes slid closed again as his mouth covered hers, hungry, needy. For the first time in her life she was grateful for her height, which made them fit together so perfectly that they could be joined at the hip and their mouths still meet for a soul-searching kiss. She felt the passion rise, felt her body shiver and shudder under the onslaught of his desire.

His body moved slowly at first, the tension building equally slowly, until it was unbearable, until she writhed beneath him, desperate for release.

''Please, Billy,'' she cried. ''Please!''

She heard a savage sound deep in his throat as his body surged against hers, as he fought the inevitable climax, wanting to prolong the pleasure.

She felt her body tensing, thrusting against his, seeking the heaven he promised, until they found it, his seed spilling into her at last.

His weight was welcome, comforting, as he lowered his exhausted, sweat-slick body onto hers, their chests still heaving to gather breath to support their labored bodies, their heartbeats still pounding to carry blood to straining vessels.

Eventually, as their breathing slowed and their hearts returned to normal, Billy slid to her side and spooned her bottom against his groin. His hand curled around her breast as though it were the most natural place in the world for it to be. ''Thanks, Cherry. I needed that. You,'' he amended.

It was more than she was willing to admit, so she remained mute. She was content to lie in his arms, saying nothing, enjoying the closeness.

It was during this quiet aftermath that she realized they had used no protection. They both knew better. Under the circumstances, a pregnancy could be disastrous. ''Billy,'' she murmured.

''Hmm.''

"We didn't use anything."

"Hmm?"

"To keep me from getting pregnant."

His stiffening body revealed his distress. "I should have asked. I should have—"

She turned in his arms and put her fingertips against his lips. "It's the wrong time of the month, I think."

"You think?"

"If there is a safe time," she amended, "this is probably it."

"Thank God," he said.

Even though she knew rationally that it was in both of their interests for her not to get pregnant, it was still irksome to see the amount of relief on Billy's face. "I guess you don't want any more children," she said.

"It isn't that," he said. "I always wanted more kids. But Laura..."

She remembered that Laura couldn't have any more. Only, that wasn't what Billy said next.

"Laura wasn't supposed to get pregnant because it was dangerous."

She felt him shudder and a thought occurred to her. "Are you saying she got pregnant anyway?"

He paused so long she didn't think he was going to answer her. At last he said, "Yes."

"What happened? To the baby, I mean?"

"She miscarried. Twice."

He pulled her close so his chin rested on her head, and she couldn't see his eyes. But she could feel him trembling and hear his convulsive swallow.

"The second time it happened I told her that if she didn't stop trying to get pregnant, I'd refuse to sleep with her anymore. I didn't want to take the chance of losing her. She meant too much to me, more than any baby ever could."

Another swallow.

"She was furious with me. She said she had promised me a houseful of kids, and she knew I couldn't be happy with just the twins. I told her the twins were enough. But she didn't believe me.

"The truth was, she had this insane idea that a woman who couldn't have kids wasn't a real woman. She refused to stop trying to get pregnant, despite the risk to her health. So I told her I was through arguing. I wasn't going to sleep with her again until she changed her mind and agreed to be sensible.''

He shuddered.

''She went stomping out of the house, furiously angry, and got into the car. And...and she was killed.''

''Oh, my God,'' Cherry breathed. ''And you're not really sure whether it was an accident, or whether she killed herself on purpose, is that it?''

''She wouldn't kill herself. Not because of something like that. She wouldn't. It was an accident.''

Cherry wasn't sure who he was trying to convince, himself or her.

''All Penelope saw the year before she died was Laura's despondency over the first miscarriage,'' Billy continued. ''Penelope knew we'd been arguing a lot around the time of Laura's death, although she didn't know what we'd been arguing about. Laura didn't tell her about the miscarriage—probably because she knew her mother would be on my side.''

''Why didn't you tell Mrs. Trask what had happened?'' Cherry asked.

''It was none of her business!'' Billy retorted. ''It was between me and my wife.''

''Maybe if she understood why—''

''It's over and done with now.''

''Perhaps if you explained—''

''Laura's dead. There's no bringing her back.''

And he wasn't sure he wasn't to blame, Cherry realized. No wonder he had gotten into so many fights in the year since Laura's death. He had been in pain, with no way of easing it. Because he would never know for sure what had happened.

''It wasn't your fault she died,'' Cherry said quietly.

''How do you know that?'' he snarled.

''You were right. It wasn't safe for her to continue getting pregnant. You had to take a stand.''

''I should have found some other way to say no.''

''Hindsight is always better. You did the best you could at the time.''

''That's supposed to make me feel better?''

She leaned back to look into his troubled eyes and saw the need in him to strike out against the pain. There were other ways of easing it. She laid her hand against his cheek and said, ''You're a good man, Billy. You never meant for her to be hurt. Whether it was an accident...or not...Laura was responsible for what happened.''

''I want to believe that,'' he said. ''I try to believe that. But...''

''Believe it,'' she whispered as her lips sought his.

His arms surrounded her like iron bands, and his mouth sought hers like a thirsting man who finds an oasis in the desert. He was inside her moments later, needing the closeness, needing the comfort she offered, the surcease from endless pain.

She held him in her arms as he loved her and crooned to him that everything would be all right. That he was a good man and a good father and he shouldn't blame himself anymore for what wasn't his fault.

He spilled himself inside her with a cry that was almost anguish. He slipped to the side and pulled her to him, holding her close with strong arms that promised always to keep her safe.

She knew it was wrong to trust in him. He would betray her in the end. Unfortunately, the heart doesn't always obey the dictates of the more reasonable head.

I love him, she thought. And then, *I can't love him. I shouldn't love him. I'd be a fool to love him.*

They fell asleep, their bodies entangled, their souls enmeshed, their hearts confused.

Nine

Over the next three weeks the twins sensed the growing tension in Billy, and their behavior grew worse instead of better. Cherry tried to be understanding, but she was under a great deal of pressure, as well, since she had to study for night school finals, which she couldn't afford to fail.

Things came to a head the day before the court hearing, when Cherry asked Raejean for the third time to take her cookie and juice snack back to the kitchen to eat it.

''I don't have to do what you say,'' Raejean said. ''You're not my mother!''

''I'm the one in charge,'' Cherry replied, using her last ounce of patience to keep her voice level. ''And I say you have to get that juice out of the living room. If it spills in here, it'll ruin the furniture.''

Cherry couldn't imagine what had possessed Laura to put silk and satin fabrics in a ranch living room. It wasn't a place to look at; they actually lived in it. If it had been up to her, she would have put protective covers on the furniture long ago to save the delicate fabrics from everyday wear and tear. When she had broached the subject to Billy, he had said, ''We live here. If the furniture gets dirty, it gets dirty.''

Cherry didn't figure that included spilling grape juice on white satin. So she insisted, ''Take that juice into the kitchen, Raejean. Now!''

''Oh, all right!'' Raejean huffed. ''Come on, Annie. Let's go.''

''I'm watching Sesame Street,'' Annie protested from her seat beside Raejean on the couch.

Raejean pinched her. ''Come on. If I have to go, you have to go.''

''Raejean,'' Cherry warned. ''Leave Annie be. Take your glass and go.''

Raejean shot Cherry a mutinous look as she snatched at the glass on the end table, accidentally knocking it over—right onto the arm of the couch.

The two of them stared, horrified, as the grape juice soaked into the white satin, leaving a huge purple blotch.

''Oh, no!'' Cherry cried. She looked for something to sop up the mess, but there was nothing handy. And by then the couch had soaked up the juice like a sponge.

''It's all your fault,'' Raejean cried, tears welling in her eyes. ''If you hadn't been yelling at me, I wouldn't have spilled it.''

''Daddy's going to be *really* mad,'' Annie whispered as she abandoned Sesame Street to ogle the growing stain.

''Go to your room,'' Cherry said. ''Both of you!''

''I didn't do anything,'' Annie protested.

''We don't have to do what you say!'' Raejean said. ''Do we, Annie?''

Annie looked uncertain, and Raejean pinched her again.

''Ow!'' she said. ''Stop it, Raejean.''

''Stop it, both of you!'' Cherry cried. She knew she had lost control, but she wasn't sure how to get it back. ''Apologize to your sister, Raejean.''

''I don't have to. Tell her, Annie. Tell her Nana's going to be taking care of us from now on, so we don't have to do what Cherry says anymore.''

Cherry couldn't believe what she was hearing. ''Who said your grandmother's going to be taking care of you from now on?''

''Nana did.''

''When?'' Cherry said.

''When she called on the phone.''

''When was that?'' Cherry demanded.

''This morning, when you were in the shower. She said that after tomorrow she's going to be taking care of us, and we'll get to play in her pool and Grampa's buying us a new dollhouse and we won't have to do chores anymore, either,'' she announced.

Cherry stared at Raejean, aghast. She didn't know what to say. The little girl had no idea what Mrs. Trask really intended. She didn't seem to realize that going to live with her grandmother meant leaving her father for good. And Cherry had no intention of frightening her by explaining it.

She was furious with Mrs. Trask but resisted the urge to criticize her in front of her granddaughters. She was way out of her depth and drowning fast. She needed help.

To Cherry's surprise, the name and face that came to mind wasn't Billy's. Or even Jewel's. It was Rebecca's.

She wanted her mother.

''Let's go,'' she said suddenly.

''Go where?'' Raejean asked suspiciously.

''To see your other grandmother.''

Both girls stared at her with wide eyes.

''We have another grandmother?'' Annie said.

''Uh-huh. You sure do.''

''Who is she?'' Raejean asked. ''Where does she live?''

''Her name is Rebecca Whitelaw, and she lives on a ranch called Hawk's Pride. It isn't far from here. Shall we go? It's either that, or go to your room. You choose.''

There was no contest, and Cherry wasted no time getting the girls into the pickup and driving to the adobe ranch house at Hawk's Pride that she had called home for the previous four years. Since Camp Littlehawk was under way, she knew where to look for Rebecca. Sure enough, she found her working with the novice riders at the corral. Raejean and Annie raced ahead of her to stand gaping at the lucky horseback riders.

''That's good, Jamie,'' Rebecca encouraged, one foot perched on the lowest rung of the wooden corral. ''Let the pony know who's boss.''

''I suppose that's good advice for parents dealing with children, too,'' Cherry said as she joined Rebecca.

''Cherry! What a wonderful surprise! Ted, would you watch the children for a few minutes while I speak with my daughter?''

Cherry noticed that Ted was on crutches. That didn't surprise her. Rebecca often found people in need and offered them a helping hand. Cherry was sure Ted was great with kids or horses or both. It always worked out that way. Rebecca's faith in people had never been proven wrong. It was that same goodheartedness that had led Rebecca to rescue a rebellious fourteen-year-old juvenile delinquent and adopt her as her own.

''I'd like you to meet your new granddaughters,'' Cherry said as Rebecca took the few steps to reach the twins. They were standing on the bottom rail of the corral with their arms hanging over the top.

''Raejean, Annie, I'd like you to meet your Grandma 'Becca.'' 'Becca was what Jewel had called Rebecca when Jewel was a child. It was also a fond nickname Zach used when he was teasing her. And it was the first thing that came to mind when Cherry searched for a name the little girls could use to address their new grandmother.

Raejean and Annie turned lively black eyes on Rebecca.

''Are you really our grandmother?'' Raejean asked.

''Yes,'' Rebecca said with a smile.

''Are you going to give us cookies and milk, like Nana?'' Annie asked.

''I'll even help you bake the cookies, if you like,'' Rebecca said. ''If you'll tell me which one of you is which.''

''I'm Annie,'' Raejean said. ''And this is Raejean,'' she said, pointing to her shyer twin.

''Raejean,'' Cherry warned.

''Aw, Cherry.'' She hesitated before admitting, ''I'm really Raejean, and this is really Annie.''

''Pleased to meet you both,'' Rebecca said. ''It's going to be fun having grandchildren come to visit.''

''Will you let us ride horses, too?'' Raejean asked, eyeing the children on horseback enviously.

''Would you like to ride one now?''

Raejean's and Annie's faces lit up as though they had been given the key to heaven. ''Oh, yes!'' they said in unison.

It didn't take long to get ponies saddled and send the girls into the ring with the other children to be supervised by Ted.

As soon as the twins were settled, Rebecca said, ''All right, Cherry. Spit it out. What's wrong?''

''Everything,'' Cherry admitted. She felt like crying suddenly. The whole weight of the world had been on her shoulders for the past seven weeks, and it was as though with that one admission she had shifted the burden to her mother.

''Tell me about it,'' Rebecca said.

And Cherry did. About why she and Billy had married and the awful wedding and the twins' resentment, how Mrs. Trask was manipulating the children's feelings, and how scared she was that Billy would lose his children.

''What about you? Would it hurt you to lose them?''

Cherry hadn't even let herself think about the possibility. When she did, she felt a terrible ache in her chest. ''Yes. Oh, yes. I'd miss them terribly. As much trouble as they are, I love them dearly.''

Rebecca smiled. ''So what can I do to help?''

Cherry shoved a hand through her tumble of red curls and let out a gusty sigh. ''I'm not sure. Could you and Zach just be there in court tomorrow? Would that be possible?''

''Oh, darling, of course we'll be there. Is that all? Are you sure there isn't something else I could do to help?''

''I think you've already done it,'' Cherry said.

''Done what?''

''Taught me to believe in love again.''

''Oh, darling...''

Cherry saw the tears in her mother's eyes and felt her throat tighten until it hurt. ''I owe you so much...Mother.'' She gave a sobbing laugh and said, ''There, I said it. Mother. Oh, God, why did I wait so long?''

It had taken being a mother herself to understand the tremendous gift Zach and Rebecca had given her. She could hardly see Rebecca through the blur of tears, and when she blinked, she realized Rebecca had her arms open wide. She grasped her around the waist and held on tight.

Cherry refused her mother's invitation to stay for dinner. ''Billy and Zach—Daddy—aren't comfortable enough around each other yet. I'd rather give them time to get to know each other better before we show up for supper.''

"All right. Whatever you think best. You can count on us to be in court tomorrow to support you both."

"Thanks, Mother. That means a lot."

"I wasn't sure before that you were ready for marriage and all its responsibilities," Rebecca said. "This visit has reassured me."

"That I'm ready for marriage?"

"That you're ready for whatever life offers. Be happy, Cherry. That's all I can ask."

Cherry smiled. "I'll try, Mom."

"Mom. I like that," Rebecca said. "Mom feels even better than Mother."

"Yeah, Mom," Cherry agreed with a cheeky grin. "It does."

Cherry spent the rest of the afternoon floating on air. She had never felt so confident. She had never been so certain that everything would turn out all right. Her youthful optimism remained firmly in place until Billy was late arriving home for supper. She waited an hour for him before she finally fed the girls and sent them upstairs to play.

She put a plate of food in the oven to stay warm while she cleaned up the kitchen. She still wasn't worried. Billy had been late once or twice before when some work had needed to be finished before dark.

But sundown came and went without any sign of Billy.

Cherry told herself, as she bathed the twins, that there was probably some good reason for the delay. Maybe he was working hard to make up for the fact he would be in court all day tomorrow. Maybe the truck had broken down and he had needed to walk home.

Maybe he had an accident. Maybe he's lying hurt or dying somewhere while you've been blithely assuming everything is fine.

Cherry silenced the voice that told her disaster had struck. Nothing could have happened to Billy. He was strong and had quick reflexes, and he knew the dangers of the kind of work he did. He was fine.

But he was very late.

Cherry read the girls two bedtime stories, thinking he would show up at any minute to tease and tickle them and kiss them good-night.

"Where's Daddy?" Raejean asked when Cherry said it was time to turn out the light.

"Isn't he coming home?" Annie asked.

''Of course he's coming home. He just had some errands to run. As soon as he arrives, he'll come and kiss you good-night. Go to sleep now.''

She turned out the light and was almost out of the room when Raejean whispered, ''Is Daddy going away?''

Cherry turned the light back on. Both Raejean and Annie stared back at her with frightened eyes. *Damn Mrs. Trask and her phone calls,* Cherry thought. She crossed and sat beside Raejean and brushed the bangs away and kissed her forehead reassuringly.

''Your daddy isn't going anywhere. He'll be right here when you wake up in the morning.''

''Nana said Daddy might be going away,'' Raejean confessed.'' I don't want him to leave.''

''Neither do I,'' Annie whimpered.

''Oh, my dear ones,'' Cherry said. She lifted a sobbing Raejean into her arms and carried her over to Annie's bed, then slid an arm around each girl and rocked them against her. ''Don't worry. Everything's going to be fine. Your Daddy's not going anywhere. And neither am I.''

''Are you going to be our mother forever?'' Annie asked.

Cherry was struck dumb by the question. She realized the folly of her promise that she wasn't going anywhere. She and Billy had a temporary marriage. She had no right to presume he would want it to continue any longer than necessary to convince the court to let him keep his children.

She was forced to admit the truth to herself.

She didn't want the marriage to end. She wanted to stay married to Billy. She wanted to be the twins' mother forever. All she had to do was convince Billy to let her stay.

When he showed up. If he ever did.

''Why don't we ask your daddy when he comes home if it's all right with him for me to be your mother forever,'' she answered Annie at last. ''Would that be all right?''

''I guess,'' Annie said. ''If you're sure he's coming home.''

''I'm sure,'' Cherry said.

That seemed to assuage the worst of their fear, and she managed to get them tucked in again. As she was turning out the light, Raejean said, ''Cherry?''

''What is it, Raejean?''

''I don't want you to leave, either.''

Cherry smiled. ''Thanks, Raejean. That means a lot to me.''

She rose up on one elbow and said, ''I'm sorry about spilling grape juice on the couch. You don't think Daddy came home and saw it while we were gone and got *really* mad, do you?''

Her heart went out to the child. ''No, Raejean, I don't think it's anything you did that's making your father late getting home. I'm sure he's been delayed by business. Go to sleep now. Before you know it, he'll be waking you up to kiss you good-night.''

As she was closing the door, Cherry heard Annie whisper, ''That's silly. Why is Daddy going to wake us up to kiss us good-night?''

''So we'll know he's home, dummy,'' Raejean explained scornfully.

''Oh,'' Annie whispered back. ''All right.''

Cherry headed downstairs hoping that Billy would arrive to fulfill her promise and waken the twins with a kiss.

As the night passed and he didn't return, she began to worry in earnest. The worst thing was, she had no idea where he might have gone. She made up her mind to wait until midnight before she called the police to report him missing. That's when the bars in town closed.

Not that she believed for one second that he had gone to a bar. Not with everything on the line the way it was. Not with everything he did subject to intense scrutiny in the courtroom. Not as determined as he was to keep custody of his children in the face of his mother-in-law's clutching grasp for them.

She sat in the dark on the front porch step, waiting for him to come home. At five minutes before midnight she saw a pair of headlights coming down the dirt road that led to the house. Her heart began to pound.

Surely it was Billy. Surely it was him and not someone coming to tell her he had been hurt.

The vehicle was headed for the back of the house, moving too fast for safety. She ran through the house, turned on the back porch light and slammed her way out the back door. She was there when the pickup skidded to a stop.

When she saw it was Billy's truck, she released a breath of air she hadn't realized she had been holding. The relief turned quickly to anger when Billy stepped out of the truck and she saw his face. One eye was swollen almost closed and his lip had a cut on one side.

''You've been fighting!'' She gasped as he began to weave his way unsteadily toward her. ''You're drunk!'' she accused. ''How could you, Billy? How could you?''

''I'm not drunk!'' he said. ''I've just got a couple of cracked ribs that are giving me hell.''

She quickly moved to support him. ''What happened? Where have you been? Who did this to you?''

She felt him slump against her. ''Aw, Cherry, I don't believe I let this happen. Not the day before I have to go to court. The judge'll never understand.''

''Forget the judge. Explain this to me.''

''I went to town to get some supplies at the hardware store and ran into that Ray character, the one who took you to the prom.''

''Ray did this to you?'' she asked incredulously.

''Him and three of his friends.''

''But why?''

''It doesn't matter why. Or it won't to the judge. All he'll see is that I've been fighting again. Lord, Cherry, I hurt. Inside and out.''

''Come on in to the kitchen and let me bind your ribs,'' Cherry said. ''Maybe I can get the swelling down in your eye, so it won't look so bad tomorrow.''

''Maybe I can say I'm sick and get a postponement,'' Billy suggested.

''Is it possible the Trasks won't find out about the fight? Did the police come?'' she asked.

''They were there,'' Billy said.

''But you weren't arrested?'' Cherry said. ''That must mean something. I mean, that you weren't at fault.''

''I wanted to fight, all right,'' Billy said flatly. ''And I'd do it again.''

''Don't say things like that. You can't keep getting into fights, Billy. Not if you want to keep custody of your girls. What could be so important it was worth risking your girls to fight about?'' she demanded.

He didn't answer her, but that could have been because he was too busy hissing in a breath as she administered antiseptic to the cuts on his face. She eased the torn shirt off his shoulders and saw the bruises on his ribs. They must have kicked him when he was down.

''Where have you been all night, if you weren't in a bar somewhere drinking?'' Cherry asked.

''I went to the stock pond to sit and think,'' he said.

''While you were thinking, did it occur to you that I'd be worried,'' Cherry asked archly.

''I'm sorry, Cherry. I lost track of the time.''

He sat stoically while she strapped his ribs. But the light had gone out of his eyes. He had already given up. He had already conceded the battle to Penelope.

''You aren't going to lose tomorrow,'' she said to him. ''You can tell the judge a bull stomped you, or—''

Billy snorted. ''Stomped on my eye? Forget it, Cherry. You know as well as I do that my fight with Penelope is over before it's begun.''

''I refuse to accept that!'' Cherry snapped back. ''You're a good father. You love your children, and you provide a stable home for them.''

''That isn't enough.''

''What more can the judge ask?'' Cherry demanded.

Billy reached up gingerly and brushed his hair out of his eyes. ''I don't know. You can believe there'll be something Penelope can offer that I can't.''

''There's *nothing* she can give them that you can't,'' Cherry said fiercely. ''And there's something you can give them that no one else can.''

''What?''

''Love. A parent's love. Don't discount it, Billy. It's a powerful thing.''

She saw the doubt in his eyes. He wanted to believe her, but he was afraid to let his hopes get too high. She lowered her lips to his, tender, as gentle as she had ever been. She brushed at the hank of hair that had fallen once more on his forehead. "You're going to win, Billy. Believe it."

He took her hand and pressed her palm against his lips. "Thanks, Cherry. I needed to hear that."

But she saw he didn't completely believe it. He believed this was the beginning of the end. He believed he was going to lose his children. That he was going to lose her. She could feel it in the way he clung to her hand.

She pulled herself free, unwilling to indulge in his despair.

"The girls were worried about you," she said as she scurried around fixing an ice pack for his eye. "I promised them you would wake them up to kiss them good-night so they would know you got home all right."

"I'll go do that now," he said, groaning as he got to his feet, the ice pack pressed against his eye.

"Don't fall coming back downstairs," she said.

He turned and looked at her. He was in no condition to make love to her, and for a second she thought he was going to refuse to come back downstairs and join her in bed. But he nodded his head in acquiescence.

"I'll be down in a few minutes."

Cherry hurried to finish her ablutions and ready herself for bed before Billy came to her room. The sexiest nightgown she owned was a football jersey, and she quickly slipped it over her head. She was naked underneath it.

She pulled the covers down and slipped under them to wait for him. She left the light burning, because she knew he liked to watch her as they made love.

It didn't take her long to realize, once Billy entered her room and began undressing himself, that he needed help. She got out of bed and came to him, sick at heart at this reminder of the fight that might cost him his children.

She took her time undressing him, kissing his flesh as she exposed it. Shoulders. Chest. Belly. She sat him down and pulled off his boots and socks and made him stand again so she could unbuckle his belt and unzip his jeans and pull them off. By the time he was naked, he was also obviously aroused.

''Lie down,'' she coaxed. ''You're hurt. Let me do all the work.''

She had never said she loved Billy in words. But she showed him with her mouth and hands and body. She eased herself down on his shaft, and when he arched his body into hers, said, ''Lie still. I'll move for both of us.''

She did, riding him like a stallion, never giving him a rest, until both of them were breathing hard and slick with sweat. She pushed him to the brink, brought him back, and took him there again. Until at last she rode him home.

He was already asleep, his breathing deep and even, by the time she slipped to his side, reached over to turn out the light, and snuggled against him.

''You'll win, Billy,'' she whispered into the darkness. ''You have to win. Because I love you and Raejean and Annie. And I can't bear to give you up.''

She felt his arm tighten around her.

At first she was terrified because she thought he must have heard her. Then she realized it was a reflexive move. He had reached for her in his sleep and pulled her close.

''You're not going to lose me, Billy,'' she murmured against his throat. ''I'm not going anywhere.''

His body relaxed, and she closed her eyes to sleep.

Ten

The day of the hearing dawned fly-buzzing hot, as though to deny the cloud of disaster that loomed over their heads. In the bright sunshine Billy's face looked even worse than it had the night before. His left eye was swollen nearly shut, and the myriad bruises had taken on a rainbow of colors—pink, yellow and purple. He walked stiffly up the courthouse steps, like an old man, an occasional wince revealing what even that effort cost him in pain.

Cherry had put on a simple, flowered cotton dress with a Peter Pan collar she often wore to church. It made her look every bit as young as she was. Billy was dressed in a dark suit that fit his broad shoulders like a glove and made him into a dangerous, imposing stranger.

The twins bounced along beside them in matching dresses and pigtails, chattering like magpies, excited by the prospect of going on a picnic after the court hearing was over. Cherry chattered back at them, putting on a cheery false front to prove she wasn't as frightened as she was.

She and Billy had exchanged very few words since waking that morning, but their eyes had met often, communicating a wealth of information.

I feel awful.

I can see that. You look like you got stomped by something mean.

What if I say something wrong? What if I can't convince the judge to let me keep my kids?

Everything will be all right.

What if it isn't? What will I do?

I'm here for you, Billy.

I'm scared, Cherry.

So am I.

I'm glad you're here with me.

He reached out to take her hand, clutching it so tightly it hurt, as they entered the courtroom. The instant the twins saw their grandparents sitting at a table at the front of the courtroom with two men dressed in expensive suits, they went racing down the aisle to greet them.

''Hi, Nana,'' Raejean said, giving her grandmother a hug. Mrs. Trask wore a sleek designer suit that shouted wealth, her short-cropped, silvery-white hair perfectly coiffed.

''Hi, Grandpa,'' Annie said, getting a sound hug from her grandfather. Mr. Trask sported a double-breasted wool blend suit, his pale blond hair cut short on top and trimmed high over his ears.

The adults exchanged not a word, but their eyes spoke volumes.

Animosity from Mrs. Trask.

Antagonism from Billy.

Anguish from Cherry.

''Raejean. Annie. Come sit over here,'' Billy ordered.

Reluctantly the girls left their grandparents and came to sit beside Billy and Cherry across the courtroom.

Billy's attorney had already suggested that Billy compromise with Mr. and Mrs. Trask and give them partial custody of the children. The lawyer had warned that with their duo of legal experts, the Trasks would very likely win full custody if Billy insisted on fighting them in court.

''Are you ready, Mr. Stonecreek?'' Billy's lawyer asked as Billy and Cherry joined him.

''I'm ready.'' Billy knew his lawyer believed they were fighting a lost cause. But he wasn't willing to give up his children without clawing for them tooth and nail.

Billy turned to find the source of a small commotion at the back of the courtroom. ''Cherry, look.''

Cherry looked and felt tears prickle behind her eyes. Her whole family was trooping into the courtroom. Zach and Rebecca, Rolleen, Jewel, Avery, Jake, Frannie, Rabbit, and Colt. She knew what it meant at that moment to be part of a family. They were there for her.

"Thank you," she mouthed.

Her mother smiled encouragement. Zach nodded. Colt grinned and gave her a thumbs-up, while Jewel mouthed back, "We're with you, Cherry."

At that moment the judge entered the courtroom, and the bailiff called, "All rise."

Cherry stood and reached for Billy's hand as he reached for hers. They stood grim-lipped, stark-eyed, waiting for the worst, hoping for the best.

"In the interest of keeping this hearing as open and frank as we can get it," the judge began, "I think the minor children should wait outside. Is there someone who can take care of them?"

Jewel popped up in back. "I will, Your Honor."

"Very well. The children will leave the courtroom and remain outside until I call for them."

"Why do we have to leave, Daddy?" Raejean asked, her brow furrowed.

"Because the judge said so," Billy answered.

"I don't want to go," Annie said, clinging to Cherry's skirt.

"It's all right, Annie," Cherry said. "It's only for a little while. We'll all be together again soon."

She hoped.

Cherry prayed that the girls wouldn't make a scene in front of the judge, proving Cherry and Billy couldn't control their children. To her immense relief, they allowed Jewel to take their hands and lead them from the courtroom.

"This is a hearing to decide whether Mr. Stonecreek's two minor children should be taken away from him and given to their grandparents," the judge began solemnly. "I would like the petitioners to explain in their own words why they are seeking custody of their grandchildren."

"It's simple, Your Honor," Mrs. Trask said as she rose to her feet. "Billy Stonecreek is an inadequate and irresponsible parent who is doing irreparable harm to my grandchildren by neglecting them. He also happens to be a drunken brawler without an ounce of self-respect. It's a well-known fact that his kind can't hold their liquor."

"His kind?" the judge inquired.

"Billy Stonecreek's mother was an Indian, Your Honor," Mrs. Trask replied disdainfully.

The judge's brows arrowed down between his eyes, but all he said was, "Please continue."

"My former son-in-law has instigated several free-for-alls over the past year since my daughter's death, for which he has been repeatedly jailed. As you can plainly see from the condition of his face, he hasn't reformed his behavior over time.

"He has subjected my granddaughters to a series of housekeepers who come and go. His latest act of idiocy was to marry an eighteen-year-old high school dropout, who was a juvenile delinquent herself."

Billy had remained silent during Penelope's attack on him. When she started on Cherry, he couldn't sit still for it. "Wait one damn minute—"

"Sit down, Mr. Stonecreek," the judge admonished. "You'll have a chance to speak your piece."

Penelope shot Billy a smug smile and continued. "This pitiful excuse for a father doesn't have the time, money, or inclination to give his children the things they need. On the other hand, Mr. Trask and I are ready, willing, and able to provide a secure and stable home for our grandchildren."

"Is there anything else?" the judge asked.

Mrs. Trask hesitated before she said, "I believe Billy Stonecreek is responsible for my daughter, Laura's, death, Your Honor."

The judge raised a disbelieving brow.

"He didn't kill her with his bare hands," Mrs. Trask said. "But he made her so unhappy that...that she took her own life."

Cherry bounced up and said, "That's not true, Your Honor!"

The judge made a disgruntled sound. "Young lady—"

"Please, Your Honor. You have to let me speak," Cherry pleaded.

The judge turned to Mrs. Trask and said, "Are you finished, Mrs. Trask?"

"I am, Your Honor." She sat down as regally as a queen reclaiming her throne.

''Very well, then. Proceed, Mrs. Stonecreek.''

''It simply isn't true that Billy is responsible for Laura's death.''

''Cherry, don't,'' Billy muttered.

Cherry looked Billy in the eye and said, ''I have to tell them, Billy. It's the only way.''

When he lowered his gaze, she turned to face the judge. ''Laura Stonecreek didn't commit suicide, Your Honor. She was involved in a tragic automobile accident. She was unhappy, all right—because she wanted to have more children, but wasn't medically able to carry another child to term. On the day she had her fatal accident, Laura miscarried a child for the second time.''

An audible gasp could be heard from the other table.

''Billy didn't want her to take the risk of getting pregnant anymore. When Laura left the house that day she was despondent, but not because Billy didn't love her enough. It was because he loved her too much to take the chance of losing her by getting her pregnant again.

''Billy Stonecreek is the most gentle, most kind, and considerate man I know. He's a wonderful father to his girls, and they love him dearly. If you could only see him with them, giving them a bath, reading a story to them, kissing them good-night. They trust him to take care of them always. It would be a travesty to separate them.''

''What you say is all to the good, Mrs. Stonecreek,'' the judge said. ''But I'm concerned about your husband's propensity to physical violence. I'm especially concerned to see his condition today. I would think he would have avoided this sort of behavior, when he knew he would be appearing before this court.''

Cherry felt miserable. Billy had refused to tell her why he had gotten into another fight. And he had said he would do it again. She could understand the judge's point. There was nothing she could say to defend Billy, except, ''He's a good man, Your Honor. He loves his children. Please don't take them away from him.''

''Excuse me, Your Honor.''

Cherry turned at the sound of her father's voice. Zach was standing, waiting to be recognized by the judge.

''What is it, Zach?''

Cherry was surprised to hear the judge call her father by his first name until she remembered what Billy had said when he married her.

The Whitelaws were well known around this part of Texas. It appeared Zach had a personal acquaintance with the judge.

"I can explain the cause of Billy's most recent altercation, if the court will allow it."

The two lawyers conferred hastily at the Trasks' table before one rose to say, "I object, Your Honor. Mr. Whitelaw has no standing to get involved in this case."

"I'm the grandfather of those little girls, too, Your Honor," Zach said. "My daughter hasn't adopted them yet, but that's only a formality. I know she loves them as though they were already her own."

Cherry's throat thickened with emotion.

"I see no reason why I shouldn't allow Mr. Whitelaw to make his point, Counsel," the judge said. "Especially in light of the consequences if I rule against Mr. Stonecreek. I'd like to hear an explanation for this most recent fight—if there is one. Go ahead, Zach."

"First let me say that I did not initially approve of my daughter's marriage. I thought she was too young, and I knew Billy Stonecreek's reputation for getting into trouble. I thought he would be a bad influence on her."

Cherry felt her heart sinking. Nothing her father had said so far was the least bit helpful to Billy. In fact, it was as though he had dug the hole deeper.

"However," Zach said, "I've since changed my mind. I did enough checking to find out that my son-in-law is a hardworking, church-going man who spends most of his free time with his children. With three notable exceptions—all occurring since his wife's tragic death—he has been an outstanding citizen of this community.

"Although my son-in-law chose to start those three fights over the past year in bars, no one I talked to has ever seen him the least bit drunk. He has never hurt anyone seriously, and he has always paid for whatever damages there were. I know that doesn't excuse him entirely."

"Or at all," the judge interjected. "What I'd like to know is why Mr. Stonecreek started those fights."

"Only Billy himself knows the answer to that question. If I were guessing, I'd say he was a young man in a lot of pain and looking for a way to ease it."

''Then he chose the wrong way,'' the judge said. ''All this is very interesting, but it doesn't explain why he was fighting within days of this hearing.''

''To defend his wife's honor,'' Zach said.

Cherry's glance shot to Billy. He lowered his gaze to avoid hers, and a flush spread high on his cheekbones.

''I'm listening,'' the judge said.

''I was in Estes's Hardware Store yesterday when Billy came in. He picked up what he needed and went to the counter to pay. Ray Estes stood at the register and began making abusive, slanderous comments about my daughter, Cherry, in front of several other men, friends of Ray's, who were also waiting for service.

''Billy asked Ray to stop, but Ray continued provoking him, saying things to sully my daughter's reputation that no man could stand by and let another man say about his wife. Even then, Billy didn't throw the first punch.

''He told Ray he didn't want to fight, that he knew Ray was only mad because of what had happened the night Billy had kept him from assaulting Cherry. Billy said he would forget the insults if Ray would say he was sorry and hadn't meant what he'd said. Billy wanted the words taken back.

''Ray called Billy a coward, said he only fought men who were drunk. Even then, Your Honor, Billy kept his hands to himself. His fists were white-knuckled, but he didn't launch a blow.

''That's when Ray shoved him backward, and one of Ray's friends tripped him so he fell. Ray came over the counter and kicked him hard, while he was down. That was when Billy came up swinging. Ray's friends held his arms, so Ray could go at him. That's when he got the black eye.

''To tell you the truth, Your Honor, I took a few swings at those fellows myself. So you see, Billy tried to avoid a fight. He only got involved when it was a clear matter of self-defense.''

Cherry gave her father a grateful look as he sat down, then met Billy's dark-eyed gaze. She reached for his hand under the table and clasped it tight. ''Oh, Billy,'' she whispered. ''Why didn't you tell me?''

''I shouldn't have let Ray provoke me,'' Billy muttered. ''But I couldn't let him get away with saying those ugly things about you. I couldn't, Cherry.''

She squeezed his hand. ''It's all right, Billy. Surely the judge won't blame you now that he's heard the truth.''

''I'll concede Mr. Stonecreek may have been provoked beyond endurance in this case,'' the judge said, confirming Cherry's hope. ''The courts have conceded there are such things as 'fighting words' to which a man may respond justifiably with violence. And I'll take into consideration your suggestion that Mr. Stonecreek's other forays into fisticuffs may have been motivated by something other than drunkenness,'' the judge said.

''However,'' he continued, ''I am concerned by several of Mrs. Trask's other accusations. Especially those concerning Mrs. Stonecreek's past behavior and her ability to function as a capable mother to two little girls.''

''I'd like to speak on my wife's behalf, if I may,'' Billy said, rising to face the judge.

''Very well, Mr. Stonecreek,'' the judge replied.

''My daughters are lucky to have someone as wonderful as Cherry to be their mother,'' Billy said. ''I feel myself fortunate to have her for my wife. Cherry was expelled from school for something she didn't do. Since then, she's taken care of Raejean and Annie during the day and gone to school every night to make up the classes she needs for graduation. I have every confidence that she'll complete her education with high marks and receive her diploma.''

''I wasn't questioning your wife's intelligence,'' the judge said gently. ''I'm more concerned about her maturity, her sense of responsibility, the example she'll set for the children.''

Cherry saw Billy's Adam's apple bob as he swallowed hard. She wished she had led a different life. What could he say to defend her? She had been a troublemaker all her life. There was some truth in everything Mrs. Trask had said about her.

''I think Cherry's actions speak for themselves. My daughters are happy, healthy, and well-adjusted. Cherry treats them as though they were her own flesh and blood. You see, Your Honor, she knows what it feels like to lose your parents at a young age. She knows how important it is to make a child feel safe and secure and loved. That's what Cherry offers my children. Unconditional love. There's nothing more important to a child than knowing they're loved, is there, Your Honor?''

The judge cleared his throat. ''Yes, well, that's true, of course.''

''But, Your Honor,'' Mrs. Trask protested, seeing the tide shifting. ''The same young woman whose merits Billy is extolling spent time in a juvenile detention facility. The fact remains, she was expelled from school. And she's only eighteen years old!''

''I will take all of that into consideration, Mrs. Trask,'' the judge promised. ''Does anyone have anything further to say? Very well. I will need some time in chambers to deliberate this matter. I'll have a decision for you shortly. Court is recessed.''

''All rise,'' the bailiff commanded.

Cherry rose on shaky legs and grabbed hold of Billy's hand for support. They had done all they could—which seemed precious little—to convince the judge they would be good parents. But was it enough?

One thing had become clear to Cherry. It wasn't only the children she was afraid to lose. She was afraid of losing Billy, too.

He had only married her temporarily to have a mother for his children. What role would there be for her in his life if his children were taken from him? Would she only be a painful reminder of what he had lost?

Cherry looked into Billy's eyes, all her fears naked for him to see. *Do you love me, Billy? If it weren't for the children, would you still want me for your wife?*

And found the reassurance she sought.

His love was visible in the reassuring warmth of his gaze, in the way he held firmly, supportively, to her hand, in the way he had defended her in court.

Without a word, Billy rose and pulled her into his embrace. His arms closed tight around her. ''Don't leave me, Cherry,'' he whispered in her ear.

''I'm not going anywhere,'' she promised.

''I want us to be together forever.''

''Forever? But—''

''No matter what happens here today, I want you with me. I love you, Cherry.''

''I love you, too, Billy.''

They held each other tight, offering strength and solace, parting only as the twins came hurtling down the aisle to greet them. Raejean leapt into Billy's arms, while Cherry scooped up Annie.

''Jewel says we have lots of aunts and uncles and cousins,'' Raejean announced. ''Zillions of them!''

Cherry laughed. ''Not quite that many.''

''How many?'' Annie asked.

''I don't know, exactly,'' Cherry said. ''But lots.''

''Can we go on a picnic now?'' Raejean asked.

''Not yet,'' Billy said. ''Soon.''

''We have to go home first and change our clothes,'' Cherry reminded her.

''Can we leave now?'' Annie asked. ''Is the judge all done?''

''Almost,'' Cherry said. ''He wants to think about things a little while before he makes up his mind.''

''Makes up his mind about what?'' Raejean asked.

Cherry and Billy exchanged a tormented glance.

Makes up his mind about whether to take you away from us.

Billy's heart had been thundering in his chest ever since the hearing began. He felt himself on the verge of panic, and the only thing he had to hang on to was Cherry's hand. So far, he had protected his daughters from knowing about the desperate courtroom struggle that would decide their future.

This morning, as he and Cherry had sipped coffee together at dawn, he had decided that even if the Trasks won custody, he would do his best to make the transition as amicable as possible. Surely the judge wouldn't deny him visitation rights, and he would continue to have a strong and loving relationship with his children.

Only, if there was one thing Billy had learned in this life, it was that there were no guarantees. He was terrified the judge would rule against him. He was terrified the Trasks would try to bar him from all contact with his children.

Right now he felt like taking Raejean and Annie and Cherry and running as far and as fast as he could. Fortunately, Cherry's family came to the rail that separated the spectators from the litigants, all of them talking at once, making escape impossible, even if he had succumbed to the urge.

He felt a hand on his shoulder and turned to find Zach Whitelaw standing behind him.

''I want to thank you for your words of support, sir,'' Billy said.

''It was my pleasure, son. I never had a chance to congratulate you on your wedding. I expect you to take good care of my daughter.''

Billy would have answered if his jaw hadn't been clenched to keep his chin from quivering with emotion. Instead, he gave a jerky nod.

''The judge is coming back already, Dad,'' Colt said. ''Wasn't it supposed to take longer?''

It had already been too long, as far as Billy was concerned, although he realized it had only been a matter of minutes since the judge had left the courtroom.

''We'd better get back to our seats,'' Zach said.

Billy was afraid to send his daughters away, afraid they weren't going to be his when he saw them again.

''All rise,'' the bailiff said.

Jewel was leading the children out of the courtroom when the judge said, ''The children can stay.''

Billy exchanged a quick look with Cherry and quickly gathered Raejean and Annie into the circle of his arms in front of him.

Cherry gave him a quavery smile. ''Surely it's a good sign that the judge let them stay,'' she whispered as she slipped her arm around his waist. It was questionable who was supporting whom.

When the judge sat, Billy and Cherry sat, each of them holding one of the twins on their laps. They could hear the clock ticking as the judge shuffled papers.

Finally he looked up and said, ''The circumstances of this case are unique. The grandparents of these children have a great deal to offer them, not the least of which is the experience to be gained with age. The children's father has shown a lack of judgment on occasion that makes his suitability as a parent questionable.''

Billy's heart felt like it was going to pound right out of his chest. *He's going to give them to Penelope. I'm going to lose my children.*

''However,'' the judge continued, ''the law favors the natural parents of a child over any other custodian. And there are other factors evident here that I believe have to be considered in my decision.''

What is your decision, dammit? Billy raged inwardly.

''I've decided to leave custody of the minor children with their father,'' the judge announced.

Shouts of joy and clapping erupted behind Billy.

''I want quiet in the court,'' the judge said, pounding his gavel.

Billy was too stunned to move, his throat too tight to speak. He saw Cherry through a blurred haze of tears. She was laughing and crying at the same time.

''We won, Billy. We won!'' Cherry sobbed.

''What did we win, Daddy?'' Raejean said.

''Did we get a prize?'' Annie asked.

''Quiet in the court,'' the judge repeated.

''Shh,'' Billy said to the girls. ''Let's listen to the judge.''

He was more than willing to listen, now that he knew his children were his to keep.

''There will be those who question my decision in light of the evidence heard here today about the actions of the children's father and stepmother. They have made mistakes in the past. However, they both seem dedicated to rectifying their behavior.

''So I have based my decision not on what either of them might have done in the past, but on what I saw here in this courtroom today that bodes well for the future.

''Seldom have I seen two individuals more supportive of each other, or more apparently devoted to each other. These children will have what too few children have these days—two parents who love and respect one another. I am convinced that these two young people are capable of providing a stable, healthy and happy home for the two minor children. Good luck to you both. Court is dismissed.''

''All rise,'' the bailiff ordered.

Billy's knees were rubbery when he stood, and he slipped an arm around Cherry to keep himself upright. He realized he was grinning as he accepted the congratulatory slaps of the Whitelaws.

''Can we go on a picnic now?'' Raejean asked.

''Soon,'' Cherry promised with a hiccuping laugh that was choked by tears of joy.

"Can Nana and Grampa Trask come, too?" Annie asked.

Billy looked across the room at the bitter face of Mrs. Trask and realized he only felt sorry for her. She had lost her daughter. Now she had lost her grandchildren, too. Because it would be a cold day in hell before he let her near his children again.

He felt Cherry's hand on his arm.

"The girls need their grandparents, Billy," she said. "And Mr. and Mrs. Trask need their grandchildren."

Billy struggled to be generous. He was still angry. And still afraid that the Trasks might yet find some way to take his children from him. But Cherry was right. Raejean and Annie loved their grandparents. It would be cruel to take them away. For their sakes, he had to forgive what the Trasks had tried to do.

"Why don't you go ask Nana and Grampa Trask if they'd like to come on our picnic with us?" Billy said to Raejean and Annie.

Billy pulled Cherry close against him as they watched the girls skip across the room to invite Penelope and Harvey Trask to join their picnic. Billy met Penelope's startled glance when she heard what the girls had to say. He saw her hesitate, then shake her head no and say something to the children.

Moments later the girls returned and Raejean said, "Nana says maybe next time."

Billy exchanged one last poignant look with Penelope before she turned away. Then he glanced down at Raejean and ruffled her hair. "Next time," Billy said.

Cherry met his eyes, her gaze proud and supportive, and said, "Next time for sure."

"Let's go home," Billy said as he reached for Cherry's hand. She reached out for Annie, and he reached out for Raejean. They walked out of the courtroom hand in hand in hand in hand, a family at last.

* * * * *